THE CALL

He stood staring at her while the air shimmered with the heat of the distant storm over Red Rock Mountain, where the slanting purple rain had begun.

She is magic, Wind Caller thought.

I called him up, Deer Shadow thought. He was surely a god. Deer Shadow ached for this man, for Coyote in his human form, for all the things that other women had that she did not.

Wind Caller moved forward. He put a hand out to touch the magic woman to see if she would vanish. Deer Shadow pushed herself against his hand.

If she had called him up, then she would have him . . .

Other Avon Books in
THE DEER DANCERS *Series by*
Amanda Cockrell
Coming Soon

THE DEER DANCERS, BOOK TWO:
WIND CALLER'S CHILDREN

DEER DANCERS

BOOK ONE

Daughter of the Sky

AMANDA COCKRELL

AVON BOOKS ◆ NEW YORK

THE DEER DANCERS, BOOK ONE: DAUGHTER OF THE SKY is an original publication of Avon Books. This work has never before appeared in book form. This work is a novel. Any similarity to actual persons or events is purely coincidental.

AVON BOOKS
A division of
The Hearst Corporation
1350 Avenue of the Americas
New York, New York 10019

Copyright © 1995 by Book Creations, Inc. and Amanda Cockrell
Excerpt from *The Deer Dancers, Book Two: Wind Caller's Children* copyright © 1995 by Book Creations, Inc. and Amanda Cockrell
Published by arrangement Book Creations, Inc., Canaan, New York, Lyle Kenyon Engel, Founder
Library of Congress Catalog Card Number: 94-96783
ISBN: 0-380-77648-0

First Avon Books Printing: July 1995

AVON TRADEMARK REG. U.S. PAT. OFF. AND IN OTHER COUNTRIES, MARCA REGISTRADA, HECHO EN U.S.A.

Printed in the U.S.A.

RA 10 9 8 7 6 5 4 3 2 1

For Marian

Introduction

Look through a hole in time.

Look through a tunnel of compressed years to a place where magic makes more sense than science; where it is possible to understand that if you dance your prayers the right way, the horned god, the deer incarnate, will come into them and speak to you.

Five thousand years ago, along the valley of the Rio Grande, the borders between the worlds were thin, and supernatural power might be in any stone. In the lightning, the rain, the animals. Any passing creature might contain the otherworld. If you lived there, the gods would move in and out of your world like unlikely relatives, troublesome or beneficent. Coyote might come, scratching fleas and trailing the stars in the brush of his tail.

And since knowledge has always been power, new knowledge may make a new god. This is the origin of myth: strange tales handed across the eons, unbelievable, laughably unlikely, still able to raise the hair on the backs of our necks.

Prologue

The old woman settles herself by the fire. Two young men attend her because she is very old and therefore very important. From her aerie halfway up the canyon walls, she can see the stars begin to stab through the night sky like thorns of light. The rest of the people of the cliffs settle around her, children in laps. She is more than entertainment on a winter's night; she is her people's history, their voice. She looks into the fire, back into the time beyond memory when the world changed and changed again, and the great gifts came to the People: maize, and music, and art. The time after the Great Mystery Spirit, who is the breath on the water, had set things moving, and the lesser gods began to be made.

Coyote was there, of course, but then he always had been.

"In the beginning," the old woman tells them, "when the people first came Up From Below, there was the Great Game, deer as high as mountains and strange, ponderous buffalo. People and animals were all one, and they spoke together about how to make the world. The Great Game bent willingly to the hunters' spears, and one would feed a clan for a year. Then came the

2

*cold time and the wandering, and the Great Game dis-
appeared, lumbering into some distant pasture. The People tried to find them. Perhaps the Great Game went
into the air, or Down Below, taking their strange ways
down the tunnels, great feet sending echoes along
smooth stone. But the Great Game was not to be found.*

*"Now there were only the small deer and buffalo, no
taller than a man, and the antelope and rabbit. Now it
took much magic to call the deer and capture them, and
the old men gave it much thought."*

*The old woman pulls a strip of memory from the fire-
light, weaving the first thread into her story. . . .*

To Daughter, who was five, it still seemed a very fine
world. In the warm, rainy summer, her red-brown skin
was bare of anything but a blue stone on a thong around
her neck. The soles of her feet were hard, and her thick
black hair was tied up with a thong because it was hot.
She had been in the river to get wet, and she glistened
like the red stone of the mountains when the long slanting rain went walking up them.

Daughter was pretending that she was a mountain.
She stood on the riverbank and cast her arms out wide,
towering over the people in her game—the turtles and
the small brown fish. The river people took no notice of
her, flipping their scales and gnarled shells in the shallow water.

"I am the god," she told them. "I bring the water."
She bent and straightened and poured it out on them
from cupped hands, flashing silver like the rain snakes.
A small turtle tipped itself into the water, out of the
shadow of the grass basket at her feet. Daughter's hand
shot out and grabbed it, tucked it in with the other turtles
bumbling in the bottom. She stretched her arms again,
pleased, trying her turtle magic, but no more turtles came
to her.

Daughter danced impatiently on the riverbank. She needed a magic, she thought, to make the turtles emerge from their little caves in the riversides. A magic like the tooth that Uncle Looks Back had. It had a double curve like a bent arm, and if it could have been straightened out, it would have been taller than Uncle Looks Back. He said it was a tooth from the Great Game, and Daughter tried to imagine what kind of animal could hold such a tooth in its mouth. She didn't think it would call turtles, though. You had to *be* the animal to call it, anyone knew that; and turtles probably wouldn't even notice the Great Game, lumbering so high above them.

Daughter bent again, hunching her back like a turtle shell, trying to feel what it would be like to live inside two stones. A stone farther along the bank was at eye level now, and she saw its true form, distinct in a moment from the smooth stones around it. Daughter scooped it up, a big one, its feet paddling angrily. There was enough for stew now, and the shell would make a good bowl. Daughter did a dance step in the mud, the way the hunters did when they came home. Her bare feet left perfect prints, heels and pads and five oval toes in the yellowy-brown mud. The sun was sitting right on top of the mountain, and its red light made the water in the footprints glisten like little puddles of fire.

Daughter admired them until the sun dipped suddenly, as if the mountains were sucking it down. She snatched up her basket of turtles and ran away from the river, back to where her mother and Aunt Four Fingers were picking berries. Looking behind her, she thought the river looked different in the dusk, gray and hidden, as if anything could come out of it. Running through the whispering grass, she spun once in her path, gave it a final retort: "Yah!" she yelled. "I got your turtles!"

* * *

"But there are worlds beyond worlds," the old
woman says. She pulls another strand of firelight and
puts it in her story. *'Worlds that Daughter had never
seen. In them lived descendants of her people who came
from the north during the cold time and the wandering.
They no longer knew one another. They were outflung
like the stars that flow along the sky road.*

*"In the south there was a wet rain forest, where the
Children of the Sun and the Feathered Serpent lived
beside a river, in the deep green where the canopy
nearly shut out the sky. They hunted the little forest deer
and the jaguar (when it wasn't hunting them), the toucans and bright parrots that squawked in the canopy.
They fished in the river and snared the long-legged her-
ons that also went there to fish. They ate roots, berries,
and fruit, and planted the thumb-sized ears of maize that
grew among the wild grasses outside the jungle. . . ."*

A ten-year-old boy in a tree was about to make a
discovery. Watching his snares, he was bored, he was
hot, and he itched. He wriggled on his tree limb and
scratched himself, rooting under the apron of leaves that
was all he wore in the summer. Hungry again, he scrabbled in the bottom of the spotted catskin bag hung over
his shoulder and scraped from it the last crumbs of dried,
cooked maize. He pulled out the bone he had brought
with him and gnawed it, not for the first time today,
pulling off the last strips of meat and gristle. It was the
foreleg of a deer, long and thin, and the boy took a stick
and poked the marrow out, licking it off the stick. There
was a bit that would not come out; angrily he blew into
the other end of the bone.

In the way that sometimes happens, when the gods
see that we are growing restless in our boredom and
likely to make trouble, and they wish to give us something to make us behave, a sop to our curiosity and our

capacity for mischief—in just this way when things and events and thoughts line up—the bone made a noise.

The bone had a hole in it, near the end, made by an obsidian knife used for dressing the meat. When the boy blew through the other end, it whistled. The sound was less like a bird than like the wind when it tried to enter a cave or squeeze through a narrow cleft in the rock. Interested, the boy blew into the bone a second time. It made a different sound, because he had taken his finger off the hole near the end. He blew into it again, finger on, finger off. Head cocked, he listened to see if it would make a noise back without his blowing into it. It didn't.

Seized with curiosity, he pulled a sharpened flint from his bag and dug another hole, a short distance from the first one. He blew into the bone and heard a new noise, but the old one came back when he covered the hole.

A macaw blundered into a snare, and just in time the boy dropped the bone and pulled the leather thong tight. He climbed down from his perch to disentangle the furious red and blue flutter of feathers, then twisted its neck and put it in his sack before he scrabbled among the leaves on the forest floor for the bone. He went home carrying the sack very carefully, as if something inside, the music or the dead bird, might break open.

"Where did it come from?" a small child demands.

"Oh, from the Moon, I expect," the old woman says. "You know how she likes to suggest things. How she quarrels with the Sun, who doesn't like change.

"The Moon laughs at him, you know. She is always drunk on fermented berries, and she'll sleep with anyone. If he didn't need her to pull the tides for the fisher people and show the women how to be, the Sun would ignore her.

" 'Look at them all,' the Moon says, 'all the separate tribes spread all over since the wandering, speaking in

different tongues. They all think that they are the only true people. When they do meet each other, they try to kill each other. They have no memory.''

'' 'And how does teaching this boy to make music help?' the Sun asks.

'' 'It is a way to remember,' the Moon says. 'There is a girl in the north who has learned to make pictures. We are making memory. Perhaps I will show them to each other, and they will see they are all one people.'

'' 'They will try to kill each other,' the Sun says.

''The Moon reaches for her cup with a long silver arm, trailing clouds from her sleeve like feathers. 'Maybe with memory, they will learn better,' she suggests.

''The Sun snorts his derision with a flare of fiery nostrils. 'They won't change. They will just know more. It isn't good for them.'

'' 'They have to learn new things,' the Moon says. 'The gods have to be born.' ''

The old woman weaves the firelight and lets the children watch. . . .

1
The Coyote

The old men were calling the deer; the young men were dancing them down the valley, holding them with the spirals of their steps. Daughter sat with the women and little children, watching the deer heads bobbing in the firelight. She could see them so perfectly—the branching antlers, the delicate line of eye and jaw. It was cold now, and the People needed meat for winter and hides for warmth.

Daughter sat bundled in deerskin and coyote fur, with Dog across her feet, his warm breath sending up little puffs of steam. Dog wasn't interested in the deer dancers; he was interested in Uncle Looks Back's bitch, who was in heat. Daughter kept a firm grip on the fur at the scruff of his neck. Father was dancing. If Dog went racing through the feet of the dancers, everyone would blame her. It might spoil the deer magic, and the deer wouldn't come.

The deer shapes wavered and swayed in the firelight, their shadows long across the dancing ground, their great heads solemnly weaving. It seemed to Daughter as if they looked right at her, as if they had something mysterious to tell her alone. She had been pounding on the ground with a stick, keeping time as the women were doing. She tried to mark the ground with it now, the way her feet had marked the riverbank, and leave the deer shape of upturned antlers and wide dark eyes.

"What's that?" A boy next to her joggled her arm. "What are you doing? You'd better not."

"Stop it!" Daughter swatted his hand away and scooted forward out of his reach. She tried again to see the deer in the scratchings she had made in the dirt.

"You'll spoil the dance!" The boy, who was the shaman's son and older than she was, tugged at the stick. All marks were magic. These might be dangerous.

"I will not!" Daughter hit him in the car and picked up her blanket of deer hide and coyote fur, trudging in it to a spot nearer the fire and the dancers. She began to dig in the dirt again. A deer head grew under her scratching: two round eyes and the spiky crest of antlers. She admired it solemnly, gave it four legs.

"You can't be here." One of the elders scooped her up by the elbows. His deer face glared at her. "Go back with the women." He set her down hard, beyond the circle of the light.

"Yah!" said the boy when she got back. "I told you."

Daughter looked at where she had been sitting. "Where's Dog?"

"You didn't watch him," the boy said.

Daughter peered through the dancing feet to where the shaman's bitch had been on the other side of the dance ground. She couldn't see her, either. Maybe they had gone back toward the caves that were the People's late summer shelter, a few hundred feet behind them, where the mountains first rose up from the valley floor in slow, sloping steps.

"You didn't watch yours, either," she said.

"It's not my job to watch dogs," the boy said loftily.

"Then what good are you?" Daughter said. "There they are—look."

Two dark shapes trotted through the dancers, dog and bitch making their own pattern. Dog drew closer to the bitch, sank his teeth into the back of her neck.

"Come on!" Daughter tugged at the shaman's son.

"Let them be." Her mother, who until now had ignored their quarrel, put a hand on her arm. "It will make more deer. It is a good sign."

It would make more dogs, Daughter knew. She supposed, then, that it would also encourage the deer, would show them how to do it, the way the dancers showed them the way to come home to death to feed the People.

She settled down again and watched the deer move in spirals in the smoky light, always moving in, always dancing home, and the humpbacked shape of the dogs, silhouetted among them.

It did make more dogs, six mewing puppies born just as the Yellow Grass People were going up the mountain for the winter, to the high ground where the piñon nuts were, when all the grasses and berries and lily bulbs were dead under the ground. Maybe it made more people, too. Daughter's mother began to swell under her fur robes, and she puffed when she walked. The people carried their bundles in deer hides, the feet laced together to make straps. What they carried was precious: baskets and grinding stones, spear shafts and cutting stones for chipping new spear points from flint, bone needles, cured deer hide and furs, and the deer masks of the dancers. Looks Back carried his giant curving tooth, and his wife carried grinding stones and stored seed. Two other men carried the magic: Looks Back's deer-hide bundle of feathers and amulets, his dried plants for fevers and broken bones, the masks he wore to talk to the gods. There were many gods, and each needed a different speech: Thunder, who made the rain and the lightning; Sun; Coyote, who was everywhere since the beginning; Uncle Snake, who put the water in the rivers; the deer themselves; and the rabbits, antelope, and shaggy buffalo, who came only sometimes in the good years.

Carrying a grinding stone, Daughter walked beside her mother and Aunt Four Fingers and Listens to Deer, who was a man but dressed like a woman, and so was sacred. Listens to Deer and the women chattered about where the best piñon nuts would be and how many more days it would take Lazy Woman to scrape her deer hide. Maybe it would sour and rot first and Coyote would steal it, Aunt Four Fingers said. In the winter the lean, gray coyotes went to the mountains themselves to eat piñon nuts—that and anything they could catch. The people's dogs kept watch, but sometimes a coyote bitch in heat would lure a dog, and then the coyotes would swarm over it, and later the people would find its eaten body. The urge to mate made you stupid, Daughter thought, and heavy with some fatal power. She scrambled to keep up with the women.

"Hop along," Listens to Deer said.

There was a taste of snow in the air, and Daughter remembered last winter, the warmth of the fires that blazed in the cave mouths where the rock had split itself open. A lion had been in one, and Listens to Deer had driven it out with a torch and a broom made of pine straw. He was very strong.

Listens to Deer had given Daughter her real first name, and she was very pleased with it. On the second night of the deer dance, she had gone again to the edge of the dancing ground to watch the deer and to try to print them into the ground under the dancers' feet. Again she had been chased away, a child making messes in the mud when there were important things to be done. The next morning, after the hunters had left with the first light, she had stubbornly pulled the deer masks from their hide bundles, set one up on a pole, and tried to see its shape so she could print it in the dirt.

Listens to Deer had caught her, taken the mask away because it was sacred, then smacked her bottom with a broad hand. But he had seen what she was trying to do and had nodded thoughtfully. That was when he had given her the name, not just Daughter, but Stubborn Mud Daughter. It was an honor to get your name from one like Listens to Deer. Daughter liked the sound of it. It sounded the way she felt.

The new baby came at the end of the winter, in the last cold snap when all the streams froze again and the water that sometimes seeped through the walls of the cave also froze, despite the fire.

Her mother lay on a pile of pine needles and deerskin surrounded by Aunt Four Fingers, Listens to Deer, and the other women. This was her fourth baby. The two that had been born between Daughter and this one had died, and Daughter made all the secret magic she could think of to help this one come out all right. The women wouldn't let her help, so she sat by the fire at the cave mouth and watched the men outside making magic in the torchlight. Babies were everyone's business. Without children, the clan wouldn't live, would go away like the Great Game.

Looks Back lifted his hands, each wrist tied with feathers, bent down, and touched them to the earth before entering the cave. He raised his cupped hands above the fire and let the pine needles he held run through his fingers into the flame, the way Daughter had poured the water when she was being the mountain god.

Daughter could hear her mother howling. She stood up and moved farther into the cave, stepping backward whenever one of the women shooed her away.

Listens to Deer, who was here because he dressed like a woman, saw her. His face was kindly under the fall of black hair that hung around his shoulders. "The baby doesn't want to come out," he said. "It doesn't like the winter; its spirit wants to stay where it's warm. We'll have to trick it out. Do you want to help?"

She nodded. Her mother howled again, a wail that broke off into a strangled gasp of pain.

"Go to my cave," Listens to Deer said, "and get my rabbit-skin bag. Find a perfectly smooth stone and a new blade of grass and put them in it. Then bring them to me."

Daughter went out of the cave, past her father and the other men trying to dance the baby into the world, and skidded down the icy slope. The cold wind whipped around her ears like frozen ghosts. No wonder the baby didn't want to come out.

The cave that Listens to Deer had claimed for himself was warmer. It was one of the best. Only Looks Back and the chief had better. It had a level floor and an overhang, which kept the rain out, and room for two or three to sleep around the fire. The fire was still burning, and Daughter stopped to put a few more branches on it so it wouldn't go out before he came back. The rabbit-skin bag was against the wall in a pile with his baskets and grinding quern. Daughter picked it up and snuggled it to her face. It was soft, softer even than Dog's fur, but there was no life in it, no warmth.

She went out to look for the stone and the blade of grass. The moon had bled half away in its monthly course, and the night was dark. Daughter knelt on the stony slope, feeling the rocks, trying to find a smooth one. There would be more nearer the stream, but she didn't want to go that far from the firelight and the People. She fumbled the rocks over in her hand, shivering, rejecting each one. It had to be right. You couldn't settle

for "almost" with magic. Only with rightness did something make a little noise in your head, like the click of
a beetle, and you knew that the thing had changed, trans-
muted itself, become the new thing, the thing with
power.

At last she found a stone on which her fingers could
detect no ragged edges, no sign of ever having been
worked by man, or by the crash of avalanche or shaking
earth, or by anything other than the slow, unending
stroking of the water. She put it in her bag and stood,
flexing her stiff knees. There was new grass beside the
path, not far from the last cave on the slope. Up here by
the caves there was only rock, the last season's dead
scrub, and the piñon pines. Grass didn't grow in the pine
needles. Daughter set off down the path, with the bag
and stone clutched in her hand.

The night seemed motionless, as if even the air was
frozen the farther she got from the fires. The grass would
be frozen, but Daughter knew that didn't kill it, not in
the spring. Listens to Deer knew that, too, so it must be
all right, as long as the life was still in the blade. Daughter didn't know what he would do with the stone and
the grass—secret magics were the most powerful—but
it didn't matter. It was up to her to bring them to him.

She came to where she had seen the new grass and
knelt again, feeling for it among the rocks. The night
was so still that she could almost hear the grass speak
under her fingers. *We are cold,* it said. *We are cold.* A
thin silvery snake flowed across the path, the sound of
its scales like the voice of the grass. Daughter plucked
a blade, then another just in case she dropped one.

She had put them in her bag when she felt a fleeting
warmth like the spark made by a fire drill, the barest
breath of something alive; its body warm inside, not cold
like the snake or the empty rabbit skin. It was on the
path between her and the caves. As she stared at it, its

shape became clear, coalesced out of the night and the half moon: a coyote, gaunt with winter, its thin ribs and matted fur flecked with ice crystals. It stared at her, yellow eyes catching the thin moon.

It was hunting. Coyotes hunted anything, even people. They sometimes ate babies who strayed too far from careless mothers. Daughter remembered when a hunter who had broken his leg had been eaten. They had found what was left, like the dogs the coyote bitches lured.

She stamped her foot and hefted the rabbit-skin sack with the stone in it. "Go away!" she said to the coyote. "I'm too big to eat, and I have a rock in my sack. Go away or I'll hit you with it!"

The coyote still looked at her. Its mouth opened, tongue lolling. Daughter shook the sack at it. "A sack with a magic rock," she said. Animals didn't always speak to people, but Coyote was an old god, and this coyote was a piece of him. "I'll hit you with it and make a blanket out of you. Yah! Go away!" She stamped and shook the sack again.

The coyote's yellow eyes caught another spark of moonlight. It turned its head to look up the slope at the caves and firelight. Then it turned off the path and trotted away into the scrub, leaving little clouds of breath behind it.

Clutching the sack to her, Daughter ran back into the tenuous safety of the fires. Something had changed. The men were still dancing, but their steps had slowed; they wove their pattern slowly now, as if finishing something. Daughter's steps slowed, too. She didn't want to go inside the cave, didn't want to know why the dance had changed. She went to Listens to Deer at the cave mouth and handed him the sack.

He looked inside. "Those are excellent. Fine magic."

"Is the baby born?"

"No."

She couldn't hear her mother howling anymore, only the voices of other women.

"She's gone Away," Listens to Deer said gently. "The baby took her."

Daughter lifted her head and howled the way the women inside the cave were doing. "It can't have her! She's mine!"

Aunt Four Fingers came out and scooped her up in her arms. "When someone wants to go Away, you can't stop them," she said.

She cuddled Daughter as if afraid she might leave, too, might slip past them into the night.

Daughter looked at the rabbit-skin bag, her face round with terror. "It's because I was too late. If you'd had it, the baby would have come out. But the coyote stopped me!"

"The coyote?" Listens to Deer said.

"I met him on the path," Daughter sobbed. "I shook the sack at him, but he just stood there. He wouldn't move. And then I yelled at him and he went away, and I was too late!" She burst into fresh howls, burying her slippery face in Aunt Four Fingers's shoulder. The lion's teeth on Aunt Four Fingers's necklace bit into Daughter's cheek, but she didn't care.

"No, Stubborn Mud Daughter," Listens to Deer said. "Pay attention. The gathering was the magic, not the stone. But dying is a stronger magic sometimes. It would not have been good for you to see how it went. If Coyote kept you on the path, he has done you a kindness."

"She can't *go!*" Daughter lifted her head pleadingly as if Listens to Deer might tell her they could change their minds. Beyond his shoulder the men's dance stopped. Her father stopped with them, his face pulled tight like a stretched hide.

He came to the cave mouth. "Was it a boy?" he asked Aunt Four Fingers.

"We don't know," Aunt Four Fingers said. "It never came out."

It had stayed where it was warm, Daughter thought. But now its hiding place would grow cold. When it was too cold, the baby and its mother would go entirely, onto the wind to where the dead lived, and Daughter would be alone. Her father didn't count; men didn't tend the children. Maybe he would take another wife to take care of her. Daughter looked at him miserably. *Don't you dare.*

"You can't sleep here tonight," Aunt Four Fingers said to him. "I'll take the girl with me. You can go to the single men."

Her father nodded again. Some men had two or three wives, but he had only one. Now he would sleep in the cave with the young men and try to pretend he was one of them, not a middle-aged man, soft and liking his comforts—the warmth of his wife on their bed of furs, the food boiled in grass baskets with hot stones, not the gristly lumps of half-charred meat he would find on the communal hearth of the young men's house. He looked at Daughter as if he didn't know what to do with her and turned away.

She woke in the middle of the night from a dream in which her mother was still here, cuddling her, her dark hair warm against Daughter's cheek, to find that it was Dog instead, lying near her in a corner of Aunt Four Fingers's cave. Aunt's babies slept beside her, and Aunt's husband was snoring the way her father always did. *Maybe I can stay here,* Daughter thought, staring through the cave mouth at the moon.

At the end of four days, when the spirits of Daughter's mother and the baby had gone out of her body, the people burned it to prevent the spirits from returning, confused, and being trapped there. They wrapped the mother in a deerskin dress and the necklace of blue stones and turkey feathers that had been part of the bride-price her husband had paid. Daughter's father, whose everyday name was Found Water, followed behind the shaman and the chief. Today they would use only their everyday names, since it was bad luck, particularly at a funeral, for a ghost to name you. Everyday names were different anyway and often changed. If Found Water didn't take another woman soon, they would probably call him Lost His Wife.

They laid Daughter's mother on the stacked wood and sprinkled her with dirt so that she could find her way Down Below to where the skeleton people lived. Found Water put the first torch to the wood, and when Daughter crept up next to him, he put his hand on her shoulder. The flames caught the deer-hide dress, and a tower of dark smoke began to rise. Daughter sniffled. The other children, ringed about the fire, looked at her solemnly. The women eyed her father, and she could tell that even the ones who were married were thinking that they might like a change. He was still a fine man to look at, and a fine hunter. He was a settled man who had wanted only one wife, and he didn't boast and strut the way the younger men did. Daughter knew it would happen, some woman would marry him, and she thought vindictively of magics and poisons.

As it turned out, however, late the next summer Found Water married four wives instead, and Daughter's hatred became so diffused among them that it lost its focus.

They had gone back to live in their old cave right after her mother's body had been burned. If Daughter had been old enough to bear children, they couldn't have, and would have had to abandon it. But since she hadn't begun to bleed yet, Looks Back said there was no danger of her catching the spirit that had killed her mother.

Daughter was glad they could return to their cave. Some trace of her mother seemed to linger there. After being in Aunt Four Fingers's cave, with Aunt's children shouting around her, she could find that whisper of her mother only in perfect stillness, somewhere between a sound and a smell. She listened for it, head cocked, while she burned her hands trying to heat stew in the cooking basket or bloodied her fingers on the quern.

"That child is too young to do a woman's job," Aunt Four Fingers said. She took Found Water's kill away and cooked it, grumbling. When the next moon came and the People got ready to move down the slopes into the valley to follow the deer, everyone said that something had to be done.

Daughter, who didn't want to leave the last echo of her mother, sat on a flat rock and sulked while the rest of the clan packed its possessions. Found Water packed theirs since she wouldn't help.

In what might have been his own burst of temper, Found Water married a widow known to be a good worker, then a walleyed woman who could cook, a girl to warm his bed, and a young woman with two boy babies who had left her other husband because he beat her.

Daughter hated them all indiscriminately. She scraped hides with Old Woman, and ground seed with Wall Eye, things her mother would have taught her, and saw with spiteful satisfaction that Young Woman was jealous of Fox Girl, who shared her father's bed most nights.

Found Water hunted all day every day to feed them all, and the clan shook their heads and said that he had the ghost sickness; his dead wife had made him crazy.

When Daughter could slip away from them all, she went to the river, where the mud was soft, and scratched her signs into it: long-legged deer with startled eyes and Dog trotting after them, or her father with his spear up. That summer they killed a buffalo, and she looked at its carcass a long time, trying to make it rise up whole in her mind so that she could take it with her to the river and dig it into the mudbank with its humped back and great shaggy head. But it wouldn't rise up for her, and she couldn't lift it, so she drew the coyote instead, the one that had stood in her path. She put him into the riverbank with his lolling tongue and bushy tail, and for a moment she thought he looked back out at her with a flicker of yellow eyes.

Sometimes Listens to Deer came to the river's edge and watched her, when he knew the others were looking for her.

"This is a great mystery, what you are learning to do," he said.

"Cat Ears says it is nothing but foolish marks in the mud, and it is either a bad magic or I am stupid," Daughter said.

"Cat Ears gives himself more credit than he deserves just for being the shaman's son," Listens to Deer said. He sat down on the muddy bank, spreading his deer-hide skirts, his elbows on his knees. "Cat Ears can't see what Stubborn Mud Daughter sees. He doesn't know how to look."

"Old Woman doesn't, either," Daughter said. "She said I was lazy and smacked me. They all smack me," she added resentfully.

"Do you do as you're told?"

"There are four of them. They all want to be first wife, so they all tell me things to do. I would put poison in their soup if I knew what was poison."

"Just as well that you do not," Listens to Deer said.

"You know what is poison," Daughter said craftily. "You could give me some."

"But I won't. You have a gift. Maybe it is going to be holy. You will have to take being different as part of that gift."

Daughter thought about that, abandoning her resentment for a moment. "Do you mean like you?" She touched his skirts. "Is that why you are the way you are?" It seemed a very daring question. Men like Listens to Deer were sacred, despite their gossip and their gentle mannerisms. You didn't ask them why they were different.

Listens to Deer didn't shout at her, the way she had seen him shout at Young Woman's son when he had asked the same thing. "I knew when I was very young," he said. "When I was a boy, maybe ten. At the time of visions. I was told that this was what I was made for— to be the one between. Between men and women, not really either one."

Daughter nodded. All boys had visions. When they began to be men, they shut themselves up in the young men's house and made magics until they had visions. Cat Ears was very superior about it. Girls had a ceremony when they began to bleed, but they rarely had visions. If a girl had a vision, she was very powerful and might be a witch. More than anything Daughter wanted a vision that would put her on an equal footing with Cat Ears, and over Old Woman and the rest. If she were a witch, nobody would smack her, and Cat Ears would be afraid of her. It was a very satisfactory thought.

"Is that why you are magic?"

Listens to Deer chuckled. "*I* am not magic. But I may see magic, because I look from a different place. What the gods give us, we are obligated to make use of."

"If I am different," she said thoughtfully, "how will it be?"

"That's hard to say," Listens to Deer said. "You are

very young—and disobedient—now. You don't scrape hides, and when you say you are going to find turtles, you make coyotes in the riverbank instead.''

"What would happen if I made turtles?''

"Try it and see.''

Daughter scratched a round shell and four feet, with the head sticking out.

"That is a turtle,'' Listens to Deer said. "Even Cat Ears could see that is a turtle.''

"He won't,'' Daughter said pessimistically.

"The turtle sees.'' Listens to Deer pointed. A big one sat on a flat stone, dripping with river water, just come up to sun itself.

Daughter eased toward it, both hands out, and grabbed it before it could paddle off the rock. She put it in her empty basket and grinned at Listens to Deer. This was better than her pretend turtle magic. She wondered if she could make something that would come and eat her father's wives. Something, of course, that wouldn't eat her, too. The coyote, maybe.

Listens to Deer seemed to hear her thoughts. He had a way of doing that, and worse yet, sometimes he could see the future. "I think,'' he said, "that you had better just make turtles for now. There are some things you don't want too soon.'' He bent forward and smoothed the coyote out of the wet bank.

II
Stepping Over the Stream

"It is a deer," Looks Back said. He stared solemnly at the marks in the mud that he and the rest of the elders stood circled around.

"It is marks in the mud," Cat Ears said. He was fourteen now and knew everything.

Looks Back ignored him. Everyone knew that the shaman and the shaman's son didn't get along, hadn't since Cat Ears had decided to know everything. "What wisdom knows," Looks Back had shouted at him one day, "is what is *not* known!"

"It is a deer," Looks Back said again. Daughter had learned some things in the last few years about creating the deer in the mud. The legs leaped forward now, instead of hanging down like sticks. The curve of the haunch was there, and the thrust of the neck. He traced the lines with his stick to teach the others how to see the deer. "The deer will see it as we do," he said.

"That is how it will be," Blue Stone Man, who was the chief now, said abruptly. The elders nodded.

Found Water seemed pleased that his apparently insignificant daughter had proved so interesting, although his four wives and their sons looked irritated. When they

23

were finished glaring at Daughter, they glared at one another.

Maybe they would fight among themselves again tonight, Daughter thought, and scream and throw the grinding stone. That would be very satisfactory.

"And how old are you, little Deer Shadow?" Blue Stone Man asked her. "Are you a woman yet?"

"Yes," she said, and realized that Blue Stone Man had given her a new name, if she chose to keep it. She decided to think about it. "Yes. We'll be made true women at the Gathering—Owl Daughter and Baby and Heron and I." She looked for her friends, standing on tiptoes on the outside of the important people.

"An auspicious occasion." Blue Stone Man inspected her. "When you are a true woman, *then* you may make your deer signs and help to call the deer, with the dancers, on the Second Gathering Day." The other tribes and clans of the People would be most duly awed by what the Yellow Grass People had among them. He would have a great name.

"An important day," Listens to Deer said. He put his hand on Daughter's shoulder as the others moved away to discuss this news further. "But you will not let it swell you up with importance like an old fish." He bent his head toward her rebellious expression. "Nor rub it in the noses of your stepmothers."

Daughter sniffed. "I made a scorpion, and Old Woman found one in her water basket. *I* didn't put it there, but she blamed me for it."

"Old Woman is no fool." Listens to Deer chuckled. "You have had enough time for such childishness. Now you will begin to use what you have been given properly."

"Why?" she demanded. "It's mine."

"Because if you do not," Listens to Deer said, "it will turn around and bite you. Just like Coyote."

* * *

The day before the Gathering, Daughter went into the corner of her father's cave and made more scorpions. She wasn't sure how many, but there was one to correspond to each of her fingers and toes and more left over. They were easy to make, creeping from a crack in the rock and parading across the floor, pincers waving, tails in the air. Her father and his wives had to move into another cave for the night, before the people moved on to the Gathering ground.

The Gathering came at the end of every summer, at the balance point of the year, when the tribes and clans of the People came together for six days of communal feasting and hunting. The old men told stories for the edification of the young; both sexes gossiped, the more salacious and embarrassing to its subject the better; the chiefs shared news of game and of the Others, the strangers who had begun to cross over into the People's territory; and the tribes made marriages in six days of raucous and uninhibited courtship.

Most bands were not large enough to marry only among their own. More often their young married outside their tribe entirely, and never within their own clan. Daughter's Yellow Grass People consisted of three clans of about twenty adults each. Her mother had been of a clan of the Red Rock People. Wall Eye was from the Blue Stone People, and Fox Girl from the Smoke People.

"Six-day marriages" were made at the Gathering, too—by couples otherwise attached who found each other attractive. But hardly anyone left his or her mate over a six-day marriage. Rather, it was considered a good way of keeping a mate from getting bored—and it provided a fertile source of gossip and jokes for the winter.

The Gathering was one of the four times in the year

when children who had reached maturity in the past months were initiated as full adults. To have your initiation at a Gathering was best, and Daughter had spent much time in fierce concentration trying to bring on her first flow of blood in time. She was jubilant at her success. It was worth it, even the bleeding and the mess and having to wash, even having to sleep in a separate cave because the blood was such strong magic that men, who had weak hearts, couldn't be near it. By having her ceremony at the Gathering, hundreds of people would be there to watch her. It was almost as good as having visions. Daughter and her friends had spent the last few days preening in eager anticipation: They braided and rebraided their hair, stuck feathers into it, and admired themselves in the river until Old Woman and Young Woman both complained about it to Found Water.

As they approached the Gathering ground, Daughter darted away from Wall Eye, dragging behind her the sack of dried deer meat, nested baskets, and bone cooking spoons she had been told to carry properly on her head. Heron loped up breathlessly beside her.

"Oh, look!"

The Gathering ground was thick with the People and their brush shelters, deer- and coyote-tail standards on poles marking each tribe. Looks Back and Blue Stone Man brought their clan into the ground with ritual gestures of peace and greeting, while Daughter and Heron looked around them avidly. They could smell the smoke of cooking fires and the strange, heady scent of unfamiliar bodies.

A boy walked by, cutting across their path going toward his own tribe. He wore a skin loincloth and had tied a cascade of turkey feathers into his knotted black hair. He eyed the two girls disdainfully, and his stride lengthened a little, shoulders thrown back, feathers dancing. He seemed coiled within his skin, the way cats were. His hair moved with the faint shimmer that brushed through buffalo grass when a breeze blew. To Daughter and Heron, on the edge of their own sexuality, he seemed the essence of boy, arrogant, aloof, enticing, stupid, and beautiful. They yearned after him without really wanting him in particular.

The girls' house was a space enclosed by hides on poles to shield them from male view until the time for their initiation, when they would undergo a transformation that would leave them no longer children, and thereafter men might look upon them with different eyes.

The girls could look out, though, and did. Besides the four girls from the Yellow Grass People, there were two from Red Rock, one from Dry Water, six from Smoke, and five each from Lightning People and the High Rock People. They lay on their stomachs where they could see under the hanging hides and watched while the women carried pitch-lined baskets to the stream for the water that would wash them and scrub away their girlhood. The boys were in another enclosure, and the men visited it with much solemnity and ceremony, carrying their magic bundles and the shamans' masks. Listens to Deer fetched water with the women, Daughter noted, but he also went to the boys' house with the men.

"What do you think they do in there?" Heron whispered.

"My brother said they dance. They dance until they see a vision," Owl Daughter said. "He said it hurt."

"Pooh. *I* would dance till it hurt if I could have a vision," Daughter said.

"You already have . . . well, whatever it is," Baby said, suddenly reluctant to name Daughter's gift and set her further apart from them.

Daughter felt oddly as if she were being pushed out,

moved into some other configuration of her people. She pushed back. "Did you see that boy when we were coming in?" she whispered. "Do you think he's being initiated?"

"No, he looks too old. And he had his hair tied up. I wish I could see him again." Baby's round face was wistful.

"Maybe next Gathering we'll be married," Owl Daughter said. "Maybe you'll marry him." She poked Baby in the ribs.

"What do you think it's like?" Baby asked.

"What?" Daughter snorted as passing feet kicked up dust that blew under the hides and into her nose.

"Being married. With a man."

"Well, you can't be married with anything else," Daughter said. "Unless one of the gods comes and gets you. And he won't if you don't quit sucking your thumb."

Baby took it out of her mouth and then put it back in defiantly. "You know what I mean. What's it like?"

"Nice, I expect," Daughter said thoughtfully. "Or people wouldn't do it all the time. People, dogs, buffalo—everything."

"My father *makes* Second Wife do it," Heron said darkly.

"Wall Eye makes *my* father do it," Daughter said with a giggle. "Or she will leave him, and she's the best cook. So Young Woman and Fox Girl have to share."

"My mother told my aunt that your father doesn't want to do it with any of them now," Owl Daughter said. "That he is tired all the time." She snorted with amusement. "She says the men call him Too Many Wives."

"Maybe he will be like the man who had eight wives, and it will fall off," Baby said.

"That's just a story," Daughter said, irritated now.

"A man can have as many wives as he can hunt for. My father is a very good hunter," she added haughtily.

"I heard that Young Woman beats you," Owl Daughter said.

"Not anymore," Daughter said. *Not since she had found the snake in her bed.* Daughter hadn't called it with a drawing. It had just appeared, looking for a place to be warm, but Young Woman didn't know that. It didn't matter that Listens to Deer said she couldn't do that anymore, Daughter thought with satisfaction, as long as her father's wives thought she could. The scorpions had been just to keep them mindful.

They could hear chanting now, coming from the boys' house.

"What are they going to do to us?" the girl from the Dry Water People whimpered.

"Nothing to be afraid of," Daughter said scornfully. "But you'll look a fool if you cry."

"All the last year's girls say it was terrible," the girl whined.

"Well, probably," Daughter said. "An initiation doesn't change you if it's just something easy." That was what Listens to Deer said. "Do you want to stay a baby all your life, or do you want to get married?"

"I don't want to get married," the Dry Water girl said. "My Uncle Swimmer already did that to me, and you don't know anything! It hurts!" She turned away from the rest of them, sniffling.

The others were shocked, except for Heron, who was more observant than most. "Men do what they want to," she said with a shrug. "It doesn't matter what the rules are."

"I know what *I'd* do to him," Daughter said.

"They're coming," one of the Smoke girls said, pulling her head out from under the stretched hide. The rest ran to peer through the seams. A procession was winding its way down the central path through the Gathering field, to the edge where the girls' house stood. All the other women of the tribe—Aunt Four Fingers, Old Woman, Young Woman, Wall Eye, and Fox Girl among them—made a long snaking line, part of a great snake that included the women of Red Rock, Smoke, High Rock, and the rest, all the married women of the People. Branches of green aspen were tied around their wrists, and they carried water baskets and dark flint skinning knives. The Dry Water girl howled when she saw the knives.

One of the High Rock girls pinched her, hard. "Be quiet!"

The Dry Water girl subsided into terrified hiccupping. Daughter decided that if your own world was wrong, then everything might be a terror to you—the unreasoning and random fear that came when you broke the pattern, when chaos came. If one thing happened that was not supposed to, then anything might. She wondered if the Dry Water girl might be whole again after the ceremony was over—if the whole woman could step out of the splintered girl. That was the way it was supposed to be. Daughter was just beginning to understand that about the pattern.

The girl was still whimpering, and the High Rock girls began prodding her, pinching her and pulling at her hair. Daughter turned on them, testing her own power to snap this one corner of the pattern straight like a hide. "Leave her alone," she said.

"Yah! Who made you the chief?" one of them asked. But they backed away.

Heron, Baby, and Owl Daughter stepped up and stood in a ring around the Dry Water girl. The way it felt to be outside that ring, to have *made* that ring, made Daughter long for a moment to pull it apart again, to fling Baby and Heron aside and pinch the sniveling girl herself. But if you had power, if you used power, then power would use you. It would set you apart. Listens to Deer had told her that, and that was the way it was. Daughter sighed. She understood now why he had been telling her these things.

The married women outside lifted the hide flap and ducked under it, their feet beating a firm, fast rhythm like drums on the trampled grass. The grass murmured beneath them as if it had something to say, as if it knew about coming of age, about change, about the flower and the seed and the winter's dying into the long slow green birth of spring.

The women crowded into the girls' house, spiraling around them, pushing them into the center, herding them the way the dogs drove the deer. Daughter stepped back and back until she was crowded against Baby with a strange girl from the Red Rock People behind her facing the other way. The girls stood tight against one another, like a bundle of sticks lashed together, while the women circled around them, tying them tighter with their singing. And then just as Daughter found herself caught up in that song, in the pattern, the women let out a long-drawn howl, the way they did when someone died, and suddenly sat down on the trampled grass, wailing. The girls, standing bunched and straight above the seated figures, stared at them, unable to move.

Are we dying? Daughter wondered. She felt as if she might be. Along with the many full water baskets, the women had brought a curved stone that held a scoop of glowing coals, and they dropped things on it that made a thick, resinous smoke. The smoke coiled around them like a snake, huge and transparent, burning eyes and noses before it rose. Daughter choked and tried not to cough. Her eyes streamed until she couldn't see what was happening. The women stood again, swaying like the grass, the aspen branches rustling around their hands.

Through the smoke Daughter caught a glint of the flint knives, and a sudden flash of fear went through her like the Dry Water girl's—unreasoning terror, fear of the unknown, the chaos in which anything might happen. For a moment she saw the coyote in the smoke, yellow eyes watching her.

Then a hand closed down on her wrist and yanked her from the bundle of girls. She saw Young Woman's face through the smoke, and Aunt Four Fingers behind her. Young Woman pinned her wrists behind her back, none too gently, and Aunt Four Fingers grabbed her thick braid of hair and sliced through it with the flint knife.

The hair fell to the ground with a thump. Daughter stared at it while she felt the strange lightness of her head on her neck, as if it might bob forward without the weight of the hair to hold it. Young Woman pulled at the thongs that laced Daughter's deer-hide skirt and tugged it down over her hips. Aunt Four Fingers ladled out water from the water basket with a bone spoon, pouring it down Daughter's belly until it ran in rivulets down her knees and thighs, and trickled between her legs. Upending the basket, she poured the rest on Daughter's head. Daughter emerged from the dunking with a sputter and a startled gasp that made her inhale water and choke.

Around her the other girls were being pulled from the group and likewise shorn and washed. When that was done, and they were huddled wet and shivering, the women wrapped them in furs and dropped more resin and feathers—bright pinkish-red ones like an autumn sunset—on the coals. The smoke wreathed around them again, thick and heady with a new smell that clung to their shorn hair and skin.

The women pulled down the hides that enclosed them, and the girls moved into the spiraling line, feet following the other women's, matching step for step. Daughter flinched when she found herself between Young Woman and Fox Girl, and then she remembered that she, too, was a woman now. She lifted her strangely light head, and her eyes met Young Woman's through the smoke. Young Woman looked away.

The procession wound snakewise through the Gathering, the women showing themselves to all the camps until they came to the dance ground. There the men were waiting with the boys from the boys' house. The boys looked like badgers just come up into the sun, their faces marked with soot and ashes. The men were intent, almost avid, even Listens to Deer. They stamped their feet and sang when the women's dance drew near.

Throwing off their furs, the new women began to dance in the torchlit dusk. This dance they knew; they had practiced it for a full moon's time, and it felt safe and familiar. They knew the linked steps, in and out of the boys' line, and they danced them with careless grace, shorn heads high; danced them for their unimportant younger sisters, for the boys with the soot marks still on their faces, for the older women whose bodies were no longer slim, their breasts no longer high. But only a little did they dance them for the men, and then only the boldest among them. Daughter saw Blue Stone Man, the chief, looking at her and wanted to draw her furs and her deer-hide skirt around her again. The men were too big, too knowing, their presence too potent a force. They were lacking the wild grace and softness of the boys.

Daughter saw Cat Ears watching her, too, and made a rude gesture behind her back that only he could see. She wouldn't have Cat Ears, she thought.

The drums spun the dancers into the night. When the Youth Dance was done, the elders began to come onto the dance ground, to step their own pattern around the spiral that was all life, and death, and life again. When

one died, another was born, and so there would always
be the People. Daughter felt caught in it, spinning like
the stars overhead, faster and faster. The meat smell
from the cooking fires made her mouth water—she
hadn't eaten all day—but the dance held her tight in the
pattern, with Young Woman on one side of her and Fox
Girl on the other. Without the weight of her hair, her
feet seemed to lift her a handspan above the ground, as
light as the blackbird's wings. Overhead, the moon spun
in a whirlpool.

Finally, breathless, she collapsed on the edge of the
dance ground, tumbled with Baby and Heron in the buffalo grass. They lay panting, looking up at the moon
where it shimmered above the mountains like a water
basket ready to tip. People were beginning to move
among the cooking fires again, eating, drinking berry
juice fermented in skin bags, tossing the leavings over
their shoulders to the dogs by the fire, who crunched the
hot bones open, nose on paws.

Daughter sighed with pure pleasure. She stretched,
easing cramped calf muscles, her head pillowed on Baby's stomach.

"This is the best Gathering ever," Baby said. "I saw
that boy again. He watched me while we were dancing."

"Everybody watched us while we were dancing,"
Daughter said. It had been as satisfying as she had
thought it would be to be the center of attention. Now
she was happy to hide from the Gathering, to let it flow
around and past her, before she was too much in the
light. She felt tentative about this new status, the way
she felt when she looked at the boys. She would have
to let it clothe her gradually, as her hair grew. She saw
a figure slip by, heard a familiar trickle of laughter, and
knew that Owl Daughter hadn't waited to get used to it.
Owl was the oldest of them. They watched her naked
form slide away into the buffalo grass with a boy from

the Lightning People. If Owl went with him, Daughter thought, they would only see her at Gatherings. Things would change now.

Daughter shivered, cold now that she wasn't dancing. She sat up, teeth chattering, and pulled Baby and Heron up. "Come on, the winter sickness will get you."

They ran toward the girls' house for their hide skirts and put them on as they hopped and stumbled along the trampled path to the brush shelter where their clans were camped. Daughter pulled her coyote furs on over the hide skirt, and her fur foot wrappings. She was ravenous now. They crowded in among the people by the fire pits, pulling meat from the roasting carcasses, yelping and laughing when it burned their hands.

"Stubborn Mud Daughter." Cat Ears stood across the fire pit from her, hungry, intent, head thrust out, shoulders bunched, a rib bone with a lot of meat on it in his hand. "Are you hungry?"

"My name is Deer Shadow," she said, pulling the new name on like her furs. Having Cat Ears call her by her old name had made up her mind about the new one. Deer Shadow twisted a rib bone of her own from the carcass and showed it to him.

"Then eat it with me." Cat Ears came around to her side of the fire pit. "I helped kill it." He had been initiated two years before and hunted with the men now. He stood over her, muscular and self-satisfied, ignoring Baby and Heron. "That's what a Gathering is for—to choose."

Deer Shadow bit into the meat on her bone, teeth snapping. It angered her that her body seemed to find him interesting, while the rest of her wanted to hit him for his smugness. "Go away," she told him through a mouthful.

Insulted, Cat Ears walked away.

"He's a good hunter," Heron said.

"He is Looks Back's son," Baby said, awed.

"Then you have him," Deer Shadow said.

Baby and Heron shook their heads. Cat Ears wanted Deer Shadow. Already they were deferring to her, giving recognition to her new power, recognition tinged with a little resentment.

In the morning Deer Shadow tried out her new name like the new dress that her father had told the wives she should have. She put them both on and went to look in the stream. Whoever looked back at her was older, with strange cropped hair and a new necklace of blue and red water-polished stones, and a very fine dress of pale deer hide, one that Fox Girl had wanted.

Looks Back and Blue Stone Man came and got her while she was admiring herself in the dawn light and walked her up before the Gathering on the dance ground. While Deer Shadow fidgeted and tried not to scratch her nose, they spoke solemnly to those assembled of a new magic, a gift to the Yellow Grass People. Then they stepped back, and Deer Shadow made deer people in the dirt. When she had finished, the images seemed to leap off the ground, antlers swaying, hooves pounding the silent dust.

The shamans of all the bands strode up portentously to look, and after that a murmur went through the crowd, like bees talking. A new magic didn't come very often, and everyone wondered aloud through which door this one had come. The borders between the worlds were thin, and there was no telling. The gods might choose anybody.

Deer Shadow, now more important than her age and sex warranted, didn't know what to do next, so she made more deer while the deer dancers emerged from their caves. If the magic was successful, the deer would hear and would begin to move in their ordained paths, trampling through the narrow reaches of the Place Where the River Runs Backward in great numbers, as they did at the turn of every year when the People called to them.

When she thought she had made enough, she sat back on her heels and listened while Looks Back waved his great tooth and talked to the gods. He reminded them of their promise that this was the People's land, and told them about the Others, in case they hadn't noticed them, being occupied in the sky. When he had explained that the Others stole the deer, he asked the gods to send the Others back to where they came from, and return the deer to the People, the true humans.

The dancers bent and swayed, antlered heads lifting and dipping, mimicking and praising the prey. The deer were venerated, respected for their willingness to feed the People. The dancers finished with a shout just as the sun lifted clear of the eastern mountains.

Deer Shadow stood stiffly, easing muscles cramped from the previous night's dancing, and watched the dark shapes of the hunters move across the grass, their dogs running ahead. The other women were at the edge of the dancing ground, and she was very conscious of the empty space around her, the still circle of magic that the others couldn't cross.

They looked at her across that space, but no one spoke to her. When they had gone back to their fires and the gossip that was the major occupation of a Gathering Day, she returned to the stream and sat beside it, picking grass and braiding it into ropes and then tearing it into little pieces. All the other newly initiated girls were huddled together comparing tales, but she couldn't go with them either somehow. Now they were all alike—even the girl from the Dry Water People seemed less tearful— but Deer Shadow wasn't. She wasn't like anybody, she thought. Was that how Listens to Deer felt? Was that the price for being sacred?

* * *

She knew for certain that she was sacred when the hunters returned dragging a kill that, butchered, would fuel another night of feasting and leave plenty to put by for the winter. But Wall Eye stuck a skinning knife in her hand. "Change out of that fine dress or you'll have it bloody."

Deer Shadow chuckled. Sacredness extended only so far, it seemed, and not past Wall Eye. She slit the hide from the hind leg of the creature that had leaped from the dirt when she called it.

Fox Girl settled next to her. "Now that you're a woman, you'll marry soon," she said pointedly. She was still angry about the deer hide.

"And leave you without any help?" Deer Shadow said, making a round, shocked shape with her mouth. Fox Girl had three children now; she wasn't as pretty as she had been.

"There are enough of us." Fox Girl tugged at the carcass. "Even with Old Woman growing useless."

"I forget. There was only one when my mother was wife."

"If it weren't for you, I would be the only one," Fox Girl snapped. "He told me. He took four of us so you wouldn't be jealous." She dug her skinning knife under the hide at the foreleg.

"Maybe it would have been Young Woman, then," Deer Shadow suggested. "Or maybe Wall Eye. *She* can cook."

"No one will marry a woman with gall on her tongue," Fox Girl retorted.

"Maybe I won't marry," Deer Shadow said, skinning. She could feel Fox Girl crackling beside her like the pine branches in the fire. "I'll just call the deer, and the People will bring me meat."

* * *

Listens to Deer watched Deer Shadow thoughtfully, her stubborn head bent over the carcass. He stared past her at the mountains until the setting sun made him see things three times, and he could see Coyote step out of the green-ringed suns.

Because dreamtime was as real as waking time, Listens to Deer didn't know that his eyes were shut, that the People stepped respectfully around him now. All he saw was Coyote beckoning to him. He went and stood beside him, looking down into the noontime when the deer were killed.

The deer were coming through the Place Where the River Runs Backward, where the water made a big loop around a tower of rock. It fell down when the world was new, because First Man hadn't stacked it properly, so the river had to back up and go around it. The deer stepped delicately, picking their way among the tumbled stones. The migration patterns of the game were mysterious, etched on the web that supported all life. The hunters of the People knew only that they came at the Turn of the Year to this riverbed.

The deer had heard the dancers, heard their names spoken by their image in the dirt. Listens to Deer watched as they were speared, pinned by flint points on shafts hurled by arms extended another forearm's length by spear-throwers—the first great invention of the People. He saw how the deer were gutted, the dogs gulping down the entrails, and trussed on carrying poles to be brought back to the Gathering ground. He saw how the women came out to meet them, and what respect was given to the woman from the Yellow Grass People for her magic lines.

"She's barely a woman," Listens to Deer said.

"It won't matter," Coyote said. "Once you have it, it has you."

And because dreamtime was like sinew, and could be

stretched or balled up, Listens to Deer looked forward and saw Deer Shadow get older. . . .

She was fourteen, and then she was fifteen, and at first she turned the boys down when they came courting because she wasn't ready for them, and she would never be ready for Cat Ears. But then, before she had ever been with one, they stopped coming. She slipped too far into her magic. The procreative force is too powerful—Coyote knew this—to cross it with any other. All the girls of Deer Shadow's year were married, but Deer Shadow had grown afraid to mate with a man. She feared that the magic would leave her. The men had grown a little afraid of her, too, and now she had become like the deer, venerated and held captive.

"She is restless," Coyote said, watching her sleeping alone in the corner of her father's cave. "See her dreams?"

The dreams were wraiths, coils of smoke like the snake-smoke of her initiation, dreams within a dream. Listens to Deer dreamed them with her. They wrapped around her sleeping body, rubbed against her insistently. Sometimes they took the form of a man, sometimes of a river. She thought that she would drown in its waters if she didn't wake.

III

The Blood Dream

Wind Caller smoothed the hole in the little bone with single-minded concentration. He had discovered that certain kinds of reed would work as well, but the bone flutes were better. He bent his head over the bone, carefully drawing a thin, cylindrical stone in and out of the hole. The parrots squawked at him under the canopy of the cedar tree. "I can make better noise than you can," he told them, not lifting his head. There was no need to watch for Jaguar while the parrots were fussing. Jaguar made the parrots very still.

It was cooler under the canopy than outside it, where the jungle met the drier savannah grasses. Most of the Children of the Sun were out in the savannah grass just now, in the field they had burned off in spring to plant the maize. The maize had to be cultivated with digging sticks, and the creepers that sprang up when the grass was gone had to be pulled. It was hot and there were biting flies, even when he covered his skin with fat to keep them off.

Wind Caller didn't have to dig creepers out of the maize like the others or pull the grasses that pushed up through the ashes, because he owned the flute magic; it

41

had come to him first. And a new flute for tonight's
prayers was more important than creepers in the maize.

Tomorrow, because it was the Rabbit Moon, the Children of the Sun would move, as they always did according to the season and the animals. In the driest
months they hunted the little jungle deer, peccaries, and
toucans. In the wettest months the squash and beans
grew, and the fish were fat and lazy and easy to catch.
Tomorrow they would go downstream for the duration
of the Rabbit Moon, to the place where the rabbits
danced, and there would be many of them to eat. The
maize would grow and be ready when they returned under the Hot Rain Moon. Six years had passed since Wind
Caller had discovered the sound that lived in the hollow
bone while trying to blow the marrow out of it, and now
he was a man and one of the council that decided when
to go and when to return. Sixteen was young for being
in the council, but he had the flute magic, and it wrapped
around him like the tamed voice of the wind and gave
him the wind's voice to speak with.

Wind Caller worked away at the flute, pleased with
himself and his own importance. It seemed to him a fine
thing to be touched by the gods in this way, and surely
he was worthy of it. He was as strong and as fast as any
of the warriors—stronger, some were saying, than Eyes
of Jaguar, the chieftain-priest who had killed one of the
great spotted spirits to earn his name. And he knew from
looking into the still blue pools that formed where the
gods had sucked the rock back into the earth that he was
good to look at: his nose long and straight, his thick
black hair braided and looped up to a knot at the back
of his head. His arms and chest bore the multitudinous
pinprink scars of pious bloodletting. He hadn't married
yet; he had little reason to, since he could tumble any
daughter of the Sun on the ferns under the ceiba trees
after a day's hunting. Or almost any other time. It was

the music; it called them in the way his own urges called him. If one of them had his son, he thought, he would marry her. That would be important.

Wind Caller put the flute to his lips and tested it restlessly. His muscles itched for a fight. It was by fighting that the Children of the Sun helped to keep the universe alive. Without battle, without blood given back to the gods to nourish them, everything—sun and moon and people and animals—would wither and die. Blood was the food that fed the world. That was why it flowed in human veins, why when they gave of it they were rewarded with visions; why, if they didn't drain it all, the body would make more, to continue to feed the gods and keep the world alive. It was perfect, symmetrical, a source of deep piety to hold the life of the world in your veins. That was what caused Wind Caller to yearn for battle; that and the fact that he liked to fight.

There would almost certainly be a battle tomorrow, or soon, Wind Caller decided. Other tribes hunted in the jungle of the Children of the Sun, and they, too, began to move under the Rabbit Moon. It was inevitable that they would cross paths and fight; fighting was something they hoped for. The gods gave good hunting to warriors who proved themselves in battle and brought captives home. In the last battle Wind Caller had brought three and killed them at the maize planting so their blood would nourish the Maize God. The Maize God lived folded inside the thumb-sized ear of grain, a mystical being clothed in green with golden hair. He was always thirsty.

Wind Caller unfolded himself from beneath his cedar tree and stood. He was clothed in a loincloth of palm fibers held at the waist with a belt of anaconda skin. His elaborately looped and braided hair was ornamented with macaw's feathers. He was very fine.

Silently he padded along the forest floor to the clear-

ing where his tribe was camped. Night was coming, and
the women were lighting the fires that kept Jaguar away.
Wind Caller sat cross-legged by his mother's fire and
blew a few notes on the new flute, ending in a little
questioning trill.

She looked up disapprovingly. "You should have a
wife to cook for you. Then I would know someone
would take care of me when I get old."

"You aren't old yet," he said. "And don't I hunt for
you?"

"I know when I am old," his mother said. "And I
am old." There was gray in her hair, and most of her
teeth were gone now. If she counted her years, she
would have marked more than three times as many as
she had fingers. Wind Caller's father had been killed in
a fight with the Upstream People two years ago. She
stood, one hand on her hip, her back bent. "My bones
ache. You marry before Jaguar eats you for your pride
and I am left with no wife's family to hunt for me."

Wind Caller laughed. He was the only one of her children who had survived to adulthood, and she scolded
him as if he were not a man. But the truth was her
brother, Ant Bear, whose wife was the chieftain-priest's
sister, would hunt for her. His mother just didn't like
Ant Bear, particularly not when Ant Bear criticized her
son. That was her privilege, no one else's.

"I will think about it," he said. "Maybe at the place
where the rabbits dance, after we have fought some, I
will think about it."

"You've thought about it," his mother snapped.
"You've tried out every girl who isn't related to you.
Now it is time to *do* it."

Wind Caller shrugged. "After the moving on."

The moving on was an elaborate undertaking because
of the nature of their gods. The land of the Children of
the Sun was rich in game—in deer; otters; peccaries;

rabbits; toucans; macaws; and ocelots, Jaguar's little brother. One had only to follow them in their seasonal migrations. Maize grew wherever they planted it, and there were wild squashes and berries and fruit to pick. The river was full of fish, opalescent creatures turning lazily in the broad pools of the lower reaches. Finding enough to eat was not difficult, and only rarely was a human taken by the jungle in return, by Jaguar or Great Snake. There was leisure to ponder where this largesse came from, to study the desires of the gods, and every act became imbued with the ceremonial, with the blood gift the gods required. There was time to make war, not over food but for honor.

The night before the moving on was one of deep ritual, old and sacred. No one ate before morning. Tonight the gods would talk to them, and no one saw gods on a full stomach.

At evening the warriors and young women returned from the maize field, chattering like monkeys, making mock battle with their digging sticks. They sobered when they saw Wind Caller, who had risen and stood rocking on his heels, the flute to his lips. Eyes of Jaguar stood at the other end of the clearing, waiting, his eyes closed in prayer, his parrot-feather banner in his hand. It was dusk. It was time.

Silent now, the men made themselves ready, painting their feet and faces with red mud, setting the ceremonial feathers in their hair, while Wind Caller's flute sent its voice to tell them it was time, to call them out. They circled around him while he stared at the gray stone jutting from the forest floor at the edge of the clearing. It seemed to have some music of its own.

Torches burned around the stone, bringing it to vivid life, so that the rivers of old blood that clothed it stood out like dark moss. In the shadows, in the darkness, the women stood apart. The warriors moved, solemn and strangely anticipatory, toward the stone.

Eyes of Jaguar opened his eyes beneath his parrot-feather banner. He spread out his hands. His wife, Lady Monkey, the privileged one, emerged from the shadows to stand behind him. Only the chieftain-priest's wife might participate in the blood gift, although women could be given to the gods if necessary when there were no more suitable captives. Eyes of Jaguar stepped to the altar stone and lifted arms high while Wind Caller played to the stone and the stone played its own tune back.

Wind Caller heard the invocation as yet another thread through the music, prayer and praise for the game and the growing things, for the air and water and the fire that were the first gifts; the propitiation of Jaguar, who was both god and demon; the recital of the birth and death of Maize, the yellow-haired, green-cloaked god; the petition that all might continue as it was; and finally the offer of food and drink, the invitation to dine at the human table.

Eyes of Jaguar took a stingray spine from between the claws of the jaguar skin that cloaked him. Taken from the salt waters beyond where the land ends, it was very powerful. While his warriors watched eagerly, he used it to prick his chest with swift jabs, creating multiple small red wounds that trickled rivulets as red as macaw's feathers. Using a firestick, Uncle Ant Bear lit the copal resin that lay in the concave mouth of the gray stone, and the smoke rose, musky with magic. Eyes of Jaguar pulled the ocelot hide from around his waist and took his penis in his left hand. With his right he pushed the stingray spine through the skin and stood, head thrown back, before pulling it out to let the blood pour into the copal smoke. Kneeling beside him, Eyes of Jaguar's wife took the spine from him and pierced her tongue. She bowed her head over the stone.

The blood streamed onto the copal, turning the smoke dark and almost viscous, it seemed to Wind Caller, who watched, waiting his turn. It wreathed around the chieftain-priest and the woman, the embodiment of Feathered Serpent, the breath of life. It clung to them, embraced them, drank their offering. The flute at Wind Caller's lips seemed to play of its own accord as he moved nearer to the stone. The music was sweet, yearning; not the terrible fierceness of battle, but an ache, a wanting, the urge to go toward the gods and be one with them.

He moved another step, the flute at his lips, and then it was his turn. Only Uncle Ant Bear had a prior place, and he scowled at Wind Caller as he handed him the stingray spine. Uncle Ant Bear thought Wind Caller didn't deserve his place in front of older warriors. Wind Caller handed the flute to Uncle Ant Bear ceremonially, with the dark thought that Uncle Ant Bear could make a fool of himself if he so chose.

Uncle Ant Bear had tried once to play the flute, and although there were others who could, Ant Bear was not among them. His breath produced thin wailing sounds, more like the mewing of kittens than music. Tonight Ant Bear declined to try. With immense dignity he held the flute across his palms while Wind Caller made the requisite pinpricks in his chest before the perforation of the penis that would send the blood pouring onto the stone. The wounds to the chest were like fly bites, the stroke through the penis a searing pain that engulfed him in the copal smoke and the gods' embrace, a flow of blood from the center of life.

Like Eyes of Jaguar, Wind Caller threw his head back, his face to the night sky above the canopy, and felt the smoke enclose him, saw it weave fantastic shapes above the trees. When he felt the blood begin to slow, he took

his flute back from Uncle Ant Bear and walked unstead-
ily across the clearing to sit cross-legged under a cedar
tree. He put the flute to his lips and saw the notes come
out of it, sinuous, rising like the smoke, bloodred and
white as they danced over his head. They twined and
parted, transparent as breath, but always coiling, coiling.
The bloodred serpent swallowed the white one, engulfed
it, and it danced in the air, weaving two heads from side
to side.

Wind Caller felt the warm pool beneath his hips
where the blood still dripped, and the sharp pain that
tethered him to the earth. The pain was all that kept him
from rising like the smoke and music, floating out of his
earthly body. The pain kept him here, kept him alive in
his body because it wasn't time for his spirit to leave.
Without the pain the spirit might go anyway, borne aloft
on the smoke and the visions.

A wasp flew erratically through the smoke and lit,
confused, on a rotting branch beside him. Wind Caller
stopped playing, the flute still to his mouth, and watched
how its wings and sleek head gleamed in the torchlight.
Its head moved back and forth like the vision snakes,
baffled, lost in the smoke, bereft of whatever interior
compass guided it. It began to clean itself, forelegs rubbing over and over the triangular head, combing the
splayed antennae, curiously mouselike in its attention to
grooming. When it was through, it sat still for a moment
and then, as if some inner vision had grown clear, shot
up suddenly into the smoke.

It caught and rode the smoky snake, and Wind Caller
blew softly into the flute to guide its way. The real wasp
had gone before he realized that what he was watching
was a vision wasp, bigger than its earthly shadow, flying
along the river that uncoiled from the body of the snake,
floating over the water, back legs trailing low. It was
thinking, Wind Caller decided. And then suddenly it

whirred into the air again, higher and higher over the river and the snake, and was lost in the sun, which had risen in a bright flare, burning in the night.

The sun closed in on itself, leaving the moon behind it, and the snake rose high above the river with Wind Caller's piping, dancing itself into a long slow road. And then, because the snake had two heads, the road split, dividing itself like a ripple running down its spine. Wind Caller stopped at the fork, one foot on each division, feeling the muscles bunched under his soles. The wasp returned, feathered like a quetzal bird, the long green tail streaming behind it, and flew down the western fork.

Wind Caller tried to run after it, but his feet were planted on the earth. The small thin pain of the stingray spine's wound pulled him back, towed him toward his body again and sewed him in it. He lifted his head to find he was still sitting beneath the cedar tree, the flute lying across his lap. The smoke roads vanished as he looked at them, and all that was left was the smoke of burning torches full of pitch.

He staggered to his feet and put a hand on the cedar's trunk until his head cleared. His muscles felt loose, knotted together with water. He walked, balancing himself carefully, to his mother's three-sided palm-thatch hut and lay down by the fire that burned in the open side. He tried to think what it all meant, but his head swam like the fish that dived deep in the rivers of his dreaming.

Wind Caller's mother watched him without comment. It was the men's business to have visions, the women's business to keep the fires burning. If she asked him what he had seen, he wouldn't be able to tell her. He would speak vaguely of blood and warriors and many captives, and then he would sleep it off, snoring by the fire while she waited for him to wake. In the morning he might not remember.

* * *

Dawn came with a pale, greenish glow like a firefly as it filtered through the canopy, accompanied by the screech and chatter of the birds and spider monkeys that inhabited its upper reaches. Wind Caller yawned, sat up, and went behind the thatch hut to make water, wincing as he did so. The night's dream came back to him, and he looked around to find the road again. He could see it clearly in his head, with the moon dancing down its length.

He went back to his mother and said, "I saw something last night. I don't know what it means."

"Tell it to Eyes of Jaguar," his mother said placidly. "He will know what it means."

"It was my dream," Wind Caller said. Eyes of Jaguar interpreted all dreams to confirm his own opinions, or so Wind Caller thought, disgruntled. Eyes of Jaguar was old, older than Wind Caller's mother, and set in his ways. Eyes of Jaguar would wait for the Upstream People in the same place that he always did, and they would fight and see who could take the most captives, just as they always did. It didn't matter that they could take more captives if they waited somewhere else and surprised them.

Wind Caller's mother was spreading a mush of ground maize on a hot stone set in the fire, and he waited impatiently for it to cook, ravenous at the smell. The rest of the men were waking now, gobbling the food the women fed them. Wind Caller got his new spear from the back of the hut and checked the bindings again while he watched the maize cake cook. The flaked flint point was leaf-shaped and to Wind Caller's mind very beautiful. It sat snugly in its haft, made of a cedar sapling, bound in place with deer sinew and ornamented with toucan feathers and an ocelot's tail. Hooked into the slot of an atlatl, the spear-thrower that extended the length of a man's arm and thus increased the force of his throw, it was deadly.

Uncle Ant Bear padded over and looked disapprovingly at Wind Caller's spear. "The binding is too loose," he announced.

Wind Caller poked it at him. "Tight enough to run down fat old men." He broke off a piece of the maize cake without waiting for it to cook and stuffed it into his mouth with burning fingers.

"Young men who insult their elders do no honor to the gods," Uncle Ant Bear said.

"I took three captives in the last battle," Wind Caller said.

"This battle you may end up on the Upstream People's altar," Ant Bear said. He looked as if that would gratify him. "It comes of not listening to the elders."

"I listened to my father," Wind Caller muttered.

"A great pity he died. Perhaps he would have taught you circumspection."

"He wouldn't have gone on doing everything the same way forever, just because it's always been *done* the same way forever," Wind Caller said. "And the binding is *not* loose. It's a new way of wrapping. It holds better."

"The way to do things is the way to do things," Ant Bear said. "That is why they have been done that way."

"Even fighting the Upstream People on the same ground every Rabbit Moon?"

"Certainly."

Thinking about his dream and the vision road, Wind Caller opened his mouth and closed it again. The dream wanted to speak to him about this, about going another way. He looked at Uncle Ant Bear and knew there was no use in trying to explain. Uncle Ant Bear was as ossified as Eyes of Jaguar. Inside them, they were shriveling slowly down to their skeletons, becoming incapable of any movement except along paths that were also old and dried up. Wind Caller envisioned Uncle Ant Bear's paunch hardening slowly into stone, a hollow case for his bones. He chuckled. When that happened, they could make a rattle out of him.

He stood up, scooping the last of the maize cake into his mouth. If he wanted to tell his vision and have it interpreted, he would have to tell it to the whole tribe, or at least the whole council—to the young warriors, the ones who weren't bones. The ones who knew that Eyes of Jaguar was growing old.

The council of the Children of the Sun made itself most important this morning. Eyes of Jaguar wore his cloak and loincloth of spotted hide and a jaguar's-head cap that reached down across his eyes. Under the cloak he wore a shirt of scarlet and yellow feathers. Uncle Ant Bear wore a cloak of ocelot skins and a necklace of green feathers as befitted the husband of the chieftain-priest's sister. The other old men wore their finest skins and jewelry, moth-eaten occasionally, as Wind Caller noted—skins that had been killed many years ago. The younger ones knew that propriety did not permit them to notice this.

"Last night the gods came to me," Eyes of Jaguar said. The others nodded. "They showed me many captives taken from the Upstream People. Many blood offerings."

The council nodded solemnly.

Now, Wind Caller thought. "With respect—" He nodded at Uncle Ant Bear, who was glowering at him. "With respect, I have seen a new vision to lay before the council."

"Indeed?" said Eyes of Jaguar.

"I saw two roads. Two ways to go. And suddenly the quetzal bird that was there in my dream took the western road. I think—'' He looked around him at the younger councillors, gathering them in with his voice, coaxing some silent echo from them. ''I think that it means there is another road to go to battle with our enemies.''

''To the west?'' Eyes of Jaguar said.

''I have thought about it,'' Wind Caller said, although in truth he had stumbled upon the unarguable rightness of the idea and clasped it to him without looking for flaws. ''Along the river to the west are cliffs. If we move along the Little Gorge by the Jaguar Stone, we can catch the Upstream People between our warriors and the cliffs and surprise them.''

''Why will that surprise them?'' Ant Bear demanded.

''Because we have been going north to wait for them since I have been old enough to remember it,'' Wind Caller said. ''It may be that they will expect us to do it again this year.''

Sarcasm was lost on Ant Bear, although a younger councillor's lips twitched.

Eyes of Jaguar closed his eyes, and the others stood waiting respectfully. Eventually he opened them and proclaimed, ''If we surprise the Upstream People between our warriors and the cliffs, they will have nowhere to escape except over the cliffs, and that is not good. That destroys the balance. If we take them all or kill them all, where then will we look next year? The gods would not approve of that way. That is not what they meant by your vision.''

''We needn't take them all,'' a younger councillor said hesitantly. ''But we might take them with less loss among our own.''

''The gods choose who is captured,'' Ant Bear said. ''The gods. Not you.''

''And maybe they choose them for stupidity,'' Wind Caller said. ''Did they instruct us to send a messenger to the Upstream People with the names of our best warriors, in case they would like to have them? Why do we deliberately make a present of ourselves to them?''

"The enemy does not change its ways," Eyes of Jaguar said. "They know and we know the way it should be.''

For how long? Wind Caller wondered. How long did you have to do something the same way for it to become "the way we have always done it"? Forever? Or only for as long as the old men's memory? Were there other ways in the memory of grandfathers now dead? Were there other ways for the future?

"Wind Caller's vision does not mean this at all," Eyes of Jaguar said. Now he had a meaning to give them, the proper meaning. "The two roads are the two ways our people may take. One represents the false way, the new way taken only for vanity and dissatisfaction with the teachings of our fathers. The other way represents the way of our ancestors, the true road. That is the road that the quetzal bird took.''

"How can you tell which road is which?" Wind Caller demanded. "Maybe the quetzal bird took the new road. With respect.''

"The gods have sent you this vision so that it could be explained to you," Eyes of Jaguar said.

No one else said anything.

Wind Caller stopped short of arguing. He was not quite ready to be the only one to argue with Eyes of Jaguar. The chieftain-priest was old and slowing, but he possessed a power that didn't come from strength of body. Wind Caller would need more men behind him to overcome it.

He looked around at the younger councillors. Their faces were tight and angry in the silence that Eyes of Jaguar left. So would the young warriors be, the men of Wind Caller's age who would be in the front line of the battle, the ones who hadn't yet earned the right to hang back and let the younger ones drive the prey. They would be the power to carry him beyond the reach of Eyes of Jaguar. It wouldn't take long for them to give him that power, not after he told them his vision and they saw what happened when they fought the Upstream People.

Wind Caller spent a great deal of time expounding his vision as the young men readied their spears and atlatls and daubed their faces with red mud. He perched a few feet above them in the crotch of a fallen gum tree and drew the course of the river in the air.

"Here we come every year. We camp with our women and children and cookfires and make a great row to be sure they notice us. And they come downstream and find us where we always are." He made a snatching motion in the air with his right hand. "First us and then the rabbits."

"How else should we go?" Parrot Tail asked.

"By *another* trail," Wind Caller said, exasperated. "So that we surprise them."

"We take the same path every year to the place where the rabbits dance," Parrot Tail pointed out. "And we always catch rabbits." Parrot Tail was short and stubborn-looking. He reminded Wind Caller of Uncle Ant Bear.

"Rabbits aren't men," Wind Caller said. "Men know more things. You have to surprise men."

"And bring back many captives," Climbs High said. His voice rose with excitement. He turned his broad face to the rest of them. "Wind Caller is right. It is time to change things."

"I don't know," Parrot Tail said. "We have always met the Upstream People in that place. There must be a reason."

"That is true." Climbs High wavered. "Eyes of Jaguar listens to the gods speak."

"*I* listened to the gods speak," Wind Caller said. "Eyes of Jaguar does not wish to listen to me because I—because *we*—are young."

"Eyes of Jaguar is losing his strength," another young man muttered.

"It is time the young spoke," a fourth man said. Up until now he had watched with silent interest.

"Maybe there will be a new chieftain soon," Wind Caller murmured thoughtfully, as if it had just occurred to him.

Bites Spear, the one who had just spoken, was a muscular married man three years older than Wind Caller. He was missing a tooth where he had clamped an enemy's spear between his jaws and snapped it. Now Bites Spear said, "Are we going to stand aside until Eyes of Jaguar is doddering and we ourselves are old men?"

"No!" someone said angrily.

"Are we going to let the old men drive us like game onto the spears of the Upstream People to take captives for them, when there is a better way?"

Wind Caller slid down from the tree, not quite liking how Bites Spear had taken over the argument. But the other young men were pounding their spear shafts on the ground and shouting agreement.

"I don't like it," Parrot Tail said just behind Wind Caller. "Eyes of Jaguar talks to the gods. And he talks to Jaguar."

That brought a short silence among the rest of them.

Wind Caller stepped into the middle, edging his way in front of Bites Spear. "It would not be good to make war within our own people. The Children of the Sun fight the Upstream People, not each other. That is how the gods say it should be. So we will not fight Eyes of Jaguar." An uncomfortable murmuring among the young men indicated their relief at that. "No, this is how it will be." He gathered them in with his hands, circling them around him. "We will do as we are bid, and go to the camp north along the river. It will be afternoon by then, and we will build the women their huts and kill the small game."

Climbs High nodded solemnly.

"That's what we always do," someone protested.

"Did I have a vision that showed me how we became toucans, or tree frogs?" Wind Caller demanded. "If we change the way we fight the Upstream People, we will not be sucked up by the sun and turned into creatures who do not have to eat. And the women will be angry if we don't hunt first."

Bites Spear nodded, arms folded. He seemed to be content to let Wind Caller speak.

"Then in late afternoon, when the old men are talking about the jaguars they killed when the world was young, we will circle west and wait for the Upstream People to pass by the cliffs above the river. They will be there tomorrow, like us. They are moving now. Hears Far told the council."

"And when we bring back many captives, the old men will see that we are right." Climbs High slapped his thigh and stood up. "It is a good plan."

"I don't like it," Parrot Tail said sulkily.

"And will you go to Eyes of Jaguar with the news?" Wind Caller stood over Parrot Tail, his voice suggestively menacing. Parrot Tail looked up at him. Wind Caller's face split into a grin. "If you do, I'll whistle up a thunderstorm and singe your tail feathers."

"No," Parrot Tail said irritably. They could tell by looking at him that he wanted to. But Wind Caller's flute might pull anything out of the wind if *he* wanted it to.

The Children of the Sun moved through the jungle with the confidence of those to whom it had always been home, tempered by a sensible caution. With this many people on the move, neither Jaguar nor Great Snake was likely to prove troublesome, but it was never a good idea to think that you needn't look over your shoulder.

The women carried the things that women always carried—the babies, the grinding querns, the stored grain, the hide scrapers and bone needles, the tools of their lives. They balanced them carefully in hide bundles on their heads while the men walked before and behind them, with what little they had—a spare pair of palm fiber sandals, spear points, finery of feathers and the teeth of kills—in packs slung from their shoulders. They carried their spears at ready, second spears lashed to their packs.

Under the leaf canopy it was hot and wet, and the people walked close to the river gorge to feel the cool spray that rose in misty clouds above the roaring water. Here the river flung itself angrily down a canyon of gray rock, rolling and tumbling over boulder-strewn rapids. But downstream it would emerge suddenly into wide, placid streams that meandered northward to where the land ended, where there were pools of fish and the place where the rabbits danced. The jungle followed the river, but in the lower reaches it became a narrow band, the savannah grasses encroaching more closely.

Wind Caller fidgeted as they went. It was a constant irritation to slow his pace to that of the smallest ambulatory child. He and the other young men would outdistance the women, but then some girl child would run up on his heels and tell him, "Lady Monkey says you go too fast."

Jaguar come and eat Lady Monkey, Wind Caller thought. It would be nightfall before they got there; the Upstream People would already be waiting for them. He danced and fidgeted until Bites Spear said, laughing at him, "You will come around a bend and surprise yourself soon, Tree Frog."

Wind Caller did not like being called Tree Frog. Tree Frog made a big noise and puffed himself up, but nothing much came of his show. Wind Caller slowed his steps and glared at Bites Spear, who had nothing more to say.

Finally the Children of the Sun came to the place by the river where they always camped at the Rabbit Moon. It was flat ground with a path, not too steep, down to the water, and a good supply of palm thatch for shelter. The women began to unpack, to set out their baskets and bone spoons, their querns and grinding stones, chattering to each other as they worked to make a habitation of the site. The smallest children dropped on the ground beside their mothers and slept, while the adults stepped over them and the older youth were sent slithering down to the stream for water.

Wind Caller cut his mother a palm-thatch shelter and wove it expertly together. She watched him with some amusement.

"You are in a hurry." She handed him a gourd scoop full of mashed beans and the fruit of the small bitter wild squash.

"You women have slowed me down all morning," Wind Caller said ungratefully. "Is this all we have to eat?"

"It is until you hunt," she said placidly, setting out her baskets and grinding stones. "I cannot grind meal and walk at the same time. And you should bring me a daughter to help me."

"I'll bring you a cavy." He took his spear and, before she could argue with him, went down by the water to look for one. He and Climbs High and Bites Spear, who were hunting too, found a nest of them on the stream bank by a quiet stretch of the river and killed four while the cavies sat up on spotted haunches and screamed and whistled at them, then tried to waddle under the rocks.

Wind Caller picked one up by the back feet, thinking of rabbits. In another moon he would be tired of rabbits, though it never seemed possible beforehand. Just now he was tired of most everything else, tired of the pattern of life and ready to force it in some other direction with all the energy and accumulated wisdom of his sixteen years.

He grinned at Climbs High. "Tell the others. It is time." Now he would show Eyes of Jaguar that he wasn't the only one the gods had put their mark on. What had the flute been for, otherwise?

Bites Spear, who had a squalling nest of children to feed, picked up a cavy in each hand. "Which way do you think we should go?" he inquired politely, deferring to Wind Caller's wisdom.

"That way." Wind Caller pointed. In his head he could see the vision road, the silver snake of the great river where the course widened between the banks and split around a turtle-shaped island. "There, across the bend where the river goes west. If we go in a straight line, we will come to the river again, where it passes the cliffs. We passed it this morning ahead of them. They won't think of us coming back."

And when they returned with captives, the council would take notice of him and begin to heed his voice, Wind Caller thought. Already the younger councillors were angry with Eyes of Jaguar. He climbed the bank quickly and dumped the cavy in his mother's lap.

"Many thanks," she said with a raised eyebrow. Cavies were rodents and not particularly good to eat, but it would have taken time to catch something more wary. He slipped away before she could think of anything else to say.

The young warriors melted into the jungle, coming together around Wind Caller in a knot out of sight of the camp. There were twenty of them, most of the fighting force of the tribe, and they looked uneasy, although Wind Caller said scornfully that the Upstream People would have no more men than that, and Wind Caller's men would have the advantage of surprise.

"While the old men are drinking and talking, we will show them how it ought to be done!"

"That is right!" Climbs High brightened. Even Parrot Tail looked morosely acquiescent.

Flushed with the excitement of leading his first foray, Wind Caller motioned them after him. The macaws in the canopy squawked and then fell silent as the warriors passed, and ahead of them a spider monkey ran shrieking up a fig tree. At that a faint unease began to creep into Wind Caller's mind, but before he could settle on its source, the jungle parted just ahead of him, and Jaguar emerged from it.

Jaguar walked on two legs, his fangs bared, his claws reaching. Wind Caller raised his spear, and the magic that surrounded Jaguar split open like a gourd, revealing the chieftain-priest, Eyes of Jaguar, in his hooded cloak. The young men behind Wind Caller drew in their breath in a single whispering intake, and Wind Caller knew that they were still seeing Jaguar in his animal form. He took a better grip on his spear and felt the sweat run down his face.

"You have disobeyed." The old and middle-aged men were ranged behind the chieftain-priest so that the two groups glared at each other around Wind Caller.

"It is time for new ways," Wind Caller said evenly. Contrition would get him nowhere, and it wasn't in his nature. He looked at the young men behind him and the old ones before him. Some of them looked uncertain, too. "It is time for Eyes of Jaguar to pass on these decisions to those whose sight is young enough to be true sight."

There was a general murmuring, not so much in

agreement with Wind Caller as in unease with the questionable strength of their chieftain-priest. As a chieftain grew strong, so did the tribe. And vice versa.

"Certainly Eyes of Jaguar can no longer keep order," Bites Spear said, and the murmuring continued.

Wind Caller looked at Bites Spear with sudden suspicion. Had he been with the young warriors? Now Wind Caller couldn't remember.

"You dare," Eyes of Jaguar shouted at him, "you dare to put yourself against the chieftain's judgment? To whom the gods have spoken?" He pulled his obsidian knife from his belt and stared, enraged, at the younger man.

Wind Caller laid down his spear and took out his own knife. Eyes of Jaguar had no choice but to fight him. Wind Caller had no choice but to respond in kind. They were caught in a tight dance of power, circling each other around dark obsidian blades while the others drew back and made a hushed ring around them. Out of the corner of his eye, Wind Caller saw Bites Spear watching them.

The chieftain lunged, and Wind Caller spun away from him, feinted, dodged at his other side. Everything above them in the canopy was silent while Old Jaguar and Young Jaguar fought it out. Wind Caller eased toward the chieftain, marking the vulnerable points at throat and groin, where blood loss would stop a man in a moment. He saw the chieftain's obsidian knife wavering toward him and leaped back as it struck.

He was caught in a net. If he killed the chieftain, they would give him to Jaguar for it. That was not how power was passed. If he did not, the chieftain would kill him—now, or later on the altar stone.

Wind Caller darted in close, aiming for the throat just as Eyes of Jaguar's hand closed around Wind Caller's wrist. They struggled, stepping back and forth, pushing, pulling, twisting in each other's grasp. The knife slid along Eyes of Jaguar's throat. Wind Caller felt the chieftain's knife dig into his ribs and flung himself backward, his arms pushing out and up. Eyes of Jaguar staggered but righted himself as Wind Caller leaped on him, the knife biting into the chieftain's forearm and then striking downward to carve a gash across his thigh. Wind Caller saw the chieftain-priest's eyes go wide with startled pain, felt him slide along his outstretched arm to the ground.

For a moment Wind Caller stood frozen, staring at Eyes of Jaguar, who lay on the ground, his thigh welling blood, his face ashen. Then he took to his heels, crashing through the silent ring of warriors, flinging them away from him, streaking like a rabbit through the jungle.

Behind him, Bites Spear looked at Eyes of Jaguar, writhing as Ant Bear tried to tie off the wound, and then at the council, undecided around him. Bites Spear pointed in the direction that Wind Caller had taken. "Kill him." He looked down at Eyes of Jaguar again. "And get the old man to camp."

"Give me the meat!" Wind Caller flung himself into his mother's hut, snatching at the cavy cooking over the fire, burning his hands.

His mother stared at the blood trickling down his rib cage. "What have you done?"

Wind Caller pulled the cavy from the dirt where he had dropped it and stuffed it into his pack. He scooped the remainder of last year's maize in on top of it. "I have to run," he said.

His mother heard the shouting in the distance and put her hands to her mouth, stifling a shriek.

"That's me they're hunting," he said. He stood, hefting the pack onto his back. Both of his spears were in the clearing where he had tried to kill the chieftain-priest, but there were two spare points in his pack. And his flute, for what that was worth now.

His mother buried her face in her hands. "You went against Eyes of Jaguar's orders," she wailed. "Lady Monkey *said* she didn't trust you! And Ant Bear, but I wouldn't listen."

"You'd better make peace with Ant Bear," Wind Caller said grimly.

His mother howled again, rocking on her heels. "He will curse you. Eyes of Jaguar will curse you. You can't get away from him."

Wind Caller felt the skin on the back of his neck begin to prickle. Uncertain whether it was the chieftain's curse or just fear, he said roughly, "If they catch me, it won't matter whether he's cursed me or not. Pray to the Moon Lady. Tell her I said to watch over you." After all, it was the Moon Lady he had seen shining on his vision road. She owed him something.

The shouting was coming nearer. He took to his heels again, dodging the creepers and the huge, protuberant tree roots. The monkeys screamed and threw fruit at him as if they knew of his disgrace. He settled into a steady run, diving through the fern and the flat shiny leaves, as broad as his chest, deeper into the rain forest.

He could hear them behind him. He parted from the way they would take to the place where the rabbits danced, heading into strange territory, hoping they wouldn't follow. His footsteps hammered in his head with his heartbeat. He waited for the sudden ripping pain of a spear point in his back, or for the unknown horrors of the chieftain-priest's curse. He felt naked and vulnerable and knew he had to make a spear as soon as he could find a hiding place. Would they give up? Would they hunt him into the night and the next morning? Across the turning year? His breath burned in his throat. The baying voices of his people stayed behind him.

* * *

There was a cliff hanging above the river gorge. Wind Caller felt as if he had been running for a day, and still his tribe was on his heels. He looked down at the water that flowed like a thrown spear through a canyon of high, gray stone walls. Beneath him the walls were covered with creepers—creepers in which there would be bees' nests. And the river was home to crocodiles who hugged the shallows just below the cliffs, where the water had worn out caves for them.

The human howling of his tribe neared behind him, and he tightened the thongs that held his pack and set it straight on his shoulders. The sky was growing dark. Maybe they wouldn't see him in the water. He turned to the river gorge far below and jumped. The water was cold, too fast-moving here to grow warm. It snatched Wind Caller like a giant hand and rolled him under. He fought it, struggling up, clawing the foaming hands away, and when his head finally broke the surface, he saw the shapes, on the towering cliffs above him, of the Children of the Sun. They threw spears at him, one last metaphoric curse, but he was already too far downriver. The spears splashed into the water upstream and were carried after him by the current.

He lifted his head, spluttering, and tried to swim. The current, swift and vicious in the middle of the river, swept him along, clawing at his hands and ankles. Fearful of rapids and waterfalls, a swift drop to death by stone and water, he aimed for the opposite shore. His lungs, already strained with running, burned, and he coughed and spat water as he swam.

Slowly the far shore seemed to grow nearer. The current slowed a little, but he could see no way to get out. The sides of the gorge were perpendicular on the western bank. Afraid to climb out on the eastern, where he had come from, he swam and floated, hoping for a hand-hold, a climbable slope.

At last the gorge spread open. Wind Caller fought his way toward the shore, his arms like stone, his throat raw. He staggered among the stones and rotting logs littered along the shallows, eyes on a narrow spit of land beneath a towering cliff of stone. His pack, heavy with water, was rubbing his shoulders raw.

A log moved. It rolled suddenly and opened its jaws wide. Terrorized, Wind Caller screamed and staggered back. He snatched up a stone and threw it at the creature, following with a bigger one. The crocodile gave an angry bellow and lashed its tail.

Wind Caller looked frantically for more stones. ''Go away!'' he screamed at it. He picked up a rock, as heavy as he could lift, and threw it at the crocodile's head, breaking open its nose. The beast bellowed again. Wind Caller ran for the gray cliffs, heaving more stones as he went, but the crocodile rumbled after him. He bounced another rock off its snout and began to climb.

The way was precarious, and somewhere above him the cliff hummed with bees. He inched his way up looking over his shoulder at the crocodile below, lumbering back into the shallows. As he watched, one of the spears thrown by his people glided past the beast, turning in the current. The crocodile opened its mouth and snapped it in two.

Wind Caller hung from the cliff face for a moment, gasping. His heart hammered as he resumed his climb, waiting next to come face-to-face with the flat, hungry head of Great Snake, or to put his hand in a beehive. This was uncharted country to him.

Finally he pulled himself up over the top of the rocks, his hands and toes raw and bleeding. He lay flat for a moment but then sat up, seized with the notion that something was coming after him. He snatched his pack off his back and spilled out its contents on the stone. The half-cooked cavy was sodden and bloody, with maize kernels clinging to it. The rest of the maize was foul from the cavy and the water. The spear points fell out, and Wind Caller looked at them in frightened indecision. If he didn't clean and dry the maize quickly, it would rot. But without a spear he felt like the cavies on the riverbank, fat and waddling and waiting to be eaten. And soon it would be night. He had to make a fire before dark. No, he needed a spear first. Suddenly all the possessions of his tribe seemed impossibly distant in time and energy.

He climbed a tree, scanning its branches carefully for snakes. After selecting a suitable young branch, he worked around its base with his knife, feeling the skin on his back crawl as if something were already putting its paw on him. He worked the branch back and forth where he had made his cuts until it snapped. He stayed in the tree to shape it, scraping away at its length with his flint knife.

He needed more tools, he thought despairingly. No doubt he could find flint among the limestone outcroppings on this side of the river, and stones to shape it, but it seemed a wearying and hopeless task, this remaking of everything he had once owned.

He worked at the spear shaft, stripping the bark from it and shaping the end to hold the point. He had no thong to wrap it with. He would take the thong from his pack, and then cut and dry more after he had killed something. He thought of the cavy and the fire he hadn't made, and cut some thin wood for a fire drill and for kindling.

Assailed by the urge to cry, to throw back his head and howl at the wilderness as he had not done since he was a child, Wind Caller climbed down. He pulled the thong from the mouth of his pack and with it lashed the spear point—in the new way that Uncle Ant Bear hadn't approved of—and set it on the rock. Then he began the wearisome chore of making a spark with the fire drill.

And what was Bites Spear doing? he thought viciously, turning the drill between his palms. Sitting by the council fire, warm and fat, explaining to the council how it was that Eyes of Jaguar had lost his strength, and would have lost his young warriors had it not been for Bites Spear. Wind Caller gave the moon an angry glare and prayed for Bites Spear to die on the Upstream People's altar. That hadn't happened to his father, he thought, hugging a small source of pride to him. His father had been killed in the battle. It was considered wasteful to kill your enemy in battle when you could take him home for sacrifice, but it was a source of honor to die in battle yourself.

A spark flickered for a moment in the drill and died. Wind Caller gave his full attention to starting the fire, turning his back on the moon. The drill began to smoke in the kindling and another spark jumped. He put some dry twigs in it, wishing for the dry grass that was kept in skin bags for tinder, wishing for resin to make a torch, for his mother to cook the cavy. At last the kindling caught, and he fed it carefully, banking stones around it before adding larger wood. Everything here was damp, and the fire smoked and stung his eyes, but it didn't go out. He found a flat stone on which he could dry the maize, and he set it near the fire. The blood from the cavy worried him. Seed that was contaminated either rotted or sprouted in its storage baskets. He looked for something to carry water in, and saw that his pack would have to do. Tomorrow he would have to find a gourd vine with some of last season's gourds still on it. It seemed so much trouble just to stay alive.

Taking the empty pack and his new spear, Wind Caller cautiously climbed down to the water. It was nearly dark, and each log looked fanged and menacing.

He drank, not knowing when he would get more, then dipped the pack into the water until it was full. Then he scuttled up the cliff, envying the monkeys their useful tails.

The pack, leaking like a badly sealed basket, was half full when he got to the top. He picked the maize from the ground and the body of the cavy and his flute, and put the kernels into the pack to wash them. Then he spread them on the stone, separating each kernel. If it dried quickly enough and didn't get too hot, it would be all right. He washed his flute, which was bloodstained and smelled, in the rest of the water, and poured what hadn't already leaked out over the cavy.

He piled more rocks on either side of the fire, cut and sharpened another stick, and stuck it through the cavy, placing the ends on the stones. He watched the fire lick at the cavy's belly. The water from it dripped and steamed in the already smoky fire, making him gag and cough. He knelt with his head away from the fire, eyes streaming, and shook as his lungs tried to push the smoke out of them again.

By the time it was fully dark, the cavy was half burned and half raw, and he ate it, tearing it off the bones with his teeth, ravenous. He spread his pack to dry beside the fire and put more wood on, enough to last the night and warn away Jaguar. He knew that the chieftain-priest's curse would have no fear of fire, but he curled in a ball beside the flames anyway, his back to the river, and watched the evening star come out and hang in the sky, solitary in the darkness. Only rarely could men see the other stars through the haze that hung above the rain forest.

Wind Caller could feel the emptiness around him, like a giant hole in the air, an absence where there should be a presence. He bit his lip to keep from thinking about tomorrow. He had never been alone before.

In spite of his fear, his eyes closed, falling upward into dreamtime. He could see Death walk across the stars, sit, with a bony rattle of legs, on the end of the Moon's crescent bed, cocking a shiny white skull at her.

"You're early," Wind Caller heard the Moon say, because now he was the Moon, or in her.

"I was wondering what you were interested in," Death said.

"Just a human," the Moon said. She folded her light a little into herself, got a shade dimmer. "He isn't very important."

Death chuckled. Wind Caller couldn't tell what he made the sound with. He was only bones.

"You always want *my* toys," the Moon said fretfully.

"Oh, this one has a long way to go," Death said. "If he doesn't come to me of his own accord." He peered at the figure on the riverbank. In the dream jungle Wind Caller could feel the stuff of his own imagining: Jaguar, the empty hunger of Great Snake, even the determined fumbling of the crocodile as it tried to go up the cliff. It butted its nose against the stone and slid back, claws scraping. The Moon clapped her hands at it. Dream animals were very powerful.

"Imagine not having any more sense than to throw rocks at a crocodile," Death said. "How did you get him in so much trouble?"

"I sent him a vision," the Moon said sulkily. "The stupid thing couldn't figure it out."

"These visions are a mistake," Death said. "Open to a great deal of misinterpretation."

"How else are we supposed to tell them anything?"

"If I were you, I wouldn't." Death stroked his bony chin with his fingers. The movement made a rasping sound, like bugs in summer. "They never listen. It's a good thing you have me," he said. "Without me, they would clog up the Universe."

He peered more closely, and Wind Caller backed away. He could feel Death's interest follow him, a faint rattle in the darkness.

When Wind Caller woke in the morning, he was hungry, and there wasn't anything to eat. He fingered the maize. It looked all right, but if he ate it, there would be none to plant, and he didn't know where he was going. He sucked the little bones of the cavy and then tipped the maize, the flute, and his spare spear point into his pack. After some searching he found more flint and with a rock gouged it loose from the surrounding limestone. He found a dry gourd, some guavas, and custard apples, still green. He got a bellyache from them.

In the days that followed he moved on, making an atlatl to throw his spear with and killing one of the little brocket deer that lived in the jungle. He used all of it: hide, sinew, bones, gut, bladder, the sprouting antlers for tines with which to flake his flint points.

He made more tools as he went: a chopper and scraper of stone, a flint blade for whittling wood, an awkward bone needle for sewing deer hide together. That was women's work, and he cursed and shouted over it when it went badly. He gathered grass and palm fiber and tried to coil a basket but gave up in a fury.

Soon he had moved west a hundred miles, and the significance of that to his westward-forking vision road was not lost on him. He moved erratically, though, looking for game, avoiding traces of humankind. The thing to do with a stranger was kill him, and Wind Caller knew this.

Slowly the sun's course shifted, and the land changed. He was moving north now, for no better reason than that it was somewhere to go. The rain forest began to give way to pine and oak, sometimes dogwood and linden and wild plum, and sometimes to trees he had never seen. He felt as if he had fallen out of his own world, spun through time and dreams into some other. He didn't know what was safe to eat and what wasn't; once he ate something that made him vomit and have terrifying visions. After that he was more cautious, taking only a small taste. If he didn't get sick, he ate a little more.

The animals were changing, too. There were deer bigger than the little jungle deer, and they were harder to catch. Once he saw a strange beast with shaggy white fur and curling horns. In the mountains he saw a huge, hairy beast that stood on two feet like a man and roared at him. Wind Caller stared goggle-eyed until it began to come after him, and then he ran. He climbed a tree, and the animal climbed it, too. Maybe it was a man, he thought, terrified. Maybe men like that lived here. He scrambled higher into the small branches and was relieved when the animal gave up. It lumbered down and walked away. Wind Caller stayed clinging to the tree until the next morning.

At night Wind Caller played his flute, the only thing around him with a voice to speak back to him. The nights were growing colder, and he wasn't sure how or why it was happening. He had heard stories of a cold time, when the world was new, but he had never known cold. For warmth he found caves to sleep in and made an awkward garment from a deerskin.

The days grew colder yet, and the trees died. He huddled in a cave and wondered what had come upon the earth, wondered if it was the chieftain-priest's curse.

In his dreams, Death watched him with continuing interest.

IV
Follow

When the long cold winter ended and the first hint of spring came, it carried to Wind Caller a sense of overwhelming relief. The first warmth came so slowly that he barely noticed it, seeping in thin sunlight through the dead trees. Only the needle-covered pines had survived the terrible cold, despite Wind Caller's many prayers beneath the dying branches of the other trees and the blood he had poured out from his own body for them to drink. On the day when he first noticed the cold was going away, he stood gaping at the bare branches above his head and saw shoots of pale green like new grass uncurling from them. In a few days they were recognizable as leaves. He laughed. He took out his flute and sat cross-legged beneath an oak to play it back to life again. He had known that the maize must be born and die again each year, but he had never known trees to do it.

Maybe it was a sign. There must be some sign to tell him how he was to be in this new world. If the trees were reborn, now was the time for the Maize God. Wind Caller looked around him. He had hidden for the winter in a cave on the slope of a hill, but not far below him was flat ground and a little stream. It would be easy to burn the grass off with a stream to contain one side. He filled a hollow stone with coals from his fire and took a torch and his water gourd with him. He poured water all along what would be the edge of his field, soaking the dry blades of the old grass. Resin from the strange needle-trees that had stayed green all winter made a fine torch. He stuck it in the hot coals and it flamed up as red as a macaw's feathers.

The field burned well, better than the wetter lands where the Children of the Sun did their planting. He beat the fire out at the edges, where the wet grass helped to stop it, and let it burn inward. A black crow sat in the still-bare branches and berated him, and a hawk swooped down and snatched up the field mice that fled the flames. The smoke made a cloud high above the little valley and hovered over the blackened ground until dusk, when the evening breeze whisked it away, tidy as a woman with a palm broom. The dew put out the last of the embers. In the morning, he could walk on it and dig it.

He had grown accustomed to loneliness. He hardly spoke anymore, becoming a creature of only occasional startled utterances, like the animals. But this morning he spoke the prayers to the Maize God aloud as he cut a branch and whittled it into a digging stick. His voice sounded strange, as if it belonged to another kind of creature, and he stopped once in despair, staring miserably around him at the empty hillside and the new green of the chaparral, strange plants whose growth he did not understand. Then he spat and swore and went on digging, chanting aloud defiantly.

The ground was easy to work, drier than the land of the Children of the Sun, but not desert. He dug it loose and mounded hills around the maize seed, offering a drop of blood in each, the Maize God's due. Ideally, there should be captives to kill over the new seed, but perhaps the Maize God would take pity on him. He dipped his gourd into the water of the stream and ladled it over the mounds. He wondered if he would have to stay near the seed to water it and keep it growing, since it didn't rain here often. And if he did that, would there be enough game to feed him? He was used to knowing things when he lived beside the river. Now he knew nothing.

Even the water was changeable. Ever since the air had grown cold, he would awake in the morning to find a watery stone inside his gourd that would not pour out. Sometimes the stream would have a skin of the same stone over it. When he put pieces of it in the sunlight or over his fire, it turned back to water again. Wind Caller spent a lot of time with the ice, playing with it, trying to understand it. When it ceased to happen as the nights grew warmer, he was disappointed, but he felt pleased with himself for having learned something. *The water turned to stone when it was cold. If it was heated, it became water again.*

He also learned to make a basket. It was lopsided but it held the acorns and bitter little plums that he found. The plums rotted before he could eat them all, but the acorns and the grass seed he gathered had survived the winter. He made a grinding stone and pounded them to mash and cooked them, as he remembered his mother doing, on a hot stone on the fire.

"Women's work," a voice snickered in the back of his head. "You'll be pricking your tongue instead of your cock to get blood next." Wind Caller was never sure if the voice he heard was his own or that of the chieftain-priest. It didn't matter that Eyes of Jaguar was probably dead by now, or at best a powerless old man awaiting death. His curse, once it was cast, wouldn't stop with his body's stopping, or with Bites Spear's becoming chieftain-priest. Wind Caller envisioned Bites

Spear with a jaguar-hide cloak around him, and a new name, calling on the gods, making the offering—maybe an offering of Eyes of Jaguar. His wife would grow fat and lord it over Wind Caller's mother, and nothing would be as Wind Caller had envisioned it. He could see it all now. He didn't even need a dream, just the memory of Bites Spear's face. He flushed. Bites Spear had had it in mind from the start.

I am older now, Wind Caller thought. *I would know better now.* Immediately he wondered if he would, and it was the first time he had chosen to question his own activity. He had misread his vision, misread Bites Spear's motives, misread Eyes of Jaguar, too—the chieftain-priest had been stronger than Wind Caller thought. He frowned. Perhaps his current condition—living alone and always being afraid of something on his tail—was the consequence of being too proud. Or was it the Moon's punishment because he hadn't listened well enough? To be thrown from certainty into a chaotic land where all was unknown and anything might happen?

Wind Caller went out hunting, wearing the hide of his latest kill although he was still cold unless he kept moving. He had done a poor job of scraping and tanning the hide—more women's work. It was stiff and rubbed raw patches on his shoulders. And it smelled.

To his relief the maize grew, and he stayed near it, eating grass seed and hoarding what little maize he hadn't planted—a talisman, a fetish, a magical link with home, the place he could go no more. He daydreamed, imagining Bites Spear dead, eaten by Jaguar. Maybe Eyes of Jaguar's vengeful ghost had gone into one of the beasts. It could happen, and then there would be a man-jaguar in the jungle, a very bad magic. Wind Caller told himself several pleasant stories in which the man-jaguar rose up from the smoke of Bites Spear's fire and tore him apart, trailing bloody pieces between the huts.

Then, sated, the man-jaguar would disappear, and the Children of the Sun would have a collective vision that told them to find Wind Caller and bring him home to lead them.

Even Wind Caller couldn't quite believe in the end of that one. More likely the man-jaguar would come after *him* next, trailing his scent west and north, his jaws steaming in the mountain cold. He stopped imagining the man-jaguar.

Occasionally he saw smoke that might be from the fires of other people, or might simply be lightning-started—the land was drier here, and he had seen the lightning touch the earth and make a forest go up in a red blaze not a mile from him. That had been before the long cold winter, when the leaves had lost their green and begun to take on red and gold with their own dying. He had run from it, smelling the smoke and seeing the small game animals scurrying through the grass with him, more afraid of the fire than of his human smell. But the distant fires he never investigated. If they were human fires, what would the humans do to him? He wondered if they were men at all—he remembered the animal that had climbed the tree after him. Only the Children of the Sun were true humans, and they had cast him out.

He would live here, he thought, by himself. There was food. There would be maize. He didn't need human companionship—since he couldn't have it. The ache for a woman arose regularly, but it was easy enough to satisfy alone. And what did he need with a woman? Women were uncaring. Which of the daughters of the Sun had been ready to run with him? (Which had had the chance? he acknowledged ruefully. But he doubted that anyone would have joined him.)

When at last he did see other humans, he was seized with an almost overpowering longing, born of constant

denial, at the very sight of them. They came up the hill
through the chaparral one day, talking excitedly and
pointing at his fire, two dogs loping ahead of them. They
looked to Wind Caller very much like his own kind,
russet-skinned and dark-haired, their flesh bare where it
showed beneath their hide garments—not like the hairy
creature that had chased him into the tree. But they carried their spear-throwers balanced in their palms, and
they shouted at him. There were five of them, probably
a hunting party. He spread his arms, empty, palms up,
trying to speak, and a spear sailed past his ear.

Wind Caller stuffed what he could into his pack as
they came running up the hill, their dogs well ahead of
them. He stabbed his spear at one dog and it backed off,
growling. He snatched up the spear they had thrown at
him and ran, leaving behind his grinding stones, his dinner, and his newly tanned deer hide, suppler and better
done than the old one. The dogs snarled at his heels,
and he turned and speared one through the throat. The
other yipped and backed off as Wind Caller pulled the
bloody spear from its mate's neck.

He ran down the other side of the hill, toward the
stream and his maize, howling with fury because it was
nearly ripe. He wished viciously that he had time to set
fire to it. It saved him, though, because when the strangers came to it, they stopped, shouting to each other and
inspecting it excitedly.

Wind Caller had seen little maize growing wild here
and had come upon none that he thought humans had
planted. He supposed that the men thought they had
found a natural growth of it and were rejoicing in their
good fortune at stealing it from the stranger. *Fools,* he
thought angrily. *They don't know anything.*

He watched from a scrub thicket, wondering if they
would go away again and he could retrieve his belongings. But his hope sank when one of them came into

view dragging his deer hide, and then another snapped a command to the dog and it began to cast around for his scent. Wind Caller took to his heels again.

After that he hoarded the few grains of maize in his pack and never again planted them. He kept them rolled tightly in a deerskin pouch, guarding them more closely than his flute. He was never hungry enough to eat them; to do that would mean that he had given up the hope of planting them, the hope of ever living among humans again. He yearned irrationally for the men who had thrown spears at him.

As spring turned to summer, he moved farther north until he came to a place of rocky hills and scrub brush. He saw no sign of big game, but a stream meandered through the land, and there were rabbits. He killed one with a sling and a stone and went under an overhanging rock that formed part of the jagged hillside to eat it and sleep for the night. He made a fire with the coals of the last night's blaze, which he had discovered could be kept alive in a handful of mud, hollowed out. Sometimes the mud would put the embers out; sometimes the embers dried the mud and cracked it so that he burned his hands. But sometimes it worked.

Wind Caller skinned and gutted the rabbit and put it on a stick. Thinking of the cold time, which he thought must happen every year (if it hadn't been a curse), he kept the skin and set about cleaning it while the meat cooked.

He had become almost self-sufficient, a strange creature able to do both men's and women's work. He seldom burned his hands over the cooking fire or burned the meat he tried to cook. The rabbit sizzled invitingly on its spit, and he had the patience to wait until it was ready. There would be more than enough for tomorrow, and cooked meat kept better. When it was cooked through, he took it off the spit and ate until he was full. He laid the rest on a clean stone—he had grown fastidious and didn't like ashes in his meat—and curled under his deer-hide blanket on a pile of leaves by the fire.

The night settled around him. The creatures whose business it was to be out at night rustled in the brush. An owl went by on silent wings like a disembodied shadow, and in a moment there was a sharp squeak from lower down the hillside. A curious burbling howl came from the other side of the valley, the hunting call of a little doglike creature that Wind Caller had seen occasionally from a distance in the dusk. The faint rustle of some browsing animal stopped and then began again. Bugs zoomed and hummed in the dry leaves.

All these sounds crossed the threshold of Wind Caller's sleep, were examined, and dismissed. Only when the faint stealthy scratch of clawed paws on stone came to him did sleep roll away. Unmoving, he opened his eyes, looking into the dark, his fingers curled around the spear shaft near his bed.

Illumined by the dying fire was a faint gray shape, its brushy tail tucked low. In its jaws was the rabbit, and with a quick flick of its yellow eyes it saw that Wind Caller was awake. Its gaze had a deviousness that was almost human. Teeth still clenched on the rabbit, it turned to run, and Wind Caller flung himself off his bed in a fury and chased it. The animal bounded purposefully down the slope, and Wind Caller flung his spear after it with all the anger of a man who sees his breakfast disappearing into the brush. The spear caught the little animal in the ribs and toppled it.

Wind Caller plunged down the slope. He stabbed it through a second time to be certain while the yellow eyes glared at him and then faded. He pried his rabbit from the slackening jaws, brushed it off in disgust, and took it back to the fire. After a moment's thought he returned to the little beast and dragged it by the hind leg up the hill to his cave. If he left it in the open, it might attract Jaguar or Jaguar's cousin, a big tawny cat he had seen in the dry hills. By the fire's dim glow he could see that his thief was one of the little doglike beasts and too thin to be worth eating. He pushed the body to one side and lay down again to sleep.

In the morning he ate the rest of his rabbit and inspected the last night's kill, curious to see one of the doglike beasts up close. The body was stiff, the jaws fixed in a frozen snarl, the legs straight as sticks. It was a female, and he saw from the sagging teats, cold and hard as rocks, that she was a nursing mother.

A whim took him, for no better reason than idleness and the lack of any other focus to his days. He took his spear and his pack and began to backtrack along the coyote's path. He supposed she had been running toward her den with the rabbit and tried that direction first but found nothing. A certain admiration for the coyote overtook him. The beast was smarter than a dog. He tried the opposite direction and finally found her tracks, faint in the dusty earth, and a bit of her fur on a bush.

It took nearly the whole morning to find her den, tucked in a little cave in the rocks below and to the west of where Wind Caller had slept, but close enough for her to have smelled his rabbit cooking. He wondered if she had watched him from the brush and waited until he went to sleep. He seemed to remember the feel of her yellow stare.

The den was narrow and too small for a man. By lying on his stomach, Wind Caller could get his head and shoulders in. There were three pups curled in a ball in the back. They sat up and crouched, snarling, against the wall. Wind Caller wriggled an arm in and grabbed one. It bit his finger to the bone, but he hung on to the pup long enough to stuff it into his pack and tie the top closed. Sucking on his bleeding finger, he thought about the other two. He would take the one he had, he decided, unwilling to be bitten further. With a shrug, he poked his spear into the den and killed the others—better than starving or being eaten by whatever would come to an undefended den.

He picked up the pack and returned to his fire. Before he opened the pack, he rubbed the dead mother's body over his arms and chest, then flung it away down the hillside. It would be gone by nightfall.

Wind Caller opened the pack carefully and inspected his prize. It looked up at him with baleful yellow eyes and flattened ears and bared its jaws, still full of milk teeth.

"No more milk," Wind Caller told it. "You'll live if you can eat meat." He pulled a bit from the remains of the rabbit and held it out on the tip of his finger.

The pup sniffed him suspiciously, and its expression grew puzzled. But its hunger prevailed, and it lunged at the meat, wolfing it down without chewing. It knew what meat was, then, Wind Caller thought, and might even be old enough to be weaned. But it would need water if it didn't have milk. He offered it more meat and it took it, with a painful lack of distinction between Wind Caller's fingers and the rabbit.

He held the water gourd out to it, and it sniffed dubiously. Wind Caller set the gourd on the ground and let the pup crawl out of the pack. It sniffed the water again and then waddled toward the carcass of the rabbit, sank its teeth around the bones, and dragged them into Wind Caller's cave. It growled at Wind Caller when he followed, but when he made no move toward it, the pup settled on the cave floor with the carcass, holding it down with both front paws and worrying it with needle teeth. Wind Caller supposed it would drink water when it got thirsty.

"I'm your mother now," he told it, trying out his voice. It cocked an ear at him but didn't stop gnawing. "I have to hunt for us. If you've got any sense, you'll stay in here and away from the fire. But I don't suppose you *have* any sense." He grinned, shaking out his pack and putting some of the leaves from his bed in the bottom. "You can come with me." He had fetched the pup so that he would have something to talk to, after all. It felt good to talk. It didn't seem to matter that it was to an animal.

He picked up the pup by the scruff of the neck, letting it keep its rabbit carcass. It growled at him but didn't try to bite him again. Wind Caller slung the pack over his shoulder and took his spear and atlatl, and stones for his sling. It wasn't going to be easy to find anything at midday, but he was hungry, and the pup would be, too, and it wouldn't eat fruit. He would settle for squirrels, he thought, or find a turtle in the creek.

When he had three squirrels by the tails, he let the pup out of the pack to wander by the creekside with him. It peered at the running water and lapped at it. Wind Caller whistled softly, and the pup stared at him. He whistled again and showed it the squirrels. It padded toward him. Squatting by the creek, he let it sniff his hands and arms, and it whined, puzzled by the coyote smell. Wind Caller scratched its ears and lifted it again by the scruff of the neck. It was a male, he saw. Just as well. He didn't want a pack of coyotes around because it was in heat, and he didn't want more pups to deal with. He held it to his face and stared at the yellow eyes until it whined. He set it back in the pack and gave it one of the squirrels to make a mess with while he walked back to their cave, carrying it in the pack.

By the time he got there, it had eaten nearly half. And it did eat fruit, as it turned out. It ate anything. It ate his dinner when he turned his back on it and didn't appear to be insulted when Wind Caller swatted it across the cave. It ate boiled acorn mash and fallen avocados, and grass. It ate mice as it grew older and began to forage for itself in the scrub. At first Wind Caller carried it in his pack, and later it ran at his heels. Because he had to call it something, he called it Follow, a word he shouted at it often enough as it strayed off into the brush. He was afraid it would encounter something bigger and more voracious than it was, but gradually he ceased to worry. Follow had the feral caution of his kind.

By the time that four more moons had waxed and waned, Follow was helping Wind Caller hunt. Together they ran down deer; teaching Follow to do that was easier than teaching him not to gnaw the carcass open in his perpetual ravenous hunger before Wind Caller could get to it. Wind Caller tried kicking Follow away or beating him with a stick, but finally he settled on cutting him a piece of the kill first thing, and knowing that it was coming, Follow grew content to wait, at least for a little while. There was never a time when he wasn't hungry.

Follow adapted to daylight hunting, having known no other way. At night he slept with Wind Caller, tail over his nose, curled against the human for warmth. But he had fleas, and before many nights had passed, Wind Caller, bitten and scratching, dragged him into a river and held him with only his gray nose out of the water until he thought they had drowned.

"If you didn't have so much hair, they wouldn't have a place to hide," Wind Caller informed him as they dried themselves at the fire and Follow glowered at him.

The night was falling fast. The dusk outside their cave—a new cave, farther north, where Wind Caller had seen many deer tracks—was purplish and chilly. Wind Caller thought that the cold time was coming again. The trees had begun to turn yellow—just a few leaves, but Wind Caller remembered that it had started that way.

A high warbling howl suddenly sounded in the purple dusk. More voices joined it, and Follow pricked his ears. The voices laced together in a cacophony of yelps and quavering long notes that made the hair stand up on Wind Caller's arms. Follow tipped his long gray nose up and howled back, tentatively at first, the sound reverberating off the stone walls.

Wind Caller clapped his hands to his ears. "Quiet!"

Follow barked, the excited yipping bark he made when he was hunting, and howled again. This one quavered like the sounds that called to him through the twilight, long and undulating. Wind Caller slapped at him, but he didn't stop. Follow got to his feet and stretched, spreading his toes, and padded to the cave mouth. He sat down just outside it and sent his newfound voice into the night.

The sound was eerie, terrifying, and Follow's adolescent shape under the half-full moon was larger than it had seemed before. He crouched on his haunches, gray nose tipped up, and sang. It was a language all to itself, one that Wind Caller couldn't speak, as expressive as his own.

He will leave, Wind Caller thought. *He will go back to his own kind.* Unlike himself, even a coyote had kin to go to. Wind Caller found himself panic-stricken at the thought. If the coyote left, he would have no one to talk to. Follow didn't care whether Wind Caller spoke to him; that was for Wind Caller's benefit and sanity. Follow had found his own tongue.

The coyote stood again, and Wind Caller watched miserably as he trotted into the purple dusk, the brushy tip of his tail a faint vanishing flicker in the brush. There was no point in trying to call him back, not from the song that moved, out of Wind Caller's reach but not

Follow's, across the twilight. Wind Caller put his flute to his lips and tried perversely to match the quavering notes. They slid from his breath like a screech, not the perfect ululations of the coyotes' song. The flute was for singing to humans, he thought. It must be some god's joke that it had been given to him. He laid it down and put his head across his knees, listening to the chorus outside in the night. They were hunting something, he supposed. Would they turn on Follow for his human smell? Would Follow know enough to be wary? Wind Caller pictured him with his throat torn out, his native caution protecting him from all species but his own.

Finally the coyote songs died away and Wind Caller slept, sitting with his head bent on his knees, too miserable even to lie down.

It was close to the middle of the night when the gray shape padded softly into the cave. Wind Caller's sleeping self knew the step and didn't awaken until the coyote sniffed at the remains of the night's meal for a bone to crunch, and settled himself against Wind Caller's rib cage with it.

Wind Caller sat up indignantly. Follow lay happily against him, cracking his bone.

"You have a big idea of yourself, skulking back to me," Wind Caller said furiously. "What makes you think I want you? What makes you think I want to feed you?" He glared at the bone. "Go catch mice."

Follow watched him with eyes that gleamed dimly in the moonlight. He folded his forepaws around the bone and tilted his head to crack the end of it with his back teeth.

"Where have you been?" Wind Caller demanded. In his head he heard his mother scolding his father, who had come reeling home one night from the men's ceremonies. Follow had that look. "Did you have a good time?'' he inquired sarcastically. ''Out with the girls, maybe?''

Follow ran a long tongue over the marrow scraps on his nose. He lifted his head and yawned, showing white teeth and pink gums.

''You're lucky they didn't eat you,'' Wind Caller said disgustedly. He lay back down and buried his face in Follow's matted gray fur. ''They wouldn't let you stay, would they?'' He was glad to have him back and still felt achingly sad, for himself and for Follow, whose true kin wouldn't have them.

Follow sneezed. It was a derisive sound, followed by a kind of snort that might have meant, ''You're too sorry for yourself.''

''I suppose you're telling me you came back of your own accord,'' Wind Caller murmured. ''I don't believe you.'' But he tightened an arm around Follow's ribs and pressed his cheek into the thick fur at his throat.

After that, through the winter, Follow sometimes stayed in the cave when he heard the coyotes sing. And sometimes he trotted off, no matter what Wind Caller said or tried to do to stop him. But he always came back; once with a bitten ear, but otherwise no worse for wear.

He was growing, too. His lanky body filled out, and the ruff of fur around his neck grew more luxuriant. He was bigger than the other coyotes Wind Caller had seen, and sleeker of coat, the result of a human hunting partner with a spear-thrower. By the time Wind Caller thought that Follow was a year old, he could have taken on the leader of any coyote pack and trounced him. By the few toothmarks that Follow came home carrying and the number of times that some other coyote's fur was in his teeth, it was clear that he knew how to fight.

Wind Caller began to think that perhaps Follow *had* made a choice to stay with him. He suspected that it had

something to do with food—Follow was still always
hungry—but it was gratifying all the same. If Follow
went away, Wind Caller knew he would be doubly
lonely.

With the notion of not staying around any coyote pack
too long, Wind Caller kept them on the move as the
weather warmed again. This time he was expecting the
spring but still managed to be afraid that it wouldn't
come. Follow had never seen winter and was as confused by ice as Wind Caller had been. He barked at it
and pawed it and then sat down and turned his back on
it as if he thought it was trying to trick him. With the
thaw he turned puppyish again, leaping after bugs and
chasing his tail in circles, and one warm spring night he
disappeared for three days. When he came back, Wind
Caller decided to move on.

They continued to go north, following a river valley
that ran between mountains. The game was scarcer here,
and so were signs of human habitation. Wind Caller both
longed for and feared some sign of man. Remembering
his last encounter, and perhaps because he kept company
with Follow, he grew as wary as the coyote. They kept
to themselves except for Follow's occasional expedi-
tions, traveling together through a strange country that
seemed to Wind Caller like the land of a vision dream.
There were no great forests here, only stands of wood-
land, and pines high up the mountains. Rain fell rarely,
when purple clouds went walking across the red landscape, the long slanting lines of rain moving as they
watched, until suddenly the downpour was over their
heads and all the dry washes filled and roared muddy
water down their courses, sweeping away anything in
their path. Once a sudden downpour caught Follow in a
dry riverbed, mousing, and hurled him nose over tail for
a long way until Wind Caller found him panting like a

stranded fish on the riverbank, soaked to the skin and throwing up water.

All the animals were different here. A long-eared, long-legged rabbit, a kind that Wind Caller had not seen before, outran Follow. He came back with sore paws, tongue lolling and very angry. Once they saw a herd of humpbacked creatures with shaggy coats and short curved horns. The beasts looked too big for Wind Caller to kill alone, and the horns troubled him. The snakes here were different, too, although there seemed to be no big ones, to Wind Caller's relief. One kind was dusty colored and hard to see, and another made a buzzing noise that stopped Wind Caller and Follow in their tracks. It was an evil sound, and they left it alone.

It grew hot as the year warmed, but it was the dry heat of a fire, not the humid, languid air that Wind Caller had known. The sky above the dry air was a blazing blue, painful to the eyes, stitched sometimes with shreds of white cloud or the infrequent dark thunderheads that built up over the raw, red mountains. At night it was dotted with the tiny floating lights of stars, more stars than Wind Caller could count or could have imagined in the rain forest to the south.

Had there been any way to make the comparison, or anyone to tell him so, Wind Caller would have seen that he had changed, too, as much as Follow had. He was taller by the width of two fingers, and heavier, his shoulders broader, arms and chest more muscular. His face had lost the last roundness of childhood, and his bones were angular and clear beneath his skin. His hair he kept braided and looped up, after the fashion of his people, and combed it out with the bone comb he had made and used also on Follow's fur. They were respectable people, he and Follow, and would stay so even in their outcast state. Besides, it helped to comb out Follow's fleas.

For another year they moved north through this country and came, three years after Wind Caller's exile, to a stream full of turtles, where reeds for baskets and plaiting shoes grew on a marshy bank. They would stay here awhile, Wind Caller decided, stay and learn the game trails and make new sandals. If they encountered no people to drive them away—or coyotes to lure Follow—they might settle for a season. He was tired of wandering and had unaccountably lost his taste for knowing what was over the next hill.

He scratched Follow's ears and the coyote yawned, curling his tongue. Follow would be happy anywhere there was food.

V

In the Rain

In the country into which Wind Caller had so haphazardly stumbled, Deer Shadow sat at the edge of her father's spring house and played with Heron's babies. A spring house was a temporary shelter of hide and brush, used when the People were on the move. The Yellow Grass People were going to their summer hunting grounds below Red Rock Mountain, and Heron's Smoke People, traveling across their path, had sent Heron for a visit.

The Yellow Grass People's camp was full of excitement and the sense of moving out of winter idleness. Deer Shadow had a pile of new rope in front of her that she was plaiting from yucca fiber cut that morning, but she had abandoned it to play with Heron's three babies. The littlest one had his first two teeth, not the front ones as they usually came in, but the canines, so that he looked like a fat rattlesnake. Heron complained loudly as he nursed, one chubby hand twined in her blue stone necklace. Heron's husband was the son of the chieftain of the Smoke People, and Heron had grown very fine and important and matronly. She wore turkey feathers in her hair and had sewn them down the front of her deer-hide dress. She was fatter, solid looking and settled, as if she had arranged the world to her liking and then plopped herself into the center of it.

But she was still Heron. If Deer Shadow squinted, she could still see the girl's face under the woman's. And there was the same familiar feeling between them that came of having grown up together, the feeling that Deer Shadow never could quite manage with the women who came into the tribe as wives.

Heron had brought honeycomb, and they shared it messily with the babies, howling with laughter when Cat Ears walked by and looked disapprovingly at their antics. Heron's other two babies, both girls, clambered about the spring house, the three-year-old stickily in and out of Deer Shadow's lap.

"Here, Disgraceful, the ants will come and eat you." Deer Shadow poured water over the child from the turtle shell she had been drinking from, then scrubbed at her face and belly with a handful of grass. The child grinned and twirled away, dancing around the spring-house poles. Her older sister was trying to build one of her own with twigs and grass, and defending it from Fox Girl's children, who sulked just out of reach, prodding it with sticks because they hadn't been given any honeycomb. Deer Shadow felt guilty about that, so she gave them each a bite. Try as she might, she couldn't warm up to Fox Girl's children as she had to Heron's or Baby's, who were almost like having her own. Fox Girl's children had been interlopers from the start and had stayed that way.

Deer Shadow pointedly ignored Fox Girl, who was grinding seed in the back of the spring house, and bent her head toward Heron. They still had news to share, and something in Heron's face was at odds with her usually placid demeanor.

"My husband's brother's wife died," Heron said, detaching the baby from her nipple and moving him to the other breast. "The brother who wanted to marry you. His wife swelled up like she was pregnant, but there never was a baby, and then she died." She shook her head solemnly. "My husband's mother says it was witches."

That was serious business. "Do you think it was?" Deer Shadow asked. "Had she made one mad?"

"Well, you never know who's a witch," Heron conceded. "And she made everyone mad. But my husband's mother always says that everything is witches."

"Listens to Deer says witches can't harm you if you don't have a wicked spot to let them in," Deer Shadow said.

Heron snorted. "*He* can say that. Even a witch would be afraid to do *him* any harm." It was all right to laugh at men like Listens to Deer now and then, but people who harmed them came to no good. Deer Shadow had seen it. But she didn't think Listens to Deer brought misfortune on them himself; she thought something else did it.

"He's getting old," Deer Shadow said unhappily. "His hair's all gray, and his knees hurt."

"You're great friends with him, aren't you?" Heron said curiously. "Of course, that's to your advantage." The last words carried a trace of a snap. Deer Shadow's status was higher than that of other women, even of women who had many babies. She was almost like Listens to Deer.

"He taught me," Deer Shadow admitted. "But I just like him."

Heron twitched a shoulder. "I don't see how you could. A man like that, with a woman's dress on. And you know the other men treat him as a woman."

"That's the way he's made," Deer Shadow said placidly. "It makes him sacred. Besides, what do you care?"

Heron puffed her cheeks out. "We have a man like

that. He is young. My husband wants to take him for a second wife.''

''Oho,'' Deer Shadow said. ''Your husband's father is old, and your husband wants to be chief after him. A wife like that would give him power.''

Heron glowered into the distance. ''My husband's brother should marry him.''

''Your husband's brother wants children,'' Deer Shadow said. She had heard the saga of Heron's complicated family relationships before. ''Besides, I imagine your husband would marry him just to *stop* his brother from it.''

''*You* should marry my husband's brother,'' Heron said. ''He told me to tell you so.''

Deer Shadow chuckled. ''It wouldn't stop your husband from marrying the soft man. You should be grateful for a second wife like that. He won't have children to compete with yours. And he won't have bleeding cramps and moan about it, or have to go away into the women's house just when you want some work done.'' She looked over her shoulder at Fox Girl.

''Listens to Deer didn't marry,'' Heron said sulkily, as if that should set a precedent.

''He did once when he was young,'' Deer Shadow said. ''He told me. But he got tired of it. He'd rather live alone and have everything the way he likes it.'' She grinned. ''He gets fussier as he gets older, too. Men come to him when they want to, though, and when he wants them to.''

Heron looked at Deer Shadow sideways. ''What about you? Do men come to you?''

Deer Shadow thought Heron knew the answer to that already, but she understood why she wanted to taunt her with it. That source of pleasure was the only thing Heron had that she didn't—that and her babies. It gave Heron a chance to know something that Deer Shadow didn't.

Deer Shadow scratched at the dirt in front of the spring house with one finger, trying to hold on to the reason why she had never lain with a man, to grasp the justification and not just the fear. The fear—that the power would leave her—was real. "I have what I do," she said. "It is better that I not do two things."

Heron relented. "Sometimes I think you are better off. Sometimes I think that I wouldn't want so much magic, especially when I see you at the Gathering, in front of all the hunters with your magic. Sometimes I see it around you like a cloud. I would be afraid of it, afraid that I would burn up in the middle of it. But then when I listen to my husband's mother talk—oh, endlessly— about witches and how the deer were all bigger when she was a young woman—as if *I* had made them smaller!—and I am so tired all the time from carrying the babies, and my back hurts, and I think that another is on the way; and now my husband wants to marry a soft man—well, when I think about all that, I would trade places with you!"

"Maybe I would trade places if I could," Deer Shadow said. "Just to see how it would be. I could have your babies to play with all the time, and you could be the one to listen to Young Woman and Fox Girl and Wall Eye. Since Old Woman died, they yammer at each other even worse, like *three* of your husband's mother."

"But do they complain?" Heron said. "It doesn't count if they only squabble."

Deer Shadow laughed. "I could teach them so you would feel at home. They complain about me already."

"Pooh. That is normal. They have to complain that the sun is too bright."

"And the night lasts too long," Deer Shadow hooted, remembering Heron's mother-in-law.

"And the hides are badly tanned and making her sick."

"The children are noisy—"

"And probably demons—"

"Or not her son's—"

"Or both."

"And someone has stolen her necklace."

"And no one gives her any respect."

They fell against each other laughing. "Oho, maybe I won't trade with you," Deer Shadow said.

Heron wiped her eyes with the back of her hand, then smiled. "I am happy enough most of the time. I have a good husband. He just has a madness at the moment. But not like Owl's man."

They sobered. Owl Daughter had married the boy from the Lightning People that she had gone with at the Gathering. But he had been crazy, or broken in some way, because he had beaten her, not just quickly in anger but enough to break her leg, and she had gone home to her mother by herself, three days' travel with a broken leg. It had never healed right, so that now she hobbled instead of walked. Aunt Four Fingers, who was Owl's mother, had gone to the chieftain of the Lightning People and gotten his permission to beat the boy in return. No one among the Yellow Grass People knew exactly what she had done to him, but he had died. Gossip had it that the Lightning People didn't make a protest over it. Everyone knew that a man like that couldn't be cured and was better off dead than loose among them.

Deer Shadow put an arm around Heron's shoulders as the baby let go of her nipple with a milky hiccup. "Let me hold him a minute."

"Wait," Heron said. She held him up, facing away from her, and a thin stream of urine arced out into the grass. "You always remember after the first one wets you."

Deer Shadow took the baby and held him against her shoulder until he belched. The two little girls climbed into their mother's lap and settled there with baleful looks at the baby.

"Do you remember before the Gathering when we became women?" Heron said. "Do you remember how we thought that as soon as we were women, we would be able to do anything we wanted to?"

"We would be grown." Deer Shadow chuckled. "We would know everything."

"Who knows everything? There must be someone." Heron sounded as if she felt it wouldn't be fair if there wasn't.

"Looks Back, maybe," Deer Shadow said. "Or Blue Stone Man. Or Listens to Deer. They know as much as there is to know."

"Do you believe that?"

Deer Shadow shifted the baby in her arms. By now he was sleeping, his thumb in his mouth, his thatch of black hair as shiny as a crow's wing. "If you ask me, Aunt Four Fingers knows more than any of them. She knew what she needed to do to Owl Daughter's husband. But if you mean who knows how the world was made or where we go when we die, then I think Looks Back can say."

"Truly?" Heron demanded. She seemed to have begun to think about this for the first time, and to be caught in it.

"I think he can *say*," said Deer Shadow, who, not having babies to mind, had had much time to think about it. She thought about it at night, when dreams and loneliness annoyed her, examining the void on the edge of which she was perched, a creature almost of its magical core.

"Well, that's no answer," Heron said.

"I didn't say it was." Deer Shadow prodded the sleeping baby's hand with her finger, and his closed around it. "He says that wisdom is knowing what you don't know."

"Then I don't want wisdom," Heron said irritably. "I want answers. I want to know what to do about my husband. Haven't I given him enough children? And have I ever pushed him away at night? And have I ever complained about what he does at the Gathering?"

Deer Shadow looked at Heron's matronly form. She was still long-legged and pretty. "Have you ever had any fun at the Gathering? Maybe you ought to give the babies to your husband's mother and go make a six-day marriage with a man from the Buffalo Leap People."

Heron giggled. Buffalo Leap men had a reputation for virility. "My mother-in-law would spread it all around the tribe and clear to where the Dry Water People hunt."

"So?" Deer Shadow said. "So your husband will look foolish, and as long as you don't misbehave anywhere except at the Gathering, he will look more foolish if he divorces you." She chuckled. "He doesn't want to anyway. He just wants more. Men do."

"How do you know? You aren't married."

"I could have," Deer Shadow said indignantly. "If I chose."

"They're afraid of you," Heron said. "Except the ones who are too stupid, like my husband's brother."

Cat Ears sauntered by again, carrying a new spear to try out, glancing at them sideways.

"You could still marry Cat Ears," Heron said.

"Cat Ears wants me for the deer magic. Cat Ears thinks he should own anything useful."

"He just wants more," Heron said, laughing. "Men do."

"You tell your husband he will end up like my father, with too many wives and a daughter he can't get rid of."

"*I* heard the daughter had a suitor," Heron said slyly, "and I didn't hear it was Cat Ears."

"Yammer, yammer, yammer." Deer Shadow opened and closed the fingers of her right hand like a mouth talking. "Don't go off at the Gathering with a Yellow Grass man; gossip is what they do best. I am teaching a boy. To make the pictures of the deer."

"Not to make anything else?" Heron chortled.

"Pictures," Deer Shadow said aloofly. "Afraid of His Mother has a gift."

"The thin boy? The one who was younger than us? His mother used to beat him."

"She was an awful woman," Deer Shadow said. "She died last fall, and the minute she was dead, the boy started to live. It was like seeing a flower uncurl. Looks Back put stones and crow feathers in the fire with her body so she couldn't come back. Everyone was terrified that she would."

"Tch." Heron clucked her tongue. "What makes a woman like that, is what I want to know. Or what makes my husband's brother's wife die." The dead were never mentioned by name, only by their relationships to the speaker and the listener. If the speaker was cautious, anyone who had recently been in contact with the dead was referred to in the same way. It would be a month or two before Heron would name her family. "Where does wickedness come from?" she demanded.

"It's just here, I think," Deer Shadow said. "Listens to Deer says it breaks off the sky."

Heron snorted. "And what does that mean?" She had a need for straight answers just now, for rules that would explain her life and tell her how to do things.

"I think it means that the world has both—goodness and wickedness, mixed up properly. It's important to keep the balance. But sometimes all the wickedness runs down into one place and a piece of it breaks off. Then there are people like that woman. Maybe when they die, their wickedness goes back where it is supposed to be, in the balance.''

Heron gave up. Deer Shadow sounded more like Listens to Deer or Uncle Looks Back all the time. It came of not having babies, Heron thought. She heaved herself to her feet, the little girls hanging from her skirts. ''If I don't go back, who knows what my husband will do.''

''Marry some more wives,'' Deer Shadow said.

Heron took the baby and stuffed him in the hide pouch that rode on her back. ''Maybe I will go and live with my brother, and let my husband see what he thinks about it.''

Cat Ears walked by again, balancing his new spear. ''He's just greedy,'' Deer Shadow said. ''All men are.''

Cat Ears bristled. ''Women should be doing their work.'' He glowered at Heron. ''In their husband's house.''

''This is woman's time,'' Deer Shadow said. ''You weren't invited.''

Cat Ears stalked off, his back stiff.

''He has a bad temper,'' Deer Shadow said. ''And Uncle Looks Back won't teach him the things Cat Ears thinks he ought to. He wants to be the next shaman.''

''Oh, no,'' Heron said, horrified. ''That would bring all kinds of bad luck.''

''He's the one who started all the stories about Afraid of His Mother and me,'' Deer Shadow said. ''Because I wouldn't have him. Afraid of His Mother might make a good shaman. I think he would. So does Uncle Looks Back.''

Heron chuckled. ''Poor Cat Ears.'' They could see him halfway across the journey camp, his back to them, pretending to inspect his spear. They both laughed, and he spun around and marched off.

Heron took her leave, setting off at an angle across

the valley with the little girls running after her. In an hour or two she would have to carry the younger one.

Fox Girl rustled her bowls of seed in the back of the spring house and glared at Deer Shadow with the anger of the bound for the free. "You should have Cat Ears," she hissed. "Before you are too old, and a laughing-stock."

Deer Shadow shrugged. "It would spoil the magic."

"Yah! Cat Ears is a shaman's son. That is magic enough."

I would be out of my father's house, Deer Shadow thought. But with Cat Ears. And there was the fear, always the fear.

Deer Shadow picked up a gathering basket and deliberately left her half-finished yucca rope for Fox Girl to put away. She went through the journey camp, feeling the eyes follow her. She trailed magic from her feet and the ends of her long black hair. She knew the men watched her because of that, and because she was good to look at, but she also knew that most of them were afraid of her.

She stopped where Looks Back's giant tooth was planted in the ground outside his spring house and made obeisance to it. It was full of magic, and one magic ought to acknowledge another. Otherwise the world got out of balance. She had known that without being taught it, but it was what Listens to Deer said, too.

Afraid of His Mother was sitting outside the young men's spring house, splitting a new spear-thrower out of green wood. He looked up at the sound of Deer Shadow's step when she was still three or four spear lengths away. When she was thinking hard, he could hear her footsteps in the earth. He was a thin boy, maybe with half again as many years as there were fingers on his agile hands. He had not counted for much before his mother's death, even living away from her in the young men's house, but the clans were beginning to watch to see what he would do next.

"You are cross," he said with the slow smile that he was just beginning to find.

Deer Shadow dug her toe in the dirt, then sat down beside him—even though it wasn't respectable to sit outside the young men's house. Young Woman and Fox Girl would shake their fingers at her if they passed by. Deer Shadow thought vengefully of scorpions or tarantulas for a moment but then stopped herself; she hadn't drawn her revenges into existence since Listens to Deer had told her not to. "I have been listening to my father's wives," she said.

"Oh." Afraid of His Mother looked thoughtful. Her father's wives frightened him, too, made him remember the constant tirade that had accompanied his mother's beatings, the constant list of his shortcomings. That her father's wives didn't frighten Deer Shadow seemed to him admirable. He whittled a little off the end of his spear-thrower. "What do your father's wives say?"

"They say I ought to—" She stopped, biting her lip. They hadn't said anything really, except for Fox Girl this morning. "It's me, I suppose. I just like blaming them."

"Whatever gives you pleasure," Afraid of His Mother murmured.

Deer Shadow's mouth twitched. "I was disrespectful, and I made fun of Cat Ears, too, so now everyone is angry at me. But Heron was here, with her babies, and it didn't seem fair not to have any of my own."

"You like babies so much?" Afraid of His Mother asked. They seemed to him a dreadful nuisance, always having to be fed or washed. Of course, the tribe needed babies, but there were lots of them already.

"Well, not babies, maybe." Deer Shadow looked darkly at the ground.

Watching her uneasily, Afraid of His Mother knew what she meant. Anyone who was old enough wanted to couple, although the idea of doing it with Deer Shadow made him distinctly uneasy. He knew the gossip, but he had dreamed of it once, when she first began to teach him: They coupled, and then she turned into a snake and ate him. When his time came, Afraid of His Mother planned to couple with younger, less potent women and marry a nice girl with no magic in her. He hoped Deer Shadow wasn't hinting at anything.

She began to draw a coyote in the dirt with a splinter whittled from his work. She had left Coyote alone for a long time, since Listens to Deer had told her to.

Afraid of His Mother watched her while he trimmed the spear-thrower. They both knew who Coyote was. "You'll call him," he said after a minute.

"I don't care," Deer Shadow said crossly. Coyote was all appetites, including the one that was troubling her now. Coyote was chaos, the god who kept things balanced. Coyote was not someone you wanted in your spring house.

"Maybe I care," Afraid of His Mother said, but she went on drawing, envisioning the coyote as a dark cloud that matched her restless mood. When she was drawing, when she was making the magic, she didn't miss anything. The magic was too strong. It enveloped her, like a bubble, like a curtain of amber with herself the magical bug transfixed inside. When she was not making magic, she wanted what other women had with a fierceness that was as sharp as an edged flint.

She watched Afraid of His Mother work. The spear-thrower was graceful, smooth, and well-balanced. It looked like Afraid of His Mother. She knew suddenly, without asking him, that he had never coupled with a girl. He didn't know it yet, but he probably never would. The magic had eaten him, too.

Deer Shadow stood up abruptly and brushed the coyote out of the dirt with her foot. The yucca soles of her sandals left a basket pattern in the dirt, as if Coyote were hidden inside it now.

Afraid of His Mother looked at her dubiously and scratched a rabbit in the untouched earth. If Coyote had something to chase, he might leave.

Deer Shadow could tell that he thought she had been reckless. She looked at the boy sitting cross-legged on the sparse grass with his spear-thrower in his lap and said breathlessly, "There's no point in having power if you don't use it. You'll find that out."

She picked up her gathering basket and went through the journey camp to the other side, daring whatever was in the wind, whatever had watched her call Coyote, to come and punish her for it.

The camp was on the edge of a river that they would follow downstream to the base of Red Rock Mountain. There in its lower reaches were wide pools and the turtle stream where Deer Shadow had first learned magic. Higher up, the river bounced through rocky beds and sudden drops sheltered on each side by stony hills softened with new grass and red bee flowers. Deer Shadow walked carefully through the humming about her ankles, swinging the basket. In the stream there would be cress, hot round leaves that gave flavor to old meat, maybe water snails and land turtles making their slow way downstream: spring foods, cool on the tongue, exciting after a winter of piñon nuts and desiccated meat hacked from a frozen carcass.

Near the streambed the rocks grew thicker, and Deer Shadow had to keep her eyes on her feet. Rattlesnakes hatched in spring, and the babies with one bare button on their tails made no sound, although there was poison in their bite. They sunned themselves on the warm rocks.

Everything was wakening. It would bite you if you stepped on it.

She scrambled down a slope, following the stream, looking for a likely place for cress to grow. It preferred running water, not too deep. She spotted its round leaves fluttering under the sunny patches as the cold water burbled by. Kneeling on the bank, she used her knife to cut a bunch and bit into the first handful, enjoying the peppery taste, surrounded by chill water. She cut more, put it in her basket, and played with the water, dabbling it with her fingers and watching the ripples pull her reflection outward, shredding it into the stream. The air on her back was warm, and she wasn't wearing much more than a hide skirt and a necklace of blue stones and eagle feathers, gifts that acknowledged her power. Their images danced in the ripples, repeating their message against the black of her hair.

The air was growing heavy. Deer Shadow felt it before she looked up to see that the wisps of cloud that spattered the sky earlier had grown into dark towers. In a while there would be spits of lightning in them, rain snakes dancing over Red Rock Mountain. She hoped Heron didn't get caught in it with the babies. When those dark thunderheads opened, the downpour would be ferocious. She made a gesture of gratitude toward the clouds that would make the grass grow and bring the deer. If it was a very good year, even the buffalo would come. She looked around for shelter, in case the storm came sooner than she thought.

That was when she saw the man standing on the edge of the water, no more than a spear's length from her.

The skin rose all along her arms, and she drew in her breath in a sharp hiss. He wasn't one of her people. His hair was looped around his head like strings of beads, and his bare chest was covered with scars.

The man stared back at her. He had been gathering

cress, too, in a lopsided basket, and he had dropped it when he'd stepped around a rock. It spilled out at his feet—where Coyote was nosing through it.

Deer Shadow felt the wild storm run down the up-raised hairs on her arms. Coyote's yellow eyes lifted and studied her, and then he sat down at the man's heels and tucked his tail around his haunches, waiting.

The air was thick and hot and gray-gold with the storm. Deer Shadow pulled her feet under her so that she was crouched by the water, poised to run. Her heart thudded in her chest. What was he doing here, a man of the Others, so close to the People's land? Could she run before he caught her? Everyone knew that the Others weren't true humans. She swallowed, tensed for flight, but he didn't move toward her, just stared.

The air shimmered around them as the rain snakes swam over Red Rock Mountain. The silvery yellow sky pulsed, flashed for a moment into something brighter than the sun, illumined them in unstable light. It made the scars on the man's chest stand out like pale rain-drops. He couldn't be of the Others; they didn't mark themselves so. Deer Shadow had seen dead ones, when a band of the People had surprised them in the People's hunting runs. She saw that this man's deer-hide leggings were crudely sewn, too, as if he had done it himself, he and Coyote on their own.

I called Coyote, Deer Shadow thought, panicked yet somehow proud of herself. *I drew him outside the young men's house and put him in a basket.* She stayed crouched, but there seemed no point in running. No one could run from Coyote. Perhaps if she drew him again, she would placate him. Coyote was vain.

She moved her hand carefully on the riverbank, look-ing for a sharp rock. The coyote watched her with nar-rowed eyes, the man with wide, staring ones. Deer Shadow made a gesture of honor at Coyote. She smoothed a patch of river mud and carved his likeness in it with swift strokes. Coyote didn't blink. She gave him a thick tail, carried high, to flatter him (Coyote wore his tail low), and a fine ruff around his neck. Maybe he would be happy with that.

Wind Caller stared at the woman on the riverbank, at first nearly choking with fear. To come so unexpectedly on another human left him panic-stricken. It was a woman, but where there was a woman, there would be men. And then the thought that it was a *woman* gripped him fiercely, not letting go. Her red-brown breasts were bare above a deer-hide skirt, and her long black hair tumbled down and flowed between them, falling like black water over her shoulder. She picked up a rock, and at first he thought she was going to throw it at him. But instead she dug it into the river mud and pulled out an image of Follow as if it had been buried there.

Follow remained unimpressed; the lines in the mud had no power to speak to him, but Wind Caller knew them. He had never seen a picture before, but he knew them anyway, leaping lines that moved on the earth the way his music went through the air. *A woman from the spirit world, maybe not a real woman at all.*

She stood, and he held his ground. It did no good to run from spirits.

They stood staring while the air shimmered with the heat of the distant storm over Red Rock Mountain, where the slanting purple rain had begun. Here the air was still luminescent with the possibility. It touched their bare skin like fingers, raising the fine hairs on arms and neck, lifting them with the force that lay coiled in the boiling clouds. Neither fled, since neither threatened. And in any case, who could run from spirits?

She is magic, Wind Caller thought.

I called him up, Deer Shadow thought.

"Are you human?" he said.

"What do you want?" she said.

They stared at each other, puzzled now, trying to hear some meaning in the garbled words. He was not of the Others, Deer Shadow realized. The People knew the Others' speech a little, and what this man spoke was different. If he was not of the Others, then he was surely a god.

Wind Caller cocked his head, trying to make the words speak to him as the lines in the mud had done. They remained stubbornly unintelligible. Since she didn't step back, he stepped forward, slowly, watching to see what she would do.

Deer Shadow took a step. The coyote didn't move but sat, pinning down the riverbank, while the man walked toward her. The wild air prickled her skin, like something pulled taut between them.

They were both young and not immune to the current of excitement that fear brings. Deer Shadow ached under her skirt for this man, for Coyote in his human form, for all the things that other women had that she did not.

Wind Caller put a hand out to touch her to see if she would vanish. Her skin was solid, as uncertain as the moment but warm, with a thin vein beating in her throat. Awkwardly, thick with hunger, his fingers closed over one breast.

Deer Shadow pushed herself against his hand. If she had called him up, then she would have him. She stared into incomprehensible eyes, heard him speak more unintelligible words. He fumbled with the thongs that held his clothing. He had been bathing in the river, she decided, since his clothes were damp and his skin smelled like cress. But the leather held the older smells of smoke and the warm, musty, bitter scent that might be the coyote.

Wind Caller pulled the magic woman to him, kicking away the tangled leggings from his ankles. He pulled the hide skirt down over her hips with only a passing thought (it would occur to him at length later) for the dangers a human man might encounter in lying with a spirit woman.

The riverbank was rocky, and they stumbled away from it, up a slope where the grass ran along the edge of a hillock. A stone overhang jutted out like a roof; not a cave, just a low shelter. She felt his weight on top of her, pressing her bare flanks into the grass. The hand he put between her legs was like the taste of cress, hot and biting, and as cool as river water. Beyond his shoulder, she saw the coyote waiting by the stream.

The air, lightning-saturated, sparked around them. The sky opened and shut as the white fires danced in it and the rolling boom of thunder tumbled after. Deer Shadow could feel it in the rocks, rumbling under her, like something trying to burst its way out. The man was trying to push himself in, and he was big and very hard, like a stone, bigger than any man of her people she had seen. She wanted him with a fierceness that didn't quite blank out the fact that it hurt. He groaned and pushed hard and then he was in her, all the way up, a column of solid flame, burning his presence into her.

The storm broke as he rolled away from her. He put out a hand to make her stay, but she said words that had no meaning for him and scrambled out from under the overhanging rock. Rain poured around her, flattening her black hair to her breasts and streaming down her face. She backed away into it, snatching her skirt from the riverbank, and ran. He started after her, but she had vanished in the sheets of rain.

VI
Afterimage

The water slid down all around her as she ran, blotting out her world. She clutched the hide skirt to her chest and stumbled through the wet curtains, while above her the thunder rolled and howled. When a flash of lightning illuminated the sky, she could see clearly each raindrop balanced in the air in front of her like an upended river.

Where would she come out, on the other side of this storm? It might be in some new place altogether, she thought, turning a terror-stricken face to the sky as a lightning bolt seared down not ten spear lengths from her. She felt its force reel her backward, lift the hair on her soaking head. It might be that her world was gone, turned away from her, or she from it, by the magnitude of what she had done with the coyote man. She ached between her legs, and she knew that there was blood and semen running down them along with the rain. She could feel its sticky warmth.

Seeing along the bank a stand of piñon pines that were stubby and thick enough not to call out to the lightning—the fire snakes liked tall things—she ducked in among them, huddling in the wet carpet of needles while water splashed off the branches overhead. She peered through the curtain of rain to see if anything was following her, or if there was anything here she knew, some small sign of her own world. She could see neither, only the furious water. She pulled her skirt on and crouched again, thinking of Heron, who would be in the open with the babies, and wondered if it was raining where she was. Poor Heron. But the gods weren't throwing fire at her.

Had *he* been a god, she wondered, the man she had lain with? Had he angered some other god, some more powerful force? Coyote was capable of it. If so, could he protect her? And did he want to? Deer Shadow had seen only hunger in his eyes, and a kind of desperate longing. Would she feel the same way if she found herself barred from the human world now? It was a consideration. There were stories of trespassers in the spirit world, or wives taken there unwillingly, who could not find their way back.

And I've left my basket! A flash of temper momentarily blotted out her fear. A fine basket that had taken much time to weave.

Deer Shadow looked behind her through the downpour and decided that she didn't want it badly enough to go back. The river might be changed, or even gone. She crouched under the piñons, taking stock of what had happened, telling it over and over in her mind like plaiting a rope while the silver shimmer of the storm boomed past.

The rain lessened at last, its curtain thinning until Deer Shadow could see through it to the stream, swollen with muddy water, plunging down its channel as headlong and reckless as she had been. The trees were sodden and dank, and she crept out from under them and washed in the roiling muddy froth of the creek. She still ached, could feel his imprint even when the signs of it were washed away. She wondered if anyone else would know, if the signs would appear like bruises, slowly from beneath the skin to mark her.

She straightened up, feeling a sharp pain and taking a deep breath until it eased. She picked her way along the riverbank, cursing her lost basket again to hold away fear. The red bee flowers were flattened, bruised and pasted to the ground. The bees were gone, and the sunning snakes had vanished. They would be underground, coiled in lithe circles, dry and watchful.

Deer Shadow scrambled upward, hoping to see the turn in the river where it splashed past a stand of cottonwoods and the ground flattened suddenly into the high valley: the place from which she could see the journey camp of the Yellow Grass People. She ran past the cottonwoods almost convinced that the People would be gone, that the valley would stretch as flat and blank as a pool, everything familiar sunk beneath its surface.

But they were there. The smoke of wet fires puffed over the spring houses, and the women were hanging sodden skins on poles to dry. The children ran muddy and shrieking through the camp, whirling clumps of uprooted grass at each other, mud clods clinging to the roots. Deer Shadow dodged a clump that whizzed past her head, then made a horrible face at the child who had thrown it, her heart in her mouth with relief at finding them.

Listens to Deer was lashing his spring house, flattened by the storm, back together again, meticulously braiding the thongs and hide and wet branches into the roof. Deer Shadow stopped to help him and saw that she looked no wetter than anyone else. Listens to Deer's gray hair dripped water, and he sneezed. His fire had gone out.

"Give me that," she said. "Go over to my father's fire and get warm." She tied the hide that formed the back wall of the spring house to the roof pole.

He gave her what she thought was a suspicious look,

and she stamped her foot at him. "You are not young. Go and get warm."

He sighed. "You will put it together all wrong."

"A roof over your head is as right as it needs to be," Deer Shadow said. "We are moving on tomorrow, and it will just have to come down." She shooed him toward her father's spring house before he could ask her any awkward questions. She never knew how much Listens to Deer could see. But she knew he saw clearly the things between men and women, because he was the one between, the one who was both and neither.

Listens to Deer shuffled toward her father's house, his coyote fur robe around his thin shoulders. Fox Girl and Young Woman would give him something to eat since the soft men were always welcome. They knew all the gossip, and they had medicines for childbirth fever and blood cramps. If Heron hadn't been so angry, Deer Shadow thought, she could have got her to talk to Listens to Deer; he would have known what to do about Heron's husband.

Deer Shadow knotted the thongs down the back wall of Listens to Deer's spring house and braced her shoulder against the central pole, shoving it into place. A year or two ago his house would have withstood such a storm. Now he was too old to lash it together properly— his hands hurt when he tried to pull the thong tight—so he spent his time braiding patterns into the thong until his dwelling was beautiful but as rickety as a dead tree.

Deer Shadow straightened the inside, making sure that his treasures were safe and finding enough dry wood to get his fire going again. Aunt Four Fingers gave her a burning stick to light it with, and Owl Daughter hobbled across the way to help her.

"Heron says to tell you she misses you," Deer Shadow said.

Owl Daughter hunched her shoulders stubbornly. "I

don't want to watch her, with her babies and her husband who's going to be chieftain.''

Deer Shadow chuckled. ''Heron has troubles of her own.''

Owl cupped her hands around the fire, and Deer Shadow told her about Heron's husband.

''Poor Heron then,'' Owl said. ''All men are crazy.''

Deer Shadow wondered if that were true, and if the man she had found by the stream had been crazy, and if so, with what. Gods were crazy, by people's standards. She wanted, needed, to think about him, but every time she did, she felt as if somehow his visage began to overlay her own and everyone could tell. Owl would see and tell her he was crazy, and that now Deer Shadow was tainted, too, broken in some way like Owl. Fox Girl would see and snicker. Listens to Deer would see and tell her what the penalty was and whether she had lost her gift, and Deer Shadow didn't want to know.

When she had straightened Listens to Deer's spring house, Deer Shadow fetched him from her father's. He was warmer now, and dry, and Young Woman had given him hot honey and water to drink. But his hands looked paper-thin, hardly able to hold the turtle-shell bowl.

''Your fire is going,'' Deer Shadow said. ''You stay by it, and I'll bring you something to eat in a bit.''

''My bones are cold,'' Listens to Deer said. He sounded weary. ''But I am not dead yet. What are you running in circles so fast to keep me from asking about?''

''Nothing at all. You're a suspicious old granny. Bide by the fire and warm those bones.''

He didn't ask anything else, but it wasn't until she had fed him, done her share of the work in her father's house, and quarreled with Fox Girl over the lost basket that she felt as if she could think about the man without her thoughts seeping past her skull for everyone else to read. By then it was dark, and the journey camp of the Yellow Grass People was quiet for the night's rest. They would leave at first light.

Out of the silence Deer Shadow managed to conjure him up again and hold him with her mind so that he would stand still and be looked at. The scars on his chest and forearms matched the pattern of the rain, as if he had been marked by the storm. Maybe he had been born of it. Or maybe it was the storm that had flung him to earth, angry over something. That seemed more likely. She remembered the coyote, tucked behind his heels, watching her. Everyone was always angry at Coyote. He kept the balance, stirred chaos when it needed it. He overset everyone's comfort, and ran, laughing. He was no fool, though. Coyote might play the fool, but he was old and elemental, and full of power.

Deer Shadow's inner eye drifted from the coyote to the man again, the man she had lain with. She could feel the bruises on her backside where the bare rock had marked her, could feel the print of his fingers on her breast, and the contrast between the heat of his skin and the cold grass. She tucked a hand between her thighs under her sleeping blanket. It still hurt, yet it was a thing she wanted to do again. She drifted to sleep thinking of the man. Across the valley she could hear coyotes howling on their nightly hunt, and she pictured him running with them, gray-furred under the moon.

The sky was dark except for the first red streaks of dawn floating over the mountain when Fox Girl shook her awake. The night's embers glowed like hooded eyes through the camp. Already the women were stirring them into flame, putting stones in the coals to heat. Deer Shadow crawled from under her blanket and yawned.

"Get some water, lazy one," Wall Eye said, stumping past with an armload of wood. Her voice didn't have the edge that Fox Girl's and Young Woman's did. Wall Eye had no children of her own and had found that she could come by a place at her husband's hearth by adopting his firstborn, insofar as Deer Shadow would let her.

Deer Shadow stretched, testing herself to see how sore she felt. It still hurt. She got up quickly before Wall Eye could wonder anything. Young Woman was shaking the children awake, and their father, Found Water, was taking the spring house down around them, anxious to be on the move.

Deer Shadow took a water basket to the river, while behind her Fox Girl complained loudly again about the lost basket of yesterday. The dawn sky was beginning to gray, and the orange puddle of the sun flowed up into it. Deer Shadow stopped and got Listens to Deer's basket as well and filled them both by the dark river. He was awake when she came back, huddled by the embers of his fire. Deer Shadow put more wood on it and looked at him suspiciously.

"You have the fever." Her voice was accusing.

"Possibly," Listens to Deer said. He coughed, a hacking sound from deep in his lungs.

"I'm going to go and get Looks Back."

Listens to Deer coughed again. "I know as much as he does." He pounded on his chest.

Deer Shadow didn't pay any attention. She rolled clean stones into his fire to heat the water and burrowed in his storage baskets to see what he had. The scent of them was pungent and dusty, a heady aroma of dried herbs and powders. She took a deep breath and felt their magic sifting into her. Some she didn't recognize, but she knew mint and willow bark, and she found honey, very old and thick, in a wooden pot. His stores looked disorganized, as if he hadn't straightened them in a long time, and she clucked her tongue over that as she brought her potion to the fire.

Listens to Deer sat very still, looking into the heart of the fire. Deer Shadow mixed the honey into the mint and bark in a bowl and set it beside him. "When the water is hot, make some willow tea," she told him.

Listens to Deer grunted something that might have been assent. Deer Shadow got up and announced, "I'm going for Looks Back."

The darkness was lifting, and she could nearly see across the journey camp. Looks Back's magic tooth was silhouetted against the flaming sky on the eastern edge of the camp. Deer Shadow stood beside it and spoke into the dimness of the house. "You are needed, Uncle."

Cat Ears poked his head out. "Who needs the shaman? My father is busy talking to the gods."

"Listens to Deer needs him. He has the fever," Deer Shadow said. *And why aren't you in the young men's house where you belong?*

"You'll have to wait," Cat Ears said.

Deer Shadow glared at him. She stalked around to the back of the spring house, where she found Looks Back sitting on a rock eating a turkey egg.

"With respect, Uncle, Listens to Deer is too sick to travel. He got wet yesterday and now he has a cough."

"And he sent for me? Gratifying." Looks Back popped the rest of the egg into his mouth.

Deer Shadow chuckled. "Actually, he said he knows as much as you do, Uncle, and can treat himself."

He chewed for a minute, then said, "That sounds more like him."

"But he doesn't. He just sits there. I made him some willow tea, but I don't know if he's drinking it."

Looks Back got off his rock. "We'll see about that." He gathered up his bundles, his own herbs and his magic fetishes and masks for talking to the gods. Anyone could make willow tea, but disease was a demon to be driven out. You couldn't do it just with willow tea.

"Bring my tooth," he told Deer Shadow. She lifted it from the soft ground and carried it reverently. Not everyone was allowed to carry the tooth. Cat Ears wasn't, for instance. He stood beside his father's house, arms folded, and glowered as they passed.

Listens to Deer was still sitting by his fire. Deer Shadow clucked in irritation when she saw that the stones were hot but he hadn't even put them in the water, much less made his tea. She scooped them from the fire with a bone spoon and blew them off, her breath huffing over the fire in little gusts of annoyance. She dropped them into the water basket and poked them around.

Looks Back laid his medicine bundles out while Listens to Deer watched silently, his face thin and pinched beside his nose. Looks Back put his head against the old man's chest.

"Cough."

Listens to Deer coughed, a hacking spasm that shook his whole torso. His breath whooped being drawn in and gasped going out.

"You are too old to get wet," Looks Back said. He began picking things out of his medicine bundle: yarrow for the cough, wintergreen to go with the willow for the pain, vervain to bring the evil up out of the lungs.

The camp was moving around them. "Go and find someone to carry him," Looks Back said.

Deer Shadow expected Listens to Deer to protest, but he didn't, which terrified her. She found her father and Aunt Four Fingers's husband and told them to make a hide litter. There was no arguing, and everyone's face fell. If a man like Listens to Deer died, the people lost something holy, a buffer between themselves and the mysteries of the gods. Also, if a man like that was angry at his death, he could be a powerful force afterward.

Deer Shadow refused to think in either terms. She

made herself brisk, businesslike, rounding up Afraid of His Mother to help. The coyote man faded from her conscious mind. He wasn't gone; she could feel him without thinking about it, on the edges of her apprehension, but she had no time for him now.

When she got back, Listens to Deer was lying flat beside his fire, the coyote robe pulled over him. Looks Back stood above him, masked and strange and far away, talking to the gods about it.

Deer Shadow put her hand to her mouth. Had *she* done this? The coyote robe over Listens to Deer's thin frame seemed to move, to ripple slightly, as if Coyote might suddenly rise up wearing it. "Not this one," she whispered. "You take me."

No one heard her, probably not even Coyote. Looks Back waved his sacred tooth and turned his thunder mask to the sky. Looks Back didn't think Coyote had done it, Deer Shadow thought. He was talking to the god Thunder. His wand was tied with eagle feathers and wrapped with a snakeskin that ended in eight button rattles, which whispered against his wrist. He told Thunder how the Yellow Grass People asked him to cure Listens to Deer, and cocked his head while Thunder spoke to him in a voice carried on the faint breeze that blew down the valley.

"Thunder Spirit sends a cure for this man." Looks Back took his mask off and looked at Listens to Deer. "Old friend, Thunder Spirit speaks words of healing."

Listens to Deer nodded. "This old man thanks the Thunder Spirit."

Deer Shadow bit her lip. A cure didn't always mean the sick person would live. It meant harmony with the universe, a proper alignment not only of body but of soul. Thunder Spirit might choose only to heal the soul, to make the sick man ready for his journey. She put her finger in the water to see if it was hot enough. When it burned her, she poured some out onto the herbs lying ready in the bowl and let them steep while the men bustled around lacing a hide to two carrying poles. After they lifted Listens to Deer onto it, she gave him the tea to drink. Afraid of His Mother began pulling the spring house down.

Listens to Deer managed to get the tea down past what Deer Shadow knew must be an instinctive reaction to gag. Not even the quantity of honey she had put in it could disguise the flavor. "I told you I didn't want Looks Back. His cures are worse than dying," he said, making a face. Then he smiled and handed her back the bowl. "Now stop fretting over me. I will be all right."

"Does your throat hurt?" Deer Shadow demanded.

"No." Listens to Deer compressed his lips firmly and dared her to argue with him.

Deer Shadow was seized with the recurring fear that she had caused this. When her father and the other men picked up the litter, she walked beside it, trying to think how to ask without telling him what she had done. She looked at Listens to Deer's thin hands folded on the fur robe. "Do you think that—that someone is angry?" she asked him.

"No," Listens to Deer said. "I think that I am getting old and lazy, and I want to be carried."

Again Deer Shadow bit her lip. Surely if there was magic in his sickness, Listens to Deer would know. But sickness was always magic—where else could it come from?

"Go and help your mothers," Found Water said. "They'll be in a temper."

"Go," Listens to Deer said.

So she went. She tried to content herself with the notion that many people got sick without her causing it. And in any case, Young Woman had had the chest sickness a year ago, and she had gotten well.

Young Woman seemed pleased with herself for that just now. "It was two moons before my chest didn't hurt anymore," she said proudly. "And did I complain?"

"All the time," Deer Shadow said, not bothering to be polite.

"She got well, though," Wall Eye said comfortably. She slung a pack over her shoulders and heaved another onto her head. "Listens to Deer is tough as an old hide. He's as tough as a woman." She grinned. "He won't die while he's still useful."

That night Listens to Deer's throat filled with the sickness and he couldn't breathe. They thought he would die, but at last he coughed it up. Looks Back dosed him with more vervain and another curing ceremony, and after that he seemed to get better. But the cough hung on and on as the Yellow Grass People moved down into summer. He was too frail to work, and Deer Shadow took him his meals every day and made his tea, seizing each minute improvement as reassurance.

She would have taken the sickness from him if she could have. She was young and likely to survive it. She tried several silent magics toward that end, and one morning when her stomach churned and she threw up her breakfast, she thought she had done it. But she never got the cough, and Listens to Deer's sickness hung on. She kept on vomiting, though, and slowly a horrible conviction dawned on her. At first she thought it was because she had been greedy and eaten too many spring greens. But it didn't matter what she ate; back up it came every morning. When her monthly bleeding was a whole moon overdue, she went into the women's house anyway and made sure that none of the others there knew that no blood came.

She spent five days in the women's house, shaking

with fear. What if it was an evil thing just to be there at all, when she wasn't bleeding? If she was pregnant, and by now she knew with absolute certainty that she was, what was she carrying? A monster? A god? A child of the Others?

She huddled to herself and went over the story again, the one she had made up in her mind. Coyote was also a man, she had decided, just as the animals had been at the Beginning. But Coyote had angered the Sky and been split into two separate bodies, unable now to rejoin. Perhaps the lightning had done it, the way she had seen it split trees. His child would be magical. She hugged the thought to herself, wore it for comfort like a blanket.

She came out of the women's house and went back to her work, making very certain that neither Fox Girl nor Young Woman nor Wall Eye ever saw her vomit again. They were not fools. They would know soon enough, but before then maybe the god might tell her what to do. Surely he must have some interest in his child.

There were times when she could contrive to forget about it for a stretch, ignore the presence within her, the sense of an invader. Listens to Deer, who was still weak, often took her attention. And there were signs that the Others had encroached on the Yellow Grass People's hunting runs. That was serious business, calling for many councils with Blue Stone Man, Looks Back, and the hunters of the tribe. Cat Ears did much shouting and angrily lifted his spear. The best hunter among the people now, he was a voice to be reckoned with, locked as he was in a struggle with his father for the upper hand at each council.

The Yellow Grass People settled for the summer in the caves that honeycombed the foot of Red Rock Mountain. They were like bees, Deer Shadow thought, homing to the familiar hive. It was knowledge of the land that counted toward survival. That was why wives went to their husband's people, and not the other way around. A boy who had spent his life learning to understand the ways of the game, the mystery of their migrations through his country, could not be lost to the band.

And where will I go? Deer Shadow thought suddenly. *Out into the emptiness?* She turned away quickly from Listens to Deer, before he could see her face, and began pounding vervain and wintergreen in a bowl. She could hear his breath bubbling behind her, always the same, never clearing.

"Cat Ears and Looks Back are shouting at each other again," she told him. Listens to Deer liked to hear the news.

"They have been shouting at each other since that boy was old enough to talk," Listens to Deer said. "What is it about now?"

"The Others have been in our hunting grounds. Cat Ears wants to go and fight them. Uncle Looks Back wants to find out why they are here."

Listens to Deer's mouth twitched. "And what does Blue Stone Man say?"

"Blue Stone Man quarreled with Looks Back last quarter moon over the place for the journey camp. So now he is listening to Cat Ears."

"When Looks Back says a place is cursed, Blue Stone Man should listen." He chuckled. "Blue Stone Man fell in the river there and lost his best spear. He should listen to Looks Back when Looks Back says a place is bad."

"Blue Stone Man thinks Looks Back did that," Deer Shadow said. "They are really in a temper because of the Others."

Listens to Deer nodded and wheezed. "I will tell you a secret thing. The Others are people too. Humans."

"They are not! They steal the game."

"They are humans. And hungry." Listens to Deer laid

his head back against the pile of deer hides and closed his eyes.

Deer Shadow poured hot water into the tea and let it steep while he slept. His eyelids fluttered, and his lips moved a little. He slept very lightly, tethered to the waking world by the pain in his chest.

She folded her arms across her belly. Her waist was getting thicker, although no one seemed to notice it yet. Whatever it was going to be grew inside her while Listens to Deer got weaker. For a moment she felt a flash of fury at it, would have ripped it from her if she could.

When the tea was a dark greenish-brown, she strained the bruised leaves from it and lifted his head. His eyes fluttered open. "Drink now."

He took it uncomplainingly. "When are you going to tell me?" he inquired.

"Tell you what?" Deer Shadow put the bowl down with a clatter on the cave floor.

"What makes you look like a rabbit with dogs on its trail."

"You," Deer Shadow said. "Worry over you. You don't eat."

Listens to Deer sighed. "I don't have any taste for it. The sickness leaves a vile taste in my mouth. It spoils food," he said fretfully.

"The tea will help that."

"It doesn't." He hunched himself under the blankets, cold even on this hot day. "I am tired."

Deer Shadow took the bowl away to wash it. The sickness had made his moods as changeable as the weather. She wondered if he remembered his questions of a few moments ago.

He never got better, but he didn't die. Deer Shadow clung to that, to the mere fact of life, as she measured her waist with her hands every morning and crept away to vomit where Fox Girl's suspicious gaze couldn't follow her. Owl helped her tend to Listens to Deer, and Looks Back made very solemn magics almost every night.

When Deer Shadow made her own magic for the hunters, she could feel its source throbbing in her fingertips, as if she had put them in the coals. It was still there. It had called Coyote, hadn't it? A magic that could call Coyote could call game, she thought defiantly. The hunters killed three deer, driving them into a high-walled canyon, and came back with tales of the Others' tracks, fresh on the game trails. Deer Shadow made them give her a liver for Listens to Deer. She stood over him while he ate it, but that night he threw it back up.

Deer Shadow lay in Found Water's cave, surrounded by her stepmothers and their children, and wondered miserably what it would be like to have a baby. Would she die the way her mother had? What if she *had* caught that evil from the cave where her mother died? There was no one to ask. She dreamed of being split open and of a snake slithering out. Of being gnawed open by gray jaws.

When dawn came she got up and tiptoed out to find Listens to Deer. Now was the time to tell him. The coyote man had sent no sign to her, and she was frightened. Listens to Deer could tell her what it would be like. He was there when all the babies were born, easing their way into the world, telling them the secrets that made them willing to come out.

The caves were as dark as the journey camp had been, dotted here and there with embers like sullen eyes, the sun still a faint wash of gray over the east. She picked her way carefully to Listens to Deer's cave and knelt in the doorway. "With respect, Uncle."

There was no sound from inside. She crept in and knelt beside him. Some sense of emptiness made her draw in a lungful of air in a sharp gasp and put her hand to his chest under the coyote skins. It was cold, and the thick bubbling of his breath had stopped.

She tilted her head back and howled, fists clenched on her knees. The sound of footsteps ran through the dark. Looks Back stuck his head in through the cave mouth, his face fuzzy with sleep, the short wisps of hair that grew along his forehead standing straight up. Blue Stone Man strode after him, fastening his collar of eagle feathers, elbowing everyone else out of the way. Behind him, Afraid of His Mother ducked in and knelt beside Deer Shadow. He put an arm around her, and she buried her face in it, hiccuping. Everyone else stood in an uneasy circle around the bed.

"I should have been here," Deer Shadow sobbed. "I let him die alone."

"He wanted to," Afraid of His Mother said. "Stop that."

Looks Back sighed, a long fluttering sound that blew through his lips. "He was tired, child. You'll have to let him go."

Afraid of His Mother made her stand up. He walked her out of the cave.

"I should have been with him." She looked back, but Afraid of His Mother pulled her away.

"Would you like someone else to see you die?" he asked her.

"Always they go when I am not there. My mother went when I was not there."

"You can't stop someone who wants to go Away. And you have to let them take their own road."

"That is what Aunt Four Fingers said when my mother died," she said ungratefully.

Her father and her stepmothers had come running with the rest to see what all the fuss was. Now they were bustling back full of chatter. A man like Listens to Deer would need a great funeral. Much respect must be given him, and many magics. Looks Back and his wife and the shaman's wife would lay out the body, and then there would be feasting and prayers, and more feasting so that Listens to Deer would not go on the road to the Skeleton House hungry. Fox Girl, Young Woman, and Wall Eye shuddered at that thought. They looked at Deer Shadow and mentally renamed her Found Water's daughter for the next month, because they could not speak her real name. She had been too close to the dead one.

Deer Shadow slumped against the cave wall, heavy and desolate, not even bothering to stand straight with her belly clenched in, the way she had taught herself to do the last months.

Fox Girl screamed. Found Water jumped and turned around to cuff her. Her shriek bit into his ears.

"Look!" Fox Girl pointed at Deer Shadow. "That's why she's been sick every morning. Don't think I haven't seen you," she hissed at Deer Shadow. "Acting so holy, like you've never lain with a man. Why hasn't he paid for you?"

"Leave me alone!" Deer Shadow spat at her.

Young Woman approached her anyway and inspected her waistline, prodding at her belly with one finger. Wall Eye came, too, and managed to elbow Young Woman out of the way. "Well, I suppose it was to be expected," Wall Eye announced, half turning her head to get the best view of the situation. "What is his clan?"

Young Woman elbowed her way back. "And why hasn't he paid your father?"

"Maybe he doesn't want her." Fox Girl sniffed. "If I were a man, I'd be afraid."

"You're afraid of everything," Deer Shadow said. "Witches, curses. Spiders," she added threateningly. Those she could produce, as big as her hand, to put in Fox Girl's dreams.

Found Water took his daughter by the wrist and looked sternly at his wives, so that they backed off. He pulled Deer Shadow out into the open, into the light. "Who is it?"

She bit her lip. "There is no law that says I have to tell you."

"Is it Cat Ears? No reason not to tell me if it's Cat Ears. That's a fine match. Very suitable."

"It's not Cat Ears."

"Afraid of His Mother, then?" His eyes narrowed with disapproval.

"No."

"Good. It will matter to the People who you marry, if you are going to. It might have been better not to, but I can see it's too late for that." He brightened. "It's Looks Back or Blue Stone Man."

"It's not—I won't tell you any more." If she went on eliminating men, he would trap her.

Her father twisted her arm. "You need a beating," he decided. He looked around for a stick. "This is going to make trouble," he said angrily, dragging her along. "Likely they'll blame *me*."

Deer Shadow stumbled after him, trying to pull her wrist free. The Yellow Grass People stared at them with interest.

"I called the deer yesterday for the People, and they came," she muttered.

"Then they won't mind if I beat you," Found Water said. "They didn't all come. Some went to the Others." He found a suitable stick of firewood outside Aunt Four Fingers's cave and picked it up, still holding her wrist.

Deer Shadow drew back her free hand and hit him, palm open, across the jaw, hard enough to stagger him. "If you beat me, I won't call the deer," she said, eyes narrowed. "Not for you or Blue Stone Man or anyone. If you beat me, I will tell them to go away."

Her father glared, and she glared back. Aunt Four Fingers stood goggling, with a crowd behind her. Afraid of His Mother stared at her as if she had suddenly turned into a fish.

"Disobedient daughters deserve to be beaten," Found Water said.

"Do it then," Deer Shadow hissed. "I told you what I will do."

There was a frightened intake of breath from those who could hear her. They had no doubt that she could do it. Slowly, as if he forcibly had to unclench his fingers, Found Water let go of her wrist.

She rubbed out the white fingerprints in her skin and let her eyes slide across the faces of the Yellow Grass People, one by one. Her father's wives looked scandalized and disapproving. Cat Ears stuck his head out at her, chin first, eyes slitted, so that his ears seemed to fold back along his head like a lynx's. "The daughter of Found Water has no right to keep this to herself," he said, closing his mouth with a snap.

Everyone knew he had wanted her. They watched, now, to see if he was going to do anything else.

Deer Shadow walked past him, putting her feet down carefully, very precisely, as if she were stepping in unseen footprints. She made the stiffness of her back as insulting as possible. The observers edged back. She had let loose too much magic here and might be marking out a path that would open up and eat anyone who followed her.

Cat Ears didn't follow her, but he managed to contrive a scornful look for Found Water. "A man who can't control his women grows too old," he said spitefully.

"And a man who tries to control them with a stick may get bitten," Aunt Four Fingers said. She gave Cat Ears a long look while the other women murmured their

assent. They had only to look at Owl Daughter and remember.

"All the same, we should know who it is," Fox Girl
snapped. She had followed Found Water and Deer
Shadow so as not to miss anything.

"We'll know when we know," Owl said. She rarely
spoke, and they blinked at her.

"Tchah! Maybe it was . . . the one who just left us."
Eyes slid toward Listens to Deer's cave.

"Never." There were suppressed giggles, despite the
power of the recently dead. The topic was too interesting
to let alone. "But it would have to be someone with
strong magic."

Their eyes slid over the men's faces, speculating.

"And not a subject for idle gossip," Blue Stone Man
said abruptly. He adjusted his eagle feather collar and
stamped his foot, scattering them.

"It must be him, then." The women were making
baskets by the river. Give Away cast her eyes at the
chieftain and lowered her voice. "You always said he
wanted her."

"I always said that Cat Ears wanted her, too," Four
Fingers pointed out. Her fingers threaded yucca fiber in
and out of the coils of bunched marsh grass.

Give Away's sister Caught the Moon said solemnly,
"*I* heard she was sitting outside the young men's house
with Afraid of His Mother."

Four Fingers snorted. Give Away and Caught the
Moon were married to the same husband. They were the
worst gossips in the band, and they never got anything
right. "Afraid of His Mother is afraid of his shadow,"
Four Fingers said, plaiting.

"Afraid of Deer Shadow," Runner said with a giggle.
She was young, newly married into the Yellow Grass
People, and afraid of Deer Shadow herself, but she was

enjoying all the speculation. This was the most excitement she had seen.

"It might be Blue Stone Man," Four Fingers said thoughtfully. "When he was young, he'd stick it in anything that moved."

They all laughed at that. It was part of the chieftain's power that he could make the game increase by virtue of his own virility, but Blue Stone Man enjoyed it more than some people thought was appropriate for the dignity of a chieftain.

"Maybe it was Killed a Bear."

"Maybe it was Walks Funny."

"Maybe it was One Ball. He's only got one, but it works!"

They wove the marsh grass in and out, giggling, thinking up names, some half serious, others deliberately silly to set them chortling.

"She'll have to tell," Caught the Moon said.

"Why should she?" Owl said. She hadn't spoken before.

"Well, really! Because it's not natural. That's not how we do things." Caught the Moon compressed her lips.

"You can't have babies and not know its clan," Give Away said. "Who would it marry?"

"Tsk! *And* how do we know the father isn't in *her* clan?" Caught the Moon sucked on a tooth with suspicion. "That would be *very* bad."

"She has more sense," Four Fingers snapped.

"Well! How do we know?"

"And why won't she tell?" Runner said, with a shiver for the wickedness of it. She put a hand to her mouth. "Ooh, suppose it's Squirrel."

Squirrel was Owl's brother, and they belonged to Found Water's clan. "If you say that again, I'll pull your ears off," Owl said.

Runner made a quick sign with her fingers to ward off evil. Anyone who was as broken as Owl was in her leg might be a repository for evil.

Four Fingers leaned forward and slapped Runner across the mouth. Runner howled, holding her lip.

"I told you it would make trouble," Give Away said to Caught the Moon, "didn't I?"

Looks Back heard the women, in the way that he heard everything that went on among the Yellow Grass People, and wondered if he ought to go and tell them to be silent. But it didn't take a shaman to know that they wouldn't stop for more than five breaths. There was too much in the air now, with the spirit of Listens to Deer still among them, and now this. They talked out of nervousness, like geese honking.

And they would expect him to do something about it, Looks Back thought. He settled himself in the back of his cave and closed his eyes until some answer came to him. Answers came out of the dreamtime, always. . . .

Looks Back opened his eyes and saw a white buffalo. He knew without doubt that it was Listens to Deer. In dreamtime, people and animals were one. The white buffalo nodded his heavy head slowly and walked away. When he was gone, Coyote sat there, tongue lolling out.

"Did you do this?" Looks Back asked him suspiciously. It had been known to happen. The Sun had mated often with human women in the Beginning.

"I might have," Coyote said.

"Might have" was always interchangeable with "is" in dreamtime. Coyote lay down with his nose on his paws, his yellow-gray furry stomach to the fire's heat. The story started like a puff of breath from Coyote's mouth, invisible in the warm air. It fell, solidifying, condensing like a cloud. . . .

When he woke, Looks Back was almost certain that Listens to Deer had sent Coyote to tell him that. But what it might mean was troubling. He thought that he would tell it only to himself just now to keep it still.

Once when Coyote was coming along, he heard of the daughter of Lives by the River. He decided to marry her. Her name was Death-Bringing Woman, and everyone said to Coyote that only a crazy person would marry her. "There is a pile of bones beside Lives by the River's house belonging to the people who have tried to marry that woman."

Coyote just laughed at them because Coyote is very pleased with himself. And also because although Coyote is often very clever and has been given many lives by the Great Mystery Spirit, the Breath of Life, sometimes he is also a fool.

So Coyote went along and he went along and he came to a place where a woman was digging for camas. He was hungry so he popped three of the bulbs in his mouth.

"Who is that stealing my camas?" said the old woman.

"It's Coyote. Can't you see?"

"I can smell you now," she said, "but I am blind."

So Coyote chewed some pine gum and spit it into the woman's eyes.

"Can you see now, old woman?"

"Yes, I can. I see you sniffing my camas bulbs." She pulled them closer to her. "You may have one more for making my eyes see, because now I can dig more of them. Where are you going?"

"I am going to marry the daughter of Lives by the River."

"Oho," said the old woman. "You'd better be

careful. She has teeth in her vagina. She'll gnaw it right off.''

''I'm not afraid of that,'' said Coyote. ''I'll take this piece of bone and knock them off.''

So he went on his way, disguised as a human, and he came to where Death-Bringing Woman lived with her father.

''What do you want?'' Lives by the River asked him.

''I want to marry your daughter.''

Lives by the River grinned. ''And what bride-price can you pay?''

''I have one camas lily bulb,'' Coyote said. ''And three deer that I killed on the way here.'' He gave him some deer that he had made out of wood.

''All right,'' said Lives by the River, ''you can marry her.''

So Coyote went into Lives by the River's spring house, and he gave a very thoughtful look at the pile of bones outside the door.

Inside he saw Death-Bringing Woman and began to understand why there were so many bones. She was very beautiful and proud, with hair like the black glass that comes out of the volcanoes. She brought game to her father simply by saying its name. She would be a fine wife to have, so Coyote said, ''I am here to marry you.''

''Then you must want to sleep with me,'' Death-Bringing Woman said, ''so come on.''

She got into a bed of sweet grass covered with a deer hide and pulled another hide up over her. Coyote could hear the grinding sound of teeth coming from under the hide, and he got into bed very gingerly.

''Quickly,'' she said. ''Quickly.''

So quickly he pushed the bone chisel in and broke

off the teeth. She was very surprised, but she wasn't really angry because she had never really been able to sleep with a man before. So they did.

In the morning, he took off his disguise and told her he was Coyote, and they were married for a long time.

VII
How Hunger Comes

"You must always go around the fire sunwise," Young Woman said to Deer Shadow. "Or you will make the cord tangle around the baby's neck and strangle it."

"My mother knew a woman who did that," Fox Girl said. "And when the baby came out it was blue, and dead, and half rotted."

"Did she die?" Wall Eye wanted to know.

"Of course. The baby's spirit was so angry it killed her."

Deer Shadow ate a handful of the grass seed she was grinding. It made her teeth hurt, but she was hungry all the time. She looked longingly at the dried meat that was Wall Eye's task, and when Wall Eye looked away she snatched a piece.

"Too much meat will make the baby kick the inside of your stomach to death," Fox Girl said. "I know a woman it happened to."

"You always know everything," Deer Shadow said, her mouth full.

"I know about babies," Fox Girl said. She turned to Young Woman. "When I had mine, I was hungry all the time, but I knew enough not to overeat, like this foolish one here.''

"It will make the labor last longer," Wall Eye said. "My mother always said this," she added when they accorded her the superior glances of women who have had babies to one who was barren.

They had been at it all morning, ever since the hunters had left. Deer Shadow had made the deer magic for the hunt with her stomach in her throat, partly because of the morning sickness and partly because she knew they were all staring at her, imagining.

Wall Eye clucked her tongue. "Sometimes, no matter how much you eat, the baby doesn't grow at all. Can you feel it moving yet?" she asked Deer Shadow. "I knew a woman whose baby didn't grow. She never felt it move, and then one day it was born but was just a pile of blood and a little sack of skin with nothing in it.''

"Like a bladder, with no bones," Young Woman said. She shuddered.

"That's witches," Wall Eye said sagely. "Or something wrong with the baby when the father puts it in."

They looked, not too covertly, at Deer Shadow.

"Well, I just can't tell you why anyone wouldn't want to tell her father what man she'd been with," Young Woman said.

"And living with her father, eating *his* food," Fox Girl said. "Not to mention not making the man pay her bride-price. It isn't as if we didn't need anything. Soon, my Eldest Daughter will be a woman and we will need new clothing for her. He should ask for good tanned deer hide. He can't bring home enough himself, when there are so many of us.''

"And so greedy," Deer Shadow said pointedly. "Perhaps my mothers should teach their sons to hunt."

"My sons can name their father," Young Woman

snapped. Her two firstborn were the only ones old enough to hunt. The rest were allowed to help butcher the meat, but not to go out with the men. "Why should they hunt for a disgraceful girl who can't do the same?"

"Why should I name a man just because *you* tell me to? Can you do this?" Deer Shadow snatched the chopper that Young Woman was using and scratched a coiled rattlesnake with it on the cave floor next to the bed where Young Woman's smallest child slept.

Young Woman threw herself on Deer Shadow, rubbing out the snake with her foot, wrestling Deer Shadow away from the bed.

"Stop it! Take it away, you witch!" She pummeled Deer Shadow with her feet, trying to get loose.

"I was *going* to take it away," she gasped.

"Witch!" Young Woman shrieked again. She kneed Deer Shadow in the belly.

"That will do." Wall Eye, suddenly forceful, stood up and pulled Young Woman away by her hair. Young Woman flailed at Deer Shadow, screaming.

Deer Shadow spat at Young Woman. Crouching on the cave floor with blood pouring from her nose, she drew the snake moving away, out into the sunlight. "I just wanted you to remember I could. Now shall I make the deer go away, too?"

"No." Wall Eye moved her bulk between Deer Shadow and Young Woman. "You go wash the blood off and behave yourself."

"My mouth hurts," Young Woman said.

Deer Shadow saw with satisfaction that Young Woman had a split lip, though her own knuckles stung from giving it to her.

She got up, her arms clamped around the tight pain in her belly. "It hurts," she said.

Wall Eye cuffed Young Woman, and Young Woman looked a little afraid. Making a woman lose a child was a crime that the chieftain had the right to punish. It fell somewhere between murder and stealing and was enough of an urge among jealous wives that the Yellow Grass People took it seriously.

"Lie down," Wall Eye said, "until it passes."

Deer Shadow tried to wipe the blood from her nose, but it coated her hands. She spat at Young Woman again and went outside instead, trudging through the sun to Aunt Four Fingers's cave. It was hot, and the sky seemed to spin in spirals of bright gold and blue that hurt her eyes.

Owl saw her coming and hobbled over to put her arms under her. They shuffled together to Owl's mother.

Aunt Four Fingers clucked her tongue and sponged water, warm from the sun, over Deer Shadow's face. "Ever since you were a child you thought you could do whatever you wanted to. Change everything to suit you. Bend everyone to *your* will. Here, Stubborn, hold this to your nose."

"I changed one thing," Deer Shadow said through the handful of dry grass that Aunt Four Fingers gave her. "Wall Eye hit Young Woman."

"Good," Owl said.

Deer Shadow looked at Aunt Four Fingers's right hand, with the twisted lump of scar along the outside. It had happened when Aunt Four Fingers was four and an older boy had set his dog on her puppy, Deer Shadow's mother had told her. Deer Shadow stuffed the dry grass against her nose and said, "Wall Eye will have a better old age, Aunt. Now that she has hit Young Woman she will have more power in the house."

"You thought of this, of course, before you made trouble," Aunt Four Fingers said.

Deer Shadow chuckled. She held the grass away from her nose and looked at it. It was scarlet, but the flow seemed to be stopping. She sniffed experimentally. "No, but Wall Eye is still to the good. *I* think that's a tally stick in my pile." She rubbed her stomach. "It still hurts."

"Are you bleeding?" Aunt Four Fingers demanded.

"I don't think so." Deer Shadow put a hand under her skirt. "No, but it hurts."

"As long as it hurts *you* and not the baby, we won't worry. Tonight you might ask the one who has just died to ease this child's coming for you. You have enough trouble already," she added disapprovingly.

"I will." Deer Shadow sniffled again, this time with tears, and put the grass down. "I don't know what to say to him. I want to say, 'Come back.'"

"No!" Four Fingers said hastily. "That is *not* a good idea."

"But I miss him," Deer Shadow snuffled. "I was going to ask him what I ought to do, the morning he went Away, and now I don't have anyone to tell me."

"You have more people to tell you than I can count on my hands," Four Fingers said with asperity.

Deer Shadow looked at her directly. "Not the ones I want. With respect, Aunt."

"You tell that to Looks Back," Four Fingers said. "He's in a temper."

"They all think it's him," Owl said with a slanted grin. "If he says it is not, that means someone has more power than he does. I think he wants Cat Ears to think it is. But his wife is getting angry."

"It's not—" Deer Shadow stopped, biting off the words. It was so easy to say it was not this man, and not this other, until there was no one left, and they would know it was not a man of the People.

A dog barked in the chaparral, and Owl cocked her head at the sound. "They are back."

Four Fingers stood up. Women were coming out of the other caves to help the hunters drag the meat home and butcher it. Whatever they had killed would be cooked tonight, to honor Listens to Deer, who lay in state in his cave, his body painted with red earth and his eyes covered with a paste of crushed blue stones. When the feasting was done, his body would go on the fire.

"You stay here," Four Fingers told Dear Shadow. "Lie down, on your back or your side." She bustled away with her butchering knife and her skinning knife, and Owl limped behind her.

"The Others were there before us!" Cat Ears had hunted long and was tired and dirty. He had killed nothing. The other men stood behind him, sullen and empty-handed. The dogs panted at their heels and snapped at each other.

"Everywhere we went, they had already been," Blue Stone Man said. He scratched his chin wearily, and the women could see that he was in a temper, too. "We found carcasses, and by the Black Rock watering hole we found tracks, but the deer were frightened off."

"Your daughter has sent away the deer." A hunter swung his head around toward Found Water.

"She *called* the deer," Cat Ears said spitefully. "But now they will not come to her. Her disobedience drives them off."

"Or the Others drive them off," Four Fingers said.

"Before, she has called them away from the Others."

"Before, the Others were not so thick in our hunting grounds."

They glared at each other, nearly nose to nose.

Someone had been quick to take Looks Back the news, and he had come stumping down the hill with his giant tooth. "This will be thought about later. Blue Stone Man and I will think," he said. His look dismissed Cat Ears. "Now we have to think of the one who has died."

"How can we send him on his road with no kill?" Afraid of His Mother asked. He was as footsore and angry as the rest of them.

"The four days have gone," Looks Back said. "And I have spent the day talking with the gods, to open the skeleton road for him. We must, or his spirit may come back into his body instead. But the skeleton road cannot stay open."

The others nodded their agreement. If left open, the skeleton road would suck everyone down into it.

"What meat we have left, we will use. And any other stores."

Four Fingers watched their faces uneasily. To use the last stores meant that they must hunt again the next day, and be successful, or begin to go hungry. The People lived just to one side of hunger as it was, at the mercy of the vagaries of game and season. But if they let Listens to Deer go hungry, he would follow them, looking for his feast.

The moon sat just over the mountain, as white and clean-washed as a skull, Deer Shadow thought. In the center of the dance ground, the fire pits glowed red and sullen, but the moon was clean. If she squinted her eyes, she could see Listens to Deer in its face. The moon was a women's place, but Listens to Deer could probably go there if he wanted to. She pictured him being welcomed by the women there, pale women, like white bones, happy to see him, wanting to give him seed to grind, baskets to weave, and their children to tend. The thought comforted her.

The smell of cooking from the fire pits curled by her on the wind and her stomach growled, but she wouldn't go to the feast for Listens to Deer yet. Wait until everyone was eating, Aunt Four Fingers had told her. Wait until the body was laid out. No one would want to offend his spirit by accusing her of calling away the deer then.

Deer Shadow wrapped her arms around her knees and watched the black figures silhouetted by the fire. Her stomach had quit hurting and there was still no blood, so maybe the baby was all right. It wouldn't help if she lost it now, now that everyone knew. And she wanted it. It was hers now, whatever it was. She thought of the man and the gray coyote face, and together they wavered in her vision. She wondered if Listens to Deer knew what she had been too foolish to tell him. She could feel no sense of his presence, pull no message from him in the chill air. She shouldn't try, she knew. Spirits who came back were dangerous.

Blue Stone Man and Looks Back brought him out from his cave on a litter of deer hide, fringed and decorated with feathers. The smell of the scanty feast lingered in the air, overlaid with the sweet, unpleasant scent of decay. Deer Shadow followed as close to the litter as she could, taking her rightful place beside Looks Back, daring him to object.

The dried meat, some rabbit, squirrel, and small birds, along with the stores of camas and berries, had been placed on top of gourds full of stones to make it look as if there were more. Deer Shadow reached for a roasted camas bulb and stuffed it in her mouth, trying not to gobble. She sat next to Owl and Aunt Four Fingers. Dried, powdered meat flavored with greens made a thick gruel, and Deer Shadow dipped some out of the gourd and sucked it off her bone spoon. They were all watching her, and she wanted to fold in on herself, pull a darkness around her until they couldn't look at her. Something was wrong, something was askew, but it wasn't her doing, she was sure of that. There was no spirit voice to tell her that, so it made it hard not to wonder, but she thought that if she were cursed, she would know. If her magic had gone, Listens to Deer would have known.

He lay on his litter on the bier of piled wood, with the moon like a white disk of shell above him. Deer Shadow thought of when they had burned her mother, with the dead baby still inside her, and of all the other fires made to send the Yellow Grass People on the road to the Skeleton House under the lake. The food was always eaten before the burning so that the spirit could have its share.

When the feast was over and nothing but stones remained in the gourds, Cat Ears and the hunters took torches of grass and pitch and laid them in the fire until they were aflame. When they were blazing, the people took them up. The men lit one end of the bier, and the women lit the other. Deer Shadow held her torch into the wood, angry as the flame that leaped up and caught his deerskin robe. Looks Back held his tooth high up toward the moon and talked to the sky spirits and the skeleton people. Blue Stone Man put turkey feathers into the fire and a handful of seed saved from the feast. Then the whole bier caught fire, and they sat back to watch it burn, and to lick out the gourds and the baskets and the stones that had been under the meat.

They went on talking, low voiced. Deer Shadow could feel the words slap up against her skin like beetles in flight.

"Maybe it *was* Afraid of His Mother," Cat Ears growled. "Slinking little beast."

Afraid of His Mother looked frightened, but he didn't deny it. None of the men whose names were raised as possibilities would deny it. No one wanted to admit that some other man was more powerful. And also, if the deer came back, the father of Deer Shadow's baby would hold some power. That was one of the reasons

Cat Ears was angry, because nobody thought it was him. Not even Blue Stone Man or Looks Back would deny it, although they professed grave concern over the situation. Afraid of His Mother thought that they would laugh at him if he denied it. They might see his dreams and know that he had been afraid of her.

"I'd bet a good spear-thrower on Blue Stone Man," Walks Funny said. "If it was the chieftain, it will be all right."

There was a murmur of assent at that. If a man of power had fathered the child, the deer would return. Today's lack of luck during the hunt would simply be because of the Others and not because of a bad magic.

Found Water didn't comment. He already looked a fool, he felt, because he didn't know. He hoped desperately that it was Blue Stone Man or Looks Back. There might be magical reasons not to speak of it yet, not simply his daughter's unwomanly will to make trouble.

The women began to take away the gourds and baskets, plucking them past fingers that reached for the last scraps of food. Despite Looks Back's edict, there was no woman present who hadn't hidden something for the morrow. The hunters would go out at dawn, and although the women would have no time for gathering camas or greens, their husbands and sons would leave with something in their bellies.

The men got up and disappeared into the night. After a while the deer dancers emerged from the darkness, swinging their antlered heads. They danced and slapped their feet on the packed earth.

Deer Shadow could see their dark eyes watching her. She prayed to them as she would to the real deer: *Come back. Come back.*

The dance spiraled around her, circling the bier, stiff forelegs tapping the ground, and all the while they watched her.

* * *

In the morning the smell of burned flesh hung over the dance ground, the sweet horrible scent of decay charred into ash. The women pushed the burned bones into the crevices among the rocks where they lived, and the hunters took up their spears. When the body was gone, the person who had lived in it was gone. His name would not be spoken again.

Deer Shadow came out of her father's cave with her drawing sticks, her hair tied up with feathers and shells. At one time there had been an ocean here, and its petrified creatures still appeared on occasion. They were valued even more highly than new ones from the now distant coast, because age is power.

She walked to the dance ground, pacing carefully as if she were on a log. Defiantly, she let her pregnancy show. She could no longer deny it, and, besides, there was power merely in the condition. That was the problem: The procreative force was so powerful that it destroyed other magic. But sometimes pregnancy could make it stronger. Deer Shadow looked at the hunters and pulled the magic around her, a blanket of force shimmering in the hot morning.

She called the deer, trying to pull them back from wherever the Others had driven them, cutting their likeness into the earth, telling them how beautiful they were, how powerful, how the People gave them honor.

Come, she prayed to them. *Come back.* Whatever was askew still felt out of balance, some ripple among the breathing forms that moved down the game trails, amid the hot hunger of the Others and the delicate quick rush of the deer. It went on silent feet, yellow-gray as the rocks in the dry wash out beyond the Black Rock watering hole.

* * *

The hunters returned at dusk, and Deer Shadow knew from the thin, angry snarl of the dogs, even before she saw them, that they hadn't killed.

"It's the witch!" Cat Ears shouted as the women ran to meet them. "The witch has taken away the deer!" He picked up a rock.

Deer Shadow slid back into her father's cave and flattened herself against the wall, terrified.

Cat Ears was yelling at the hunters, waving his rock and his spear. The hunters and the women met each other on the slope below the caves. The chieftain's wife and the shaman's wife had the rest of the women gathered around them, howling out their grievances.

"We have empty bellies because the woman didn't keep her magic holy!"

"Flaunting herself, and no man even willing to pay her father for her!" the chieftain's wife snapped. She flung a black look at Blue Stone Man. She had heard the gossip.

"Then let *him* pay for the deer!" Cat Ears pushed through the hunters and caught Afraid of His Mother by the shoulder, fingers digging in deep. "Here's the one who put the baby in her!"

"No!" Afraid of His Mother said, startled. "No—I didn't."

"You never said you didn't until now," Cat Ears snarled. "Do you think I'm a fool?"

"Yes!" bellowed Looks Back, who had been hunting all day with the others and was hungry and footsore. He tried to pull Cat Ears away from Afraid of His Mother, but Cat Ears elbowed him out of the way. Afraid of His Mother was trying to twist out of Cat Ears's grasp. Cat Ears raised his stone and knocked Afraid of His Mother down with it.

"Let be!" Looks Back shouted, but the other hunters

clustered closer to Cat Ears, their empty stomachs howling for someone to pay.

The women licked their lips, excited and fearful, but no one intervened. The wives of the shaman and chieftain looked at each other with a kind of furious satisfaction, as if Afraid of His Mother held their errant husbands' spirits, taken into him for punishment.

Afraid of His Mother was trying to crawl out through the hunters' legs, scrabbling in the dirt, his spear gone. Another rock hit him in the back.

Four Fingers looked at Blue Stone Man, whose face was impassive. If the Yellow Grass People wanted to do this thing, it was beyond him to stop it. They were hungry and frightened. If Looks Back could not stop them, then it was meant to be.

His arms over his head, Afraid of His Mother pushed through a crowd of younger children. A rock thrown by a small hand flew after him.

"Kill him!"

Cat Ears's voice went through them like lightning. They picked up stones and flung them, men and women both.

Deer Shadow heard them howling after Afraid of His Mother and saw him stagger up the hill in a rain of stones. She ran out of the cave and down the slope, her grass sandals sliding on the rock. "No!" she shouted. "It isn't him!" But no one heard her, or no one wanted to.

Afraid of His Mother ran blindly, staggering, tripping, stumbling as rocks came down around him. Now the whole band was surging after him, oblivious to Deer Shadow's screams of protest. They picked up stones as they went.

"No! It wasn't him!" She sobbed, gasping, trying to catch them. They bayed past her, their snarling dogs at their heels. Blue Stone Man and Looks Back strode after them, not throwing rocks but trying to hold some control.

Deer Shadow ran up to Blue Stone Man and clutched at his arm. "Please, stop them! It wasn't him!"

Blue Stone Man shook her away.

"Get out of sight," Looks Back said to her. His face was furious, and he ran ahead trying to catch Cat Ears.

Owl hobbled at the rear, with Four Fingers holding her daughter's arm. They pulled Deer Shadow away toward the caves. She twisted her head frantically and saw Afraid of His Mother fall as a rock hit him on the head. And then they were on top of him.

Looks Back thought of Coyote's story and shivered.

Deer Shadow shut herself up in her father's cave, insofar as she was able since caves have no doors, and made a door of magic that her stepmothers were afraid to cross. They came looking for her, to tell her with relish what had happened to Afraid of His Mother for her wickedness, and she threw stones at them and spat in the fire, cursing them until they were afraid to go in. They went off to complain to one another until Found Water returned and they could unleash their tales of Deer Shadow's irresponsibility on him. Found Water had gone to the hills with Blue Stone Man and Looks Back, who needed to consult with the gods about what the Yellow Grass People had done.

Owl and Four Fingers had left Deer Shadow alone, too, and she huddled against the far wall and pondered how she had killed Afraid of His Mother without even lying with him. Maybe she should lie with Cat Ears, she thought vindictively. Maybe she could kill him if she did.

Her stomach knotted up. The women had found greens, half-ripe berries, and one small turtle while the men were hunting, and Four Fingers had killed a rabbit with a sling. But Deer Shadow was still empty, as ravenous as Cat Ears was for something to kill.

Cat Ears was outside, trying to persuade the Yellow Grass People to kill Deer Shadow next. She could hear his voice, spitting and strident.

"Who can believe what a witch says?"

The younger hunters nodded. They especially did not wish to believe her when she told them they had killed an innocent man by mistake, particularly when that man might have had power. Before Looks Back had gone to consult with the gods, he had called them fools in a furious voice and shaken his tooth at them.

"What if it wasn't him?" Squirrel said, uncomfortably doubtful now.

"Then it was someone else she wished to hide—a man from the Others most likely." Cat Ears stood up on a boulder so they could see him better. "That's where our deer have gone! To the Others!"

"Never!" Squirrel said. After all, Deer Shadow was one of his clan. "That's an insult."

"Now, now, she could have been raped," Walks Funny said. "It happens, a woman out alone, and that one's too independent."

"Does it matter how it came on her?" Cat Ears said disgustedly. "She's tainted, and the magic is tainted. She'll never get clean of it, and the child won't be human. We should have killed her first."

There was a murmuring of assent among them, but slowly it grew less certain.

"She could curse us," Walks Funny said uneasily.

"She belongs to the deer. If we kill her, they might go away forever."

"The deer aren't here now," Cat Ears said furiously.

"Wait until tomorrow," someone said. "Maybe what we've done is enough."

"Yes." They grasped at that, that maybe it was good, what they had done. Maybe it was enough.

"We could wait until tomorrow," Walks Funny said. "And look for a sign."

Cat Ears was growing livid. "You're *fools*!"

"Why should we do this just to salve *your* pride?" Squirrel asked.

"He's been as jealous as a fourth wife," One Ball said. "Ever since he found out some other fellow's been at her." He shook his head, and some of the older hunters chuckled. They thought Cat Ears considered himself too highly, and thus they begrudged him both the virility and the arrogance of his youth.

"Cat Ears may be lucky he didn't get her," Found a Snake said. "She's a curse. Cat Ears is right."

"If she's a curse, we'd better be careful," Walks Funny said. He stumped up to the front of them, bow-legged and beefy. "Who wants to do it?" He pointed at them. "You? How about you?"

They muttered and backed away a little, like jittery antelope, swiveling their ears.

"I've got no wish to have her shrivel the one I've got," One Ball said. "Cat Ears has one to spare."

They were still on edge with the killing, with the thing that the People became when they acted as one, even if they turned on their own. It was the feeling that the hunt gave them, or the deer dance, of coming into the heart of some greater organism, of being a piece of some larger, greater entity. Also, they had eaten nothing but greens and sour berries, which for a people accustomed to meat might bring visions. But now that the heat was gone from their blood and Afraid of His Mother's wailing aunts were laying out his body, their visions were not so strong.

When Blue Stone Man and Looks Back came down the slope from the place where Looks Back talked to the gods, with Found Water walking between them, their people were still making angry noises at each other, blood and hunger rising and ebbing by turns.

"Sometimes the gods will these things," Blue Stone Man said. "If he were not the evil, he may have stood for it."

The people listened with relief. What their chieftain said made it official.

"It is wrong, even so, to do the gods' will before you have asked them about it," Looks Back said acidly, eyes on Cat Ears.

"Perhaps the gods no longer speak to you, old man," Cat Ears said. "Perhaps they speak to me now."

Looks Back pointed his tooth at Cat Ears. "You disgrace me. Be quiet." He had made his peace with Blue Stone Man so that they could keep order. Their pact didn't include Cat Ears.

Blue Stone Man held up a hand. The rest subsided, grumbling. "Found Water asks, and has a right to ask, because he has hunted many years for the Yellow Grass People, that we purify ourselves of blood and make the dance again tonight. It may be that it was wrongly done in some way, or it may have been done too close to a death."

"And since when does Too Many Wives decide that the dance is wrongly done?" Cat Ears said. "Is the shaman ready to give up his place?"

The women who had prepared the body were pushing themselves into the crowd around the chieftain and the shaman. "One of these days your teeth will bite your tongue," Wall Eye snapped at Cat Ears. She had grown more confident since she had hit Young Woman, and it pleased her to chasten Cat Ears, who made fun of her.

"The shaman knows these things," Caught the Moon said.

"Certainly," Give Away said. She and Caught the

Moon had no patience for Cat Ears, who swaggered and made fun of them, too. "If the shaman says that Found Water may be right, then Found Water may be right." She clucked her tongue at him. "Young men always think they know everything. What does our husband say?" They looked expectantly at Turtle Back, who had married the two sisters because their father wouldn't give him only one.

Turtle Back looked startled. He was getting elderly, and his left ear didn't hear very well. But as the former hunting companion of Blue Stone Man's father, he was respected and respectable. "The gods say," he said, with a deferential glance at Looks Back, "that the way to be is the way of harmony. If we stray off that path, then we make the world top-heavy, and, of course, things may go awry. Now our young people stray off the path and do not listen to their elders. What are we to do about this? The gods say that we must come back to proper behavior."

"Thank you," Cat Ears said caustically.

"The young people must listen to their elders. The young woman must listen to the shaman, who knows what she ought to do. Most important."

Caught the Moon and Give Away beamed at him admiringly. Cat Ears snarled at them. He had lost the moment and he knew it, despite the fact that the two sisters had held stones in their hands when the tribe had hunted down the one who was dead now, the one whose name could no longer be spoken.

"We must listen to the shaman," the sisters said. The people around them looked a little relieved. It was growing hard to heat up the blood for a second killing.

"We must listen to the shaman," they said to one another.

"Go and purify yourselves. Go and wash," Looks Back said with disgust. "You have blood on you."

VIII
Coyote Followed a Sign

The woman in the rainstorm never came back, never brought her angry husband or brothers or tribe to kill Wind Caller. Follow, who had seemed oblivious to her presence, went off on his own affairs for three days and left Wind Caller to think. Surely she was magical for *him,* a sign, the first human he had touched in three turns of the sun—a woman so beautiful, with magic flickering off the ends of her hair, waiting for him on a streambank. When Follow returned, and Wind Caller had dreamed of her for three nights running, he went to look for her.

The Yellow Grass People had gone, but he found their journey camp. So she had come from people and was not just a magic woman made out of the rain. He decided that she must be a sign for him, to lead him back into the company of humans.

Several bands of humans roamed these broad, interconnected valleys, and he trailed the Yellow Grass People cautiously, uncertain of his welcome among them. To trust in signs was to give up a solid certainty for an elusive one, as thin as fog. If he came upon any of the other peoples, he was certain they would kill him. It was a possibility that the woman's people would, too. Only the dreadful aloneness drove him on, became something he could feel, like water closing over his head.

Wary but determined, he followed his sign and the tracks of her people. In his search, he saw that two bands were hunting the same runs and that there was bad blood between them. He watched the tracks carefully, afraid of landing in the wrong camp. The game was flighty and erratic, skittish about their old watering holes. He and Follow had discovered that the deer were trampling out a new trail in the canyons to the east, and between them they ran down an old doe and ate.

Wind Caller tied the rest of the deer in the skinned hide. "You don't have to come," he said to Follow.

Follow scratched his ear and hung his tongue out at him.

"I won't leave you any of the deer, though."

Follow closed his jaws with a snap. He stood up and stretched.

"Well, come on then." Wind Caller shouldered the deer-hide bundle along with his pack and his spears, and they made their way west to where he had seen the prints of the Yellow Grass People. This time he would follow them home.

The sun was low in the west, ready to slide into twilight. Her people would all be in their camp, he reasoned. He had to make sure that the woman was there. If she could pull coyotes out of the earth, she could keep her people from killing him. Besides, if someone brought meat, you were not allowed to give him to the gods. That was the rule among Wind Caller's people and the Upstream People, and he saw no reason for it to be different here.

He could see the smoke of their cooking fires against the sunset blaze of Red Rock Mountain. There was no smell of meat in the air, only the charred scent of old bones. Long shadows moved across the ground, flickered and bent at the cave mouths. He moved a little closer, trying to see if the woman was there, his woman, and braced for the barking that would erupt when the dogs smelled Follow. He saw a pair of children chasing each other through the camp, and the silhouette of a woman bent over a grinding stone. Behind her, a man cocked his arm back, and then forward, then back again, testing a spear-thrower's balance.

Wind Caller's throat knotted, and his eyes filled. It had come on him so suddenly, the longing to be a part of that life. Follow looked at them suspiciously, and at Wind Caller with further suspicion, but Wind Caller shifted the bundle on his back and went on.

It was the children who saw him first. They stopped chasing each other and, shrieking, pointed at Wind Caller. The Yellow Grass People's dogs backed away from the fires and sniffed the air. Three of them barked furiously, and one ran yelping into its cave. The people stood up and stared at Wind Caller.

One of them shouted something, and the next moment they were pouring out of their caves to encircle him. With growing unease, Wind Caller looked for the woman from the rainstorm. A man his own age prodded him with a spear and demanded something unintelligible. An old man carrying a giant curved tooth that spiraled into the sky over his head asked him in slow and serious tones something equally unintelligible. That man pointed at Follow and made a sign, then muttered, but neither he nor anyone else would get near the coyote.

Wind Caller lowered his bundle carefully and laid it down. His spears were still strapped to his back, but there were so many of the woman's clan that they could kill him whether he had a spear or not. He spread his hands open wide to indicate that he wanted to give them something, then untied the deer hide.

The man who had prodded him with the spear did so again and shouted what sounded to Wind Caller like a question, but he had no idea what the man wanted to know. Still Wind Caller looked for the woman. They were all crowded around him now, but he didn't see her.

The man with the tooth, who Wind Caller thought might be the priest, came forward slowly to inspect him. He was old, but his eyes were bright and intelligent. His gray hair was bound up into a topknot of turkey feathers with a black crow's tailfeather in the middle. He pulled this out and pointed it at Follow. Follow yawned at him. The old man looked grave.

Suddenly an argument broke out, the old man shouting at the young one with the spear. The women began to talk all at once. Another man, with a string of blue stones around his neck, shouted at them. Wind Caller pushed the meat wrapped in the hide toward them.

Where was the woman? *You have to be real,* he thought.

Deer Shadow sat in the back of the cave while Wall Eye, Young Woman, and Fox Girl fixed what little there was to eat. After her father had come home and shouted at her what Blue Stone Man and Looks Back had said, she had let the wives in but had stayed on her bed by the back wall, away from them. They looked happy enough with that.

It wasn't until the dogs began to bark, and her father and his wives went out and did not return, that she got curious. All the children had gone, too, and when one came back in, saying breathlessly, "Father wants his spear," she caught him by the arm.

"What does he want it for?"

"There's a man out there. He brought most of a deer, but we don't know him and he doesn't say anything.

Maybe he's from the Others. Cat Ears wants to kill him.''

Deer Shadow got up. It was undoubtedly a man from the Others, but why would he bring them meat? Perhaps what Listens to Deer had said was true, and they really were human. Perhaps he wanted to make peace. If they made peace over the hunting runs, the deer might come back. *Yah, and the sun might come out at night, too.*

Deer Shadow started for the cave mouth, curious to see what he looked like. And if he had brought meat, she wanted some. ''Did he bring anything else?'' she asked.

The child's eyes opened wide. ''He brought Coyote.''

Deer Shadow left the child behind and raced toward the crowd milling on the dance ground. Some of the women were already carting the meat away to cook it.

''Nothing of the sort,'' Give Away was saying as she passed. ''Perfectly good meat whether they kill him or not.''

Deer Shadow pushed her way through the people, and when they saw who it was, they backed a step away from her as if her skin might burn them. Curses were known to be catching.

Cat Ears was standing with his spear prodding the stranger's throat. The stranger held his head back and glared at Cat Ears in a way that made everyone else think that harming him might not be a good idea. The other men shifted from foot to foot, and their dogs looked at the coyote with hackles raised.

The coyote stared back at them with narrowed eyes and a show of teeth. Looks Back and Blue Stone Man stood in the spiral of Looks Back's tooth. The chieftain looked startled, outraged that something else should come to trouble him. Looks Back appeared grave.

Deer Shadow shoved her way between Four Fingers and Wall Eye and peered into the stranger's face. A look of relief crossed it, but he didn't move because of Cat Ears's spear.

"Stop it!" Deer Shadow stamped her foot at Cat Ears.

"This isn't women's business," Cat Ears said contemptuously.

Deer Shadow stalked over until she was eye to eye with him if she looked up. She lifted her chin and did so, knowing that Cat Ears didn't like that. "This is my business," she said between her teeth, pulling as much power around her as she could. She could see the coyote out of the corner of her eye and thought some of the power came from him. She spoke to Blue Stone Man and Looks Back.

"Call off your puppy before this man gets angry." Listens to Deer had always said you should start from a position of strength. "I have not spoken of the father of my child because it was not yet time. Now it is time."

"I told you!" Cat Ears shouted. "I told you it was a man from the Others!"

"Yah, and you are as blind as Old Mole," Deer Shadow said to him. "You can look at him and see that he doesn't belong to the Others. Put your spear away."

Cat Ears braced his feet, spear still pricking the stranger's throat.

Deer Shadow caught Looks Back's eye with hers. "Call him off, Uncle," she said ominously, "before Coyote grows angry."

There was a sharp intake of breath all around her at the name. Satisfied, she waited while the Yellow Grass People thought about that, and Looks Back and Blue Stone Man both motioned for Cat Ears to back off.

Found Water bustled up beside them, paternal obligations suddenly recollected. "Well, Daughter?" he said.

"With respect, Father," Deer Shadow said, letting them see that that was a formality, "this is my husband, father of my child. He came to me in the great storm. He has angered the Sky God and is thus divided into his two halves, the two pieces of his nature. It was the lightning that did it,'' she added, finishing off the story she had spun for herself. She glanced at the man. Cat Ears had backed off an inch or two, but he still gripped his spear with both hands and glowered.

The stranger watched him carefully, only letting his eyes stray to hers every now and again. She gave him a look asking for corroboration, but he didn't speak.

Wind Caller listened to the woman telling them something. About him, he supposed. She didn't seem to be telling them to kill him. The spear point in his throat pulled back a little. The woman was glaring at the man with the spear, snarling at him. Wind Caller could nearly see the sparks that flew off her long, dark hair.

The man he thought might be a priest was looking at the sky as if he were talking to it. The man with the blue stones around his neck was listening to the woman go on with her telling. Every so often he would peer intently at Follow, where he sat stone-still beside Wind Caller's legs.

"Yah, let him prove he is your husband," Cat Ears said angrily. He felt the People slipping away from him, from his energy, his fierce will to drive them to do what he wanted.

"You wouldn't like the proof," Deer Shadow said.

One Ball and Walks Funny nodded sagely at that. Coyote was a notorious trickster, not always malevolent but never benign, either. You didn't want Coyote proving anything to you.

"Then I'll kill him," Cat Ears said. "He can't be Coyote if I can kill him."

Looks Back snorted derisively. "If you had listened

to your elders instead of preening and thinking how fine you are, you would know that Coyote has died many times. Always Coyote is killed, because always Coyote takes chances, the way he has done today. *If* this is he," he added with a harrumph at the back of his throat to show that he was not entirely to be taken in. "When Coyote is killed, it is not good to be the man who has done it."

"Pah, I have killed a coyote," Cat Ears said. He waggled his arms in his deer-hide sleeves, which had yellowish-gray fur around the edges. It made the spear wave back and forth. Follow tracked it with his head.

"I would not be the man to brag about that just now," Looks Back said. The others glanced uneasily at their clothing. Coyote's many children were a useful source of fur, and they competed with the People for game; for these reasons the People killed them when they could. That was understood. Coyote understood, but perhaps not just now.

"Have you ever *tamed* a coyote?" Deer Shadow demanded. "Does a coyote follow at your heels like a dog? Yah, you are too stupid to talk to."

"*Look* at it, sitting like a dog," Four Fingers said.

"That is true, I never saw a tame one."

"I heard of a man who tamed one once."

"I heard of a wolf, but never a coyote."

"That is because Coyote's children are tamed only when Coyote wishes," Deer Shadow said loftily. "Give this man to me. He is mine. I will make a new magic tonight. And Coyote will make the deer run onto your spears in the morning."

"That is what the witch said last night!" Cat Ears snapped.

"Kill him and Coyote will run the deer into the sea and you will starve," Deer Shadow said, "and he will haunt you. I will call him back to haunt you, and if you

kill me, we will *both* haunt you!" She flung her hands
out wide toward the Yellow Grass People as if flinging
a curse, and they flinched. Blue Stone Man stepped back
a pace, and then forward again, determinedly.

Looks Back nodded, power acknowledging power.
"There is much to be heard here. But the man has not
spoken."

"He can't," Deer Shadow said. "The lightning has
made him deaf to our tongue."

Looks Back scratched his chin. "That might be," he
conceded. "I myself have seen a man struck by lightning, and he was addled in the head. Simple, like a child.
Is this one simple?"

"No, he just can't speak as we do." Deer Shadow
looked at the stranger again. *You could be simple for all
I know. You could be Coyote for all I know.*

"I have asked the Sky God about your tale," Looks
Back said suddenly.

Deer Shadow flinched. Had the Sky God told him that
she made it up? But it might be true anyway.

"And what does the Sky God tell you, old man?"
Cat Ears demanded.

"That the deer know the answer," Looks Back said.
"So we will wait."

"The deer are gone!" Cat Ears said. "We will wait
forever for them to come and tell us."

"Until tomorrow," Looks Back said, and Deer
Shadow felt her stomach knot up. She had one night to
find a magic that would call them. She put a hand on
the stranger's arm to tell him he should come with her.
Maybe he would know.

"Are we going to let this man in among us?" Cat
Ears howled.

"He brought us meat," Walks Funny said. They
could smell it cooking now.

"What else has he got with him?" Runner said, pointing at his pack. "We should see." Her eyes were bright. This was even more exciting than speculating about the father of Deer Shadow's baby. Who would have thought it would be a god? Or even a stranger with a tame coyote?

Cat Ears grabbed at the pack, but the stranger put his hand out hard into Cat Ears's chest and shoved him away. Deer Shadow tugged at the stranger's arm and then at his pack, which he shrugged off before Cat Ears could come back. He gave it to her warily, one eye on Cat Ears.

Deer Shadow opened the pack. Looks Back, Blue Stone Man, and her father knelt down beside it. The coyote opened his mouth to pant. They could feel the hot moisture of his breath. The dogs crept a little closer, whining, a half-growling singsong.

Deer Shadow pulled things out of the pack: a second shirt, roughly stitched, two lopsided but tightly coiled baskets, a handful of dried meat, and two spear points. She puzzled over the bone flute, and Looks Back took it, turned it over, and peered through the end. It was a spell-caster, maybe, through which a person could look at his enemy.

Found Water seemed annoyed. There was nothing here to make a bride-price, certainly not one that would keep his wives quiet. Looks Back would keep the spell-caster.

The stranger bent down and took the flute out of Looks Back's hands. Looks Back held on, even when the stranger tugged at it, but after a moment the old man let go. The stranger put it to his lips.

It sang. His breath sang in the bone. Deer Shadow gaped at him. If she hadn't known him to be magic before, she was certain of it now. Even Looks Back was greatly startled, and the rest of the Yellow Grass People were fashioning little gestures designed to make him keep his magic to himself. Cat Ears's mouth snapped open and then shut again without comment for once.

Wind Caller began to feel more certain that he would survive at least this first meeting with the woman's people. He saw her gawking expression with satisfaction. *This is something I can do that she can't.* He watched her with interest, and then with greater interest saw her waistline clearly for the first time now that no one had a spear at his throat. For a moment he felt as if the spear had suddenly been stuck back. Was she sacred? Was that why they wanted to kill him? He felt certain that she must be, since she could dig living animals out of the dirt. Plainly she had power. Had she told them that he was responsible for her pregnancy? He wished for a moment that he had decided to stay lonely.

He stopped playing, and Found Water upended the pack to see if there was anything more of interest in it.

"What else does Wind Caller bring with him?" Looks Back asked Deer Shadow, inadvertently giving him the same name as his old one.

Deer Shadow held out a handful of grain, small kernels that she didn't recognize. Looks Back examined them, while Found Water sat back in disgust. Nothing but magics. Magics only worked for the person who owned them, or maybe for shamans.

"What grain is this?" Looks Back asked Wind Caller, and the stranger said something that no one understood.

"Poison," Cat Ears said.

Murmurs of suspicion echoed him.

"Maybe it's a charm," Deer Shadow said dubiously.

They've never seen it, Wind Caller thought. *It doesn't grow here.* He said, "Maize."

"What?"

"What did he say?"

"Maize."

"What?"

He put the flute back in the pack with his shirt and his baskets. The women were pulling at them, criticizing the workmanship, he imagined from their tone. He stuffed them farther down in the pack, then took the maize from Deer Shadow's hands and put most of it back in the pack, too, closing it firmly. "It's maize," he said. "I will plant it for you. It grows seed on ears like this." He held his thumb up to indicate their size.

They started to argue with each other again in words he didn't understand. He took a seed and mimicked putting it in the ground. They watched him as if he were mad. He lifted his hands upward, trying to make the plant grow in their eyes. They looked blank. These people didn't plant anything, he decided, just foraged for what they could find. He had seen no signs of human cultivation since he had come north from his own country. Maybe northern people didn't know about seeds. The thought crossed his mind that he could outdo in magic even the old man with the tooth if he grew maize for them. And certainly the young man who had wanted to kill him.

Wind Caller dug a real hole this time and put the seed in it. He pointed at the moon just rising and held up three fingers. He held his hand above the ground to show how high it would be, then made grinding motions as if with a quern. That they recognized.

"It's food!" Runner said.

The women pushed forward, interested and suspicious.

"He has come to bring us a great gift," Deer Shadow said, without knowing how she knew. There was something reverent about the way he handled the shriveled grains. *There is power in this food,* she thought.

She pointed to it and waited for him to tell her again what it was called.

"Maize," he said.

"Maize. Coyote has come to bring us this food. We must do as he tells us with it."

"Are we fools?" Cat Ears demanded.

"You may be," Deer Shadow snapped. "We are hungry, and he has brought us meat. In this grain he brings us a new kind of food. Coyote is very generous to the Yellow Grass People, and you are a fool."

"You are a fool if you think you can lie with some stranger like a bitch in heat and then try to pass him off as Coyote Spirit."

"That will do!' Looks Back shouted. He dug up the grain of maize from under the dirt and handed it to Blue Stone Man so that he would feel important. Then he got up and pushed Cat Ears out of the circle. "You bring danger to all of us. If Coyote eats you, I want it to be away from the People."

"Coyote, yah! You will see!"

The rest of them began to argue among themselves again. If it was a gift, did they want it? Was Coyote ever to be trusted? They would see if he drove the deer in the morning.

Blue Stone Man stood up, too, and bellowed at them to be quiet. They subsided. He put the grain of maize in the pouch that hung from his belt and turned to Deer Shadow. "Looks Back says that the deer will tell us tomorrow. You may keep him tonight."

Deer Shadow took Wind Caller by the arm, his pack in her other hand, and pulled him through the crowd, Follow sticking close to his heels. Some of the people reached out, touching Wind Caller as he went, patting him to see what he felt like, but none of them touched Follow. As he went by, Runner snatched up one of her children.

"He doesn't eat babies if he's fed," Wind Caller said, but no one understood him. Blue Stone Man still had the kernel of maize, and Wind Caller wondered if he knew that it had to be planted. The rest was in his pack, which the woman had. He was assailed by a sudden terror that it might not sprout. It was old. He made a prayer to the God of Maize in his mind, extravagant promises of ritual devotion, of blood. Maybe he could offer up the man with the spear. But Wind Caller didn't know whether the god could hear prayers from this far north, or whether the maize would even live here.

Deer Shadow led him into a cave, and he saw with some trepidation that one of the men who had been talking to her, three of the women, and a brood of children all followed them in. She sat him on a bed of reeds at the far end of the cave, and the children stood in a half circle in front of him, staring.

Deer Shadow clapped her hands at them. "Go away! Go and bring us something to eat!" She looked at Follow, who had curled himself on the end of the bed as if he had always lived there. "And for the coyote, too."

They scattered, and Young Woman said, "I'm not living in a house with a coyote."

"You live with dogs," Deer Shadow said.

"The dogs won't come in," a child said. Follow opened his eyes and closed them again.

Deer Shadow sat down on Wind Caller's other side. "We are here," she said. "Tomorrow we will find another house. Tonight we are here." She sat back, a little closer to Wind Caller, presenting him to them, an acquisition they couldn't argue with.

Wind Caller couldn't understand the words, but it was reasonably plain to him what was happening. She had kept them from killing him, and now he belonged to her.

* * *

There were many ways of making magic, Looks Back had said. "First there is the good-luck piece. The power of the universe is in everything, and some objects bend it to human use.

"Next are spells, and third, the prayers to animals to be killed. Then, fourth is the power of life's changes: death and the menstrual blood of women.

"Fifth, these are the things we know: that like imitates like. Lightning resembles snakes, and snakes bring rain. Once-joined things are never separate. If you burn my cut hair or my nail clippings, you will hurt me."

In all these things Deer Shadow's people believed implicitly. They were the foundations of the natural world, the key to the cipher of the Universe. Everything had power, locked in its heart. The trick was to know whether that power would harm or help.

Looks Back knew this. Deer Shadow wasn't sure she knew. She felt she had been reckless.

The man sat beside her eating a handful of meat and boiled greens. There wasn't much. Everyone had been given a taste of the deer he'd brought. Follow had a pile of bones and gristle and was cracking them with his teeth. The two of them were like two ends of a spell she couldn't pronounce, an amulet of unknown origin. Magical surely, but with what results? What results were growing in her right now?

The sun was all the way down now, and the fire on the dance ground was burning, flaring up like whatever it was that she was about to do next. It dwarfed the light of the hearth fire, by which she could see the whites of Wind Caller's eyes, like white stones against his skin, and the hundreds of tiny raindrop scars on his chest and arms. She touched them with one finger, curious.

Wind Caller thought she wanted to know what they were, since the men here had none. But he had no way to tell her. Didn't the people here give their gods blood?

What did the gods live on then? Maybe that was why these people were so backward; their gods were starving.

She took him by the arm again and led him out of the cave toward the dance ground. Wind Caller pulled away from her and went back for his pack. He wasn't going to leave it here; it was all he had. Follow trotted at his heels. Follow wasn't going to let Wind Caller leave him there, either. When they stopped, the coyote peered out from behind Wind Caller's legs, his gray nose suspicious.

In front of the fire on the dance ground was smooth mud, a spear's length watered and scraped, ready for what her magic would pull out of it. Deer Shadow saw that it was Looks Back who had prepared it for her. (Afraid of His Mother had always done it.) The shaman stood in the great spiral of his tooth, linking the people to the days of plenty and the Great Game. The women and children were sitting along the sides of the dance ground with a handful of men. The men were cross-legged, their legs wrapped around hollow logs with deerskin stretched across the top. The palms of their hands tapped quietly, imitating the distant footsteps of the deer.

Wind Caller stared at them and knew they were staring back, the women watchful, the children curious, the men pretending not to see him. They were solemn, silent, except for the faraway drumbeat. Their work was serious, bringing the deer step by step out of the earth as they once came Up From Below, making them many. Wind Caller didn't know what this ceremony was going to be, but he felt its importance in the hairs on the backs of his hands, in the tightening of the scars on his chest. Whatever it was, it might be the way they fed their gods.

Deer Shadow sat cross-legged on a deer hide in front of her smooth space of mud and pulled at Wind Caller's hand to make him sit down with her. Follow sat on his other side, gray coat lapped red by the flames. Besides the bonfire burning in the center of the dance ground, there were torches dipped in pitch set into the ground along its outer edge. They lit the faces of the people like rippling red water. The air was dry and filled with the scent of pine smoke. Wind Caller watched intently to see what would happen, but the deer materialized in front of him before he had even seen them approach.

They circled sunwise around the fire, their antlered heads lifting up and down, their forelegs tap-tapping the earth. More followed them out of the caves, and Wind Caller saw that some of them had deer-hoof rattles instead of the foreleg sticks. They clacked together like bones rattling, or hooves on stone, dancing to the drumbeat. In the darkness they came leaping out of the earth, looking more real than actual deer. They circled, always sunwise around the fire, keeping to the outer edge, where the children reached their hands up to touch them. Leading them was a woman without a headdress, a white deer-hide cloak swinging from her shoulders, its ends cut like flying legs and tail. The Mother of Deer. She swayed, stamping her feet. Her long black hair was tied with spruce branches, trailing down the white cloak. Her hands shook deer-foot rattles.

Deer Shadow saw that the woman was Four Fingers and thought that was a good sign. The disfigurement of Four Fingers's hand had never been seen as a hindrance to magic because she had defeated the dog that gave it to her. Four Fingers was the strongest woman Deer Shadow knew, except for herself. She saw her as a great white deer, stepping on the sky. She wanted to make her magic tonight instead of waiting until morning, to erase what wrong they had done in killing one of their own today for no good reason. The people believed that woman power was dangerous to the hunt, but tonight it seemed that the procreative force might be the one that would balance things again. She suspected that Looks

Back thought so, too. Looks Back knew magic could be turned in on itself, sent backward toward its origin.

Wind Caller saw only a middle-aged woman in a white deerskin, but his breath tightened in his throat as she passed by him, leading the deer inward, spiraling toward the fire. He knew who she was then, knew that she was old, old as the deer, and that they came from her.

The spiral swung inward, the Deer Mother moving beyond the fire, her children at her heels. As the deer moved, their polished antlers glowed, and the dark sockets of their eyes gazed out over the dance ground. The movement was a ripple of sound, a pattern of drum and rattle, hoofbeats heavy on hard ground. It was a song.

Wind Caller took his flute from his pack and put it to his lips. The music was almost inaudible at first. Only Deer Shadow and Follow heard it, and Looks Back standing above them. Then it grew and danced with the deer, calling them in toward the fire, singing them home. The sound was something that could almost be seen, like a thin silver band that moved in the torchlight, rising, falling, twirling among the dancers, lifting their heads and feet, calling them: *Come. Come.*

The deer circled inward, called by the flute. They packed tighter and tighter together around the fire, barely skimming the edge of Deer Shadow's smooth mud. They lifted their heads, tossing them, prancing, their breath heavy in their throats. The Deer Mother lifted her deer-foot rattles to the dark sky where the mantle of stars was thrown and said, "We come. We are as many as you, our reflections in the sky."

They crowded around Deer Shadow and the man, pressing in on them, asking for something. Deer Shadow wasn't sure what, but something felt different to her; something askew slid back into balance.

She took her drawing stick and began to pull deer

from the ground. The man beside her put the flute to his mouth again to give them music to run with. The deer came scrambling up out of the mud, leaping, running, dancing in a spiral out from the center. Deer Shadow moved ahead of them, crouching, digging them up with her stick. She was the Deer Mother now, setting free her children, bringing them up to the surface of the world for the People to eat. When they died, they would go Down Below again to be reborn, so that they would always live and the People would always have food.

They came and came until the entire expanse of smooth mud was filled with them. Deer Shadow stood up and looked at the people become deer who were gathered before her, at the ring of women and children beyond them. Except for Four Fingers she couldn't see any of their faces. The men were unknowable in their deer heads, great horns branching against the sky.

"Go now," she said to her creation. "Go out to your trails, and the People will meet you in the morning." The deer obeyed her, moving back into the darkness, Four Fingers lost among the jostling antlers.

The dance ground was empty suddenly, swept clean as if a wind had lifted them all. The women who ringed the bare ground moved away, too, and then there were only Deer Shadow and the man. Looks Back, who knew that something more was going to happen and that it was not his magic, had gone already. They saw his great tooth moving up the slope in the darkness, a wavering curl of white behind the torches. The torches had nearly burned out, and Deer Shadow motioned to Wind Caller to pull them out of the ground for her. They let them drop, shaking little wisps of fire from them, and rolled them on the dirt until they were out. Follow padded behind them as they circled the dance ground, walking into darkness. When the last torch was out and only the dying fire remained at the center, she took his hand again, and they walked into the blanket of its warmth.

Wind Caller knew what was going to happen. The dying light streaked the skin of her belly, showing him the first luminous outlines of the child within. His child.

Whatever magic they had made with their coupling, they must make again here on the dance ground, for the child, for the deer, for these people he had come to live among. He knew there would be a hunt tomorrow, and Wind Caller's people, like Deer Shadow's, never mated on the night before they hunted, for fear of woman magic overpowering the hunters' strength. But tonight they had to turn the power backward, inside out, call up the offended deer with their union; do the thing that created life to counteract the death they had caused.

Wind Caller didn't understand this as clearly as Deer Shadow, but he knew what she wanted from him. Her hands were pulling at his leggings and his loincloth, reaching under them for him, insistent. His blood was hot—he'd dreamed about her since the day she came from the storm. It didn't take much to arouse him. Not even the feel of spirits breathing down his neck could distract his body from what it wanted. He could feel the slight hardness of her thickening waist under his hands, the roundness of her breasts. She was life. She was beautiful, and her skin was hot with the fire when she pulled him into her. Coupling was the oldest of magics, the most powerful force. He lay down on the ground with her under the open sky and showed the deer how life was made. Entwined, they taught them to be fruitful.

IX
War Came

Wind Caller woke when the sun began to poke its fingers in his eyes. He was lying on the hard-packed dirt of the dance ground, dimly aware of the stones beneath its surface, clothed in dirt, a skeleton under the earth. He remembered the fierce coupling with the woman and knew there had been power in it. But now in the bright morning he had the uneasy sensation of having been more sacrifice than lover. The woman was curled beside him under the deerskin they had sat on last night, her head on his outstretched arm, which had gone numb.

She woke when he pulled it out from under her, her expression unreadable to him through the tangle of her hair. He raised himself cautiously and looked around. Follow was sitting by the embers of the dead fire, watching them. He scratched his ear haughtily as if to remind Wind Caller that he was not so reckless in his own affairs. There was no sign of movement near them, but Wind Caller knew that the people in the caves on the slope above them were awake and getting ready to hunt. He knew what last night's dance had meant, just as he knew what his coupling with the woman had meant.

He sat up, his breath quickening. Something in his

mind said, *This woman will own you if you are not careful.*

She also sat up and wrapped the deer hide around her, twisting it over one shoulder and under the other. She pointed at him to put on his leggings. He leaned forward, still naked, and pressed himself against her, against the protection of the deer hide, to let her know what he remembered. Then he sat back and put his leggings on.

His compliance didn't make her less imperious. She said something to him that he thought must mean, "Come on," and they walked up the hill to the caves while the Yellow Grass People tried not to look at them. He saw them make gestures as they passed, warding-off motions, as if the magic were contagious. Deer Shadow stalked past them regally, the ends of the deer hide swinging against the backs of her legs. Wind Caller felt as if she was wearing him, too, or was carrying him as a sign of potency like the old man's tooth.

She took him into an empty cave and motioned to him to give her his pack. Follow slipped in behind them and settled himself in a corner. He pricked up his ears when Deer Shadow pulled out the spears lashed to the back of the pack and handed them to Wind Caller.

Wind Caller grinned and looked at Follow. He suspected that he and the coyote were now supposed to prove their usefulness to her people. He thought they probably could. They knew where the deer had gone.

Deer Shadow left him there, after gesturing for him to stay, and went to her father's cave. She found him inspecting the binding on his spear and wearing the expression he wore when he wanted to convey to his wives that he was a busy man not to be bothered. When Deer Shadow walked in, the wives stopped talking and stared at her with suspicious curiosity. A little current of veiled excitement ran through them. Were there bite marks on her arms? Traces of soft gray fur on her calves? If Coyote could take human and animal form, could she now, too? What kind of child would she have? Fox Girl sniffed suspiciously to see what she smelled like.

Deer Shadow took a cooking basket and stuffed a handful of greens into it. Young Woman opened her mouth and snapped it shut again when Deer Shadow looked at her. Deer Shadow added to the basket a bone with some meat on it from last night and a handful of camas bulbs.

Young Woman shrieked in outrage. "Put it back! We haven't enough as it is!"

"I dug these," Deer Shadow said. She took some more bulbs. "Be quiet or I'll send the coyote to get them."

"Take only enough to feed you this morning," Wall Eye said firmly. "If you have a husband now, he should hunt for you, and you find camas for him. Find camas where they grow, not in here, not after this morning."

Deer Shadow smiled, amused. "As you wish, Mother. After this morning."

"He hasn't paid for her!" Fox Girl said.

"That is not your affair," Found Water said abruptly. He looked disinclined to cross his daughter, who had suddenly become something beyond his knowledge. Not, at any rate, until he found out exactly what that something was. "We will discuss payment after we hunt. Hunting is more important." And if they didn't find the deer, he supposed everyone would want to kill the coyote man *and* his daughter.

Deer Shadow set the cooking basket in a water basket on top of her grinding stone and added her bone comb and a long bone spoon to its contents. She picked them all up together. She could feel the eyes of her father and his wives on her as she left.

The man was still waiting for her at their cave. When she set her booty down in front of him, he chuckled.

Deer Shadow unwrapped the hide she was wearing and laced up the skirt she had retrieved from the dance ground. She picked up the water basket, pointed at the darkened ring of stones on the floor, where the last inhabitant had made fires, and motioned for him to come with her. It was woman's work to set up a house, but not this morning. Today everything was aslant, her work mixing with his, their forbidden coupling on the dance ground the night before the hunt—it was inside-out magic, reversed and pliable, like long springy grass weaving some new basket to hold things she hadn't thought of yet. She wriggled her shoulders. There was no sensation of something crawling between them, her own physical test of wrongness. The morning didn't feel wrong or dangerous by anything more than its sheer power.

They walked to the river together like any newly made couple, with Follow trailing his scent at their heels and setting the dogs to barking. The coyote caught a mouse and ate it while Deer Shadow filled the basket with water. Wind Caller picked up an armload of wood from the pile near the dance ground, which the young boys were expected to keep supplied. The women, who had come to get wood for their fires, stopped talking and stared at Wind Caller. Then their voices rose again in a flurry, like excited birds. Fetching wood was *their* job.

"Stupid turkeys," Deer Shadow said. "Gobble, gobble."

Wind Caller laughed. The scorn in her voice gave clear meaning to her otherwise incomprehensible words.

"I should talk to you. You would learn if I talked to you," she said.

"Do you think I can understand you?" Wind Caller muttered. "Do you think all people speak the same language?" Maybe they did, here.

"We come here every spring," Deer Shadow said

chattily. "This is our summer place. Then we go to the Gathering in the autumn, and then we go where the piñon nuts are."

"I don't know what you are saying," Wind Caller said.

To Deer Shadow, his words sounded like an exasperated noise. *Too fast*, she thought. *I have to teach him words. Like a mother with babies.* She pointed at the bundle in his arms and said, "Wood."

"Wood," Wind Caller said dutifully. He pointed at a tree. "Wood."

"No, tree."

Wind Caller glared at her. He shifted his burden so that he had a free hand and stuck his finger in the water basket.

"Water," Deer Shadow said.

"Water."

She pointed at other things, but she told him too many and he mixed them up. When they got back to the cave, the Yellow Grass men were ready for the hunt and Looks Back was talking to the gods about it. Wind Caller dumped the wood on the ground and took Deer Shadow by the shoulder. He made her look at him.

"I know where the deer have gone," he said.

She shook her head, uncomprehending.

He put his hands to his head and made antlers with his fingers, making himself a deer.

"Deer," she said.

"Deer." He bent down and made walking away motions with his fingers on the ground. He stood and imitated a hunter looking desperately for deer and finding none. He pointed to himself, went to where the deer he had made with his fingers had gone away, and pointed at their hiding place.

She cocked her head at him, puzzled, and then looked at him with dawning comprehension. She left him there and whisked across the stony slope to Looks Back. Wind Caller heard her talking excitedly.

He wondered if she had understood what he meant to tell her. He might have told her that dancing trees went south at night and grew from his fingers. How had people talked to one another before there were words? Had some god brought them language? Or did they sit down by themselves and decide what sound should mean what thing? He had never thought about it before.

"Deer," he said to himself, hoping it meant what he thought it did.

"He knows where the deer are," Deer Shadow said fiercely, stamping her foot at Cat Ears in case he even thought of interrupting. "He knows where the deer have gone. You have to follow him."

"Yah," Cat Ears said as soon as she paused for breath. "We will follow him—into the dry lands while the Others kill our deer in peace!"

"He knows where they've gone," Deer Shadow said insistently. "You know they move on sometimes!"

"When the grazing is bad," Looks Back said.

"Or when there is no water," One Ball said. "But it has been a wet year."

"When they are frightened," Deer Shadow said. "He knows where they have gone. He killed one yesterday."

"Did he tell you this?" Looks Back asked her.

"Yes! Well, I think so." She couldn't think what else he could have meant.

"He doesn't hear our speech," Cat Ears said. "So tell me how you understand him, witch!"

"Call me that again and I'll show you if I am!" They glowered at each other, and Looks Back stepped between them.

"There are more ways to talk than with your tongue," he informed his son. "Sometimes better ways, although it may take wisdom to know them. What kind of speech was this?''

Deer Shadow thought. She waggled her fingers over her head as the man had done in imitation, then crouched and walked them away.

"Those are deer," Walks Funny said.

"Very clever," Turtle Back agreed. He sounded as if he thought that might be sinister in itself. "Why should we trust him?''

The Yellow Grass men began to argue again.

"Because he brought us a deer yesterday."

"It could be a trap."

"It could be magic."

"For a magic deer, it tasted a lot like a real one.''

"How do *you* know what a magic deer tastes like?''

"If he could magic up one deer, he can magic up more. *I'll* eat them." The speaker's stomach growled loudly at that, and they laughed in spite of the seriousness of the question.

"*I* think he comes from the Others," Cat Ears snarled. He glared at Looks Back, as if defying him to object. "We all do.''

"He knows where the deer are!" Deer Shadow said furiously. "I called them for you, and he will take you to them. If you return hungry tonight, it will be *your* fault, Cat Ears, and maybe we will do to you what you did to Afraid of His Mother!''

"Enough!" Looks Back shouted at them. "Be quiet!" He put on his sky mask to talk to the gods about it. The mask was made of bark, with pale grass springing from its four sides, like the four winds, and eyes of blue stones, pupilless and enigmatic.

Wind Caller saw them from the cave and decided that it might be better to join them than to let the woman do the talking for him. He had eaten a handful of the greens she had brought and bitten into the cold slickness of the camas. His stomach was rumbling, and he envied Follow his mouse.

Wind Caller picked up his spears and spear-thrower and whistled to Follow. They went over to where Looks Back was talking to the sky and stood carefully outside the circle until someone noticed them. When Looks Back did, Wind Caller put his antler-hands up again and said, "Deer." He pointed out to the southeast.

"There," Deer Shadow said to Cat Ears. "I told you."

Cat Ears folded his arms and fumed. He thrust his chin out.

"We will follow this man," Blue Stone Man said suddenly, before Looks Back could offer his opinion, or the gods'. It was important to be the one who decided. Cat Ears had influence with the younger hunters, and that made him useful, but Blue Stone Man was careful not to let that influence grow too great. Blue Stone Man wasn't old yet; the Yellow Grass People didn't need a new chief.

Blue Stone Man lifted his spear. He nodded at Wind Caller and pointed. They eyed each other solemnly and fell into step together.

Deer Shadow watched them go, and then her stomach curled into a ball and she threw up uncooked greens and camas. Industrious women had been up since before light, cooking a journey meal for their husbands, while she had been asleep like a slut on the dance ground. A magic slut, but a slut all the same—she knew that's what the women were thinking as they stood there chattering and squawking about whether the men would find meat. She could feel their thoughts on her skin.

She wiped her mouth on the back of her hand and got

up. They edged away from her a little—they could feel her thoughts, too.

Stupid hens, she thought. *Gobbling and fussing until the men come and tell them what to do. What would you do if you didn't have any men? Gobble and fuss until the Others came and got you?*

'There's no need to gawk,'' Four Fingers said briskly, cutting across their chatter.

"Certainly not," the shaman's wife said. Remembering their dignity, she and the chief's wife made shooing motions at the other women.

"An idle woman invites in mischief," the chief's wife pronounced. She and the shaman's wife gave Deer Shadow a triumphant glance and went back to their proper work: digging camas, looking for berries and greens or turtles in the stream, making sandals, mending clothes, cooking what there was to cook, until the men should come back and tell them what would happen next.

"Where is he taking us? Blue Stone Man must have the madness to follow this one."

"You saw the tracks."

"The deer have never come this way."

"Our deer. Maybe it is some other deer."

"I have heard stories about when the deer went away—and someone had to go after them, where they were being kept."

Wind Caller assumed that the muttering behind him had to do with the wisdom of his choice of direction. Or the wisdom of letting him choose, judging from the expression on the man with the blue stone necklace, who Wind Caller had decided must be the chief. It seemed that the chief and the priest were two different people here. No wonder they argued all the time.

To the east of the caves the land was covered with

grass and small scrubby trees, the low foothills of the mountains rising in the distance. In some places, the land approaching these mountains rose gently in undulating hills like a cupped hand turned upside down; in other places, it leaped fiercely upward, clinging to the sky on the hooks of sharp mesas and bluffs that closed in their sheer walls to exitless canyons. It was at the open end of one of these that Wind Caller and Follow had seen the deer and run one down. Wind Caller had thought then that with many hunters, the deer could be run to the back of the canyon and trapped under the high bluff at the end.

He stopped and looked at the trail, and one of the Yellow Grass men knelt beside him. They both saw the footprint at the same time, and the Yellow Grass man snapped his head around to stare venomously at Wind Caller.

Wind Caller twisted his head to look at it from every angle. Maybe it was his own, but he didn't think so. Whoever it belonged to had been stalking the deer, too, probably this morning. He held up a hand, and the men behind him muttered at having to wait. Whatever was up ahead, Wind Caller wanted to know about it before it knew about him.

He let the chief look at the footprint for a moment and then slid forward silently. The deer trail was new, not yet worn to earth, and the prints of human feet were hard to see in it. It wound through the yellow scrub grass under a high sandstone bluff. Wind Caller listened. He thought he heard faint sounds ahead, a murmuring beneath the birdsong and the distant ripple of water.

He faced into the morning sun and tried to see the source of the sound, to see where the deer went on their delicate hooves, perhaps bounding away, startled by the scent of humans. They were lucky, though. The wind was blowing toward them, sweeping their scent behind them, allowing the dogs to smell deer on the wind. The dogs whined and looked for the deer.

Follow's yellow-gray nose twitched. He had kept close to Wind Caller, well away from the dogs. Follow knew they would like to kill him, and there were enough of them to do it. He sniffed again and made the low sound in his throat he made when he was angry.

Wind Caller glanced at Follow and went on cautiously, slipping past the bluff into a little shallow valley that tapered at one end into the mouth of a canyon. A stream ran through it, and a little way into the canyon there were wild plum trees and a spot where the stream widened into a pool. Here the trail vanished in the grass. The deer spread out here to browse and eat the wild plums when they ripened. Wind Caller stopped so abruptly that Blue Stone Man walked onto his heels and cursed him.

The deer, if they were there, were well into the canyon, but when Blue Stone Man looked where Wind Caller pointed, he saw with infuriating clarity a man of the Others slipping through the canyon mouth with two men behind him. Blue Stone Man hissed at the rest of the hunters to be still. They were still shadowed by the bluff and were downwind of the Others' dogs.

Wind Caller stuck his spear-thrower in the waist of his breechclout. He had only two spears, and he didn't want to throw them. Not until he knew how many more men there were.

Blue Stone Man looked grave, and Wind Caller caught a flicker of indecision on his face. "We're going to fight them, aren't we?" Wind Caller demanded, forgetting that no one could understand him. They seemed to be debating it among themselves.

What was the matter with these people? Was there some curse on them that kept them from fighting the Others? In his silent, secret observations of both Deer

Shadow's people and the Others, before he had mastered the courage to come out of his solitude, he had not noticed a reluctance to fight on the part of the Others. They fought each other and were the aggressors when they met these people.

Fools, Wind Caller thought scornfully, to cover his growing unease. If they were going back without meat, after the woman's extravagant promises, he might do better to take to his heels now and hope he could outrun them. They wouldn't have any compunction about killing *him.* And there would be no more hunting with men again, no hope of learning to speak with them, no nights with the woman in the warmth of a grass bed. They would probably kill his child, too, and that mattered greatly.

Wind Caller thought that he might as well die at the hands of the Others here as of loneliness somewhere else. He grabbed Blue Stone Man's spear-thrower from his hand and poked it through the man's belt. Blue Stone Man looked startled, too startled to protest. Wind Caller went down the line of hunters behind him, doing the same thing to each. That seemed to encourage them. When he came to Cat Ears, he halted; that one was ready to fight. Cat Ears jerked his spear back and leveled it at Wind Caller. With his other hand he was fitting it to the atlatl.

Wind Caller chuckled. Cat Ears spat some angry words at him, and Wind Caller left him.

Blue Stone Man seemed to have made his decision. He spoke quietly, and then they moved forward, shadows in the long grass. Looks Back had a quick word with the gods and fell into line. Cat Ears shouldered his way to the front, but he had sense enough not to push past Blue Stone Man.

The Others had disappeared into the canyon, and the Yellow Grass men padded cautiously down the trail be-

hind them, hoping to surprise them. Wind Caller kept a
wary eye on the thickets of chaparral that climbed the
slope. If the Others had seen them coming, the surprise
could be on the wrong side. He doubted that Blue Stone
Man had considered that; these people didn't fight. Wind
Caller contemplated the strangeness of that while he listened. He heard no shouting and concluded that the Others were still stalking the deer. The canyon mouth was
wide, and they would drive the deer gently until they
were bunched too closely to turn and bolt. There were
only a few more than twenty of the Yellow Grass hunters, the Others probably likewise. If they moved too
soon, the deer might get around them.

The canyon narrowed as they went, until it was barred
with light and shadow, the sun bouncing off the contorted shapes of the wind-eroded rock and twisted trees
that lined its uppermost edge. It swam glaringly in their
eyes. Deer and men might come and go unseen in those
barred shadows. They passed the pool where the deer
drank and picked their way through thickets of stunted
plums. On the riverbank they could see the marks of
hooves and sandals, the hooves skittering away upstream, the sandals following deliberately.

Wind Caller stopped again suddenly, but it was too
late. They had come unexpectedly on the last straggler
of the Others, and he had seen them. He shouted, saw
their number, and turned to run. The Yellow Grass People ran after him, and Cat Ears hurled a spear. It drove
through the fleeing back, spinning the man down, transfixed on the shaft.

Cat Ears started toward him. The hunters of the Others
howled back through the canyon, abandoning the deer.
They hurled themselves on the Yellow Grass People before Wind Caller could try to tell them where to make
their stand.

Wind Caller saw a spear coming toward him and

knocked it away with his own. The point went past his
eye so close that the binding scraped his ear. He jumped
back to give himself room enough to cock his spear arm
and lunged forward, trying to pin the other man with the
spear. The point went into the Other's shoulder, and
Wind Caller yanked it out before he lost it. Then he saw
a Yellow Grass man standing alone, looking wildly
about him for what he ought to be doing, and Wind
Caller drove his spear through the thigh of the Other
who was coming up on his back. The Yellow Grass man
turned a startled face to Wind Caller and dived into the
melee of thrashing spears, waving his. Found Water
puffed by him on the other side, breathing hard just to
keep up.

Jaguar take them, Wind Caller thought. They didn't
know how to fight. They drove their spears at the Others
with no idea of parrying the Others' blows. When they
lost their spears, they flung themselves at their enemies,
knocking them broadside, and tried to beat their heads
in with rocks.

Wind Caller got back his spear. He saw Blue Stone
Man thrust a spear again and again into a man who was
already dead, propped up by the thicket into which Blue
Stone Man had driven him. One of the Yellow Grass
men was dead, his body sprawled underfoot.

The dogs of both groups were fighting each other, but
Wind Caller saw Follow dart through the dust, sink his
teeth into the back of an enemy's knee, and give a quick
snap of his head. The Other's knee buckled. Follow
backed off then and waited for Wind Caller to put his
spear through the man's throat.

One of the dead man's fellows came at Wind Caller,
holding a heavy spear in both hands. Wind Caller
brought his own spear up, but the blow went wide. He
dropped it and caught the enemy's spear just as it came
at him. For a moment they struggled, tugging it back

and forth, snarling at each other like the dogs. The dust billowed around them in heavy clouds as they blundered through the chaparral and the scrub. The sun had grown hot, and breathing the dry, dusty air was like breathing sand. Wind Caller felt himself slide in the blood beneath his feet and let go of the spear shaft. The Other, suddenly freed, stumbled backward and fell. Wind Caller righted himself and jumped on him, pulling his skinning knife from the waist of his breechclout. He drew the knife across the twisting neck.

Blood spurted from the cut throat, soaking Wind Caller until his hands were slippery with it. Another Yellow Grass man had gone down, and two of the Others were dead as well. Wind Caller killed one of their dogs as it came at Follow and saw Follow about to sink his teeth into another knee. The man howled and kicked at him, and Follow ran into the thicket.

Wind Caller got away from the blood, before he slipped in it again, and rubbed his hands with dirt. He retrieved his spear and found Cat Ears beside him, flung by the chaos of the battle against Wind Caller's shoulder. Cat Ears's spear was gone, and he was lashing desperately with his knife at a big man who was backing off along the shaft of his heavy hunting spear with obvious purpose.

Wind Caller drove his spear into the man's belly before he could turn away from Cat Ears. The man grunted with surprise, his breath flying outward into Wind Caller's face, and his spear sank away from Cat Ears.

Cat Ears turned furiously on Wind Caller. He snarled something angry, and spat at him. Wind Caller prodded Cat Ears with his own spear until he backed away.

The Others were moving now, Wind Caller saw with satisfaction, stumbling past the Yellow Grass People toward the canyon mouth, dragging their wounded with them. Wind Caller prodded Cat Ears again. ''That's why you shouldn't use an atlatl,'' he said, poking Cat Ears again to make his point. "Someone will take your spear and gut you with it.''

Cat Ears said something furious. Wind Caller didn't think it needed translation. He walked down the spear a little, hand over hand, careful to stay out of reach of the skinning knife Cat Ears was holding, and said, "You don't know how to fight, little man. You should listen to your betters until you do.''

That didn't need translation, either. Cat Ears knocked the spear point away and limped off—he had a gash in his left leg—daring Wind Caller to come after him.

Flown with their victory, the Yellow Grass men chased after the Others until Wind Caller set out after them, catching One Ball and old Turtle Back by the arms, pulling them back. "Let them go!'' he told them.

They looked at him blankly. Found Water huffed up beside them.

"Let them go unless you want to eat them! Hunt the deer!'' He shouted at them, waving his arms up the canyon. Blue Stone Man joined them, breathing hard, most of his spear shaft bloodied. Wind Caller remembered the word the woman had taught him. "Deer!'' he said. "Deer!'' He lapsed into his own tongue again, shouting in exasperation. "If you chase these men, they will be waiting for you. Let them go! You don't know how to fight.''

Blue Stone Man understood. He was of much the same mind. The Yellow Grass hunters looked as flighty as untrained dogs, ready at any moment to run after the wrong thing. "Let the Others go,'' he said.

"I want to kill them,'' Cat Ears said. "We should go and kill them.''

One Ball and Turtle Back looked disappointed. They had killed an enemy each and were elated. "We should chase them,'' One Ball said.

"We have driven them away," Looks Back answered. "It is they who have taken the deer. Now we should take the deer back."

Slowly they nodded, grumbling, as their blood cooled.

"What about our dead?" Walks Funny asked, frowning. Among the dead lying in the canyon were three Yellow Grass men. One of them was his brother.

Blue Stone Man considered this for a moment and then pointed at the youngest hunter. "You. Watch from the thicket, in case the Others come for their slain while we go after the deer. If they do, run after us, but I think they will wait until we're away. When we come back with the deer, we'll carry our dead home."

"If there *are* any deer," Cat Ears said, still angry because he wanted to fight. "Leave *me* here with them."

"No!" Blue Stone Man said. To soften it, he added, "You are the best hunter. We need you. And if the Others were not driving deer, they had no reason to be here. There are deer."

Cat Ears decided to be mollified by the compliment. "Come, then," he said loftily to the rest of them. He had retrieved his spears and carried one cocked into the atlatl.

Wind Caller chuckled. A spear-thrower was very useful with deer. Deer couldn't throw them back at you.

Cat Ears heard him, spun around, and pointed at Wind Caller. "*He* brought them here! *He* called the Others here with that piece of bone!"

Blue Stone Man halted in exasperation. "He fought them. He is wearing their blood. He killed two, maybe three."

"He kept one of them from killing Cat Ears," One Ball volunteered. "I saw him."

"You saw your own backside!" Cat Ears snarled.

"Enough!" Blue Stone Man snapped. He looked from Wind Caller to Cat Ears. They were probably of the same age. And of course Cat Ears had wanted the woman. Their discord was to be expected. "Keep your tongue behind your teeth until we have fed our people," he said to Cat Ears. "That is more important. I was young and randy once, too, but eating is more important."

"Especially when you get old," Found Water said, and they laughed.

Found Water was battered but in one piece. As the hunters fanned out across the canyon to drive the deer, he took his place in the net with relief. Maybe the urge to kill someone to account for their troubles would go away now, and they could resume a peaceful life. The strange man might even be a suitable son-in-law. He could fight, and perhaps that would be useful. The People were not warriors. There had always been enough room for everyone and no reason to fight. Greed and covetousness were considered bad manners. The Others seemed to like to fight, which baffled Found Water. Two young men with their blood up, fighting over a woman—that was understandable. But one clan deliberately setting out to fight another, as he had heard that the Others did, made no sense, not when there were so many better things to do in the world, like hunt, or make babies, or listen to the stories of when the world was new that Looks Back told around the fire. It was a fine world, Found Water thought, if only it didn't have the Others in it.

Perhaps this new man could make them go away. That would certainly make Found Water important, too.

They were far into the canyon before they found the deer, who had bounded up the slopes into the chaparral, frightened by the fighting. The sides of the canyon were too steep here to climb, and when the deer saw the hunters, they leaped back to the canyon floor and scattered through the low thickets. They were tawny like the canyon walls, and it was easy to believe that a magic could have made them out of mud. Their bright eyes gleamed through the dappling shadows of gray-green sage and the tall spines of yucca. Looks Back sang a chant, apologizing to the deer for the battle, for the intrusion of human quarrels into their world.

The hunters were closer together now, walking in a line across the canyon floor where scrub and small trees grew beside the trickle of a stream. Thornbush scratched their arms and legs, and Wind Caller gave a wide berth to a cactus with strange fat oval leaves studded with small spines. He had touched one once and been in misery for days. Like all lands, this one was armed against strangers and might eat its travelers.

He quickened his step, almost unbearably glad to be among humans again. Follow still looked suspicious. But in this battle and hunt Wind Caller felt a swift joy that he hadn't experienced since he had hunted with his own people.

Ahead, the deer were crashing through the thickets, heads up, eyes wild. At the end of the canyon a rock wall rose bluntly, blocking their way. The stream had its source there, a thin thread that ran from a cleft in the rock, snowmelt from some distant mountain. The thunder of hooves grew louder as the deer found themselves trapped, swung back toward the hunters, then retreated again toward the canyon's dead end. They leaped and bounded, soaring frantically, running in a circle, trampling and biting the ones in their way.

The hunters closed in and began to throw rocks, driving the deer in upon themselves, into a maelstrom of hooves and horns. Wind Caller nocked his spear into the atlatl, drew his arm back, and snapped it forward with a quick turn of his wrist. The spear flew away, whirring like an insect. A deer went down, the others leaping around and over it.

Spear after spear flew into the trapped herd. One deer sought to break away, but a thin gray shadow drove it in again. Follow bit at the deer's haunches and slunk away, leaving it hobbling. The hunters shouted, driving in closer and closer, dangerously unwary, Wind Caller thought, until he saw how they danced just out of reach of the sharp hooves and antlers. These were not the little brocket deer his southern people hunted. These antlers could pierce a man as easily as his spear could impale the deer. No meal came free in this country.

Finally, panic-driven, the remaining deer flew right at the hunters, and the hunters pulled away to let them go. Deer must be spared to make more deer, to keep their part of the compact with man that was made when the world was new. The Yellow Grass men circled their kill, warily dispatching any that still breathed. There were six, an unheard-of number for a single hunt.

They gutted the deer and let the dogs eat their fill. Follow stuck his gray snout in the offal of the deer that Wind Caller gutted and gulped it down without chewing, disinclined to share it with the dogs. Wind Caller put the liver, heart, and bladder back into the carcass. The first two had magical properties, and the last was useful. The hunters cut apart two of the livers and gave each man a piece. Wind Caller bit into his hungrily. It was frightening how little time it would take to starve, a realization that had never occurred to him in the jungles to the south, where food was always abundant. This dry land felt alien to him, as if he had suddenly found himself in the sky, scattered among the stars.

The hunters tied the hooves of the gutted deer together so that they could be carried on spear shafts, two men to a deer. The three dead humans were more troublesome, for they must be shown respect. With two men to carry each body, only a handful were left to scout ahead for signs of the Others.

Five of the Others lay dead, sprawled in the scrub. They had seemed surprised to find the People ready to fight them, Wind Caller thought. He was also aware that he had done a great deal of the fighting himself and that Blue Stone Man and the rest of the People knew it. That might be useful to him, but it might also be dangerous. If Blue Stone Man thought Wind Caller was gaining too much influence . . . Well, he remembered what had happened when Eyes of Jaguar had thought that.

When Blue Stone Man pointed at him to help carry a deer, Wind Caller didn't object. He could always drop the deer if he needed his spears, which were slung across his back. Cat Ears strode grandly beside the procession, his spear at the ready. Wind Caller noted with amusement that this time it wasn't nocked into the atlatl, but he didn't let Cat Ears see his grin.

It was a laborious trip back with the weight of the dead and the deer. The canyon was much farther from the summer caves than the old deer runs had been, and it gave them time to crow about their victory.

"Yah! We are great fighters!"

"We have killed all the Others!"

"They'll be back for their dead," Cat Ears said, his head cocked for any whisper in the surrounding scrub. "We should go back and wait for them and kill some more."

"Maybe they won't go back," Walks Funny said.

"Just leave them there?" One Ball said. He looked uneasy. If the Others did that, who could tell what they might do?

"They aren't human," Found a Snake said. "Maybe they don't care."

"If they aren't human, then it should be all right to kill them," Cat Ears said stubbornly.

"Young men should have respect for the commands of the spirit people," Turtle Back said. "It is a mistake to kill for no reason."

Cat Ears spat into the dirt.

One Ball chuckled. "And weren't you just about to chase them, too, Uncle?"

"I was excited by the heat of battle," Turtle Back said with dignity.

"We drove them away!" Walks Funny said. He made it a victory chant. "We drove away the demon people, and our dead will go to the Skeleton House in triumph!"

"We drove them away, and we killed many deer!"

"They took away the deer, and we have taken them back!"

They chanted it over and over, building a new ritual, a way to tell the gods of their exploits, a spell to bring victory next time. Slowly Wind Caller began to distinguish one word from another. He didn't know what each one meant, but he began to chant them, too. Collectively the words meant victory, he was certain of that much.

They sang the deer and their dead home until they crested the last hill beyond the summer caves, and the women and old men and babies came pouring down the slope to meet them and hear the tale.

X
Burning the Field

Butchering the deer was a task for the women and children, and in the heat of late afternoon it was hot, sticky work, and brought flies. Deer Shadow pushed stray hair back from her face with her arm, holding her bloodied hand away. The livers and hearts were already piled in baskets ready for cooking. One of her small half-sisters picked up a basket to take to the fire pits, waddling under her burden like a duck. The men were in the cool of the caves, resting after their hunt and the fight, honoring the dead hunters, and, Deer Shadow supposed, telling the hunt story over again. She wondered how the stranger was doing among them. She had seen him go off with the rest while the coyote slunk into the brush to wait for him. It might be that men were the same everywhere, and he didn't need to understand their talk to know how he should be.

"Is that man really the father?" Owl whispered to her as they worked on opposite ends of the deer.

Because Owl had never asked her before, Deer Shadow answered in a voice that let Owl know it was true. "Yes."

Owl worked her knife under the hide and detached

196

the skull with it. This was a particularly fine deer, worth saving so it could live again in the deer dance. "Squirrel says your man had a big fight with Cat Ears," she said when she had finished the tricky part.

"Cat Ears doesn't like him. Why should he like Cat Ears?"

"Squirrel said he made fun of him."

Deer Shadow chuckled. She would rather hunt than butcher the kill, and when she was irked by that, she chose to roll all men, whose idea it was that *they* should be the hunters and leave the mess for the women, into the arrogant symbol of Cat Ears.

"What did he make fun of Cat Ears about?" Deer Shadow asked curiously.

Owl turned the detached head over to clean it, cutting the tongue out and putting it into the basket with the liver and the heart. She saved the brains to use for tanning. "Squirrel said it was when they fought the Others. Cat Ears wanted to throw his spear at them. I don't suppose he thought about getting it back."

Deer Shadow hooted. "No wonder he looks as if he just ate ants. I don't suppose I would think of that, either, though." She pulled the last of the hide loose from the hindquarters. "I don't ever remember fighting people. Listens to Deer said the Others are humans, too, but I don't see how they can be. Humans don't steal and fight each other."

Owl gave her a somber look. She knew what humans could do to each other. "Look what we did yesterday."

"That's not the same," Deer Shadow said. "I mean wars. Looks Back says there have been wars. You've heard him tell about them. But they were in the First Days. The People don't make war now."

"We will if the Others do," Owl said. "Looks Back said the men who fought yesterday are unclean now and will have to purify themselves."

"Just to be sure they can't help scrape hides," Deer Shadow murmured. "Have you ever noticed how when there's nasty hot work to do, the men have to purify themselves? Or go into a trance somewhere inside, where it's cool?"

"Then what did you want with one?" Owl's face screwed up in anger. "I thought you weren't going to have a man."

"I didn't mean to. He was just there." Deer Shadow felt foolish. "I don't know what happened exactly."

"You don't remember it?" Owl was scornful.

"No, I remember it. That's why—well, I wanted to!" She looked at Owl as she scraped the skull and said tartly, "You wanted to, too. You were dying to go with that man. You just didn't know what he was going to be like. They aren't all that way."

"No," Owl said shortly. "They aren't. But mine was."

"I'm sorry," Deer Shadow said.

"You aren't broken," Owl said bitterly.

"No, I just nearly got killed like Afraid of His Mother. And it wasn't just men that did that."

"Now you're defending them," Owl said. "I don't think you know what you want, except the man. It's that wanting that makes people careless. It's too strong. I *saw* that boy beat his little sister; I just never thought he would do it to me."

Deer Shadow began to cut the meat off the haunches and put it in a basket. She cut the tendons out and laid them to one side. Everything would be used. The bones would be made into tools, the bladders waterskins, and the sinews thread. It would be disrespectful not to use every part of an animal that had sacrificed its life.

The child returned for the next basket of meat. Deer Shadow could smell it cooking on the fire pits that other women were tending. The day was still hot, and sweat rolled down into her eyes, but the smell made her stomach growl. She wiped her forehead with her arm again and waved away the flies. The next time the child came back, Deer Shadow whispered, "Steal me a piece, if you can do it without getting caught."

The little girl grinned. Her mouth was greasy. She trotted off again and reappeared with a piece of half-cooked meat hidden in the empty basket. Deer Shadow sank her teeth into it and tore off a bite, ruffling the girl's hair with a greasy hand. Now that she was going to have a child of her own and didn't have to live with these, she found herself resenting them less.

"Can I have a piece for my puppy?" The girl looked wistfully at the carcass.

Deer Shadow gave her a chunk of the raw flesh, and the child went off to some hiding place with the puppy waddling after her. There were plenty of places to be alone in among the caves that honeycombed the yellow tufa cliffs. As a child, Deer Shadow had known most of them. She wondered which one her little sister had picked for her own.

Attracted by the smell of meat, the men were beginning to emerge from the caves. Deer Shadow saw Wind Caller watching her, but he didn't come over, probably because he was unsure of what he should be doing. He followed the men.

Owl and Deer Shadow set aside the useful bones and put the rest in a pile for the dogs. The coyote appeared from out of the brush and snatched one, but it wouldn't come to her, even when Deer Shadow offered it meat.

"Yah, then, go and eat your bone," she said, affronted.

The coyote looked at her over its shoulder and slunk away into the brush again. She had the feeling that it didn't approve of her. *I don't like you, either,* she thought.

"You'll have to compete with that thing for him," Owl said. "I wouldn't have it sleeping in the cave with *me*."

It had watched them all of last night. It was like having another person watch you, not like a dog.

The dogs didn't think it was like them, either. They no longer growled at it but had developed a tendency to turn tail and skulk off when it came near them. Instead of growing less afraid of it, they were growing more so, as if its mere presence somehow established its dominance.

Deer Shadow stood up, rubbing her aching back. She had other things to do besides think about the coyote. Tomorrow the hides would have to be pinned down, scraped, and soaked in wood ash to remove the flesh and hair. She looked at the hides with loathing. The one they were saving for the deer dance would have to be treated with special care to leave the hair on the outside. Then all the hides would have to be rubbed with the brains and then worked to make them supple. It took more time to tan the deer than it did to kill it, she thought irritably.

"Enough for tonight," Owl said. "Eat before you put yourself in a temper."

Tonight and tomorrow the People would eat their fill of fresh meat. What was left over would be cut into thin strips and dried for the winter. When the meat was dry, they would grind it into fine powder and mix it with the fat. A handful in a pot of water would make a meal. It didn't taste like fresh meat, though. Nothing did. The voices around the fire pits had grown loud with relief that the deer had come back.

Deer Shadow found Wind Caller and sat next to him. He smiled at her, which startled her. He was gnawing pieces off a rib bone. He handed her another, and she bit into it ravenously. She couldn't remember being this hungry even as a child; she was hungry all the time. Pieces of baked cactus had been piled onto a hot stone, and she stuffed one of those into her mouth, too. Then she remembered her manners and solemnly offered a piece to Wind Caller.

He looked at it with revulsion and at Deer Shadow with suspicion. She was prepared to be insulted until she studied his expression. Then she understood. Once, when she was little, she had grabbed a cactus and learned what the spines could do. She mimicked pulling them out with pincers.

"You don't eat the needles," she told him, laughing helplessly. "You don't come from here, do you?" She put the piece in his hand and took another for herself before they were gone.

Wind Caller took a bite, gingerly.

The night was growing cool, as arid country tends to do even in summer. Wind Caller settled himself cross-legged in front of the fire pit's heat and watched the woman eat. There were more things to eat here than he had thought, things he never would have tried. He supposed Deer Shadow would be as lost in his country as he was in hers. More so, maybe. Hunting was universal, even if there were new game trails to learn. A man could eat nearly any animal if he was hungry. But knowing what plants to eat, that was another matter. He remembered the times in his wanderings that he had spent delirious or throwing up because he hadn't been careful enough.

He smiled again. If he hadn't been certain that the woman was pregnant before, he was now. Only a pregnant woman could outeat men. He found himself reasonably content with that, here in the warmth of the fire, under the scattering of stars that had begun to fill the sky—so many stars here. Where the Children of the Sun lived there was too much haze to see the stars. Wind

Caller had been afraid of those stars when he had lived alone under them. Now he watched their sweep with astonished delight.

He hadn't learned the language of her people yet, so no one could have told him that Coyote was supposed to have put them there.

The Yellow Grass People burned Afraid of His Mother that night in a more elaborate ceremony than would ordinarily have been accorded him. Now that the deer were back, his aunts had wanted reparation. The rest of the People were uneasily aware that Deer Shadow said the baby was the stranger's.

"It is possible that his death has brought the deer anyway," Looks Back said solemnly. "He had power. He may have belonged to the Deer Mother. He may have gone to speak to her."

Wind Caller's people would have understood that idea immediately: They sent the dead as messengers to the gods. But the Yellow Grass People were prepared to believe that possibility only by believing the messenger to be something more than human. All the same, they looked relieved. Maybe they hadn't been quite so wicked as Looks Back had said at first. The urge to self-justification is as old as human nature.

"We must do the proper thing so that one does not become angry and come back," Blue Stone Man said.

The Yellow Grass People were quick to agree. Any ghost lonely for its earthly family might return and try to take someone with it. But a vengeful ghost could bring sickness and terrifying visions. No one who had thrown stones at Afraid of His Mother wanted to be visited by him.

Because it was risky for men to touch a corpse, Afraid of His Mother had been laid out by the women, but the bier had to be carried by men. It was decided that one of them should be Looks Back, since a shaman's powers could counteract any malign influences; the other should be the stranger, since he had arrived after the death and was in any case expendable.

Wind Caller didn't argue when Looks Back pointed at him. He thought perhaps he was being honored. He noticed how they all stepped away, though, as he and Looks Back came down the slope with the bier. The women walked beside it with torches, allowing Wind Caller his first good look at the body. It was mottled, blackened in places, and crusted with dried blood. He nearly dropped the bier, and Looks Back shouted at him angrily.

Wind Caller righted himself and saw that Deer Shadow was among those walking to one side, her face streaming with furious tears. Again the urge to ask questions and the knowledge that it would be futile maddened him. He might as well be the coyote, with no speech at all except for yaps and howls. Something evil had taken place here before he arrived, he was certain of that. Did it have anything to do with the reception he had received, or with the woman? There was no way to tell with people as odd as these; they never behaved as they were supposed to.

They laid the bier on the pile of sticks, and Looks Back put on his skeleton mask. Wind Caller felt relieved; the mask he recognized. Looks Back put a black crow's feather in the corpse's folded hands, so that he could not fly back from the dark, then placed one of his precious eagle feathers next to it, so that the spirit should not be offended. He covered the body with a deer hide in case Afraid of His Mother belonged to the Deer Mother after all.

Wind Caller watched curiously. Were they leaving the body to lie in state before they buried it? Already it was beginning to stink. His nose twitched at the smell, which was not overborne by the spruce branches and sage packed around it. And what about animals? Would someone guard the body all night? He thought uneasily of Follow, who ate carrion indiscriminately, and wondered if he should tie the coyote up. He had tried it once before; Follow had transformed himself into a thrashing, snarling tornado in the dirt and had clawed and bitten his way through the rope in moments. Then he had stayed just out of Wind Caller's reach, growling his high-pitched singsong growl until all of Wind Caller's hair stood up on end.

Deer Shadow handed Looks Back her torch, and the sticks beneath the body were burning before Wind Caller realized it. Was *this* what they did with their dead? How could you go to the place of the dead if you had no body to go in? He stared, queasily, and wondered how he could persuade them not to do that to him when his time came.

The fire was licking the spruce and sage around the body, sending up puffs of pungent smoke. Little lines of flame ate at the edges of the deerskin. The smoke grew blacker, and Wind Caller began to smell hot flesh. He backed off, gagging, driven away by the smell, and pushed through the crowd. They made way for him without noticing who he was, their eyes on the bier. A number of them made warding-off gestures at it, middle finger crossed over forefinger. Wind Caller wanted to do the same.

When he got away from the crowd, Follow appeared out of the dark, carrying his bone. The coyote looked toward the bier and sniffed, curious.

"No!" Wind Caller said violently. "You stay away from that!"

He went into the cave that the woman had shown him that morning and found that it now contained a wide bed of sweet grass, a waterskin hung from a peg driven into a crack in the stone, and a functional fire pit, newly lined with stones and banked with embers. An array of storage baskets and leather pots stood against the far wall, and Wind Caller, forgetting his revulsion, wondered how much argument it had taken the woman to get the things out of her father's house.

He went out of the cave, made water, then went back in and sat on the grass bed. It was covered with a hide, a blanket of otter fur, and another of coyote. Follow sniffed the furs and decided to ignore them. He curled at the foot of the bed and put his tail over his nose.

"I don't know how she's going to like you," Wind Caller said.

Follow yawned and snapped his white teeth closed.

Wind Caller lay down on the bed. The smoke drifted up the slope and crept into the cave, thick and unpleasantly sweet. He buried his face in the grass.

In the morning he woke to find the woman sitting up beside him, watching him, as if she was waiting for him to wake up. Her feet were tucked up under her. Follow was sprawled on the end of the bed, snoring. With every wheeze his muzzle twitched, showing the ends of his teeth.

"It slept where I put my feet," she said as soon as Wind Caller's eyes opened. "When I moved my feet, it bit me."

Wind Caller shook his head. "I don't know what you're saying," he said sleepily.

The woman got up. She snatched the coyote fur robe off the bed, wrapped it around her, and padded out of the cave. Wind Caller tried to wake himself up. It had been a long time since he had slept in a bed with the warmth of any other body besides Follow's next to him, and the luxury of it had left him groggy.

After quite a while the woman reappeared with wood and began to poke at the fire. The smell of burned flesh was still in the air, but it was cold now, and the smoke from the hearth fire wiped it away. Deer Shadow put the wild grapes and half-dried berries she had picked yesterday in front of him. "We could use a rabbit," she said.

Wind Caller ate a handful of grapes.

Deer Shadow drew the picture of a rabbit on the cave floor. "Rabbit," she said. She found his sling in his pack and laid it in front of him.

"Ah." Wind Caller made a gesture of respect, fingers to bowed forehead. "I hear and obey, Most Important Lady."

She also pulled the rest of the maize from the pack and balanced the grains in her hand. "Looks Back says it is time to see what this is," she informed him.

The translation of that was made plain when Looks Back and Blue Stone Man appeared at the cave mouth, the rest of the Yellow Grass People hovering excitedly behind them.

It seemed late in the year to plant maize, Wind Caller thought, but he couldn't be sure. Where he came from it would grow almost anytime, but he had learned that it was different here. Plants had to ripen before the cold weather came, and maize took three moons. He looked at the avid faces crowded in his doorway and knew that there was no way to tell them that it had to wait until after winter. They weren't going to let him.

He picked up the stick that Deer Shadow used to dig for camas and set out down the hill, with everyone behind him. "It isn't magic," he told them irritably, "it's seed." He led them a long way from the cave through the already yellowing grass, to a flat place on the stream bank, where water would be just under the surface. He paced off an area a hundred times the length of his foot on each side, trampling down the grass. "Burn this," he said.

They looked at him blankly. He might as well be speaking to lizards. Exasperated, he went back up the slope, and some of them trotted after him again, not wanting to miss anything, while he got a torch from last night's burning. Giving a wide berth to the charred bones on the ashes of the bier, he returned to the cave and stuck the torch in Deer Shadow's fire until it was ablaze. He picked up a water basket while he was there. His adopted tribe trailed behind him like a comet's tail as he retraced his way to the stream, discussing whether the stranger was mad or dangerous or about to do great things.

Wind Caller handed Deer Shadow the torch, and she held it, puzzled, while he dipped water from the stream and poured it along the boundary lines he had stepped out. With one water basket, it was laborious, and he got irritated quickly. He tapped three of the men on the shoulders and pointed at the stream. "Get some baskets and help."

"What's he saying?"

"Does he want more water?"

"I'm certain it's a curse, Husband." Caught the Moon clutched Turtle Back's arm. "Don't listen to him."

"He just wants water, you silly hen," Deer Shadow said.

Caught the Moon fluffed herself up like a turkey in indignation.

"Water!" Wind Caller said, remembering the word from yesterday. He pointed at his basket and at the stream again. "Water."

"I believe it will be safe," Turtle Back said solemnly. He detached himself from his wife. "Go and bring me something to carry it in."

Caught the Moon scooted up the hill, and the men

waited until she returned with two baskets and a water-skin. They filled them, and Wind Caller pointed at the other sides of his field. They watched while he wet the grass down outside his border, and then went and did likewise.

"Why is he doing that?" Give Away asked Deer Shadow.

"So the fire doesn't jump past the part he wants to burn," Deer Shadow said. She gave Caught the Moon a repressive look to forestall any more questions. Sometimes the People cut firebreaks when they wanted to drive the game with fire. For a small area, water would work just as well. But she had no idea why he wanted to burn it in the first place.

"Why does he want to burn it?" Caught the Moon said, echoing her thoughts.

"Because the Fire God has said to," Deer Shadow said loftily. Maybe when she had taught him to talk, she thought, she wouldn't have to make everything up.

When the men finished wetting down the perimeter, Wind Caller took the torch from Deer Shadow. She felt the quick flare of its heat move away from her to him. He walked along the wet grass, setting the dry thatch beyond it on fire. It went up furiously.

Wind Caller held up a hand to the wind and dipped up more water just in case. The fire burned inward, eating up the grass, sending pale smoke boiling into the sky. The flames had a voice, a hot whisper in the still air that could be heard above the nervous chatter.

The blaze met in a tower of red heat in the center of the field, licking up the grass until nothing was left. It fell in on itself. Bright sparks rose in the smoke, winked out, and were gone. Wisps of smoke rose here and there in the blackened field, and once in a while the red eye of a sullen ember popped open and died.

The Yellow Grass People pressed around Wind

Caller, wanting to see what would happen next. He stepped forward as if he were going to walk on the hot ground, and they gasped. He stepped back again, hopping, as if he had tried it and burned his foot. That they understood: No one but a shaman could walk on fire. They had entertained the notion that Coyote could and had wondered if that was the reason the stranger was burning the ground, but it seemed not.

Wind Caller pointed over the eastern mountains to the sun, then toward the west, where it would go to lie down. He pointed at the burned field and the digging stick he had left lying with the water baskets.

"He says," Looks Back announced, "that he will bury the grain when the ground has cooled." He thought a moment. "Otherwise it will be parched."

"Oh," they said. "Of course." After they gathered wild grass seed, they parched it to keep it from sprouting in the storage pits. Then maybe he *could* walk on fire after all, if he wanted to.

Wind Caller and Follow returned with a rabbit in the late afternoon, to their mutual satisfaction. These rabbits were the long-legged, long-eared kind that could run like the wind, and he and Follow felt pleased with themselves for their cleverness when they caught one. They also killed a turkey, but Deer Shadow wouldn't cook it, although she was happy to have the feathers.

"We don't eat those," she managed to convey in sign language, although Wind Caller never understood why not. He gave the turkey to Follow, who had no such scruples.

While he had been gone, he saw with amusement, she had made another bed, coyote-sized, on the opposite side of the cave. Follow ignored it and lay down on their bed with his plucked turkey and proceeded to eat it noisily, beginning with the head. Deer Shadow followed Wind

Caller with alacrity when he gathered up the maize and set out for the field.

People were already there, watching the cooled ashes as if they expected jaguars to pop up out of them, Wind Caller thought. He took a stick that he had split into thin fingers at one end and raked the ashes smooth with it. When he got tired of that, he gave sticks to two of the other men and indicated that they should do it instead. They tried to hand the sticks to the women, but Wind Caller wouldn't let them. Men planted maize.

When the ground was smooth, he took the digging stick and dug holes two feet apart in rows down the field. There wasn't enough maize to plant the whole field, but they would need the space next season. He knew that the Yellow Grass People supposed him to be working some spell, and he stopped to think about what he should do. There was a proper ceremony for planting maize, but he had never done it himself, only listened and watched when Eyes of Jaguar had done it. Wind Caller stood thinking for so long that the people began to mutter.

"This is dangerous," Cat Ears said stubbornly, arms folded over his chest. "Anything new is dangerous."

"It's food," Deer Shadow said. "You like food well enough."

"Oh!" Give Away said. She put a hand to her cheek. "What if it's like the madness weed? We might eat it and die!"

"I told you," Cat Ears said.

"There has been too much change," Turtle Back said. "It is not good to change the way we do things. We have changed enough already." He looked at Deer Shadow. "One new magic at a time may be enough. It is unwise to draw the spirits' attention too closely to us, by untrained people. Only the shaman knows the proper way."

Looks Back nodded his appreciation of this sentiment. He studied Wind Caller, who stood now, hands upraised, in the middle of the field and talked to the Maize God in an unknown language. "I have made certain to tie his magic down," Looks Back said. "There is no danger. This new man has power, but it does not smell evil."

"Maybe the shaman's nose is old," Cat Ears said. Everyone looked at him disapprovingly, and he puffed out his chest to show them that he wasn't afraid, that he had as much power as his father. Looks Back gave him a long black stare.

Wind Caller stopped his chant and turned to face them. There should be a war captive present, to give his blood to the ground, but he hadn't thought to try to catch one of the Others, and he didn't suppose these people would let him kill one of them. He peered wistfully at Cat Ears. No. Regretfully, he took his knife out of his belt, slashed his thumb with it, and squeezed a drop or two of blood into each hole. They watched him, silenced.

The sun was falling as he moved down the rows, his long shadow stretching black behind him across the burned ground. His skin caught the red western light so that he appeared to be bathed in the blood.

Deer Shadow held her breath. This was beyond mere ritual, the repeated pattern of an act old and familiar. This was the coming of a new thing never known in their world, watered by true life blood. Was that what the scars on his chest were from? The small hard ridges and bumps her hand had encountered on his penis? Suddenly he was a creature as unknown and distant as the stars. He moved down the rows, bending and straightening, scarlet and black among the ashes. What wonderful and terrible thing might come out of those holes?

* * *

In the weeks after the planting, Deer Shadow took to going the long way home from the stream and her foraging to stop and look at the field. At first the maize was only tiny green shoots. She would sit cross-legged in the grass and watch them, her hand on her swollen belly. She and the maize were both growing something new.

Wind Caller remained as mysterious to her as ever. In the same instant he was both human male and someone who could bring a new plant up out of the earth as First Creator had done. She studied the maize for clues.

When weeds began to sprout up through the ashes between the little shoots, Wind Caller chipped out a hoe blade and lashed it to a stick with deer sinew. He showed the Yellow Grass People how to use it, making it very clear that he was not to be the only one who did the hoeing. Instead he would play the flute, singing up the maize, as he explained it haltingly with the words of their tongue that he knew. The men quickly gave the job to the women. Summer was the best season for hunting, and they might be gone three or four days at a time. Women had time for things like hoeing.

"Women gather plants," Deer Shadow complained. "But a *man* brought this plant." She looked at Wind Caller accusingly.

He didn't answer right away, though he was slowly learning their language. After he had learned enough to be told what he was supposed to do, he had paid her father three deer hides for her. He had kicked the coyote out of their bed, too, and made it stay in its own, where it watched her resentfully.

"Men plant maize," Wind Caller said. "Women hoe maize."

"Why?" Deer Shadow demanded.

"Why not eat turkeys?" he asked.

"Because we don't. They are—" She searched for a

word. Not poisonous, or tabu, exactly. "We just don't."

They looked at each other, mutually baffled.

"Where I come from," Wind Caller said, "the gods have told us what to do."

"These are the gods who want blood?" Deer Shadow asked. They had had a bewildering theological discussion in which each had concluded that the other's gods were so alien as to be unknowable. Thus they accorded each other's gods great respect, moving warily in the presence of the other's magical possessions or skills. Deer Shadow granted Wind Caller's flute great reverence and was secretly proud when he would play it for her at night and the other women could hear and be jealous. Even as she neared the sixth moon of her pregnancy, it made her blood sing and made her want to lie with him.

The coyote she feared, even though she still thought it was his other half; and because she had tried again to make it come to her hand and it wouldn't, she treated it with defiant disrespect. At night when it stuck its gray nose into the pot where she was boiling yucca root for soap, she hit it with the stirring spoon and it sank its teeth into her wrist. Wind Caller found them that way, the woman with the upraised spoon, and the coyote holding on to her other hand, the yucca root in the ashes of the fire.

"Drop it!" he said in the same voice he used when Follow stole meat from the fire. Follow opened his jaws. He stuck his nose in the yucca root again, decided he didn't like it, and got up on their bed to scratch fleas. Deer Shadow glowered at them both impartially. The discovery that he had barely broken her skin did nothing to mollify her. Nor did it improve matters when Wind Caller laughed. Repentant, Wind Caller drove the coyote off their bed and onto its own, where it lay cracking a bone. The People's dogs didn't have beds, Deer Shadow thought. If you were going to be a coyote, you ought to live like one.

She looked sideways at Wind Caller, who took his flute down from the niche he had chipped in the cave wall, where it lay with a sprig of sage and a brown-and-white turkey feather. He put it to his lips, and the music sang through the cave. Follow pricked up his ears. Deer Shadow put away the mess of yucca root and the hide she was stitching for a pack to carry the baby—she was tired of it anyway, and her fingers were sore—and sat with her hands folded around the unborn child, her fingers laced. Wind Caller was very beautiful in firelight, the mysterious unearthly scars making him look as if he were standing in the rain. Her body, lifted out of its growing awkwardness by the music, began to ache for him.

While they coupled, Wind Caller could feel the child kick under his hand. He had never lain with a pregnant woman before, and it had begun to unnerve him. Their couplings were as intense as that first one in the spring rain, or the night they had spent on the dance ground, as if he held more than just the woman in his arms. What else might be taking part in their joining he didn't know. The animals she called up out of the earth, maybe. As soon as he had been fluent enough to understand the gossip, he realized she had bought his life with magic.

What kind of child would such a woman give birth to? he wondered. A monster? A god? The gods had strange births from stones or waterspouts or balls of feathers. That might be more dangerous yet. Gods were not necessarily benevolent. None of his thoughts kept him from wanting her, from his flesh tightening when he saw her. None of it made him understand her any better.

* * *

As the summer grew hotter, and the child heavier, her mood grew more volatile. She moved with the ease of flowing water from whispers of delight when they coupled to imperious demands for rabbit, quail, or deer liver, or whatever else she fancied, to a sort of sly warfare with Follow. When she was in a wild temper, she would go away, and he learned that she went to watch the maize.

He found her there sitting quietly just outside the field, her hands as empty as the sky, when any industrious woman would be about her work, pregnant or not.

An hour before, a thunderstorm had boomed its way down the valley, bringing what the Yellow Grass People called the male rain—the hard, pounding rain that dug the washes deeper and filled them with roiling brown water. The sun was out again now and the battered leaves of the maize steamed dry in it. Tufts of what looked like yellow hair were beginning to show at the tops of the little pods that grew between the leaves and the stalk.

"It won't grow any faster if you watch it," Wind Caller said.

"Neither will this." Deer Shadow slapped her stomach irritably. "Maybe that is why I like it. We have something in common."

"Oh," Wind Caller said, bewildered again. "Am I going to get anything to eat?"

"Maybe," Deer Shadow said. "If the coyote hasn't stolen it."

"You left him alone with it?" He stamped his foot in aggravation. He had gone to bathe in the river, and Follow had declined to accompany him. No wonder. "Aaheh!" he said, grinding his teeth. "I bring you a perfectly good turkey and you won't eat it. I bring you squirrels and you leave them on the fire with that sneak thief in the cave!"

"We don't eat turkeys," Deer Shadow said.

"Bah," Wind Caller said. "I have eaten them."

"Very likely they gave you a fever and made you unclean. But you were ignorant," she added tolerantly.

He was standing in the stream, just in the rippled edge, the cold water bubbling around his ankles. On impulse, she scooped up a handful of water and splashed it at him, to see what would happen.

He turned around, startled, and scooped a whole handful up quickly, splashing it upward, drenching her. She spluttered, dripping, delighted that he would play with her. Another handful of water brought her one in return, and she flung herself at him, laughing, delighting in the cold water, trying to trip him down into it.

Instead he caught her by the shoulders. "Be careful of the child," he said. His eyes softened. "Now you look the way I remember." He chuckled. "Dripping wet!"

"Tell me why you were there, again. By the river," Deer Shadow said. She still wasn't sure she believed his stories of a strange people to the far south.

"Looking for you," Wind Caller said. It made his heart beat harder when he thought it.

"Why?" Deer Shadow demanded. He was still holding her, hands around her heavy waist. "My father told me you said Coyote told you to marry me."

"Maybe he did," Wind Caller said. He had heard the gossip about how he might be Coyote. Coyote, he had come to understand, held a place in their pantheon comparable to that of Jaguar. Coyote ate people, too, literally and symbolically. When an unexpected and terrible fate befell someone, the Yellow Grass People said that Coyote had eaten him. Therefore Coyote was distrusted and was sometimes even killed. But he also had great power. "Maybe he did. Maybe we felt that you would be wasted on Cat Ears."

"Cat Ears, pah!" Deer Shadow said. "Would I have had Cat Ears?"

"It depends on how lonesome you got, Most Important Lady," Wind Caller said. He dipped his chin and kissed her forehead, an unexpected gesture. Usually he kissed her only when he wanted her to couple with him. "We are the strangers," he said quietly. "You and me. Maybe Coyote thought we needed each other."

Deer Shadow rested her forehead on his chest. She felt as if they were in a basket, they two, enclosed and safe, able to tell truth. She could hear his heart thump under his skin, under the raindrop scars.

And then the moment was gone. She couldn't tell what cracked it, maybe only that it was too fragile. Give Away and Caught the Moon went by with gathering baskets full of greens. The sisters ducked their heads together and whispered when they passed.

Wind Caller lifted his head. When their backs were to him, he let out a yip that made Deer Shadow jump, a hunting coyote's singsong yelp. Give Away and Caught the Moon spun around like rabbits. Wind Caller grinned at them, showing his teeth the way Follow did. They bolted down the path.

Wind Caller chuckled. He yipped one more time.

Deer Shadow glowered at him. "And maybe Most Meddlesome Coyote should have saved his trouble," she muttered, angry at the breaking of something she couldn't define. She felt heavy again, and cumbersome. She waded out of the stream and waddled back toward the caves in the tufa cliffs.

She reminded Wind Caller of a duck from behind. He outpaced her to the cave, expecting to be in a fury at what he would find, but Follow had left the squirrels roasting on a stick and wasn't to be seen.

Deer Shadow poked the squirrels with her finger and stirred a pot of mush made from ground grass seed.

"Turtle Back's bitch is in heat. I saw the coyote going off down that way." She gave him a mischievous smile. "Perhaps Turtle Back will want three deerskins for his bitch."

Wind Caller laughed and squatted down beside her by the fire. She was as changeable as the weather. Whoever among her people had decided to call the hard pounding rain the male rain, and the soft soaking rain the female rain, had perhaps not known women well. "*My* people consider it an honor if their bitch attracts a good hunting dog."

"Turtle Back won't," Deer Shadow said. "Not if the pups come out looking like coyotes. What good will they be? They won't even pull a load." The people used dog power to drag their belongings on hides. Follow had reacted to that idea much as he had reacted to being tied. Not even Wind Caller had been willing to try it a second time.

"They will be smart," he offered.

"Crafty," Deer Shadow said. That was not a virtue in dogs, although certainly it was Coyote's main characteristic.

"If I can lie with you," Wind Caller said, "Follow can have his woman."

"You can't lie with me," Deer Shadow said irritably. "It is hot and I itch. And my back aches." She looked at him balefully. It didn't hurt to do it anymore; it felt good when she wasn't so tired. But almost always now she was tired, and she felt big and ugly, and anyway it only left her wanting something more. She thought of asking Aunt Four Fingers if she was doing it right, but she was ashamed to, since she had made herself so important over it and over the man. "I hoed maize all day," she said sulkily, unwilling to admit the rest of it.

Wind Caller looked enviously at Follow when he trotted in later under a full moon. "I suppose *you* had a fine time," he said. "Did old Turtle Back say, 'Here, take my daughter'?"

Follow yawned and closed his jaws with a snap. He cocked his head at Wind Caller, who watched him sleepily. Deer Shadow was already asleep and the cave was dim, only a faint silver thread of moon coming through the mouth to touch the guard hairs on Follow's coat. Wind Caller closed his eyes.

When he opened them again in dreamtime, he saw that Follow had gone out to the maize field and was talking to him there.

"This is like watching rocks take a walk," Follow said. He prodded at the maize to see if it would grow faster, but pawing at it just broke off the tassel at the top.

"Now you've done it," Wind Caller said. "There is a proper way to do things. Some things take time."

Coyote grinned at him. Coyote could turn time inside out, and impatient with waiting for it, he showed Wind Caller what the maize would be later: as many colors as there were stones in the earth—black and red, yellow, white, blue, some mixed up together, all spotted like turkey's feathers. There would be dances to it, and ceremonies for it. It would be used to feed the sacred masks and make magic, to paint with and give blessings. It would change the People in ways they had not dreamed of. It would make new gods.

But that was all in the future, which Coyote had reeled in over the seasons, dangling the years on threads of light. Just now, the little ears that Wind Caller had planted were thumb-sized, harder to make a meal of. They were a beginning, but Coyote was impatient.

Wind Caller thought he knew what was going to happen. There was too much of Coyote in these people. But Coyote wasn't the only one who could tell stories. Wind

Caller knew one now. He began to tell it to Coyote as he danced among the stars.

> A long time ago when all the animals talked like people, Turkey and Bear heard the People complaining because they were hungry. There were some things that Coyote, Old Man I-Thought-Up-the-Universe, hadn't thought of. He'd made sure there was sex and plenty of game, and that had kept him happy so far. But the People wanted more.
>
> So Turkey and Bear shook themselves, and all sorts of wild things to eat dropped out of their feathers and fur. There were juniper berries and prickly pear cactus, wild mulberries, saguaro fruit, piñon nuts, acorns, wild plums and yucca fruit, and little bitter squash.
>
> Then Turkey shook himself again, rattling his feathers, and maize fell out. He showed two of the People, a brother and a sister, how to make digging sticks and make holes for the maize. They dropped the seed in, and the next day it was knee-high. The People asked Turkey for more seed, and he gave it to them. At the end of four days, the maize was ripe, but Turkey told them this would be the only time that it would come up and ripen in four days.
>
> "After this, it will take a lot longer," he said, and it did.
>
> By this time the brother and sister had planted maize three times and had begun to give away seed to other people. It was a lot of work. They hoed the weeds between the stalks so that the maize would have enough water and sun. When it didn't rain, they watered it. By the fourth day their garden was really quite a showplace.
>
> That was when Coyote came along. He stopped and stared, smelling the mush that the sister was

cooking over the fire. His mouth watered, and he licked his muzzle. "That maize you planted looks very fine," he said. "I'd like to have some."

The sister gave him a meal of it, and the brother gave him some seed and tried to tell Coyote how to plant it. But Coyote didn't listen because he always thought he knew more than everyone and he was very lazy besides.

"These people plant their maize and do all that work, and then when it's ripe, they still have to cook it," he said to himself. "I'm not going to do it that way. I'm going to cook it first, then plant it, so when it's ripe I won't have to take the trouble."

So he cooked his maize and ate a lot of it. He would have forgotten about saving some to plant except that he got full, because he had already eaten three mice and a snake and some garbage. So he scratched holes in the ground and planted what he hadn't eaten and felt very pleased with himself.

"You people will have to cook your maize when it's ripe," he told everyone. "But I've saved myself some trouble."

Nobody argued with him about it, because you can't argue with Coyote. The next day, all the People went off to gather saguaro fruit to make liquor with, and Coyote went along. They came back with many baskets of fruit and decided to have a big time to celebrate all the things that Bear and Turkey had given them. But there wasn't anything growing in Coyote's field.

Coyote was angry and went around telling everyone that the People must have taken the hearts out of the seeds that they gave him.

"We tried to tell you," Sister said. "You just don't listen. You burned the heart out of the seed when you cooked it. You have to plant first and cook second, the way Turkey showed us. You always want to stand everything on its head.''

"He didn't tell me that," Coyote said. "If I see Turkey, I'll bite him. Give me some more seed.''

So Sister gave him some more seed, and Coyote planted it, sort of. He scratched out little shallow places in the ground instead of digging proper holes, and he didn't hoe the weeds but once. But the maize came up anyway. The day after it was planted, it was a foot high. Coyote felt pleased with himself that he hadn't wasted his time on all the other things that Sister had told him to do.

But Brother and Sister and the other people that they had given seed to were already harvesting their maize and tying it into bundles to dry. Coyote could smell it cooking, and his mouth watered. He went around begging some from people until they got angry with him.

"I just want a few ears to feed my children,'' he would tell them. "I'll pay you back as soon as mine is ripe.'' Every time he asked for maize he seemed to have more children.

The other people had all their corn harvested and stripped by now, but Coyote snuck into their camps at night and stole the meal.

Finally the People came to Coyote's camp. "Are you the one who's been stealing our meal? Someone is leaving tracks like yours.''

Coyote licked the meal from between his toes. "I don't see why you are accusing me. You are always turning against me. There are lots of other camps over that way. Why don't you accuse them instead?''

"Because you have meal in your toes.''

"We can see it in your whiskers, too.''

"Stay away from our camp!''

"That's right, go away and make your farm some-

place else. From now on, don't make it near us!''

They were very angry and shouted at him, waving their digging sticks.

''Well, all right!'' Coyote said in a huff. ''I was going to repay you double when my maize got ripe, but I won't do it now that you've treated me that way.''

''That's fine,'' they all said. ''Just move away somewhere else.''

So ever since then, Coyote's family has always lived a very disorderly life, and they never bothered to cook anything before they ate it.

Wind Caller turned in his sleep, murmuring, oblivious to Follow's snores.

XI
Berry Juice

The maize began to ripen at the tail end of summer, just before the Gathering. Deer Shadow wanted to look inside the pods, which Wind Caller said were called ears because of the way they stuck out, but he wouldn't let her. He went down to the field every day to inspect it, followed by a handful of curious souls including Cat Ears, who examined the maize with suspicion, as if scorpions might drop out of it.

Wind Caller watched the little pale hair at the tops of the ears turn brown and then dry up. "If I pick it green, it won't sprout," he said over and over, but no one knew what he was talking about.

"We have to leave this place at New Moon," Deer Shadow said insistently.

"It will be ready." Wind Caller hoped so. If it wasn't, the people would tear open the ears just to see what was inside and spoil the seed.

There was distraction in the necessity of laying in meat for the winter. Soon the deer would move on to eat acorns in the oak woods and then higher yet for the piñon nuts. They were harder to hunt in the mountains and never as fat as they were in the lowlands. Wind

224

Caller left to hunt for three days, taking with him, to his relief, all the men he considered most likely to trouble the maize. They returned to report that there had been signs of the Others but no more direct fighting. The deer were not as plentiful as they had been last fall; the Others were taking them.

When Wind Caller was alone with Deer Shadow and had given her a bedraggled buck to skin, he told her the maize was ready.

She left the buck where it lay and hurried down to the field with him. Everyone else came, too, alerted by the sixth sense that people in small villages possess. They saw Wind Caller's basket and brought their own.

Wind Caller twisted one of the little ears off the stalk and pulled back the husk. The ear lay in his palm like an unwrapped baby, folded in green. The pale hair that was brown and dried at the top lay as yellow as thin sunlight along the inside. Under it, the ear was thumb-sized and studded with golden kernels.

Wind Caller handed it around, and they inspected it from every angle. Give Away sniffed it. "How do you eat it?" she said.

"You can roast it and bite the kernels off the cob," Wind Caller said, "or cut them off. But mostly you dry it and make meal with it."

She looked at it dubiously.

"We will cook it now," Blue Stone Man said. "Then we will know if this is good."

"No," Wind Caller said. "Not this year."

"He's going to keep it all for himself!"

"I told you it was a trick!"

"Maybe it's poison!"

"Be quiet!" Wind Caller shouted. He spoke well enough now to understand the babble of voices. "This is *seed*! This isn't enough maize to feed all of you for a moon. You have to save this and plant it next spring. *Then* you can eat it.''

"We did the work!" they protested. "You sat down and played the flute at it. *We* cut the weeds.''

"It won't grow if you don't sing to it," Wind Caller said, not so sure that what he said wasn't true. "And you can't eat the first year's crop from a new field anyway," he added, struck by inspiration. His wife was not the only one who could concoct a story to suit her, he thought, pleased. "The Maize God will sicken you if you do, and tie your insides into knots so that it won't pass through. You must use it for seed.''

"Pah! It's a spell," Cat Ears said. "This isn't food. It's something he's brought to harm us. If it were food, we could eat it!''

"Why can we not eat *some* of it?" Blue Stone Man asked. "Then we would know if it was good, and there would still be some left for seed.''

"Because we need it *all* for seed if we are to have enough *next* year for meal *and* seed." Wind Caller looked serious. "With respect, Chieftain, there is also the Maize God's prohibition—my people have known of this for many years. Although I cannot stop the chieftain from doing as he wishes.'' He looked past Blue Stone Man to Cat Ears with an expression that said plainly he would very much enjoy it if the Maize God tied up Cat Ears's insides so that nothing would pass through.

Blue Stone Man winced. He was not as young as he had been, and some things gave him the cramp lately.

"Are we afraid of some god we have never heard of?'' Cat Ears demanded.

"That might be prudent," Looks Back commented.

"Strip the ears from the husk, like this," Wind Caller said, deciding to take Looks Back's words for assent. He bent to show Give Away and Caught the Moon how to do it. "You ladies with quick fingers will learn soon."

He gave them each an ear and watched approvingly as they pulled the husk off.

"Exactly! And then you tie the ears together and hang them from a pole to dry—being very careful this first year not to get any in your mouth."

They looked at him wide-eyed, and he patted their shoulders.

He grinned. "Women know how to take care of the maize. Women know how to wait. And make hungry husbands wait."

They smiled at him tentatively, clutching their ears of maize. Caught the Moon looked over her shoulder for her husband. Deer Shadow's stranger was very handsome, except for those funny scars. Too handsome—he made her nervous, talking to her like that, but it was exciting, too. She fluttered her hands and dropped her ear of maize.

"Show me," Runner said. Wind Caller made Runner nervous, too, but she liked it. She wondered if it was true what they said about him, that he turned into a coyote at night. She wondered if he did it in bed.

Wind Caller showed her how to strip the ear and where the kernels would come loose when they had dried. In a few moments the rest of the women had crowded around him, while the men went on arguing among themselves. Deer Shadow stood a little to one side and watched.

The women were the savers, the keepers, the authority who rationed food when it was scarce. The men wouldn't go against them now. But neither would they forgive Wind Caller for charming the women. A respectable man didn't cajole women; he gave them orders. Women had too much power already. In a temper, the men went away and left the women to the maize.

* * *

Deer Shadow learned the quick shucking motion that pulled the husk off, like someone pulling a hide shirt over his head. She and the other women carried the little ears up to the caves in baskets, tied them in bunches, and gingerly hung them to dry, mindful of Wind Caller's warning.

"Was that true?" Deer Shadow demanded of him when they were alone for a moment. "Will eating the seed make you sick?"

"Probably," he said. "It's going to make Cat Ears sick."

"Cat Ears will do something."

Wind Caller whistled between his teeth. He was fitting a stone into the side of the big new storage pit he had dug in the cave floor. "How many days before we leave?" he asked. "The maize can't go in before it's dried, and if it doesn't go in, the mice will eat it."

Deer Shadow looked at the late afternoon moon, as opalescent as a shell against an aqua sky. "We'll leave in seven days, most likely," she said.

"That will be enough. Everything dries here like the water is sucked out of it. What will Cat Ears do?"

"I don't know. Something. Make trouble. Try to prove you're lying. He sits around the fire at the young men's house and tells big stories that get bigger with every telling. Cat Ears says you're a witch. Or one of the Others. He says he saw you putting a spell on the soft man, and that is why he died."

"The old man who died before I came?" Wind Caller said.

"Cat Ears says you were here then. He says he saw you."

"And how do you hear what goes on in the young men's house?"

"Squirrel," Deer Shadow said.

"Tell Squirrel not to eat the maize in the young men's house." Wind Caller gave her a sly smile.

Deer Shadow hated to leave the summer place. She always loved the Gathering, but this year she was heavy with the baby and the heat, and she wanted to go nowhere. The last kill had been dried and wrapped in hide, the maize dried and left in stone pits for their return in spring. She suspected that Looks Back had had his wife grind some and had tasted it, but he didn't say anything. He and Wind Caller seemed to have reached some silent understanding that had to do with the web of authority that held the Yellow Grass People together—the lines of power both physical and magical that linked to keep them all from flying away into a world where every man could do as he pleased; the web that kept them all from chaos, from Coyote. Coyote himself was part of that web, and Looks Back knew it.

But it seemed that Coyote was nipping at Cat Ears's heels just now. Cat Ears had the surly, snappish expression of a lynx who had been mousing and caught nothing. He watched Wind Caller as if protecting them all from him and had more than one young hunter convinced that his last missed kill or his sore tooth was the doing of the stranger.

"There is something we are not seeing," Cat Ears said. "Because of the witch. If he does not want us to eat this new food, he must have a reason. It may be magical, and he wants it all for himself."

"What do you suppose it does?" one of them asked.

"It must make you powerful," Cat Ears said. "Otherwise why would he want to keep it for himself?"

"He gave it to us to keep," another said.

"Yah! Because he wanted *us* to dig the storage pit! And are not *your* fingers sore with the digging? He gives himself airs as if he were the chieftain. Blue Stone Man should drive him out.''

"But first we should make him tell us what magic is in this food we may not eat,'' another one said.

They looked at Cat Ears expectantly. The next morning they would be leaving this place, not to return until late spring. Cat Ears pulled the stone cover off the storage pit and pulled out one of the dried cobs.

"There is great magic in this.'' Cat Ears held it out on both palms, waiting to feel the magic. He knew that if he ate the magic food, he would be as powerful as the stranger; as powerful as Looks Back, his father, the shaman who could eat fire. That must be the way it was done. You found a magic and you took it and made it work for you.

He turned the cob in his hand and bit at the end of it, hurting his teeth. Those around him gasped at his audacity. When he remained unharmed, they stepped a little closer. Cat Ears laid the cob on the stone lid to the pit and smashed it with a rock, grinding down the kernels. He stuffed some in his mouth and swallowed.

It began slowly, as a mild unease after the young men had lain down for the night, the feeling of something perhaps not right. A tickle in the throat, a faint movement in the belly. It communicated itself in some strange way so that most of the young men were lying awake and wondering why, when Coyote finally sank his teeth all the way into Cat Ears, and Cat Ears rolled on the floor, howling and vomiting.

Squirrel went running from the young men's house through the darkness as if the unknown god were behind him, hand reached out to grab his own stomach. He danced up and down outside Looks Back's cave, howling for him to come out. "It's Cat Ears! Cat Ears is sick! He's making a horrible noise.''

The shaman stumbled out sleepily and peered at him. Cat Ears's mother was behind him, wrapped in a fox-fur robe. "What is the matter with him?"

"It's just as Wind Caller said," Squirrel babbled. "His insides are tied in a knot so it won't go down, and it's all coming back up!"

Cat Ears's mother put a hand to her mouth.

Looks Back roared, "He ate some? And he's sick?" He burst into laughter.

His wife cuffed him. "Shame! Shame! Go see to your son."

"There may be nothing I can do," Looks Back said. He didn't seem in a hurry. "I do not know how to propitiate this new god. I must speak with Wind Caller."

"Then *speak* with him!" his wife shrieked.

Looks Back wrapped his hide blanket around himself with dignity. "Get me a torch," he said to Squirrel. They set out at a stately pace while Cat Ears's mother ran toward the young men's house.

Half the Yellow Grass People were awake by now. Follow stuck his nose out of the cave mouth and bared his teeth.

"With respect, Uncle," Looks Back said to him, "we have need to speak to your master."

Follow sat down on his haunches. He and Looks Back seemed to have an understanding.

Wind Caller got up, rubbing his eyes. He peered at Looks Back in the light of the torch that Squirrel held just outside the cave mouth. Squirrel wasn't at all certain that the coyote's invitation extended to him.

"What is it?" Wind Caller demanded. There was a lot of shouting and movement outside, but it didn't appear to be directed at him. He relaxed a little. Deer Shadow crawled out of bed, and he touched her arm to reassure her.

"Oh, please," Squirrel said, "Cat Ears ate the maize and now he's dying!"

"How much did he eat?" Wind Caller asked.

"Two whole ears, because he said . . . he said they were magic, and he would prove it to us . . . and that's why—"

"Did you eat any?"

"No," Squirrel said thankfully. "None of the rest of us did. I don't think he wanted us to."

"And what is he doing now?"

"He's rolling on the ground. And screaming. And it keeps coming up because it can't go down, just as you said."

"Thank you," Looks Back said, and Squirrel subsided. To Wind Caller the shaman said, "With respect, I come to ask what may be done. My wife is distraught." They could hear feminine wailing in the distance.

"The Maize God must be propitiated," Wind Caller announced solemnly.

"And how may that be done?"

Wind Caller hesitated. The Maize God might not take these things lightly. He discarded the attractive ideas of making Cat Ears crawl around the maize field naked or paint his balls black with soot. "He must fast for three days, while the knot unties. And then purge himself with greasewood." Cat Ears would probably not want much to eat for a while anyway.

"I thank you," Looks Back said. "Will you speak to your god and tell him that it will be done?"

"I will," Wind Caller answered. He was getting worried. He feared that he had come a little too close to being disrespectful to the Maize God. He touched Looks Back on the arm. "Cat Ears must open his thumb with a knife, as I did when I planted the maize, and leave the blood on the lid of the storage pit. That is important. I will do this as well," he said by way of penance.

They set out in a procession to the biggest of the caves, where the unmarried men lived in common. Deer Shadow was not allowed in, nor was Cat Ears's mother, who stood outside and called to him. Nearly everyone else crowded around the entrance as well. Cat Ears was inside, clearly visible, crouched on hands and knees, head hanging. Every few minutes a spasm shook him, and he collapsed, vomiting. The other young men stood well away from him in case the god should reach for them, too.

Wind Caller pushed his way importantly through the crowd and spread his arms over the maize in the storage bin. In his native language, he spoke to the Maize God. "Take blood for my blessing and offering. Take blood to eat and feed us again." He cut his thumb and dripped its blood over the stone.

Wind Caller went to Cat Ears and stood over him. "I told you not to eat the maize. Can you walk?"

Cat Ears only glared at him.

"Come." Wind Caller and Looks Back took him by the shoulders and heaved him up, dragging him to the storage pit. They dropped him again, and Cat Ears retched.

"Cut your thumb over the stone," Wind Caller said. "You have to do it yourself. If you don't," he added in a dark whisper, "nothing will ever come out the other end again. Everything you eat will come up this way."

Wind Caller handed him the knife. Cat Ears moaned but took it and held his thumb over the stone. His hands shook as he punctured the skin and managed to get four drops of blood out. He gave Wind Caller a look of vicious loathing and crawled away.

Wind Caller and Looks Back, united for the moment, turned to peer with severity at the Yellow Grass People.

"That which is unknown," Looks Back solemnly proclaimed, "is always worthy of respect."

It took four days to reach the Gathering ground, and the Yellow Grass People at first thought they were going to have to carry Cat Ears. But driven by furious pride, he managed to stagger along. He quit vomiting on the first day, and by the second he was hungry and in a temper.

When they stopped for the night, Wind Caller and Looks Back held another long consultation and brewed the greasewood leaves to be administered the next night. There was something odd about Looks Back's expression—a tightness around the mouth as if he were trying not to laugh. His wrinkled chin was pursed.

Deer Shadow, consumed with curiosity, grabbed her husband's arm as he crawled into the brush-and-hide shelter that was their journey hut. "What did you do to Cat Ears?" she demanded. "And don't tell me you didn't. You and Looks Back have been laughing like fools together. Two respectable men with a position to uphold, it's disgraceful. You look like that thing." She jerked her head at Follow, curled too close for comfort in the journey hut. The coyote opened his mouth and produced the smile she was alluding to.

Wind Caller grinned, too. "I told him not to eat it."

"You said the Maize God would make him sick."

"I am the servant of the Maize God," he said.

"What did you do?"

"I rubbed it with green alder bark. It won't hurt the seed."

"Oh, poor Cat Ears!" Deer Shadow burst out laughing. "Oh, what I would have given to get into the young men's house and see him thinking his insides were tied in a knot."

"I imagine they felt as if they were. And certainly

you can't go in the young men's house. It's not decent.''

''Neither is poisoning people. If anyone finds out, they will say you're a witch. I'm not going to have people saying I'm married to a witch.''

Wind Caller chuckled. ''If you didn't want people to talk about you, you shouldn't have lain with some stranger out in a rainstorm.''

''I wish I hadn't,'' she said darkly, rubbing her belly. She kept turning over and around the way the coyote did, trying to get comfortable. ''I wouldn't have if I had known I would feel like this,'' she muttered.

At the Gathering, Looks Back set up his tooth in the ground so that everyone would know where the Yellow Grass People were camped. Wind Caller looked around him curiously. He had never seen so many of Deer Shadow's people together at one time. He knew that all the old women could tell you who was born to which tribe, whose father had been whose nephew or brother. They were like a basket, and the old women kept all the strands straight. How would they plait him into it? he wondered, cutting brush for Found Water's journey hut. Found Water and Blue Stone Man were doing something more important, talking with three strangers who looked neither like them nor like Wind Caller. They had their hair cut off very short, and their noses were fierce, arched like a hawk's beak.

''Hummph!'' snorted Wall Eye. ''We don't need them!''

''Maybe they've brought red dye,'' Young Woman said.

''Who are they?'' Wind Caller asked them.

The women eyed him the way they always did, as if a frog had spoken, but they answered him. ''Men of the Others,'' Wall Eye said, crossing her fingers to ward off any evil that might have floated in on the wind with them. "Our men trade with them." She spat.

"And you don't approve, Grandmother?"

"They steal our game. Why should we let them in our Gathering to rob us here, too?"

"I want some red dye," Young Woman said. "They know where to find it."

"There are only three of them," Deer Shadow said. "And they are not the tribe that you fought with. These are from the north. I've seen them before."

"Not human." Wall Eye spat again. "No business trading with people who are not human."

"Tell your husband," Deer Shadow said. She passed Wall Eye a bowl of the fermented berry juice that was circulating freely. Wall Eye drank it and heaved herself back to her cookfire.

Smoke was rising from hundreds of fires, and the other bands' totems leaped up against the low sun: an antlered deer skull on a pole, coyote tails, an eagle's wing. It wasn't long before Heron came, towing her babies with her and shrieking when she saw Deer Shadow.

"Yah-ah! What happened?"

"What does it look like?" Deer Shadow said grumpily, but she patted Heron. "It is fine to see you. Is Baby here?"

"She's just coming." Baby had married a man of the Dry Water People. "And where is Owl? I want to see Owl whether she wants me to or not."

"She will, she's promised. Just don't look at her leg."

"You can't help looking at it," Heron said practically. "But nobody thinks about it. And where is your man?"

"Over there." Deer Shadow gestured toward Wind Caller, dutifully helping to put up his father-in-law's brush house. Heron goggled at him.

Baby came running up, as pregnant as Deer Shadow and with a three-year-old at her heels. "Oooh!" she said when Heron clutched her and pointed at Wind Caller.

"Hush," Deer Shadow said, laughing. She pulled them into her own brush house, where Owl was waiting for them, and settled herself on the piled furs. "News for news," Deer Shadow said. "Did your husband marry the soft man?"

"Well!" Heron said. Deer Shadow had a waterskin full of fermented berry juice, and she poured each of them some in a turtle-shell bowl. Heron drank hers and giggled. "Well!" she said again. "No! The soft man wouldn't do it. He said he didn't want to be married, because it was too much trouble!"

They all howled with laughter, even Owl. "So you don't have to take a lover from the Buffalo Leap men?"

"I may anyway," Heron said, and they howled again.

Baby clutched Deer Shadow's arm. She held out her cup for more juice. "Who is that *man*?"

"I found him," Deer Shadow said. "I don't know who he is. He lives with a coyote."

"What?"

"I live with it, too," Deer Shadow said. "It's run off right now. There are too many people here for it." She filled her cup again.

"With a *coyote*?"

"Everybody here thinks that he *is* a coyote," Owl said.

"*What?*"

"So what are *you* going to have?" Baby said, poking Deer Shadow's stomach. "Puppies?"

"We think parts of him are human," Owl said solemnly.

For some reason that struck Deer Shadow as hilarious, although in her secret fears she had imagined furred monsters biting their way out of her. But here with her oldest friends, women she had become a woman with, it didn't seem likely. "I'll tell you about him," she said, and hiccuped.

Wind Caller finished getting Found Water's journey hut up and listened to the shrieks of laughter coming from inside his own. Everyone got drunk at a Gathering. He was a little drunk himself. Night was falling, and fires were beginning to blossom over the darkening ground. He wondered what Deer Shadow was laughing about. It made him feel cut off from her, set at a distance, and he wondered when the women would leave. With him her mood had been fractious lately, and as her time drew near she had been less inclined to couple with him and more inclined to blame him for her condition. He itched for her. Or for someone.

When he stuck his head inside their journey hut, the laughter stilled into an immediate silence. The women all stared at him, openmouthed, then burst into giggles again, howling and burying their faces in their hands. Stung, he withdrew, taking a second skin of berry liquor with him as he went.

They were laughing at him, he thought. Well, then, she could spend the night with her friends if she wanted to. He took a swig from the skin and hung it over his shoulder. Most everyone was going down to the dance ground to watch the girls who had been made women and the boys who had been made men today. He would go, too. He could hear the drumming and the stamp of feet. There were plenty of other women, he thought, who weren't sullen and disrespectful. Plenty of food and plenty to drink. (It turned to vinegar in a few days after it fermented, so you might as well drink it now.) Old Turtle Back lurched by with a skin in his hand and a disapproving wife on either side to steady him.

The dancers glowed in the ring of torchlight, their newly shorn black hair bobbing about their faces. Wind

Caller found himself caught in the ring, pulled in by the spiraling dancers. He lifted his flute to his lips, letting the rhythm and the dancers carry him wherever they wanted to.

A woman in a line of women opposite was watching him. Wind Caller knew he was an oddity, was used to being stared at, but now that he could speak their language and had the protection of the Yellow Grass People, no one offered him hostility. Rather, he was a strange and unruly element in their midst, prized for his magic, which might or might not be holy but was certainly powerful.

The woman kept her eyes on him. She had a kind of leonine grace, big-boned, with long rippling muscles in her arms and her nearly bare thighs. A long curtain of hair swung behind her as she danced. Then his line and hers moved away from each other, and he lost sight of her in the smoky darkness.

When the dance ended, he found himself still in the center of the dance ground, the stars overhead moving too slowly to see, but always moving. He tilted his head back and watched them until he thought he could see them move. He took another drink out of the skin and went over to the fire pits where women from all the clans were cooking meat. Deer Shadow wasn't there.

Wind Caller gnawed a piece of rabbit, hot and greasy from the fire, and looked around him. Blue Stone Man was conversing very solemnly with the chieftain of the Smoke People. They were nearly head to head and staggered every so often, to keep upright. Each had a skin; it was beneath the dignity of a chieftain to let another chieftain outdrink him. Next to them, Squirrel was hacking a piece of meat off a deer carcass to give to a girl from the Red Rock People who had just become a woman today. She was very young, tiny with big eyes and a thick cap of shorn hair that ended at her ears. She ate it solemnly, and they went off hand in hand.

Wind Caller saw Walks Funny's wife go off with a man of the Lightning People. He had heard of the Gathering custom of six-day marriages. Sometimes they didn't last six days, either. One-night marriages.

It was in the air, the urge to couple and make the world grow, the plants sprout, the animals thrive. It was what the initiation dance was all about. It was what Wind Caller and Deer Shadow had done the night before the hunt, but that had made him feel more like an offering.

Now, she was in their journey hut, telling her friends about him, laughing, no doubt, at who knew what. Irritated, he took another sip from the skin until that feeling went away and the itch he had felt earlier came back again.

The woman he had seen in the dance stepped into the firelight, calling over her shoulder to someone going the other way. She reached for a piece of meat and singed her fingers. On impulse, Wind Caller took his knife and cut it for her.

Her eyes widened and grew interested. "What people are you from?" she asked him. She didn't touch the meat. Her speech was a little different from Deer Shadow's, but understandable.

"The Yellow Grass People," he said.

"You don't look like them."

"I am—I was—" He searched for the word and finally said, "I came to them from someplace else."

"Oho, then I have heard of you." She looked him up and down and took the meat. "Me, I am from the High Rock People."

Wind Caller cut himself another piece of meat, and they walked away from the fire pits, eating. The grass in the valley rustled with a faint breeze and the sounds of other couples. They found a spot under a gnarled oak tree and sat, chewing. Wind Caller took a drink from his skin and passed it to her. She laughed and drank deeply, letting the red juice run down her chin. She wiped her hand across it.

"I do not know some things," Wind Caller said. "Do you have a husband?"

"Somewhere," she said. "Not here."

Wind Caller laughed, relieved. He didn't want a second wife. One was almost too many tonight.

"I have a wife," he said. "Somewhere, not here." *In our hut, laughing at me.*

She wiped her hands on the grass and drank from the skin again. This far out from the fires, there was only moonlight to see by, and it washed her brown skin with silver so that she might have been made out of sand, or aspen leaves. Aching for her and wanting to prolong the moment in the magic dreamtime of a Gathering night, Wind Caller took his flute from his belt. He hoped he wasn't so drunk his cock wouldn't stand up, but he took another drink from the skin anyway and began to play a song, a new one he was making just for the moment.

The music rippled over the grass and wound itself around the other couples in the night, half heard over the chatter and laughter from the Gathering ground. Deer Shadow heard it, too, when she and Heron and Baby and Owl came out of her brush house, arms around each other, all staggering like Owl. Baby and Owl were yawning, and Baby's daughter was asleep over her shoulder. They moved away into the firelit camp, and the silence they left behind was like clear water. Deer Shadow heard the flute's thin voice beyond its edges.

She stiffened, mortified that Wind Caller was out there making the flute sing, probably for somebody else, and looked to see whether Owl could hear it, too. But Owl had gone inside Aunt Four Fingers's brush house, only a few feet away. Deer Shadow went in her own hut again, snatched up her coyote-fur blanket, and wrapped it around her in a fury that was partly due to thwarted ownership and partly to the berry liquor's unaccustomed effect.

Warmer, she stalked to the edge of the fire pits and looked around, but she didn't see Wind Caller. Her father was there with Walks Funny and One Ball, throwing knuckle bones with some men from the Falling Water People. They didn't even look up as she stumbled past them, stubbing her toe on a stone and trailing her coyote furs behind her.

She peered at the figures still weaving on the dance ground. None of them was Wind Caller. The dancers swirled past her, eyes bright, caught in the dance, spun out along the spokes of its web. A couple broke off from the men's and women's lines and darted into the darkness, the trickling voice of the flute driving them.

Deer Shadow walked uncertainly away from the dance ground toward where she thought she had heard it. Everyone else could hear it, too. He wasn't even sorry he had humiliated her. She knew he wasn't and gritted her teeth. She walked with careful, waddling dignity, clutching her furs.

And then the flute stopped.

Wind Caller pressed the High Rock woman's body down beneath him in the grass. She was as warm as the berry liquor, and she clung to him, arms around his neck, legs around his hips. He had had just enough to drink, he'd discovered; his cock stood up fine. Now their bodies moved as if they were part of the dance again, carried on the thin moonlit flute notes that still hung in the air unheard. It was *his* choice, no one else's, to be here. He owned himself tonight.

She yelped and bit his ear, then whispered in it the

things that must always be said in a whisper, and he clutched her tighter, shuddering, and dropped his face into the hollow of her throat while the tide of their dance ebbed out slowly, like the flute notes returning. He took a deep breath of night air, lifting his head above hers, and was surprised to see his breath come out in clouds of steam. He didn't want to move. He didn't feel cold yet and supposed that she must not, either, with him on top of her. He propped himself on his elbows, thinking that in a while they could do it some more.

A rock hit him in the back. He flew off her, wincing, and looked wildly into the darkness. He could just see a shape under the moon, human height, wrapped in something that dragged in the grass and tripped it. It threw another rock.

"Yah!" it shouted. "Go and do it in the bushes like a coyote! Dirty, smelly coyote!" It threw another rock, and the High Rock woman screamed and ran into the brush.

Deer Shadow was asleep when he got back to the brush hut. Or at least she was lying down with her back to him, acting as if she were asleep.

Wind Caller sat down next to her. She pulled the furs more tightly around her, leaving him none. She was rolled in them like a cocoon. He tipped the skin so that the last berry liquor slid down his throat. Except for the bruises where the rocks had hit him, he felt fine, even peaceful. Maybe she wouldn't be angry when she woke up. Maybe the sun would go backward into summer tomorrow, too.

When he had finished the berry liquor, he went outside and made water, then lay down beside her, warily, hoping she didn't have a knife under those furs.

He awoke with a pain in his head and the aggrieved sensation of having been done out of something: He could have spent the night with the High Rock woman, who at least wanted to do it.

Deer Shadow was sitting in the doorway of their journey hut staring at him. She was eating the last of a bowlful of meal, scooping it out of the turtle shell with her fingers, and he didn't see any prospect of her making some for him. He saw Cat Ears and Walks Funny go by the door carrying their hunting spears and knew he should have been up sooner. The sun was climbing the sky.

"Why didn't you wake me?" he said. He reached for his spears and his sandals.

"Yah, you have other things to do besides hunt," Deer Shadow said. "Stick it in strange women, for one."

"What makes you think I was doing that?" he asked her, aggrieved again now that he thought of it. He knew who had thrown rocks at him, but how had she known where to find him?

"I heard you! Everyone heard you out there like the coyote with your flute, making music for some other woman!" She picked up the flute on the ground by the bed and threw it at him, then folded her arms and looked out the hut door.

"You didn't want me!" Wind Caller said. He felt sulky. "You had plenty to do, getting drunk with the ladies and telling lies about men!"

"They are old friends."

"And I'm a new husband. Who needs more looking after?"

"You do, obviously!" she screamed at him. "You were just looking for an excuse!"

"You wouldn't even let me in!" he said. "In *my* hut that *I* built. After I helped your father put his up!"

"Hah!"

"Yah!"

"Coyote!"

"If you turn your back on me at night, I'll find some one else who won't!"

"If I'd turned my back on you more often, maybe I wouldn't look like this, and you wouldn't go looking for sluts in the bushes," she screamed at him. "Playing that *thing* for her"—she grabbed the flute and threw it again—"so that everybody would know it was you!"

"You were pregnant when I got here," Wind Caller said, snatching up the flute. "So how do I know it's even mine?"

"You don't!" she screamed. "It's Bear's! Or maybe it's Buffalo's! Or maybe the Wind God came in a big storm! I hate you! Dirty coyote sticking it in every slut at the Gathering! Go stick it in a knothole!"

She crawled over and began pummeling his chest and then his back when he tried to get away from her. "Get out!" She kicked him in the tailbone, and then her fist connected with his ear. He smacked her back and rolled out of the hut with his spears in one hand and his sandals in the other. He sat in the trampled grass to put them on while a great many people who had been standing nearby watching suddenly realized they had other things to do.

Found Water stood outside his hut looking bemused. "Always been like that," he said. "Stubborn Mud Daughter." He took his spear and set out after the departing hunters, while Wind Caller knotted his sandals.

When he stood, Walks Funny came up and slapped him on the back. "They get like that. Mine's had three babies. Got like that every time."

"Hah," said a woman who was filling a basket with dirty bowls to take to the stream. "Men get a woman big-bellied, and they go around barking about it. Then they go off with another woman and leave her by herself!" She nodded vigorously at an old woman who was passing, and the old woman nodded back. They both seemed to know all about it.

"She was talking about me," Wind Caller muttered. "To her friends. Laughing. Wouldn't let me in."

"She's had too much freedom, that one," Walks Funny said. "You ought to make her mind you."

"How?"

Walks Funny appeared to have no constructive ideas. "No harm in going off for a bit at a Gathering," he said finally, brightening. "You tell her that."

By nightfall the story was all over the camp. Wind Caller had been certain that Cat Ears would spread it, but it hadn't needed Cat Ears. Gossip was the most highly traded item at the Gathering. Shells and obsidian and blue stone and good flint blanks were bartered for hides and furs, but gossip flowed freely, the added fillip to any transaction, a store of stories to last the winter. It was easy to recognize Wind Caller, even for people from Dry Water and Red Rock who had never seen him. They shouted advice as he passed, and good-natured suggestions for places where his wife couldn't find him.

Deer Shadow, he discovered, had the women staunchly on her side. They glowered at him when he slunk home from the hunt with his head still aching. Deer Shadow received him with elaborate politeness and handed him a bowl of mush.

"No meat?" he asked her.

"There is meat at the fire pits. I assume you will go down there anyway, to see what you can find." She proceeded to ignore his presence.

Wind Caller ate the mush and handed her the bowl. He stood up.

"Where are you going?"

"To the fire pits to see what I can find." He stalked

out. He had been prepared to make amends, but if she didn't want it—well, Walks Funny was right.

He ate moodily at the fire pits, and a number of women looked at him with interest, but he couldn't tell if they were amused or amorous. He saw Heron and Baby, two of the women he had seen in his journey hut, and they greeted him gravely, but as he walked away he heard a stifled giggle. His back stiffened.

He cut himself another piece of meat and filled his waterskin from a big pitch-lined basket of something that looked as if you could get drunk on it. He set out away from the fire, hoping he wouldn't fall over a coupling pair. The grass was full of them, like grasshoppers in summer. He sat down under the tree where he had lain with the High Rock woman the night before, and found Follow beside him.

"Where have you been?"

Follow yawned at him. He looked well fed.

"Stealing meat from the camp at night." Wind Caller cut him a piece of his own anyway.

Follow ate it, snapping it down in one quick bite.

Wind Caller finished his and drank from the skin. He wasn't sure what was in it. Cactus fruit maybe, or yucca. Almost anything could be fermented. He offered some to Follow to see what the coyote would do, but he sniffed at it and declined with canine lack of tact. He opened his mouth and made retching noises.

Wind Caller settled his back against the tree and picked up the flute. Follow turned himself around and around in the grass and finally flopped himself next to Wind Caller. He yawned again, showing all his teeth, and put his head on his paws, ears up. Wind Caller thought that he liked the flute.

Wind Caller played the song he had made up for the High Rock woman. He could have found another woman for tonight, maybe even that one again, but hadn't wanted to. He would rather sit out here with the coyote. Maybe Deer Shadow would think he was with a woman, though, he thought with satisfaction. Maybe she would think he was out here with three women. He hoped so.

XII
Turning the Sun Around

After the six days of the Gathering, the Yellow Grass People moved through their fall hunting grounds and slowly followed the deer up through the canyons and foothills to the higher slopes, where the piñon nuts grew and the honeycombed rock faces caught the low winter sun. As soon as the Yellow Grass People split off from the rest, Follow came out of the brush and trotted at Wind Caller's heel. Deer Shadow wasn't pleased to see him.

She was still in a temper, although she and Wind Caller were able to speak to each other politely now and shared the same bed without any rock throwing. There was no use in making yourself a laughingstock, Deer Shadow said huffily, pinning her hair up in the morning. Particularly, and she gave Wind Caller a haughty glance, when someone else had already done it so thoroughly.

But it was hard to put the journey hut up and down together and share the same bed without relaxing, and sometimes they grew nearly companionable before Deer Shadow remembered she was angry. Once he rolled over in the night and grabbed her before she was really awake, and she let him couple with her, although in the morning she claimed she hadn't.

As she lit the fire, she made much of being sore and having been roughly handled. "What choice did I have? Men are all alike at night."

"How do you know?" Wind Caller asked suspiciously.

She sniffed. "What do you think women talk about? But maybe I'll go try another, just to be sure."

"You should wait till the baby comes," Wind Caller said, tightening the binding on his spear. "You will be in a better mood. No one but me would lie with you now."

"I'll hit you if you do it again," Deer Shadow said. "It hurts."

"I hear and obey, O Most Powerful," Wind Caller said. Then he went to find some men to help scout a deer trail they had seen yesterday.

Game was growing scarcer. The urge to make one more kill before winter was strong. Squirrels and birds denuded the landscape of seeds and nuts that the People didn't get to first. Snakes slithered into their deepest burrows and stayed there, suspended in the cold. At last the Yellow Grass People arrived at the shelter of their winter caves and burrowed in, the first snow falling practically on their heels.

Blue Stone Man took stock of his people and decided which ones would bear watching during the winter. Forced together by cold for three moons at a time, the People knew there was always some bad blood, new or old, that would erupt under pressure. Cat Ears was already complaining.

"We made a mistake to let that one in," he said. He was hunkered by the chieftain's fire with his father, the shaman. As chief of the hunters, Cat Ears had a right to a place there. The chieftain's wife was at the back of the cave, pretending not to hear the conversation the men were having, in accordance with custom. But it wouldn't stop her from telling the shaman's wife and Aunt Four Fingers tomorrow.

"We should have killed him," Cat Ears said. "Or made him a slave, the way the Others do. It wasn't a good idea to give him the deer magic woman."

"She did that herself," Looks Back said.

"Yes, and now they are angry at each other," Cat Ears said with satisfaction. "That is dangerous. There is too much power there. It will upset the balance, and things will go wrong."

Blue Stone Man turned to Looks Back and asked, "Is that true?"

"Only if they use it on each other." Looks Back chuckled. "So far she has only thrown rocks."

"That will change," Cat Ears said, convinced. "And anyway, there is too much power there. A man who can make *me*"—he thumped his chest—"sick is dangerous. He might turn it on anyone next."

"The gods made you sick," Looks Back said flatly. "You are a great hunter; we know this. But you are not a man who thinks. You were told not to eat that grain."

"By this Wind Caller!" Cat Ears said, as if that clinched it.

"And what are you proposing?" Blue Stone Man said. He had to be somewhat more conciliatory to the chief of the hunters than Cat Ears's father did.

"Drive him out. If you won't let me kill him, drive him out. The storms will do it for you."

Looks Back raised his eyebrows. "And give you the woman? She wouldn't have you before the stranger came."

"I don't want her."

"Very likely that is wise of you," his father retorted. Blue Stone Man paused for a while and stared into

the fire. Then he looked up and said, "We will wait.
We are not like the Others. When we have taken someone in, he is ours. We do not kill him."

"Yah, you will be sorry," Cat Ears said, standing up.
"Don't say I didn't warn you." He stalked off, leaving
the two older men to sit at the fire.

"I am old," Blue Stone Man said presently. "But I
am not so old that I wish to stop leading the Yellow
Grass People. I do not know what to do."

"You are not so old as I am, so I will tell you. We
will wait. Something will happen and you will not have
to decide."

"And if Cat Ears is right?"

"Then Cat Ears will be right," Looks Back said. "It
is not time for us to guess about this."

"If Cat Ears carries any more tales to the chieftain,
something will twist Cat Ears's gut up again until he is
dead," Deer Shadow said viciously. She had cornered
Cat Ears by the young men's house and backed him up
against the wall just inside the cave mouth—a full, disgraceful two feet inside the cave mouth, but no one
wanted to touch her and tell her so. She was at the end
of her ninth moon, her belly already big enough for the
tenth. A woman that close to giving birth was sacred,
holy, and dangerous. She could curse a man or shrivel
his balls.

"No woman has a right to know what the chieftain
and the shaman and the chief of the hunters talk about,"
Cat Ears said.

"*I* know," Deer Shadow said. "Women always
know. You are a fool if you think women don't know.
Next time I will put a curse on you, too." She wrapped
her arms around her belly as if something hurt, but she
didn't back off.

"Get away from me," Cat Ears said uneasily.

Her face twisted into a grimace, and she made a sound that wasn't quite a cry.

"Get away from me!" Cat Ears said again.

Deer Shadow saw with satisfaction that a muscle beside his mouth was twitching. "Yah! You are stupid. Men are stupid." She turned away and went through the light powdering of snow to find Aunt Four Fingers. The baby was coming. Or something was. A pain ground across her body, clear through to the backbone, from one side to the other. She nearly howled with it.

Aunt Four Fingers was brisk. "I thought so. Nearly a full moon early, but you are big enough. Maybe you miscounted."

"I didn't miscount," Deer Shadow gasped. "How *could* I?"

"Never mind," Aunt Four Fingers said. They were both wondering the same thing, which neither of them cared to admit: What kind of baby was this? "Walk around for as long as you can," Four Fingers said. "It will ease it."

More women bustled into the cave, and Wind Caller was put firmly out. This was not business for men, except for the shaman and men such as Listens to Deer had been. Deer Shadow wished he were here. She could almost see him when the pains came. And what if the same thing that happened to her mother happened to her? She looked around the cave, terrified, waiting to see her mother's ghost. All the women made soothing noises. Looks Back arrived and threw pine needles into the fire as he had done for her mother. Outside, she could hear the men dancing, trying to dance the baby out. She supposed her father was among them. He could do the dance in his sleep, she thought, after all the babies he had had. And was Wind Caller with them?

She howled as a pain worked its way from one side to the other, then doubled over, kneeling on the bed that had been made ready. *Why did I want a man?* she thought, furious at the pain and the indignity. It was only as her pregnancy had progressed that she had fully grasped the fact that once the baby was there, there was only one way for it to come out. All of Fox Girl's and Young Woman's stories of monsters with no bones returned to haunt her.

Deer Shadow rolled over on the bed and doubled up as if she were a baby being born herself. Four Fingers gave her a hand to hold, and she squeezed it until Four Fingers gave her a rock instead.

"It hurts!"

"The first one is always the worst," Four Fingers said.

"I'm not going to have another one!" She wished violently that she could make Wind Caller have this one.

"Let the pain come. Don't fight it," Four Fingers said. "You always try to fight everything."

Deer Shadow remembered trying to fight the night her mother died, screaming for her to come back. Some things you could fight, but not that. Maybe not this, either. She tried to relax, to let the pains wash over her. It didn't feel any better, but it wasn't worse.

"Good," Four Fingers said approvingly.

The pains came closer together until they nearly doubled her up, and then something started happening. The bed was wet with blood, and Four Fingers was pulling the baby out of her. It gave a thin wailing cry, loud enough for Deer Shadow to hear. She let out her breath all at once.

"It's a girl! She looks healthy." Four Fingers pressed on Deer Shadow's stomach to make the afterbirth leave. It hurt but not as much as the baby being born.

Deer Shadow chuckled weakly. "No fur?"

"Hush. The gods will hear you," Four Fingers said absently. She had a puzzled expression as she felt Deer

Shadow's belly. "Push," she said suddenly, just as another contraction told Deer Shadow the same thing. "There is another one!"

Deer Shadow shrieked and tried to push the baby out, but it didn't want to be born. But Four Fingers saw the head and reached for it, and the baby was born anyway, shrieking furiously, gasping in cold air.

"This one is a boy!" Four Fingers announced. She felt Deer Shadow's belly again uncertainly. "No, that is all. No wonder you were big as a buffalo."

Deer Shadow whimpered when Four Fingers pushed down again and said, "It has to come."

Deer Shadow could see Wall Eye and the shaman's wife cuddling the babies. The cords had been tied off and cut, and Wall Eye was washing the boy with water heated by stones. The girl was already bathed and bundled in the fur bunting that Deer Shadow had made.

The afterbirth finally came, and when it had, they let her get up and wash, too. Looks Back took the afterbirth and cords and put them into the fire, while Four Fingers went outside to tell the men all about it.

The men crowded around the cave mouth. Twins were a magical event, a portent of some kind, and they waited for Looks Back to tell them what it meant. Wind Caller pushed his way through, his eyes wide, nostrils flared. The women let him in.

He knelt down beside Deer Shadow. "What will happen now?" he said.

"Maybe all these people will go away," Deer Shadow said with a faint smile. "I am tired. It hurt," she added, sleepy and accusing.

"The babies. Which one was first?"

"The girl."

Behind him Four Fingers gave a snort of laughter. "Your daughter. It would be."

Looks Back finished asking the gods to take back the

afterbirth and the cords so that they couldn't be used to harm the children later. Snow was falling harder now, but people were still standing outside the cave in it, shivering and curious.

Finally Looks Back raised his arms. "This is a holy thing that has happened. I cannot say what will come of it, but these children will be important to the People in some way." He glanced at Blue Stone Man. "Did I not tell you that the answer would come?"

Blue Stone Man grinned. The Yellow Grass People gained much importance by having twins born to them. Especially if they lived. "Is all well with them?"

"Nothing is certain in this life," Aunt Four Fingers said briskly. "But they look all right. And they are big. She is lucky to have carried them this long. Now, with respect, go away and let her sleep."

Found Water came in anyway. "I am the grandfather of twins! Hah!" he said, beaming. He touched Deer Shadow's forehead awkwardly. "I will give you fur for another bunting." He beamed at Wind Caller, too, and went out again, pleased.

"You would think *he* had had them," Deer Shadow muttered, but not loud enough for him to hear. She looked at Wind Caller. "And what is wrong with you? *You* didn't have two babies." He looked wary, like the coyote when too many people were around.

"Among my people," he said hesitantly, and stopped. Then he blurted, "Is it thought a *good* thing here to have twins?"

"Well, certainly," Deer Shadow said. "It means they're holy." Coyotes always had more than one, she thought, but her babies looked like people. She looked at him, puzzled. "Isn't that the way with your people?"

"No," he said shortly.

"Well, what do their gods tell them?"

"The first one is the true child. The second is a demon, and they kill it.'' He didn't notice that he said "they" instead of "we." Deer Shadow was outraged anyway.

"Who are these *people* you come from? They aren't people, they're witches, or worse. You aren't going to *touch* my babies!" She gathered them up tightly.

"I didn't say I was," he protested. "I didn't say I was."

"Gods that drink blood! You aren't even civilized."

"*I'm* not civilized? You people don't even know how to plant food."

"We don't drink blood."

"Neither do I! That is for the gods. If they feed us, then we must feed them. Can't you see? Otherwise they will grow weak, and there will be no maize and no game."

"You stay away from my babies," Deer Shadow said. "If you touch my babies, I'll curse you."

"They're my babies, too. And I'm not going to hurt them, you stupid vixen. I was *afraid.* I was afraid *your* people were going to."

"Oh. Well, who knows what to expect from someone whose gods eat blood?" She unbent a little and unwrapped the boy and then the girl so that he could look at them. She glanced at him sideways, trying to see what he thought.

Wind Caller put a finger into the girl's tiny hand. She grasped it and held on. The boy was asleep, but when Wind Caller bent over him, he opened his eyes and stared back.

A gray shadow slipped through the cave mouth now that the fuss was ended. Follow sidled up cautiously to the bed, and Deer Shadow snatched the babies close to her again. "Tell it to keep away!"

Follow gave her a guarded look, but he didn't back up. He stuck his nose into the bundle of fur and sniffed while Deer Shadow glared at him. He sniffed the other one.

"Get it away from them!"

"He's only curious," Wind Caller said.

"He's a coyote," Deer Shadow said.

"Not a hungry one. Has he ever bothered a child here? You would have heard about it fast enough if he had."

Deer Shadow said, "Maybe. Tell it to get on its own bed." Follow had curled himself at the foot of hers.

Wind Caller pointed at the other bed. "You can't sleep there. Move." When Follow didn't, Wind Caller took him by the scruff of the neck and dragged him across the cave. Follow lay down, but he watched the babies.

Deer Shadow's oldest brother, Young Woman's son, came in with an armful of otter furs. "Father said to bring you these." He peered at the babies. "They look like skinned rabbits."

Deer Shadow made a face at him.

"You are not so beautiful yourself," Wind Caller said with a grin. Relief had made him cheerful.

Oldest Brother reached out to touch one of them, as curious as Follow had been. The next moment he was screaming.

"*Owww!* Get it off me!"

Follow's teeth were in his arm. A singsong growl came from the coyote's throat.

"Let go!" Wind Caller cuffed Follow's nose. "Stupid coyote!"

Follow loosened his teeth just enough for Oldest Brother to get his arm out. The coyote snarled, gums pulled back, more teeth showing than before.

"He's decided they're his," Wind Caller said, amused. "You had better warn people."

Deer Shadow didn't want Coyote for a guardian spirit.

You called him up, a voice in her head said.
So I did, but now I don't want him.
Nobody does. He came anyway.

Oldest Brother was rubbing his arm, aggrieved, and Wind Caller was assuring him cheerfully that Young Woman would put something on it for him so it wouldn't fester. Follow's yellow eyes held the expression of someone who had a job to do and had done it.

Maybe I could make a truce with it, she thought, since nothing seemed to make it go away.

Winter closed down around them, and for a long time there was no more hunting. The women watched over the stored food and were sparing with it to make it last. Everyone was always hungry in the winter. Nursing two babies made Deer Shadow thin, but both of them lived, and Looks Back proclaimed that to be a sign, too. Children died too easily, early babies the easiest of all.

At the winter solstice, when the sun stood still, the men went into the sacred cave, the one that went deep into the heart of the mountain, and danced out the ceremony that would turn the sun around. Women were not allowed—the sun was masculine, and woman magic might injure him—but Wind Caller went to take his place as a proper man of the People. Looks Back unlooped and unbraided his hair and made him wear it knotted the way the People did, although Deer Shadow suspected that after the solstice he would braid it to please himself again.

Locked in by the cold, the Yellow Grass People talked the winter through, telling stories of spring to make it come and tales of old hunts while crafting new spears. Gossip gleaned from the Gathering enlivened the circle around the fire, and hungry children were coaxed to sleep with stories of Sky God and Rain God, of Grandmother Spider, and of how the world was made.

The women banded together for company, to teach their daughters to sew and weave baskets while there was time to guide fumbling hands. They talked freely in the presence of the girls, as if their daughters were other adults; there was very little that the children of the People didn't know anyway.

All of the women wanted to see the babies.

"With your gracious permission," Deer Shadow said to Follow. The coyote backed off, outside the circle of the fire. He didn't seem to mind women handling the twins. But when Blue Stone Man had wanted to touch them, Wind Caller had had to hold Follow by the throat, digging his hands into the yellow-gray fur.

The women passed the babies around, cuddling them and examining them for signs of magic, remarking, "And the girl was born first."

"I knew of a woman who had twins when I was a girl," Give Away said. "They were both boys, just alike. All the men wanted her for a second wife after that, in case she did it again."

"Did she take a new husband?"

"Well, yes, but that was because her old husband beat her. She wasn't pretty, and until then no one else had wanted her."

"What did the old husband do?"

"He ranted and roared, the way men always do if it's the woman that leaves. But he didn't do anything else. The chieftain saw to that."

They all nodded. The People had no more of a ceremony for divorce than they did for marriage. You simply took a mate, and if you grew unhappy later, you could leave. Some did, but not often. A woman or man who left too many mates was considered flighty. Sometimes bloodshed did occur, but it was punished.

"Did she have more twins?" Deer Shadow asked Give Away.

"No, she never did. But the new husband was happy with her anyway. She had other babies for him, and nobody *stays* pretty, anyway."

They nodded again. Youth bloomed quickly and faded, along with nursing mothers' teeth. Wrinkles were respected. Youth very often had no sense, the women told their daughters, clicking their tongues.

Deer Shadow took up a half-finished yucca basket while the women held the babies. Her fingers moved in and out, almost like a dance, and she was pleased with the basket's wide, shallow shape. Weaving it was almost like drawing the animals, except that the basket wouldn't bring anything except grass seed to thresh in it, and a place here at the women's fire, doing the things that women did. Being among them was comfortable and peaceful. It had been a long time since she had felt like one of them, not set aside by magic or scandal or disgrace.

"My bones ache for spring," Four Fingers said, bouncing Deer Shadow's son on her knees. Tickling him, she told him, "There will be plenty of babies born next Gathering for you to lord it over, Small Important One, if the weather doesn't break and let the men go hunting soon. This is true. Men are all alike. Even my old husband."

"And mine!" someone else said.

"He wakes in the morning with it ready and comes home at night with it ready," another woman said. "Isn't there some way to make him *tired*?"

"Only that way," Four Fingers said. She kissed the baby on the nose and handed him on to Runner.

"I *like* winter," Runner said with a giggle.

"That is because you are young and don't have any babies to mind yet," they all said to her.

Runner unwrapped the baby's bunting and looked at him curiously. "He's very nice. Big for his age." She glanced slyly at Deer Shadow. "What was it like, making them?"

"Making them?" Deer Shadow took Son and Daughter back into her lap and put them to her breasts. They were always hungry.

Give Away giggled. "Yes, does he really turn into a coyote in the bed at night?"

"Does he bite?" Caught the Moon asked.

"Certainly not," Deer Shadow said repressively.

"*I* heard that he changes when the sun goes down," Runner said. "Tell us what it's like."

"Where did you hear anything as foolish as that?"

"You told us yourself," the chief's wife pointed out.

And it might be true, Deer Shadow thought. But maybe not the way that they imagined. "The half of him that is Coyote," she tried to explain—and bit her tongue when she saw Follow watching her, cracking a bone just outside the circle of the fire. He looked as if he were listening, and she didn't like it.

Give Away followed her glance. "Oh, we know what it does," she said, giggling. "It chases all the bitches."

Wind Caller, opportune but oblivious, walked past deep in conversation with Looks Back. "If I were a bitch, I'd let it catch me," Runner said wistfully.

Oh, would you? Deer Shadow thought. She eyed Runner with suspicion and said, "It's dangerous."

"Then he does bite!" Caught the Moon said.

"There are some things," Deer Shadow said, "that I may not speak of."

Son and Daughter were sleeping. It seemed to Deer Shadow that they *never* slept, but now they were both making small whispery snores in their bundles of fur. Snow fell in big feathery flakes that caught the moonlight and looked like down from some plucked bird. It wasn't as cold as it had been, and Wind Caller stood in the cave mouth watching the snow just because it was beautiful.

Deer Shadow watched him. He was beautiful, too, she thought. She had thought so when she'd found him in the rain. It made her irritable that the manner in which they had found each other had not made them a perfect pair, attuned in some way beyond flesh. She thought again of the women, envious and curious, who had nibbled at her with questions all morning. She wiggled her toes under the furs, almost warm with the fire close by and the babies beside her. She wished Wind Caller would get in with her.

"You will take a sickness," she said softly.

He turned, surprised. "Are you awake?"

"For once." Usually she drifted off as the babies did while she fed them, falling into a dark heavy sleep from which only their voices could awaken her. Tonight Runner's voice had kept her wakeful.

Wind Caller shed the hide he had wrapped around himself, and got under the furs, bare skin to bare skin. It was warmest that way. He reached for her to see what would happen, and she didn't push him away as she had ever since the babies were born.

"Is it possible, O Most Important One, that all your sore places have healed?" he said into her hair.

"Is it possible, O Most Hungry One, that you have any to spare after licking your chops over other women?"

One hand tightened on her breast, and the other ran between her legs. "What other women?"

"The ones who are licking their chops over *you* and wanted me to tell them what it is like to mate with you. How long your teeth grow and whether there is fur on your feet."

Wind Caller said something in his other language that sounded like a curse mixed with laughter. The curse had something to do, he had once said, with someone being eaten by jaguars, which were like the big mountain cats, with spots like a lynx. They lived mostly to the south. Deer Shadow hoped one would come north and eat Runner.

"What did you tell them?" he demanded.

"I told them it is very dangerous to couple with you. I told them that you bite me on the neck and hold me down, and that it takes till sunup."

Wind Caller sank his teeth into her neck and climbed on top of her. He pulled her legs apart, and she let him, laughing.

"*You* thought up that story," he said. He pushed himself into her and began to rock back and forth. "You should be careful what you make up. It might come true."

She put her hands around his hips, feeling the muscles move under the skin and the angle of the bones. She tried to imagine fur and the sharp backbone of a coyote, the brush of a tail between her legs, and closed her eyes to see what would happen. But she felt only skin. Looks Back the shaman could turn himself into a bear without fur; she had only seen the long teeth, but she knew it was a bear. Maybe that was what happened with Wind Caller.

Their coupling hurt her at first, the way it had hurt when she had found him in the rainstorm, but after a bit it began to feel good. Without babies inside to make her heavy and clumsy, she felt light, as if she could float in the cold air with Wind Caller, like coyotes chasing each other in the sky, their fur powdered with snow.

When he had finished, shuddering and pressing his face into her hair, she felt something similar happen inside herself, like carefully balanced stones toppling or the earth quaking under her. She let her breath out, not knowing she had been holding it, and yelped in surprise.

Wind Caller's arms tightened around her in what might have been acknowledgment or answer; he sighed deeply and started to snore.

She had waked the babies. Son was screwing up his face and fussing. Still flushed by what had happened, Deer Shadow pried herself out from under Wind Caller and unwrapped the babies' furs. She pulled out the soiled dried grass she had stuffed inside the bunting, and put the baby to her breast. Daughter was awake, too, demanding her share, and Deer Shadow tended to her with one hand while she held Son with the other. Little tics of feeling, of that earthquake sensation, kept returning as he pulled at her nipple, and Deer Shadow looked at his father with a new appreciation, although somehow mixed with irritation that she was awake and feeding babies and he wasn't. But she liked the little recurrences that kept happening now, slowing, farther and farther apart, like rain stopping. She felt possessive. There were other men she could have, if he ran off with Runner, but they might not make her feel that way.

In the morning she woke before Wind Caller. She fed the babies and heated some water for cooking dried meat and withered squashes from the winter store. Then she got another pitch-lined basket, filled it with snow, and put more hot rocks in to melt it. She had decided to wash her hair, and it made her feel happily vain and foolish. Most people washed in the river in warm weather or not at all.

She hummed something that might have been an echo of Wind Caller's flute while she heated the water and scrubbed yucca soap into her hair, kneading it with her fingers, bending over the water to keep her clothes from getting wet.

"Haven't you got anything better to do?" her father asked, making his morning rounds to see that everyone he was connected with was all right and behaving properly.

"If I want to be clean, it's my business."

"Very unhealthy," Found Water said. "You'll get a disease in your head in this weather."

Deer Shadow ignored him. She scooped water out of the basket with a shell and poured it through her hair. It took three basketsful to get it rinsed. Afterward she sat by the fire with a bone comb, untangling the long wet strands and drying them. Once dry, they were full of little lightning prickles in the cold dry air and fanned out from her face, clinging to her fingertips.

Wind Caller watched her, bemused. Those long strands of black hair looked like a net, a web that might hold the universe. She combed magic through it with a crackling bone comb.

Then she put on her best furs. This was the day for making women and men of the children who had come of age since the Gathering. There would be extra to eat tonight: hoarded deer meat from their one successful winter hunt, buried in snow to keep it, and the last of the dried fruit from summer. The women would cook it with piñon nuts to make it go farther, but it would be a festival, and who knew what might happen at a festival?

Wind Caller wondered what Deer Shadow thought might happen. She was carefully not looking at him but at a knot of men trampling down the snow on the dance ground, moving rhythmically, beautifully, as if they were the dance to come. Now that the babies were born, she would take part in the girls' initiation, in the making of women, as he would take part in the making of men. Wind Caller had braided his hair back the way he was used to it, but in all other respects he was a man of the People now. They would meet each other on the dance ground, he thought with a little flicker of excitement.

* * *

That night, after the boys in the boys' house had had their visions, brought on by fasting, Deer Shadow was at the dance ground with the new women, shorn-headed girls only as tall as her shoulder. She danced among them, her sleek, crackling hair floating in the torchlit cold.

From where he stood in the men's row opposite the women, Wind Caller saw her dancing before two young men who were not of her clan. There was nothing disgraceful about that, but Wind Caller took an instant dislike to it. She was watching them with the same interested eyes with which the High Rock woman at the Gathering had watched him. And the two young men, who *had* been watching the girls, small, slender babies with new breasts, now were watching Deer Shadow. Anyone would be.

I threw rocks at him for this, Deer Shadow thought. *Now I am doing it. The doe can have what the stag wants.* She looked at the men, assessing them. Did she want any of them? She thought that she probably didn't, but who knew what would happen at a festival? She caught Wind Caller's scowling face out of the corner of one eye. It wouldn't have been any fun if he hadn't been watching.

"Where are your children?" he said when the dancing was ended.

"Aunt Four Fingers has them," Deer Shadow said.

"So you can cavort about like a bitch in heat?"

"Poor bitches." Deer Shadow giggled. "They can't have fun but twice a year."

"Poor things," Wind Caller said. "Maybe women should be made that way."

"Maybe men would be sorry. A bitch will bite you if you try to mate with her any other time. Ask your gray friend about that."

"He can usually find *some* bitch in heat," Wind Caller said, goaded.

She burst into laughter. "And does she clean his kill and make his sandals? And tell him which pups are his?"

"Coyotes don't care."

She looked him in the eye. "Do men care?"

Wind Caller watched the young men swagger by, sleek in the firelight, younger than he was. "Men care," he said. "I have been thinking, and what I think is that I am sorry we first came to each other the way we did. I don't know if I am lying with some magical omen or with a woman."

She sighed, some of the laughter falling away. "I don't, either. When you are not there, I think the coyote watches me, and I don't know what I am married to."

Wind Caller nodded. "If you didn't choose me," he said, "and I didn't choose you, maybe now we will choose each other. Maybe you will stop looking at boys whose brains are still living under their breechclouts and we will leave the babies with Aunt Four Fingers for a little longer."

"Maybe," Deer Shadow said. "Maybe we will do that." They walked away from the fire pit into the darkness, where the glow of their own fire could just be seen on the night's face. As they passed Runner, Deer Shadow flashed a quick triumphant smile that Wind Caller couldn't see.

Looks Back saw them go. Something shimmered about them, he thought. A thin veil of moonlight maybe. He blinked beside his fire, dozing, and saw that the woman *was* moonlight, hand in hand with Coyote.

They were the light and dark, the copulation and the babies. In order for chaos to bring balance, it took the Moon and Coyote both. Her light became him; his fur was all silvered with it, and he looked very respectable. His tongue hung out in a grin while he watched the man and the woman down below.

Bending down beside him, the Moon looked, too, saw what they were doing, and got interested. "I suppose you are pleased with yourself," she said to him. "Father of twins!"

"I have lots of children," Coyote said, and Looks Back saw Follow trotting through the dreamtime camp, purposeful.

"It's a fine thing to make children," the Moon said. She sat, trying to get a better view. "And her people didn't kill him."

"It was close. They may still do it, but not until he leaves a part of himself with them."

"What do you think will happen now?" the Moon asked.

"Why, the world will change," Coyote said grandly, as if he had arranged it.

"The world's always changing."

"Now it will change faster. And faster. In a while there will be all kinds of things."

"Why is that good?"

"It isn't good," Coyote said. "It just is."

The Moon watched the two little figures down below. She felt a tickle of excitement that started at the tips of her bare toes.

Coyote was watching, too. He sat a little closer to the Moon and put one hand in her lap. He was hairy but not unhandsome in this light.

The Moon let him stroke her. She felt herself being shaped by his hand. "Is this part of the change?" she said.

"Certainly," Coyote said. His hand pushed a little deeper. "It makes things happen, doesn't it?"

She reached out and grabbed hold of him, a very wonderful sensation, like holding a hot coal. Sex was one of the glues that held the Universe together, a force like lightning or gravity. It kept everyone from spinning off alone.

Coyote licked her ear. They lay down on the sky and forgot to watch what the humans were doing.

It was a power, one that made the maize stand up like Coyote's penis. It made men and women want each other. It made Life. Now they were joined like the humans, rolling across the sky, lighting the stars.

Looks Back smiled to himself in his sleep.

XIII
Outcast

It stayed cold long after the sun had turned at the solstice, until everyone was twitchy with it, and Wind Caller was certain that this year no warmth would come again. He said so to Looks Back, who said gravely that it was always possible, and that was why the men helped to turn the sun in the sacred cave. But every year of his life, the warmth had indeed returned.

"Where I lived, there was no cold," Wind Caller said, and Looks Back tucked that information away to mull over later. Certainly he knew that where the spirit people lived it was always warm and that it was Coyote who had brought winter by stealing the sun and the moon and turning them loose to wander.

"You live among us now," Looks Back said, to indicate that Wind Caller, whoever he was, would have to put up with human life if he was going to be human. "Be grateful that you are young, and there is still warmth in your bones."

It was the old, those who were forty or more, who felt it most. Four or five of the Yellow Grass People always died in the winter, mostly the old and the babies. The first thing everyone asked at the Gathering was who had died in the past year, and then there would be mourning for people whose bones had been burned sometimes as long as ten or eleven moons ago.

With spring came the hope that no more would die for a while, except for the hunters that the horned deer or the puma might kill, or the women who died in childbirth, or the injured who died of festering wounds. There were many ways to die. Life for the People was short, and they clung to it with a tenacious joy that knew its brevity.

At last the sun climbed high enough to suck the chill from the lower valleys, and the People packed their belongings and hurried down the slopes, leaving the patchy snow and dank caves behind.

The sky was blue stone, more brilliant than the pieces of it that the earth hid. Sun-colored poppies and blue lupine carpeted the ground, and horned lizards emerged to bask on the rocks, warming new life into themselves. Walking through the new grass with a baby on her back and Wind Caller beside her with the other, Deer Shadow could find nothing amiss with her world. She felt as she had when she was five, standing on the riverbank in a hot summer rain, arms spread to catch it, wet and shiny as a fish.

The berry bushes had begun to sprout pale buds along their branches, and the stream they were walking by dipped into pools where trout glinted in the sun among the shiny pebbles. Willow and alder and chokecherry were leafing out, and overhead came a great flapping of wings as ducks flew over on their twice-yearly migration. Lower down, where the river slowed and widened, they would stop to rest, and someone who was good with a sling might kill one.

The People moved slowly, gathering what food and things they found, hunting the spring deer as they went, crossing paths with the Smoke People and stragglers from the Buffalo Leap People on their way to their own summer grounds. The Others were everywhere, the Buffalo Leap People said, like a sickness on the land. That was how these Buffalo Leap People had gotten separated from the rest of their band, during the fighting.

"There was fighting?" Blue Stone asked.

Oh, yes, there had been fighting, and the buffalo would not be this far west again this year because of it. The buffalo were sacred—they lived on the plains to the east where the spirit people roamed, and only once in a while did they move west for the human people to kill them. When they did, all the tribes of the People would band together, as they did for the Gathering, to drive them. But now that the Others had come, the buffalo would not.

The deer were moving, too. As they had stayed away from their summer runs last year, they had not returned to their spring ones. The hunters felt the world moving under their feet, as if either they or the deer had stood still and the landscape had moved. They grumbled and were gone for days at a time, trying to learn new patterns.

At least there was no sign of foreign people when they arrived at the caves in the tufa cliffs. The women settled into their familiar places, chattering uneasily about the Others. If the men found no game, the People would have to move, to wander and live in brush shelters until they found a new summer place, to learn a new land.

Deer Shadow left the babies with Aunt Four Fingers—whose bones hurt her more and more, even in the warmth—and went down to the river with Owl and Runner and a sling to see if she could kill a duck. She had lived here every summer of her life and thought possessively that they would never find another place as good. And there was the maize Wind Caller had set them to planting only yesterday. Cat Ears had grumbled about it, as usual, but Wind Caller insisted that in three moons there would be food from it, food that didn't have to be searched for. What would happen to the maize if they had to move on?

Who were the Others to spoil her fine summer? Deer Shadow looked back at the cliff face, golden in the afternoon sun, and tried to think of a magic to make the Others go away. It was harder to send something away than to call it, she had found. She slipped through the brush that grew around the river, and into a willow thicket, where she could wait silently and listen for the sound of wings. The ducks would come at late afternoon, up from the south, and darken the sky, sweeping down to the water with a sound like deer hides flapping in the wind.

She could catch a corner of the sky through the willows to see them coming. She heard their rush of wings and crouched, waiting, willing them to land. A circle of round stones waited at her knee, and in the center of it she had scratched a duck, trapped him there to draw the others.

The ducks circled down, feet stretched for the water, wings beating, and they settled onto the surface, where they bobbed, quacking to themselves. Deer Shadow put a stone in her sling and slid cautiously toward the water, carrying two more stones with her. She set them at her feet and aimed. If she missed these, there probably wouldn't be any more. It was late in the season. She had thought that the men would be back from their hunt by now so that they could line the river on either side and kill many ducks, but they hadn't returned. More likely than not, they would be empty-handed when they did.

So now there was only herself, and Runner and Owl, who were waiting in the thicket on the other side of the water. None of the other women were good enough with a sling.

She whirled it above her head, fast, and let it go, knowing that Runner and Owl would hear it and fire, too. She fitted another stone into the sling without waiting to see if she had hit her duck. She had only a few seconds. The ducks rose in the air with a great quacking and flapping, and she let fly with another stone, then another, that one futile but she flung it anyway, upward into their departing flight.

When the ducks had gone, she saw that between them they had killed four.

"Yah!" Deer Shadow did a little victory dance on the river's edge, while Runner and Owl waded across. She went into the water to meet them, and they snared the floating ducks before the current carried them away. Two were drakes with shiny green feathers on their throats, iridescent in the sun. The women grinned at one another. They could divide the feathers to decorate a dress and tie the tail feathers into their hair. Since no men had had a hand in the killing, no man could decide he needed them more.

Deer Shadow took a duck and a drake in each hand while Runner helped Owl up the bank. Grudgingly, Deer Shadow had decided that Runner was a reasonable person, even if she did lust after Deer Shadow's husband. Runner's husband was solemn and took life seriously.

They climbed to the top of the bank and shook themselves like dogs, laughing and dripping river water. "Yah hah, we are fine hunters," Owl said, but then she screamed.

Deer Shadow spun around. There were men coming across the valley, more men than she had fingers and toes. At first she thought they were the Yellow Grass men, but they weren't.

"The Others," Runner whispered, frozen.

Deer Shadow clenched her fingers into Runner's arm. "Stay here with Owl. Hide in the brush." She turned and ran for home, for the caves, for her babies, with only one terrified look over her shoulder.

Her breath came in gasps of fear. She didn't know whether they could see her. She flew past the turtle pond and the fishing hole, past the empty land where the maize was still underground. The women at the caves were beginning to cook the evening meal, and two small boys tottered along, their arms full of firewood.

"Put it down!" Deer Shadow screamed at them. "Leave it! Come with me!" She took them by the hands and dragged them, stumbling, along with her.

The women saw her running and stood up, their faces searching for what she was fleeing from. One of them looked past her and screamed.

"The Others!" Deer Shadow shouted. "They are coming this way, they are coming here!"

Aunt Four Fingers ran toward her, carrying the babies. "You keep them!" Deer Shadow said. "Take them and run."

"Where is Owl?"

"Hiding by the river. Try to go that way and take her with you." She wished now that she hadn't told Runner to stay with Owl. Runner could have handled a spear. Deer Shadow darted into her cave and grabbed the one spear that Wind Caller had left there. The old men who had not gone on the hunt were doing the same thing, and Deer Shadow shouted at the young women, "Give the babies to your mother! Get a spear!"

Some of them listened to her, some of them clutched their babies and ran. Older women ran past her, too, carrying baskets, furs, anything they wouldn't part with. They scattered, wailing, toward the river.

There were maybe fifteen of the Yellow Grass People left, old men and young women, no match for the Others but enough to hold them off for a while. They could see the Others clearly now. It was a hunting party or a war

band, all men, moving through the long grass with de-
termination. One of them started to break off, to chase
the women he saw running through the brush, but another shouted at him, and he turned back. They marched
on purposefully toward the caves.

"Thieves!" Deer Shadow shouted. It was plain what
they wanted, not the game but the People's living place
with its good river and warren of caverns. She shook
her spear at them, almost more furious than frightened.
"Yah! Thieves! Sneaking, thieving rat people with no
manners! This is *ours!*"

"We want to let the women get away before we fight
them," old Cloud Catcher said. "There are not enough
of us to hold them back for long." He looked with dis-
may at his gnarled hands, clasped around a spear. He
was Turtle Back's father, nearly the oldest of all of them.

"I want to kill them," Deer Shadow said fiercely.
"*We* live here."

She braced herself furiously for a fight, hoping Four
Fingers and the babies were safe, hoping Runner and
Owl were. The only way not to be frightened, not to
turn tail and run, was to hate them.

The Others were loping up the slope, waving their
spears and howling in a language that was not the People's. They were young, strong men, their mouths pulled
back in snarls as they ran at the People, spears leveled
to scatter them. Deer Shadow stood her ground, stabbing
and hacking at them, pushing them back down the loose
rock on the slope below the caves. They came up again,
clawing their way. Deer Shadow drove her spear again
and again at the face of a man who parried it with his
own and each time climbed another step up. Beside her,
two women who had no spear were pelting the Others
with rocks.

For Deer Shadow, the fight became the piece of
ground she stood on, the piece of their summer dwelling

that she held here, now, with her feet. But slowly she was forced up the slope, and slowly the Others came after her in a haze of dust and blood. Old Cloud Catcher was dead, and so was a girl who had only been a woman since the solstice. Her hair hadn't even grown out.

The ground was turning under Deer Shadow's feet, familiar places pulling away from her. The numbers of the People were thinning. Below her a man stumbled, went down on one knee, and Deer Shadow drove her spear into his breast. He slumped forward on the shaft, and she had to twist it to get it out again, so that the blood pooled at her feet. *Die,* she thought with savage satisfaction, but the Others kept coming.

They were nearly up the slope; it was time to run. Deer Shadow felt a pain in her chest, and her breath was coming in gasps. She saw blood on her leg and wondered where it had come from. As soon as she saw it, the gash it flowed from began to hurt.

"Don't let them get around you!" she screamed to those who remained of her people. "Stay together! Run for the water!" She didn't know if the Others would chase them. She didn't know what they wanted—to kill them all, make them slaves, or simply take their dwelling place. Listens to Deer had been wrong; the Others couldn't be human.

The Yellow Grass People ran before the Others could press them against the rock face or trap them in the caves. They fled down the east side of the slope, forced by necessity to leave their dead behind them. Deer Shadow could feel blood running down her leg, could feel the cold touch of her hide skirt, still wet with river water. Everything was stronger, more powerful—from the wild thudding of her heart to the pain in her ribs when she took a breath. She could hear the Others howling after them.

The People flung themselves into the river at the ford

and splashed across, gasping for air. A spear flew past Deer Shadow's head and caught Fox Girl in the back. Deer Shadow tried to pick her up and pull her along, but she couldn't. Fox Girl was dead.

She ran out of the water and raced on with her people while Fox Girl's body drifted away on the current. Ahead now they could see the other women and the children, slowed by their burdens, running east. With every step she took, more blood flowed out of Deer Shadow's calf. How much could you lose before you died? she wondered.

The defenders caught up with the straggling women and children, snatched up some of their burdens, and ran on. Deer Shadow took one of her babies from Aunt Four Fingers. She pulled a heavy grinding stone out of an old woman's arms and threw it on the ground. "Run!" she shouted at her.

The buffalo grass that grew so thickly on the valley floor seemed to pull at their legs, and jumping mice flew out of it, leaping in terror. Deer Shadow felt like a mouse in a coyote's path. She could feel his hot breath on her shoulder.

Where were they going? She could see no answer except to run until the Others gave up. She looked over her shoulder and saw them still behind. The sun was falling, and her own dark shadow ran on before her, elongated as lines of rain. She clutched the baby she was carrying tighter and plunged on. Owl was running beside her, her face contorted with pain. It hurt Owl to walk, much less to run.

From up ahead, Give Away shouted something that Deer Shadow couldn't make out. A child stumbled and fell and no one noticed. They were looking ahead. The purple dusk made it hard to see, but there were shapes coming toward them.

The shapes wavered, indeterminate as spirits, and then

coalesced into human people who ran shouting through
the scrub that grew beyond the edge of the grassy valley.
Deer Shadow was afraid it was more of the Others, but
it was the Yellow Grass men.

The Others dropped back. They had wanted only the
tufa cliffs and had waited until only the women were
there to fight for them. Scornfully now, they left the
Yellow Grass People free to wander away, shelterless,
from where the Others would live. They shouted something across the valley. Deer Shadow didn't have to
know the words to understand that it meant, "*We* are
here."

The women staggered on, sobbing, toward the men.
The men encircled them, furious, belittled, battered from
a fruitless hunt.

By nightfall the Yellow Grass People had fled into the
scrub and the dubious protection of a low mesa. They
clambered to its top, built brush shelters, and made new
fires, the men cursing the Others and the women wailing.
Three children had been lost in the flight, and their
mothers had to be held down to keep them from going
back.

There was nothing to feed the rest but a pair of rabbits, a desert tortoise that had had the misfortune to be
in their path, and a badger they had dug from its burrow.

"The deer are gone." Exhausted, Wind Caller
crouched by a fire at the front of a hastily made shelter,
shivering more from weariness than the cold. Deer
Shadow had put both babies to her breast, and Wind
Caller had tied up the gash in her leg. Looks Back had
no medicine with which to wash it. They were outcast,
dispossessed. A low murmur of despair whispered
among the fires.

"The Others drove the deer off," Deer Shadow said
with conviction, "so that our men would be gone and

they could kill the women." She spat, then told him with savage satisfaction, "I killed one of *them*."

Wind Caller looked at her respectfully and touched her cheek, wet from her tears.

"We had to leave our dead ones," she said. "My father's youngest wife is dead. They will do something horrible to the children they took. They are not humans. The old soft man was wrong."

To the Yellow Grass People, the Others were a force of nature, like a flash flood or an earthquake, Wind Caller thought. There was nothing to be done but endure, and their helplessness made them angry.

The sense of bearing a curse grew over the days that followed, festering with the waxing and waning of the moon. The Yellow Grass People moved on to their fall camps with a feeling of wrongness, of being out of step with the season and the sun and the proper ways. Game was scarce—it was not the right time of year—and they pursued it into country they had never seen before. Against the distant mountains, the Others' fires burned in the caves the People had been forced to abandon. One Ball and Cat Ears went there to count the interlopers and came back to say that nearly twice as many were living in the cliffs now as when the People owned them.

"What about the maize?" Wind Caller demanded. "Is the maize growing?"

"The maize is growing. Whatever it is." Cat Ears made a warding-off sign at Wind Caller. To Blue Stone Man, he hissed, "I told you. I told you in the winter that he was a witch. It is this *thing* he has planted that has brought the Others."

"The Others began to come in our grandfathers' time," One Ball said. "I don't remember a time without the Others."

"Do you remember a time when the Others were in your dwelling place? Using your skins and baskets and fire pits? That one has called them in!'' Cat Ears pointed to Wind Caller, avoiding his name.

Blue Stone Man looked solemnly at Wind Caller. "What do you have to say?"

"I'd say you're a fool," Wind Caller said in his first language. Deer Shadow, who understood a little of that speech now, prodded him as if to say, *This is serious. A curse isn't to be joked about.*

Wind Caller saw the hunters watching him with uncertainty. "How long do I have to live among you before I no longer have to prove that I am not a witch?" he asked them angrily. "Is there a law about it? A certain stretch of time? Or shall I plan on spending the rest of my life offering this gift and that gift and this other proof, to pacify people who think their own shadow is a witch for following them?" He looked disgusted.

"Where then do the Others come from?" Looks Back said.

Wind Caller thought that the shaman was giving him an opening, a chance to speak truth to the Yellow Grass People. He suspected that the shaman would as soon not do it himself. Truth-telling is not always well received.

"They come because they are hungry. And because our dwelling places are better than theirs." He was careful to say *our*. "Because someone else is pushing them out of their dwellings. Because something stronger is driving them out, they come to drive us, like stupid rabbits."

"We are not rabbits, and they are many more than we!" One Ball protested.

"They aren't human. Human people don't steal from each other!" The rest of the hunters took up the argument.

"We have always hunted this land, we and the rest of the People. The Others took only a little."

"Well, now they are taking more," Wind Caller said.

"Shall we lie down like upended turtles and let them?"
What was wrong with these people? They didn't want
to fight their enemies; they wanted to find witches and
curses to blame and then go off in the dry lands and eat
sand. *Bah!*

'What can we do about it?" Squirrel said.

"We can fight them!" Wind Caller roared. "Or we
can put mud in our hair and wait for the spirits to see
that we are hungry and drive them away. Which one do
you think will work better?"

"The deer woman is supposed to call the deer,"
Found a Snake said.

"I can't call them into a land that is not theirs," Deer
Shadow snarled. "The Others have taken the land where
the deer are."

"They are many more than we," One Ball said again.

"What of the other Peoples who come to the Gathering?" Wind Caller asked Blue Stone Man. "Together
we are more than the Others. Why do we not go to
them?"

"We do not do that," Blue Stone Man said. "We
must take care of our own, or they will laugh at us."

"They will laugh less when the Others take *their*
land," Wind Caller said. He wondered how many bands
of the Others there were. "The Buffalo Leap People
have fought them."

"The Buffalo Leap People did not ask for *our* help,"
Blue Stone Man said.

Wind Caller ground his teeth. When the spirits had
given the Yellow Grass People their world and taught
them how to live in it, it appeared that none had remembered to teach them to fight. He threw his arms out,
disgusted. "Then by all means let us go and eat mud,
since we cannot fight the Others. No doubt the Buffalo
Leap People will also be eating mud, but we will all be
proud and no one will laugh at us. Yah, you are all like

the monkeys when Great Snake comes to look at them.''

''What are monkeys?'' Squirrel said.

''Silly creatures that live in trees and throw fruit at each other.'' Wind Caller glared at them. ''Never mind. I hunted alone before. I can hunt alone now.''

Deer Shadow grabbed his arm. ''Stop it! This is serious. It is law. We cannot ask other bands for help. It is not the way we do things. You couldn't change the way *your* people do things—'' She had heard the story of his exile by now and half believed it. ''What makes you think you can change us? Are we children then, and not so important?''

''Oh, certainly not, Most Important One, but your chief of the hunters''—he jerked a thumb at Cat Ears rudely—''wants to kill me for being a witch. The rest of your people can't see what's under their noses—that they must take back the caves *and* the maize from the Others before they lose this gift, which I am sorry I ever brought to you.'' He had given up on saying *we* and *our*. He folded his arms.

''And how is that to be done?'' Looks Back said. ''Are you telling us that you know the way to drive off a people who outnumber us?''

''Oh, no, I am saying that we should sit down on stones here and wait to starve.''

''If you know how it is to be done, then say,'' Looks Back said angrily.

''You will not call on the other People for help? Not even the Buffalo Leap People?''

''We will not.'' Looks Back also folded his arms. *He is as stubborn as Wind Caller,* Deer Shadow thought. This was the first time the two men had opposed each other, Looks Back having always taken Wind Caller's part before, maybe because of Cat Ears.

''I told you,'' she said to Wind Caller, trying to convince him, ''that we cannot do that.''

"Very well," he said. "I still know how to drive the Others away, but it will be harder. Is there some rule your gods have made for you, that you have to do everything the hard way?" Perhaps that was the result of not giving them blood, he thought. Or maybe—the thought occurred to him uneasily—this was Eyes of Jaguar's curse come down his trail at last. Eyes of Jaguar would like to see him trying to change these stubborn, ignorant people who couldn't even fight. Eyes of Jaguar might be laughing from the greasewood bushes.

"We will never drive the Others out unless we drive *this* one out!" Cat Ears swaggered to the front of the arguing group of hunters, pushing the women aside until he came to Deer Shadow, who didn't move. She picked up a stick and made drawings in the air with it.

Cat Ears held up a warding-off sign but didn't back up. Behind him were Dancing Bear, a tall, hulking boy who had been initiated at the solstice, and Found a Snake, Cat Ears's chief supporter. What Cat Ears wanted done, Found a Snake would second, or be sent to do. The three of them turned and faced the hunters, putting Wind Caller between them and the rest.

Wind Caller's eyes snapped, and Deer Shadow laid a hand on his arm again. Follow threaded through the legs of the crowd until he was at Wind Caller's heels.

"When we have killed him"—Cat Ears pointed at Wind Caller—"the Others will go. They are not human people, not real. They come because he brings them. If we kill him, they'll go."

"And then we will burn this thing he has planted," Found a Snake said. He looked at Cat Ears almost pleadingly, wanting his assurance.

"Then you will starve!" Deer Shadow said, furious. "It is food! It is power over the Others because they do not know how to grow it!"

"They will grow it after these fools have killed me,"

Wind Caller said. "The maize will ripen, and the Others will figure out what it is for. The *Others* can think of new ways to do things! Yah! That is why they are in your caves." He looked at Cat Ears, and Follow's head also swiveled in his direction. "And you can try to kill me, but remember this: I was taught to fight, not to throw my spear at the first enemy I saw, and then try to kill the rest with bragging."

Several of the hunters snickered. Cat Ears spat, "I can kill a witch!"

"But can you kill a man who can fight better than you?"

"You can't kill a witch so easily, you know," One Ball said. "It's very hard. Dangerous."

"My husband is not a witch!" Deer Shadow objected. "That is Cat Ears's tale because he wants to be most important among the Yellow Grass People—and he is not!"

"If he is not a witch, why have the Others come and the game gone away?" Cat Ears asked the rest of the Yellow Grass People. He made it sound reasonable, as though one was linked to the other.

"That is true. We never had these troubles until he came," Dancing Bear said.

"We never had these troubles until you became a man, either," Deer Shadow said. "Maybe that's the reason. Maybe *you* are cursed."

"This is not an argument for women," Dancing Bear said.

"This is not an argument for boys who have not seen their first Gathering as a man," she said scornfully. "I am older than you, and even if I were not, I would still know more."

"You're a woman," Dancing Bear said.

"I call the game. What do you do besides follow Cat Ears like a tame buffalo?"

Dancing Bear's face remained expressionless. "This is for the hunters to decide. Not for women."

No one argued with him. Deer Shadow watched the faces of the men, furious that they were not letting her have any say. She called the game for them, but when the game didn't come, she was just a woman. That stung like salt sweat in a cut. Hadn't she fought the Others while the men who were ignoring her had been gone? Hadn't she killed one of them? That was more than Cat Ears had done. That was more than any of them had done. She had a purplish scar down her leg to prove her right to speak, but they weren't interested in it.

"There has been enough talk of killing," Looks Back said, overriding the men. He thumped his staff on the ground, lacking his great tooth, which remained in the tufa cliffs, making power for the Others. "If the stranger who has come to us can show us the way to take back what is ours, then let him. What is more important— that or young men's pride?" He looked at Cat Ears.

Cat Ears ignored him. The father and son had never understood each other, and since Cat Ears had become chief of the hunters, they had been constantly at odds, vying for Blue Stone Man's agreement. The shaman was old and set in his ways, and Cat Ears wanted change— but change led by Cat Ears, not by Wind Caller. He demanded of the hunters, "Do we listen to old men, and women?"

They murmured, exploring the notion that Cat Ears might be right. Old men had wisdom and were supposed to be listened to, but where had listening to the old men gotten them? Maybe they should listen to Cat Ears now.

Deer Shadow could see their intention in their faces: They would kill her husband. They would leave the cliff caves to the Others, and she would never see her summer place again, never grow the maize, which had power, power that she could feel when she touched it.

She cast a pleading glance at Blue Stone Man, but his face was impassive. He was thinking, listening to it all. Looks Back lifted his arms toward their home, toward the deep blue, saw-toothed heights that guarded the slope of Red Rock Mountain. Even if they let Wind Caller go, outcast with the coyote, they would never let her go with him, not so long as they thought she could still call the deer. And they would never let her take the babies. *I am human, too!* she wanted to scream at them. *What I want matters as much as what you want!* But she knew that it didn't. What she wanted didn't matter to the men at all.

The rest of the women were behind the hunters, waiting for the men to decide. They would go where the men told them to, dragging their grinding stones and newly made baskets, hoping the men would kill enough deer before winter, hoping to keep the children alive.

Looks Back turned toward the People again. "Let the stranger show us the way to drive the other strangers off. That is what the gods say." He thumped his staff.

Blue Stone Man looked from one hunter to the next, marking their expressions. He watched them until they noticed him doing it and quieted. "Although I am not as powerful with a curse as the shaman, I am strong enough to curse any man who goes against me. We cannot afford to be divided now. This is what I have decided. We will let the stranger we call Wind Caller tell us how he thinks we may defeat the Others, and we will try it. If he leads us properly, there will be no more talk of witches. If he does not, I will decide what to do with him. Talk is ended."

Blue Stone Man's ruling was not to be argued with, not now anyway. The hunters and the women walked away, leaving Deer Shadow sick with mingled relief and fury. The outcome would have been the same had she

been up in the sky with the nighthawk that was beginning to swoop about in the dusk, scooping up bugs in
her big mouth. *Yah,* she thought, *may you all wake tomorrow in the skins of women.*

XIV
Blood and Stone

Wind Caller spent the night sitting by the fire outside the fragile journey hut he and Deer Shadow sheltered in with Follow and the babies. The brush and leaves used to build it were too dry to be close to the fire, and Deer Shadow shivered as she watched him and fed the babies, who squalled with hunger because her milk was thin. He had become all men to her tonight, almost of a part with the men of the Others who had invaded her world and stolen it.

He sat with his chin in both hands, peering into the fire as if he saw people in it. Sometimes he picked up his spear and atlatl and looked at them as if they were something he had never encountered before; and once he collected pebbles, arranged them in a straight line and half circle, then moved them very fast, the way One Ball could do with snail shells until she forgot which shell had the bean under it.

She gave up watching him after a while and went to sleep, snuggling the babies against her for warmth. Even in summer, this land was cold at night, descending on them like a hand as soon as the sun went down. She thought vengefully of the woman of the Others who was sleeping in her furs, and wished she had had time to draw a rattlesnake under them.

In the morning Wind Caller went to Blue Stone Man. The chieftain was gnawing at the same bone he had gnawed on last night, and his hair, normally neatly knotted and tied with many feathers, was unkempt. His wife was grinding unripe seed on a stone not yet worn down into a quern, so that the hard seed kept sliding off it into the dirt. She was crying with vexation.

"I need two men to come with me and look at the land," Wind Caller said.

"Sit down," Blue Stone Man said. "Don't start telling me what you need while my stomach is growling."

Wind Caller joined him. "With respect, the chieftain's stomach will growl until we take back our own hunting runs. Or until we move on to another place entirely where there is game and no people, and I assure the chieftain that that is not such an easy place to find."

Blue Stone Man nodded. "It is getting harder all the time. The world is becoming a wicked place."

"Certainly," Wind Caller said, forcing himself to be patient. He was growing tired of lamenting change, disguised as wickedness, instead of fighting it. "Perhaps there are just more people living in these days."

"If you can't find a place with no people, why do you want two men to look at the land?" the chieftain asked him.

"To find a place to trap the Others. We don't outnumber them; we shall have to hunt them like game."

Blue Stone Man peered at him. "You know how to do this?"

"Certainly," Wind Caller said, hoping that he did. This was the idea that Eyes of Jaguar hadn't let him try. At least he knew how to fight.

"You can have Cat Ears," Blue Stone Man said with a twitch of his lip.

Wind Caller chuckled. It was the first time he had heard the chieftain make a joke. "With respect, I might not bring him back again. I want One Ball, and another of your choosing."

Blue Stone Man thought. "Squirrel," he said finally.

Wind Caller didn't ask why. Squirrel was related to Deer Shadow. Maybe that was the reason. "We will be gone a long time, maybe a moon. We will need to know that other men will hunt for our families." One Ball was married and had children. Squirrel had a new wife from the Red Rock People and hunted for his mother and Owl as well.

"When we are hungry, what we have we divide," Blue Stone Man said. "They will be fed as well as any of us."

"There is another thing. The men should make throwing spears while we are gone. Many. Enough to waste. Each man should have as many as he has fingers."

Blue Stone Man put down his bone and furrowed his brow. "You think of too many things for us to do."

"Let my wife teach the women to use a sling. If my wife can kill ducks, the women can kill quail, maybe rabbits."

"If they can find them." Blue Stone Man looked as close to despairing as Wind Caller had ever seen him. The Yellow Grass People stayed, by orders, away from the hunting runs of the other bands of the People—apparently intruding there was not done any more than asking for help—and it left precious little worthwhile countryside to hunt. The land where they were now was evil country, with black stone and dry scrub poking dismally through it and almost no water except for stinking springs that bubbled boiling out of the rock. If they couldn't beat the Others, they would have to go elsewhere, far away, and take land from someone that the People didn't count as human.

"Set the women to making spears, too," Wind Caller said.

Blue Stone Man appeared to be shocked.

Wind Caller shocked him further. "And teach them all how to fight."

"How to fight?"

"We'll need all the warriors we can get."

"Women?"

"It's not unknown. Looks Back has told me."

"That was in the old times. Before the grandfathers' times. That was not now." Blue Stone Man fidgeted, as if he had inadvertently sat on something with thorns. He looked at his wife uneasily.

"If women fought then, women can fight now," Wind Caller said. "My wife killed a man with my third-best spear when the Others attacked."

Wind Caller thought the chieftain was about to say that Deer Shadow was not a proper woman anyway and had caused a great deal of trouble despite giving birth to twins. But Blue Stone Man seemed to bite back the words, then looked again at his own wife, a plump, weathered woman with badger stripes of gray in her hair. Not so plump now, not after a moon of hunger. Her breasts were wrinkled, her wrists bony.

"Raccoon, will you fight the Others?" he said, almost gently, his voice low.

"I will fight them sooner than starve and watch my grandchildren starve," she said, not gently at all. "Better we die that way."

Wind Caller hid a smile. He was learning something about women, and their possessiveness of the place in the tufa cliffs was only part of it. He touched Follow, lying beside him as usual, just out of Blue Stone Man's reach. "I killed this one's mother," he said. "She stole a rabbit right out of my fire to feed her pups. Tell the women that if they want to feed their children, they will have to kill the Others.''

"The women don't need telling," Raccoon said, breaking all precedent by acknowledging that she had heard tribal matters not addressed directly to her. She flushed, embarrassed, and turned back to her grinding.

Blue Stone Man looked as if a rock had spoken. "Woman magic takes man's strength away." He looked at Wind Caller, waiting for him to find a way to deny that.

"Then we will turn it on the Others!" Wind Caller answered. "You said you would give me a chance to say how we may beat them. Did you expect it to be by shouting bad names at them? We cannot fight them in an open battle, men against men. They are too many."

"It is dishonorable to let women fight," Blue Stone Man said.

"Why? Because it isn't the way you do things?" Wind Caller thought of the turkeys. It was just as well there were none in this place, or they would have had another cause of disagreement.

"There are reasons why things are done in certain ways," Blue Stone Man said. "It is to prevent us from being dishonorable.''

"Are the Others human?" Wind Caller asked craftily.

"No."

"Then we can be dishonorable to them. We aren't going to eat them, so we don't even have to be grateful.'' He got up, made a gesture of respect to the chieftain's authority, and was gone before Blue Stone Man could think of another argument.

"This is how you bind a spearhead," Wind Caller said. "You've watched your father and me do it enough times.''

Deer Shadow wrapped the sinew tight and pulled the knot.

Wind Caller shook his head. "That is loose. It will come out."

Deer Shadow snarled at him but wrapped it again. "And where will you be, while we are making spears? And who is going to flake the spearheads? That is even harder to learn."

"The old men will flake the spearheads. Do you have to arrange everything, or can you trust some of it to me? I am going to find a place to fight the Others where it won't matter so much that there are more of them."

"How will you get them there?"

"I'm thinking. Here, pull the sinew so. Then the knot will tighten."

"And while you are *thinking,* I am to make spears and teach the other women to hunt with a sling, and the old men are also to teach us to fight? We are most humble and grateful that you have consulted us about this."

"Rattlesnake," Wind Caller said. "Why are you so angry? I know you are hungry."

"Yah, the men are hungry, too," Deer Shadow said. "We are all hungry, but the men are told things. The men have most important councils while the women sit to one side and are told by cubs who are barely men that they are not allowed to speak."

"And when have you not spoken?" Wind Caller said affectionately. "Most Wise, you are permitted to speak all the time. For that matter, you speak when you are not permitted, as befits a magic woman."

"What is the point in speaking if men don't hear? They let us speak and then go on with what they are saying, as if we had been a dog barking. That young lout Dancing Bear doesn't listen, and neither do you. Did you *ask* us if we wanted to fight?"

"Do you want to fight?" Wind Caller asked her.

The sage that roofed the brush shelter rattled in the dry wind, and leaves drifted down on her hair. She brushed them away viciously, crushing them in her hand, so that he could smell their pungent scent. "I want to fight somebody," she said. "Right now I want to fight you, so maybe I should fight the Others."

"Maybe you should." Warily he put an arm around her shoulders. "You said you wanted to kill them, when they drove us out."

"I know," she said mournfully, fists clenched. "I never wanted to kill people before."

Wind Caller found that incomprehensible, but then he found Deer Shadow's people largely incomprehensible. "You want to kill *these* people, not everyone."

"I know. But what will happen then? Will the deer still hear me if I kill people? If I *want* to kill people? You aren't supposed to kill things you aren't going to eat, or use in some way. Even then you must honor them."

"Do the deer hear you now?" Wind Caller asked her.

"Couldn't we drive them away?" Deer Shadow asked. "As they did to us?"

"There are too many of them. They would just come back. We have to kill them."

Using the point of the spear she had been binding, Deer Shadow scratched into the dark sand the image of something she had never made before: a man with arms, legs, and a spear at the end of one arm. He was driving it through another man. She looked at it with horror for several moments and quickly wiped it out again.

The idea might upset Deer Shadow, but to Squirrel a scouting expedition to find the proper spot to ambush the Others seemed a fine plan. Despite having to leave his new wife, which was the subject of numerous ribald jokes as they set out, he felt it was an adventure, the sort of thing not ordinarily given to a man. He followed Wind Caller uncomplainingly, not even asking where they were going.

One Ball and Wind Caller put their heads together the first night out and made more arrangements of pebbles and dry sticks beside the fire, while Squirrel fed the flames to keep them going. There wasn't much to burn, and the wind whipped through the flames, trying to snuff them out. Coughing, Squirrel finally got the heart of the wood burning, skinned the snake they had killed, and put the meat on a stick. Snake wasn't bad; it tasted better than lizard. The coyote had gone off somewhere to hunt on its own, suspecting, rightly, that the humans weren't going to give him any of their snake. Squirrel heard more coyotes off somewhere in the distance, where the foothills ran down to the desert. Their warbling, undulating conversation lifted the hair on the back of his neck.

He looked at Wind Caller curiously, wondering if he really was one of them. Did he remember running with them, back before he had become human? To fight a battle with someone like that, who might be Coyote himself—Squirrel shivered excitedly.

"We want a canyon," One Ball was saying. "Put half of us at one end to wait for them, and half of us to come after."

"They are still too many," Wind Caller said. "We need to do more than just surprise them."

"There is also the matter of how to get them *into* the canyon."

"We will think about that when we have found a place," Wind Caller decided. "I want a place with a lot of big stones, high up. The way the Place Where the River Runs Backward looked before it fell down."

"Oho," said One Ball.

Such a place was easier to describe than to find. It

took ten days to get back across the black stone country without starving or dying of thirst on the way. The land was studded with strange wind-carved figures, tall thin points of rock balancing egglike stones on their finger-tips; mesas undercut by wind and water long since vanished; softer stone blown away from beneath heavier formations. Wind Caller had seen these over and over in his wanderings through this land and regarded them as a kind of god or totem—landmarks with something to say. Eventually, if he searched long enough, he would find a canyon wall riddled with them.

They took much care not to be seen by the Others, although once they stumbled upon a group of women picking yucca. Follow saw the women first and flattened himself in the chaparral. Wind Caller had learned long ago to pay attention to Follow, and One Ball and Squirrel learned it now, dropping to peer over the ridge that Follow had been trotting along.

There were four women, plainly of the Others, according to Squirrel, although they didn't appear that different to Wind Caller. All northern people differed so much from his own people that he had trouble telling them apart. The women had children with them, a fat toddling boy and two babies in packs; a fourth child, a girl with a face of defiant misery, stood staring at the ground, moving only when the women shouted at her.

"That's Rainwater's girl," Squirrel whispered. "We can—"

"No!" One Ball said.

"She's ours!"

"And she isn't the only child they took, or the only thing they took. No!" One Ball said.

Wind Caller put a hand out toward Squirrel. "Later we can get them all back. They haven't hurt her. And how far do you think we would get with her now?"

"They've hurt her if they've made her one of them,"

One Ball said unhappily. "I had an aunt the Others took. When she came back, she was crazy and kept trying to run away to them."

"How did she come back?" Squirrel asked, diverted.

"Her father and her father's brothers went and got her. There was a big fight. It was a long time after they took her. They found where she was from someone at a Gathering who had traded with the Others."

"The Others are not so new here, then," Wind Caller muttered.

"We told you," One Ball said. "Since the grandfathers' time. But never so many of them."

"And you trade with them."

"Sometimes. Before they stole our dwelling. I didn't, though," One Ball said. "Trading with people who aren't human is risky. But sometimes they have blue stone and red crystals to make paint."

"Mmm," Wind Caller said. He motioned them back from the ridge despite Squirrel's protests. Rainwater was part of the same clan as Squirrel and Deer Shadow. Wind Caller hadn't worked out how they defined clans yet, but he was beginning to understand some of the relationships. "We will try to get the children back when we have beaten the Others," he said. "At least you can tell Rainwater that her daughter is alive."

One Ball, Squirrel, and Wind Caller ate better once they were back in their familiar hunting runs, although they spent much time dodging the hunting parties of the Others. Then they would track them, and finally they found that the Others used some of the same game trails that the Yellow Grass People always had; and some new trails, because much of the game had been driven elsewhere by the encroachment of the Others, hunted from two directions at once. Wind Caller and the other two fanned out, each going a different way, covering all the

ground they could before converging at nightfall, searching—searching for where the gods had built them the
place they needed.

"Which gods should we ask for it?" Squirrel said,
baffled.

"If you ask me," One Ball said, "it's the kind of
place Coyote would build. So I don't see why we
haven't found it."

"I do—he only comes to me sometimes," Wind
Caller said. How could he tell them he was not Coyote
when he wasn't sure himself? He looked at Follow. No
one, Deer Shadow had told him, had ever tamed a coyote
before, not even a pup. And half-coyote dogs (the males
would occasionally sneak into a camp if a bitch was in
heat) were unreliable. If he was Coyote, if he and Follow
together were Coyote, they were only a piece of him.
*And where should the piece look for what the whole had
created?*

Wind Caller thought about that at night, while One
Ball shuffled a pebble under some dry seed pods and
won a deer hide from Squirrel with it.

"I don't have a deer hide," Squirrel said.

"When you get one," One Ball said.

"You bet me a catskin breechclout, and you don't
have that either."

"I was going to get one," One Ball said, "if I lost."

"You never lose," Squirrel said suspiciously.

"That ought to teach you not to play with him,"
Wind Caller interjected. "His fingers are too fast." He
went back to thinking.

"Good. Teach me to do it," Squirrel said to One Ball.

"Why? Then I can't win from you anymore."

"I won't play with you again anyway," Squirrel said.
"I am not stupid, but I will give you two deerskins to
teach me how to do it."

"When you get them?"

"When I get them."

"All right. There isn't anything else to do."

Wind Caller watched their fingers moving in and out, flying, making a pattern that was like stitches. Squirrel would fumble, and one of the pods would leap into the air. Patiently, One Ball would set them up again. In, out, around, across. Up and down, until Wind Caller couldn't follow the pods, and his head would spin.

"There!" Squirrel said. "Do you know which pod it's in?"

"Here." One Ball picked up the pod and tossed the stone in his palm.

Squirrel did it again, stitching the pattern together until it burned like the trail that a torch left in the dark when a man ran with it. Wind Caller watched until it made him dizzy.

"Yah!" he said finally. "I am going to sleep. You are making my eyes cross."

He rolled on his side under the thin hide that was all he had for a blanket, edging closer to Follow for warmth, the way they had done before he came to the Yellow Grass People. Follow's fur was smoke- and sage-scented, a faint overtone across the coyote smell. Wind Caller buried his face in it. He should know the right place by its smell, he thought sleepily.

Wind Caller dreamed that lines of light streaked across the darkness, like watercourses filled with fire. Rolling among them was a big rock, and wherever it rolled, another stripe of light rolled out under it. Wind Caller stood in the darkness. He had tried to follow the light, but it burned his feet because he was not a shaman and didn't know how. He didn't know the pattern; it had never been stitched into his skin. All *his* patterns were different, scarred lines all pointing south. They were no use here. Even in the dark he could see dust boiling up from the big rock as it rolled on, shooting sparks, leaving its snail trail of light. Wind Caller put his foot out again and it burned, but he kept it there. He took one step and then another, and he saw that it was Coyote who was pushing the rock, his brushy tail stuck out behind him. Coyote rolled the rock with his front paws, his ears pricked forward as if he heard something ahead of him. He trundled the rock toward it.

Wind Caller shouted at Coyote to wait for him, but Coyote wouldn't. Suddenly Wind Caller was loping, chasing the rock, while ahead of him he saw it burst into uncounted tiny pieces, bright as sparks. They shot into the sky, splattering the blackness there, and Coyote leaped after them, into the stars.

Wind Caller woke with the place in his head. He had seen it in his wanderings. Amazed, he pulled it from his memory and examined it. It had the shape of the path Coyote had traced in his dream, a canyon with a sharp bend in it and then another, so that it curved like the meandering river that had carved it. Above the rim, just where the bend began, were balanced wind-carved rocks, eroded from the bottom, top-heavy and precarious. And he knew where it was, because he had gone from there straight west to the river where he had found Deer Shadow. The way to it was written in the pattern of his dream.

One Ball and Squirrel were impressed by the dream, which was an accepted way to gain knowledge. All the same, it took two days to find the place, and when they did, they indignantly demanded why he hadn't remembered it to begin with.

"I didn't know I was going to need it," Wind Caller said, standing with hands on hips to peer up at the canyon rim. Above them, the red sandstone boulders nodded like a row of heads. "I haven't ever wanted to drop rocks on anyone before."

"Let's go up," Squirrel said, excited.

"How?" One Ball demanded. The rock face was sheer, without even a stunted tree clinging to it.

"We have to go out again and climb from the other side," Wind Caller decided.

One Ball groaned.

"Not you," Wind Caller said with a chuckle. "You stay here. We have to have someone to throw rocks at."

"Most amusing," One Ball said, but he looked happy enough to sit in the shade and let them claw their way through the cactus and thorn scrub to the top. He filled his waterskin at the thin stream that trickled through the canyon and sat down with his back to a gnarled piñon pine, where he could watch the canyon entrance.

Wind Caller didn't bother to mention to him that the water here was acrid and tasted of the rocks it flowed through. One Ball would find out.

"Shout when you find the top," One Ball called after them comfortably.

They dropped a rock on him instead. Only a small one, but he leaped up angrily from a dream in which he had been squeezing his wife's breasts (in the form of the waterskin). He shook his fist at them.

"Yah!" Wind Caller shouted down at him. "The Others might have come and eaten you. You wouldn't have noticed until they got to your head."

"I have been watching," One Ball yelled up at them. "No one came except some women looking for you because they heard it's that long." He held his hands an arm's length apart. "I told them we didn't know you, and anyway your wife throws rocks."

"Yah-ah," Wind Caller said. "Now we will throw

rocks at you. Go to the dead cottonwood at the first bend and start running up the canyon.''

"How fast?"

"As if you were chasing the Others."

"Do I want to catch them?"

Wind Caller threw another rock. One Ball set out down the canyon and ran back up it, a wary eye on the canyon rim.

"We have to know when to drop the rocks," Wind Caller said. He and Squirrel were hunkered on the canyon rim, Squirrel picking cactus spines out of one palm. "Things take time to fall." Wind Caller selected a fist-sized rock and let it drop, careful to avoid One Ball this time. One Ball was past by the time it landed.

"Go and do it again!" Wind Caller shouted.

One Ball shouted what was probably a curse and trotted back down the canyon. He ran again, watching suspiciously as Wind Caller dropped another rock, a little sooner this time. It splattered in the rubble below, just on One Ball's heels.

"Close! Do it again!"

"Do it with your backside!" One Ball yelled, but he went down the canyon a third time. He discovered Follow watching him from a nest he had dug in the wet sand by the stream, and he laughed. "Even your stupid coyote has more sense than to climb up there with you!" he yelled at the two above him. "One more time! Here I come! If you hit me with a rock, I'll climb up there and throw you off myself!"

He raced up the canyon, feet pounding while Wind Caller waited, rock in hand. When he dropped it, it hit a single foot's length ahead of One Ball. Wind Caller whooped.

One Ball stopped, panting, and retrieved his water-skin. He drank from it and made a face while he watched Wind Caller gesticulating to Squirrel on the canyon rim.

"Push the rocks over when the leaders are at that bent piñon," Wind Caller said "It will take a little longer to push these big rocks."

"We could shove one over on One Ball just to be sure," Squirrel suggested.

"Let's go down and tell him that, for a true test, he has to climb up now and drop rocks at *us*," Wind Caller said.

"He might do it."

They slithered down in the rough scree that littered the mountain, trying to avoid the cactus. It was a long way around and down, and when they got to the canyon floor, One Ball had built a fire and was cooking half a ground squirrel. "He ate his half raw," he said, pointing at Follow. Follow ran a long tongue over his gray chops and stuck a little closer to their heels on the journey back.

Blue Stone Man surveyed the women lined up in front of him. Deer Shadow and Runner and Four Fingers grasped their spears like men. Blue Stone Man wouldn't have wanted to fight any of them. Give Away and Caught the Moon held theirs as if they had picked up dead rats. His wife, Raccoon, gripped hers fiercely but with her hands the wrong way around so that she was going to end by jabbing the haft into her belly. Blue Stone Man sighed. Did he really *want* a tribe of women who could fight? Some of the men were complaining already.

Blue Stone Man adjusted the women's grips on their spears. "It isn't just a thing you are holding," he said. "It has to be part of your arm."

"Why can't we throw them with atlatls like the men?" Runner demanded.

"You will," Blue Stone Man said. For this battle there would be enough spears to waste. Everyone in the band was making them. The black rock here made fine points. "But first you have to learn to use a spear in your hands. Pretend I am the enemy. Come at me."

Runner lunged at him. Blue Stone Man knocked her spear upward with his own, but he waited a moment too long. A thin streak of blood ran down his chest, the skin scratched open.

"Hah!" Runner said.

"Hah yourself," the chieftain said. "Very good. Raccoon, come and try it."

Raccoon blinked. "I've sometimes wanted to," she said with a half-laugh, and the women around her grinned. There weren't any of them who hadn't wanted, on at least one occasion, to take a spear to their husbands.

When they had all had a turn at him, Blue Stone Man called out the other hunters to spar with them, resisting the temptation to pair Cat Ears with Deer Shadow for amusement.

He watched them with growing unease as their abilities improved. The women were learning to fight from men who were almost equally unaccustomed to it and therefore condescending, but it wasn't long before the men ceased to laugh and grew respectful, at least while their wives had spears in their hands. The women, given this unaccustomed respect, began to demand it. The men complained again to Blue Stone Man.

"It is only for this battle," he said, suppressing his own unease. "Afterward your wives will be as they were."

But when Wind Caller came back with One Ball and Squirrel, Blue Stone Man said to him, "You have upset the balance. This is not the way we are supposed to be. Anything may happen."

Certainly Deer Shadow found that to be so. When the three returned and the People made ready to follow them back to fight for their land, she discovered that her husband's coyote half had decided, for reasons best known to himself, that One Ball was a person he would take food from. He still would not take it from Deer Shadow, which incensed her.

"It likes One Ball!" she said indignantly. "It acts as if it owns the babies! What has it got against me?"

"Probably because you are mine," Wind Caller said with a grin. "He's jealous."

"I am not yours," Deer Shadow said. "You are mine. I found you."

"Your pardon, Most Wise." Wind Caller laughed and didn't argue with her. Deer Shadow laughed back at him, her indignation forgotten. Both were in an unusually fine mood—the Yellow Grass People were going home.

That they would have to fight the Others to get there was for the moment forgotten. They set out purposefully, and with every step north they took, the sense of home grew stronger, and the more willing they were to fight for it.

"I can't breathe here," Deer Shadow said of the ancient black lava flow they had trudged wearily across, growing hungrier. It was as if the old burning stone that had made the mountains was still there, underground, its vapors hissing up through the ground, choking off the air. It felt like breathing in the boiling waters of the sulphur springs, though without the smell. Now as they passed out of it, she took deep lungfuls of air as they walked and saw that the other women were doing the same.

They moved slowly, of necessity, bringing the old and the children with them. There would be no leaving them alone in this desolate place, without even the women to care for them. If the young men and women died, the grandmothers and grandfathers could at least go with their grandchildren to other bands, where kin would take them in. That much, honor permitted.

The journey home lasted one moon, almost as long as it had been in flight, but something seemed to loosen, some bony fist to unclench. In some way they were different, changed forever, even if they lost. Give Away killed a rabbit with her sling and danced, shouting, across the desert with it to show her husband. Turtle Back clapped her on the back as if she were a man.

Three moons after they had been driven out of their land, the Yellow Grass People camped on the edge of it, as far from the canyon Wind Caller had chosen as a man could walk from sunup to noon. Now there was the matter of getting the Others into it.

"There is only one way," Wind Caller said. He looked at the Yellow Grass People and asked, "Who runs the fastest?"

Runner wasn't named so for compliment's sake. Runner, Wind Caller, and a boy named Flycatcher set out in the predawn darkness to lie in wait on the Others' hunting trail. It ran not far from the canyon, but the Others rarely ventured in, as the People had never done, because what little water there was ran out into sand halfway down the canyon and had a bad taste. You could drink it—One Ball, Wind Caller, and Squirrel had—but the game knew of better water elsewhere. Only a stranger, unknowing, would stumble on it.

Runner's husband hadn't liked her going, hadn't liked her learning to fight, either, but she had ignored him. Wind Caller suspected that her presence also annoyed Deer Shadow, who was not particularly fleet of foot, but Deer Shadow hadn't objected. Going home was what counted. She could bend a jealous eye on Runner there, safe for now in the knowledge that no man who was going to fight a battle would disarm his power by sleeping with a woman. Wind Caller had assured her of this, although she couldn't banish the notion that he had sounded a shade too self-righteous.

The three, who were bait, hid in the chaparral and hoped that the Others would come along this trail today. They should. There was fresh deer sign, which was why Wind Caller had picked today.

"Our deer," Flycatcher said grumpily. Even at rest he seemed to move faster than anyone else and was always hungry.

"You are not to jump up until I say to," Wind Caller instructed, grabbing Runner and Flycatcher each by the wrist to make sure they understood him. He had left Follow behind, persuading him with difficulty to stay with One Ball at the canyon's mouth, where he would do some good.

It was hot as soon as the sun was up. Wind Caller could feel the sweat trickle down his neck, as well as the stinging of the biting flies it attracted. He slapped at them. A muscle in his leg began to twitch. A hornet circled them, droning, looking for a place to light. Wind Caller willed it away, but it lit on his back, where he couldn't reach it and was afraid to slap at it with a branch. He could feel its feet investigating him.

Flycatcher stiffened and said, "Ssss!"

"They're coming," Wind Caller said. "Or something is."

But he knew. A hunting party makes a sound in the earth unlike that of a single wolf, or even a bear or big cat; a sound of many feet, moving at once but not together. He crouched, willing himself to forget the hornet. From the spot he had chosen they could see a long way down the game trail. The faint murmur of sound grew louder, still indistinguishable to anyone not listening for it. Then the Others came soft-footed into view.

As he had expected, nearly all of the men were with

them—their numbers double that of the People. The deer trail showed signs of a big herd, and with summer already waning, they would hope for a kill to last them into the fall.

Beside him, Flycatcher wanted to run, to take to his heels. The Others were getting close.

"Be still," Wind Caller said. "Not yet."

Runner seemed content to wait. She took a deep breath, slowly filling her lungs. They could see faces now. Wind Caller tried to think of them as he would the Upstream People, just another enemy to be fought in a world populated with enemies. Someone to give to his gods.

"Now!" He jumped from the chaparral. The hornet, startled, sank its needle into his back, and Wind Caller howled more loudly than he had intended to. Flycatcher and Runner jumped up shrieking, shouting insults the Others might or might not understand.

"Yah! You are masterless dogs!" Wind Caller shouted, dancing backward as the Others started to run after them.

Runner waved her spear at them. "Yah! Bah! Our women beat your warriors! Your warriors are all soft men! Send your women to fight us next time!"

The Others howled and surged toward them.

"Now we know your women are alone!" Flycatcher yelled.

The three turned and raced away, flying down the trail, the Others baying after them. As long as they didn't stop to think, they would keep running, Wind Caller knew. That was what the insults had been for, to send the Others into a fine fury before they wondered why, if the People were trying to catch the men out hunting and the women alone, as the Others had done, they would let themselves be seen. He turned, dancing backward again for just a moment, and made an obscene gesture with his hands.

"Deer lice! Thieving rats! You can't catch us! Lice can't run!" He turned and plunged on again, hearing them pounding behind him.

Runner was a step ahead of him, Flycatcher in front of her. They sailed down the trail, plunged off it into the brush, heading for the canyon. The hornet sting burned like a torch stuck to Wind Caller's back, and he wanted to plunge into a cold river. If he ran fast enough, the pain seemed to stay a finger's width behind him.

Runner stumbled, and the Others howled and picked up speed. She righted herself, flashed Wind Caller a grin, and flew on ahead. *Just to keep them encouraged,* her expression seemed to say.

They tumbled down a slope of loose shale and pounded across a little valley that whispered with dry buffalo grass. A dark shape soared interestedly overhead, wings spread on the air. It recognized a hunt even if the quarry was man.

Wind Caller's breath burned in his chest now, but he knew that the Others were winded, too, and they would have to fight afterward. He turned and saw them plunging grimly on, although some looked ready to stop.

Summoning more power than he felt, he capered in front of them, taunting them. "Worms! Go and eat dirt! The People curse you! Yah-ah, you are too stupid to be human!"

A spear sailed toward him but thudded in the grass short of its mark. He and the other two had been careful to stay out of range.

They streaked across the valley, heading for the canyon mouth, careful to approach it in seemingly blind flight. The Others were hot on their trail now, their fury renewed. They had been insulted by a lesser people, made fun of, and that had to be wiped out, given back on the end of a spear. They were reputed to be proud that way, and Wind Caller was relieved to find that it was so.

Finally they were running up the canyon mouth, and Wind Caller searched as he ran for some sign of the Yellow Grass People waiting for them. He saw none—he wasn't supposed to—but thoughts of betrayal, of Cat Ears somehow convincing them all to abandon him, crossed his mind, barbed fears drawn in with the breath that burned his throat. He had left most of them at the canyon mouth. A handful were up the canyon to drive the Others back when the rocks had fallen on them, and another handful were on the canyon rim to push the rocks over.

Wind Caller's eyes went upward in spite of himself. If they timed it wrong, he and Flycatcher and Runner would be caught under a falling boulder too easily. He had put Four Fingers, who was too old to fight, up there because she had sense, and Dancing Bear because he didn't but was strong enough to shove rocks. One Ball and Blue Stone Man were in charge of the fighters at the canyon mouth, and Squirrel, to Squirrel's great satisfaction, of the handful inside the canyon. *Great Jaguar, let this work. Please.*

Conscientiously, Wind Caller added a prayer to Coyote, who probably didn't listen to prayers, but who had shown him the canyon. He ran beneath the looming, nodding heads of stone above him. They seemed to wobble in his peripheral vision, leaning out over the canyon, suspended in air, waiting to bury him. The Others were yowling after him, close on his heels now, Runner and Flycatcher a bare pace ahead of him. Wind Caller risked one more glance over his shoulder at the lead hunter of the Others and could see sweat pouring from his face, his mouth contorted in fury. He was close enough to throw a spear. Wind Caller could feel it in his back like the hornet sting, but he had risked their wanting him alive, alive to tell them where the rest of the People were. *Alive to torture.* It was said that the Others did that, too.

Where were the stones? As he thought it, he heard them, a deep rumble like an earthquake, shuddering the canyon walls, shattering them like clay as the big rocks tumbled down, bouncing against the slope, booming and rushing. Wind Caller ran with his heart in his throat, flinging himself from their path, stumbling against Runner and Flycatcher.

He turned and saw the leaders go down under the falling rocks. More broke loose from the canyon walls, creating a river of boulders that smashed bone and skull, burying the howls of the injured. On the canyon rim, he could hear Four Fingers and the rest yelling their satisfaction.

Squirrel and his band came down the canyon and ran past them, spears nocked into atlatls. Now they could throw. They had made enough spears to waste, and the Others had no more than one, maybe two apiece. Squirrel's band flung spears, stumbling over the stones and bodies, climbing the wall of boulders. The Others spared by the avalanche had turned and run, bumbling against each other when the rocks came down. Disoriented, they fled for the canyon mouth, with Squirrel's band behind them. Squirrel pushed them hard, driving them toward One Ball and Blue Stone Man before they could turn and fight.

Wind Caller bent over, hands on his knees, drawing in deep breaths, his lungs still burning. Runner was leaning against a rock, hand on her pounding chest. Flycatcher watched the canyon rim nervously. It looked unstable, as if more pieces might crumble from it.

"Go," Wind Caller said. "Out. Now." He straightened and pulled them up, too, with a gesture. "Get away from this place."

They climbed on hands and knees over the tumbled stone, hearing the dying men under them as if the stones spoke. Wind Caller put his hand on bloody flesh and saw a shattered face under it. He clambered past it, down the other side, tripping over arms, legs, a broken torso pinned by rocks. The smell made him gag. He fled down the canyon, leaving the stones moaning behind him.

Her back to warm stone, Deer Shadow crouched in the brush, safe, enclosed, listening for the rumble of the earth. When she heard it, she would have to leave this place of safety, confront the Others pouring back through the canyon, and kill them. She had seen Wind Caller go past, had heard his breathing even from where she hid, and was obsessed with the idea that Dancing Bear, who was as stupid as a rock himself, would time it wrong and kill him.

Then it came, the sound that made the stones behind her hum. Blue Stone Man stood, spear in his atlatl. "Now!" The Yellow Grass People surged from the chaparral. From the other side of the canyon, One Ball's warriors rose with a roar and streamed to join Blue Stone Man's. They moved up the canyon until they blocked it, jammed like a plug in a waterskin. Deer Shadow saw Cat Ears, mouth snarling, his anger at Wind Caller forgotten for the moment. The plan had worked, and Cat Ears was doing what he did best: hunting.

The Others spilled down the canyon, and Deer Shadow fitted a spear to her own atlatl and cocked her arm back. The Others leaped toward her like deer, and she threw. A man went down, clutching his throat, blood pouring around his hands. Squirrel's men came pounding after them, and Blue Stone Man shouted to watch their aim. After the first volley of thrown spears, the Yellow Grass People moved in on the Others, hurling spears at any who tried to escape, driving the rest in on

themselves at spear point. Follow had his teeth in someone's leg, and One Ball drove a spear through the man's
chest. Follow picked another target, and One Ball followed. The women were shoulder to shoulder with the
men, in One Ball's group and in Blue Stone Man's, and
the Others were even more afraid of them than they were
of the men. Deer Shadow could see it in their eyes:
Women didn't fight. These might be demons.

She could see the chief of the Others trying to keep
his men in order, keep them around him. He must be
the chief. His necklace was even finer than Blue Stone
Man's, and his spear was tied at the haft with eagle
feathers. Cat Ears watched him hungrily, waiting his
chance.

The canyon was thick with dust and the smell of
blood and dying bodies loosening their grip on life. The
Others called to one another with shrill cries like birds
and words that Deer Shadow didn't understand. With a
relief that nearly toppled her, she saw Wind Caller,
caked with sweat and dust, loping along the side of the
fighting, trying to make the Yellow Grass People tighten
up their circle.

"Keep them together! Don't let them get past you!"

The Others were battering at the People's spears with
their own, trying to force their way through. They were
hard to hold, desperate and with not much to lose. The
People began to edge backward toward the open valley.

"Bunch them together! *Kill them!'* Wind Caller
shouted.

Cat Ears leaped for the Others' chieftain, the eagle
feathers marking him tantalizingly as a prize. Two or
three hunters followed him.

"Get back!" Wind Caller shouted, his mouth twisted
in unbelieving rage as the Others pushed hard against
the hole that Cat Ears had left in the People's line. Cat
Ears was battling his way through them toward the chief.

"Jaguar eat you, you poisonous toad, *get back*!" Wind Caller hurled himself into the gap that Cat Ears had left, but it was too late. The Others were pouring through it, pounding past him. Turtle Back, on Cat Ears' other side, had been knocked flat, and they trampled him. Someone reached down to help him, and again Wind Caller yelled, "Get into line!" But it was too late. The line was broken, straggling. Deer Shadow flung a spear at one man as he went by and Follow brought another down for Wind Caller to kill, but the Others were running, ten or more of them, while those still trapped kept the People from following.

Slowly they closed the ring on those remaining, and slowly each bloodied hunter was driven down. The Yellow Grass People yipped triumphantly, dancing around the last of them, driving their spears into the falling bodies.

Cat Ears lifted up the chieftain's eagle-collared spear, his feet thumping the ground.

Wind Caller spat at him. "They got *away*! They got away, thanks to your stupidity, you thieving snake's ass!" Wind Caller jumped at Cat Ears, bare hands outstretched, and Blue Stone Man shouted, *"No!"*.

Wind Caller stopped, a foot from Cat Ears, breathing hard and cursing him.

XV
The Flute Birds

The People went home. Behind them, in the blue stone sky, the buzzards circled. The People drove the Others' women and children from the caves in the tufa cliffs, sweeping them out with spears the way a woman would with a broom.

"Out! Get out of my place!" Deer Shadow screamed, jabbing her spear at a terrified girl with a baby clutched in her arms. "Get out of my place! Your men are dead!" The girl fled, abandoning possessions as Deer Shadow had abandoned hers.

All along the cliffs, old men and women were being driven out, crying children running lost behind them. They tumbled down the slopes with the vengeful Yellow Grass People in pursuit. The People found a baby they recognized, a boy, and snatched it from the arms of the woman carrying it, but no one saw Rainwater's daughter. Either she had been dragged off in the Others' flight or she had escaped from them before now; no one knew. Rainwater ran through the melee with a spear, killing any woman she could catch. Someone snatched a girl of the same age as Rainwater's daughter from the Others and flung her at Rainwater, saying, "Here, take this one." And then Deer Shadow had to stop her from killing the child.

"You have no sense!" Deer Shadow screamed at the one who had taken the girl. It was Walks Funny—a man, naturally. She dragged the terrified child into her own cave and sat her down in the shambles on its floor. Deer Shadow didn't want the girl, but she couldn't turn her loose. The Others were too far scattered now; she would never catch up.

"I don't want you," she said, but she knew she had her whether she wanted her or not.

She left the child sitting there, half hoping she would run away, and went back outside. Wind Caller and One Ball were methodically killing the wounded of the Others, and Looks Back was seeing to the People. They had lost three of their fighters in the canyon and there were five wounded here, including Give Away, who had a gash across one breast and didn't know whether to be proud of it or to howl with the pain.

No one knew where the Others who had escaped the canyon were, only that they had scattered into the foothills. The People had been careful to stay between them and the tufa cliffs to keep them from going home. *Not their home now,* Deer Shadow thought with satisfaction. The cliffs were the People's again—they had only to be cleaned of the Others' taint.

Deer Shadow looked at Wind Caller to see if his mood had changed any in the last few days. Only Blue Stone Man's direct orders had kept him from trying to kill Cat Ears. He looked scornful, she thought, the face he adopted when he was angry and couldn't afford to show it. She had seen him slit the throat of a wounded woman of the Others without flinching. Now he and One Ball were dragging away the dead of the Others who had been killed in the camp and taking them to the dance ground, where other men were setting fire to them to purify it. Their own dead would have a proper burning later when the burning place was clean. The People had carried their dead home from the canyon but had left the Others to rot there. No one would go there now but the hungry buzzards.

Dancing Bear looked about with immense satisfaction. He had been resentful of having been sent to push rocks down on the enemy instead of fight them, but here at the caves he had killed three people, two women and a toothless man, and now he felt better. "Yah!" he chanted, stamping his feet. "We are a great people! We have killed them all!"

Wind Caller, dirty with blood and ashes, choking on the greasy black smoke that rose in the air, spun around to face him. " 'We have killed them all'!" he mimicked him, stomping his feet and dancing in imitation. "Yah! We let this many of their men go!" He held his hands, fingers spread, in Dancing Bear's face, shoved them at him so that Dancing Bear stepped back a pace. "This many! We have no more than twice that of fighting men ourselves! Or are you planning for our women to fight for us forever?"

"I thought it was a mistake to have women fight," Dancing Bear said stolidly.

"You thought with your backside!" Wind Caller said. He looked at the people who were watching them with interest, tired, bloodied, but not beyond observing someone else fight. "Do you understand? Because fools wanted a prize, wanted to be able to yammer at the fireside when they are toothless that they killed the chieftain, we let the rest go! And now they will find their women again, and probably their kin from other places, and they will come back."

"They are not enough to hurt us now," Found a Snake said angrily. He knew Wind Caller wasn't really talking to Dancing Bear. Everyone could see Cat Ears a few feet away, cleaning his spear and glowering, but Blue Stone Man had forbidden Cat Ears and Wind Caller to speak to each other directly.

"Not this year," Wind Caller said with scorn. "Or for a few years—unless, being less honorable than we, they ask their kin for help." He included Blue Stone Man in his glare this time. "But they will come back. I told you we had to kill them all."

"And what do you suggest we do now, Most Wise?" Found a Snake said sarcastically, and Dancing Bear guffawed.

"Learn to fight." Wind Caller gave Cat Ears a scathing glance and a rude gesture that didn't quite qualify as speaking directly to him, and stalked off to throw more kindling into the horror on the burning ground.

"Let him go!" Blue Stone Man shouted when Cat Ears started after him.

"We have this place to purify," Looks Back said. He had found his great tooth and stood in its spiral, pulling the Others' magic out of it and throwing it away. When the tooth was purified, it would make magic for the People again. It circled him like a blessing.

The People nodded. The world was out of balance. It must be tipped right again, and that couldn't be done by quarreling. The men would go with Looks Back to sanctify the sacred cave and the women to scrub the smell of the Others out of their houses.

Deer Shadow picked among the rubble of what had been her cave, looking for a waterskin, and saw that the child was still there. Deer Shadow took her by the hand and pulled her along after her. She was as likely as not to poison the food while Deer Shadow's back was turned. She took her to Aunt Four Fingers, who had Son and Daughter with her as well, and said, "Here."

"What is it?" Aunt Four Fingers said, eyeing the child distrustfully. Follow, who had been driven up the

hill by the scent from the burning ground, and had come
to make sure that Four Fingers hadn't eaten the babies
yet, stuck his nose out from behind a rock shelf and
sniffed the girl. The child screamed and flung herself in
the other direction, trying to pull free of Deer Shadow's
grasp.

"Someone tried to give her to Rainwater," Deer
Shadow said. "Some fool of a man, when Rainwater
couldn't find her daughter. Rainwater was going to kill
her, so I took her."

"Better you had let her," Four Fingers said. "What
are we going to do with her?"

"I don't know," Deer Shadow said. "But she's a
baby. I don't kill babies. I am bloody enough today."

"She's a baby like that one was." Four Fingers jerked
her head at Follow. The child had much the same feral
quality.

Raccoon, Blue Stone Man's wife, stuck her head in
the cave mouth. "What's this?" she said.

"Another coyote," Four Fingers said disapprovingly.

Raccoon looked at the child writhing at the end of
Deer Shadow's arm. She clucked her tongue.

"Walks Funny thought Rainwater would want her,"
Deer Shadow said.

"Men are fools," Raccoon said briskly. Household
matters, children, were her business. Here she held
power. "Well!" She inspected the child. "Who does
want her?"

"I don't want her," Deer Shadow said sourly. "I kept
Rainwater from killing her."

Raccoon chuckled. It did her good to see Deer
Shadow stuck with something she didn't want. Deer
Shadow got what she wanted too often, in Raccoon's
opinion. "Well, that makes her yours," she said.

"I *have* babies," Deer Shadow said.

"And a husband who isn't one of the People. That

makes you the best person to have this one."

Deer Shadow let go of the child, who sat down with a bump on the floor. She howled again when Follow stuck his nose in her face, but when he didn't bite her, she snuffled into silence and stared at him.

"There," Raccoon said. "See?"

"I don't want her," Deer Shadow said. "I didn't want the coyote, either."

Raccoon dusted her hands briskly. "Some things are meant." She bustled off to see what else needed straightening out.

Aunt Four Fingers burst into laughter. "Yah, if you could see your face."

Deer Shadow scooped up the babies. They were getting big in spite of being hungry most of their lives, and wriggled like rabbits under each arm. "Come." Deer Shadow motioned at the child with her head. The girl stared at her uncomprehendingly until Follow nosed her toward the door. Then she came, clutching a handful of his fur.

"Ssss," Aunt Four Fingers said. "She *is* a coyote."

Probably, Deer Shadow thought. Whatever she was, Deer Shadow didn't want her. Had her stepmothers felt that way about *her*? she wondered suddenly. Probably. She felt a flash of pity for Fox Girl, who had died trying to let her children get away and who wouldn't ever know that they had taken their summer place back again. She looked at Others' Child, shivering in the cave mouth. How dangerous was she? How dangerous had she herself been, at the age of six, when she had learned she could call animals?

"Watch her," she said to Follow.

Follow snorted at her, surprised that she had spoken to him directly. He nosed Others' Child into a corner by the storage pits. Deer Shadow put Son and Daughter down next to him and began to clean.

"Yah, you are dirty people," she said over her shoulder to the child, but it was mostly temper. The cave was swept, and only a little pile of rubbish and bones remained at the front ready to be taken to the midden. The rest of the disorder was the result of the fighting. Deer Shadow herself had done most of it when she had driven the woman and her baby away, smashing open baskets of grain, ripping the deer-hide hanging that curtained off the back of the cave, slicing it through with her spear. She wished now that she had been less furious. She looked at Others' Child, deciding that *she* could sew it up again.

Deer Shadow scrabbled among the stores and found dried meat, camas bulbs, and a basket of half-cooked squash and some sort of meat—squirrel, she thought—that had spilled in the fire and put it out. She righted the basket. It was cooked enough, she thought. She felt disinclined to eat the Others' food, which might be dangerous to human people, so she handed the basket to Others' Child and Follow. It wouldn't poison them. She ate a handful of camas bulbs raw and began to put things where they belonged, where *she* had kept them.

The rest of the women were doing the same, sweeping their caves with rush brooms and washing the floors with water carried up from the stream in baskets. Looks Back and the men came out of the sacred cave and went from dwelling to dwelling, chanting to the gods that they were home. Deer Shadow lugged a basket of water past them and wondered how long it would take them to forget that the women had fought beside them. Not long, she suspected. The People's dogs walked stiff-legged up and down the cliff face, sniffing and claiming their territory again. Deer Shadow chuckled.

The sun was low now, orange as fire. Tonight they would put out all the fires and make a new one. That was the last step in cleansing a place. Wind Caller held his flute to his lips, and she felt the music pick her up like dry leaves and carry her so that she felt light, as if she could dance in the air. Anger slipped from her. Others' Child came to the mouth of the cave and stared, and Wind Caller stared back, the music faltering.

We are all strays and strangers, Deer Shadow thought. *What difference does one more make?* The child still had her hand twisted in Follow's ruff.

The men's procession went on, chanting, Wind Caller looking over his shoulder. It wasn't until he turned back again and the procession continued to Aunt Four Fingers's cave that Deer Shadow saw Cat Ears drop out of line.

She watched him, hesitant, wondering why he would leave something so important, and why he would be at the end of the line in the first place when he had enough importance among the People for a place at the front. Cat Ears was jealous of those things. He was being careful, she thought. He looked as if he were hunting.

Owl was coming up the hill, hobbling with a heavy water basket. "Here," Deer Shadow said to her. "Watch these." She pointed at the babies and Others' Child and ran before Owl could argue with her.

Cat Ears had almost disappeared into the bluish dusk when she caught the flicker of his movement in the willows by the river. She slid after him. Cat Ears should be with the men. Therefore Cat Ears was going to do no good to someone.

He moved along the riverbank, in the shadow of the trees, upstream. Surely he wasn't going to the Others. Deer Shadow found herself unable to believe that even of Cat Ears. He made no sound, his skin almost bluish in the twilight like the shadows. Deer Shadow kept her distance, afraid he would hear her. Had he hidden something? Some poison he had stumbled on, during the journey, maybe? Some amulet or charm, a magic to sicken someone?

The willows thinned and gave way to scrub, and then the land around the river opened suddenly into flat flood plain, and she knew why he had come. By the time she caught up with him, he was in the maize field.

The maize had grown, and the Others had been tending it, she thought. As Wind Caller had said, they were not stupid. Only a few weeds, grown back from chopped-off stalks, were snaking between the rows. The maize was higher than Cat Ears' shoulders, with thick green leaves folded back from the stalks and fat ears poking between them. Cat Ears was slitting the pods open with his knife, slicing through the outer husk into each ear.

Deer Shadow sucked in her breath with a hiss, and he turned and saw her. She ran at him, fingers clenched on her knife, pushing her way through the rough stalks with the blood buzzing in her ears.

"Thief! Thieving rat! You'll never lie down in peace until you're old and your teeth have fallen out! I'll see to it!" She advanced on him, knife in her hand, but it was the expression on her face that he was looking at.

"Get away from me," Cat Ears said. "Do you think you can beat *me* with a knife, even if you do think you've learned to fight? Pah!" He spat.

"I don't need a knife to cut your balls off," Deer Shadow said. "Or any other part of you that I want to shrivel and drop off like deer antlers."

"Deer antlers grow back. Bigger," he said, trying to make a joke of it.

"Yours won't."

"Go home, woman," Cat Ears said. "I am letting the curse out of this plant so that it doesn't poison us. If you are lucky, when we have killed your husband, some other human man may want you." He reached for another ear.

"Stop it!"

"I told you, go home," he said, but he kept swiveling to face her as she moved around him, knife point out, level with his heart. He could see the whites of her eyes and the snap of her teeth in the dusk, and they seemed to have some life of their own, as if they might come out of her dark face and bite him while she just stood there. As if they might be the tangible body of her curse, hovering between her face and his, ready to slip down his throat.

"You go home," Deer Shadow said. "Go to Blue Stone Man and tell him what you've done. Or I'll kill you."

Cat Ears froze for a moment, and then, as if he had come to some decision, gathered some stored and secret courage, he backhanded his fist hard against her face, scratching himself on her knife without caring. She stumbled backward and fell in the dirt, and he started cutting into the ears again.

She was still crouched, gasping, when a thrashing in the rows startled them both. Wind Caller went pounding past her and flung himself on Cat Ears.

They rolled in the dirt between the rows, howling and hacking at each other with their knives, while she pulled herself to her feet, one hand on her aching jaw. She could taste blood and feel it on her fingers. Realizing she had dropped her knife, she threw herself down again, searching for it in the fading light, cursing.

Cat Ears pinned Wind Caller in the dirt, and Wind Caller kneed him in the groin, rolled him over, and banged his head on the ground. Cat Ears sank his teeth into Wind Caller's shoulder and forced his knife hand out of Wind Caller's grasp. Deer Shadow gave up look-

ing for her knife and searched for a rock to use against
Cat Ears instead.

And where was the coyote when she actually wanted
him? she thought savagely, and felt his warm breath on
her neck. She shrieked in spite of herself, and he went
past her without stopping, purposeful, his scent like a
color in the air.

Follow had no trouble telling one man from the other.
He sank his teeth into Cat Ears's thigh, and the man
screamed. Wind Caller twisted out of his grasp and bent
his knife hand behind his back.

"I'll kill you!" Cat Ears turned his head, screaming
in Wind Caller's face. "Witch! Get it off me!" He
kicked at Follow. The coyote hung on, growling in his
throat.

"If I *were* a witch," Wind Caller panted, struggling
to hold Cat Ears, "you wouldn't know it." He kneed
him in the back and twisted Cat Ears's wrist until he
dropped the knife.

Deer Shadow had found hers. She came toward them
with it, wiping her bleeding mouth with the other hand.

"Get back," Wind Caller said. He kicked Cat Ears's
knife away.

"Why?" Deer Shadow demanded.

"Because I tell you to," Wind Caller said. "Just this
once, Most Important, will you do what *I* say?" He
struggled with the writhing Cat Ears and got his arm
around his throat.

Deer Shadow halted, not letting go of her knife. Cat
Ears was howling and cursing. They looked like a writhing monster in the dusk, all arms. Wind Caller pressed
his knife against Cat Ears's back. "Drop it," he said to
Follow.

Follow unclenched his jaws and waited. Cat Ears's
blood dripped from the coyote's teeth. Follow hadn't
been playing.

"I don't want to kill you," Wind Caller said to Cat Ears, panting, "because it will make trouble, and the chieftain has said I am not to."

"*You* attacked *me*," Cat Ears said spitefully, "and I will tell Blue Stone Man *that*."

Wind Caller ignored him. "The maize is ready to harvest, and if I catch you near it again, even at the harvest, I will stuff five ears down your throat whole, and five more up the other end. Do you understand me?"

Cat Ears was silent, stiff and furious.

"Get away," Wind Caller said to Deer Shadow again, and this time she moved back. He shoved Cat Ears away from him, hard, so that Cat Ears stumbled toward the river. "Go home. Tell your father the shaman to put something on that bite, if you want to explain how you got it."

Cat Ears stared at him in the gathering dark. "I will kill you," he said distinctly.

"Yah, one day we will all do great things," Wind Caller said.

Cat Ears spun around and limped toward the path to the cliffs. Deer Shadow felt Follow brush past her and saw him trotting after Cat Ears. To be certain where he went, she thought.

"Now he will start telling tales again," she said. "You made him look foolish. Why didn't you let me kill him?"

"Maybe I didn't like hiding behind my wife. You bought my life once. That is enough for any man."

Deer Shadow thought about that. "And how did you know to come here?"

"Owl. She said you ran off after Cat Ears and left her with the babies. She was put out, and thought he would do you some evil."

"Not me," she said. "The maize."

"When I saw you had gone this way, I thought so,"

he said. "And what," he demanded suddenly, "is that child?"

Deer Shadow laughed. "I think Coyote sent her."

He looked at her oddly for a moment. "He might have."

"This is what Cat Ears was doing." She twisted off one of the ears that Cat Ears had cut into and handed it to Wind Caller. He looked at it, squinting, holding it up in the failing light. The hairs that sprouted from its top were dry and brown. He peeled back the husk. The ear lay in his palm, fat and pale under the rising moon. He bit into it, and the juice ran down his chin. "Here."

Deer Shadow bit the kernels off the ear with her front teeth as she had seen Wind Caller do. It was faintly sweet, dusty in her nose as a dry summer, laced with the scent of grass. She thought of the Maize God, yellow and green as Wind Caller had pictured him, sleeping in each seed. The wind ruffled her hair around her face and stirred the stalks in their rows. They said, *We are life.*

The People would cut the maize. They would roast the ears and eat them, magic running down their faces, dry them and grind them into flour. They would save some for next year's seed, and when the game was scarce, they would have maize. None of the wild seed they gathered gave this much grain. None of it sprouted tamely at man's command, called from the ground as she had called the deer. She looked at her husband and heard the stalks whispering all around them. "Are you really a god?" she asked him, awed.

Wind Caller pulled his flute from his belt and put it to his lips. He blew a few notes from it. They rose like birds and perched along it. "I don't know," he said at last, shaking his head, and the birds whispered in the maize. "Do the gods know what they are?"

Deer Shadow thought. She supposed they might not. Dreamtime and real time alternated with each other, flowing over and under, each with its own words to say, until it might be hard to tell.

"Are *you* a god?" Wind Caller asked, startling her.

Maybe, Deer Shadow thought. Here among the rows, with the flute birds whispering to the maize, it seemed possible. Possible to be more than just a basket to hold the magic; possible to *be* the magic. That was frightening, but she liked it.

"Maybe," she said. She put her hand in his. "Maybe."

Epilogue

"Is that all?" the children ask the old woman indignantly. They can see Wind Caller and Deer Shadow, bathed in the firelight, hand in hand in the maize field. The flute notes flutter up and sit on the old woman's feet.

She stretches old bones. *"There's always more,"* she says. *"But time unrolls slowly. Those two are still human people, mostly. Nothing much will happen to them for a while."*

"What will they do then?"

"Eat. Make love. Bathe in the river. Have babies. Die."

"When do they get to be gods, then?"

"Oh, after they die. Becoming gods is a slow process."

The old woman laughs. Her laughter startles the little flute birds, and they mingle with it, silvery feathered notes. *"There is always Coyote,"* she says.

Coyote wants. Coyote is hunger, for what hasn't happened yet, for what might happen, and even for what we pray will not happen. Coyote keeps the balance. Even the adventurous Moon has her path in the sky, but Coy-

ote ranges the wild lands as he pleases. He comes when
we call him and sometimes when we do not know that
we have called.

"Watch him," the old woman says, and the children
see him bunch his haunches and leap out into the stars,
falling nose over tail, growing smaller as he falls, tumbling to Earth, until he fits inside Follow, trotting after
Cat Ears in the dark.

It is harder to see from inside Follow. The world is
smaller and flatter, and many of his memories make no
sense. He trots behind Cat Ears until Cat Ears goes into
the young men's house, because that is what Follow has
to do. But then he turns back and goes into the other
cave, where Owl is still minding Daughter and Son and
Others' Child. Others' Child—still fierce and rebellious,
making child magics in her head. Coyote lies down beside her.

Author's Note

There are as many variations of the oldest Native American tales as there are of *Cinderella* or of *Little Red Riding Hood*. Stories evolve. They are told and retold with embellishment and adaptation. The stories of Coyote planting maize and of Coyote and Death-Bringing Woman in this book are adapted from tales recorded in *American Indian Myths and Legends*, edited by Richard Erdoes and Alfonso Ortiz, and I owe them a debt of gratitude for a wonderfully rich and comprehensive book.

I also owe my thanks to Sonja Halsey for inspiration, information, and sheer nerve; to Lynn Dunbar of the Archaeological Conservancy; to Pamela Lappies of Book Creations, Inc., editor extraordinaire; and to Ellen Edwards of Avon. And always, for everything, to my husband, Tony Neuron, who first introduced me to Coyote.

The flute notes beat upward in the hot, dry air, carried on the updraft above Wind Caller's head. To his children watching from the greasewood bushes, the notes seemed to tumble down like raindrops, kicking up puffs of dust at his feet. But no rain fell after them, no clouds massed in a sky that was as hot and empty as a baked blue stone.

"It's not going to rain," Mocking Bird said pessimistically. "It isn't working."

"The song isn't *for* rain," Follows Her Father informed him. Mocking Bird was her twin brother, and she was inclined to be scornful of him because she had been born first, a circumstance to which she attributed superior knowledge of almost everything. It helped make up for his being a boy. "It's to make the maize grow." Singing up the maize, Father called it.

"Well, it won't grow without rain," Mocking Bird said.

"Sssh!"

They sank lower in the greasewood bushes. Father had said not to come with him while he was trying to talk to the Maize God. Apparently that was like when he was trying to talk to Looks Back, the old shaman. Children were not allowed to interrupt.

Others' Child peered over the heads of her brother and sister, pushing them down. She was two years older than they were and felt that her advanced age gave her privileges, so that they were all reasonably content with their positions in life, even though Others' Child had not been born to the Yellow Grass People. "If the Maize God wants it to grow," she said, "and it needs rain, maybe he'll send it. If he doesn't, we'll have to move early this year. The deer will leave if all the streams dry up."

"Oh, no." Follows Her Father looked horrified. She had helped to plant the maize, and envisioned the tiny ears shriveling in their husks, withering for lack of water. The land had been dry all summer, and they had dipped water from the steadily shrinking river to keep the maize alive. "If we go, it will die." She could feel herself drying up like the maize.

"Looks Back is going to try to make it rain tonight," Others' Child said. "And Mother."

The twins nodded solemnly. Even the Deer Dance and their mother's magic were beginning to fail at calling the game. There were no turtles in the river, and the fish people died when their streams sank into the sand. The Yellow Grass People were living close to hunger, and they expected Looks Back and Mother and Father to make that different. The twins felt very important about that. Others' Child was beginning to be afraid.

The children watched their father again, silhouetted by the low sun against the yellow tufa cliffs where the Yellow Grass People lived. He was muscular but more slender than the other Yellow Grass men—as if his bones were smaller, Others' Child thought. He was magically different, from his slightly slanted eyes, which were vaguely like Others' Child's, to his aquiline nose. Others' Child silently fingered the small bump on her own nose. Wind Caller had a determined face, the kind that very often had no patience with fools. Bent over his flute, his body had the curved shape of a cupped hand, and his nose jutted out fiercely, the way that Cat Ears's chin did. When Wind Caller and Cat Ears argued, which was always, they seemed to Others' Child to be standing nose to chin.

Wind Caller stuck his flute in his belt and pulled his hunting knife from it. He lifted his arms upward, and the looped braids in which he wore his black hair, unlike those of any of the Yellow Grass People, crisscrossed the dark pattern of his arms like a spiderweb. While the children stared, he pricked both thumbs and squeezed them until they dripped blood. Onto each of the hills in the maize field he squeezed a drop, bending and straightening rhythmically, up and down, his voice rising and falling in a chant the children didn't understand, in a language that Wind Caller no longer spoke.

"That's what the Children of the Sun do in the south where Father and the maize came from," Follows Her Father whispered. "They give the Maize God blood."

"Mother says they are uncivilized," Others' Child said. Deer Shadow, their mother, still found her husband's gods incomprehensible.

"No, it's what they have to do," Follows Her Father said somberly. She was slender, but with the compact muscularity of the People, and she moved inside her skin like a small cat.

Once again Others' Child, angular and bump-nosed, was aware of her Otherness. She watched Wind Caller bending, straightening, turning through the rows, doing what the men of the Yellow Grass People could not: calling up the maize that would feed them. He turned sideways to the slanting flame of the sun, and it licked at the old scars on his breast, rows and rows of them like silver raindrops against the red-brown skin. Others' Child saw fresh blood there, too, to feed the maize. . . . All to feed the maize.

"He has to do it, too," Follows Her Father whispered, "because the maize says it's time."

Other's Child felt the skin on her arms tingle. Mocking Bird shifted under her hand, coiled like an impatient russet snake, his round face turned toward his father. They both knew that Follows Her Father was right. Wind Caller was a god, a gift-bringer for the People. They all knew that to be a god meant also to be a sacrifice.

At night Wind Caller sat silently by the fire with his scarred hands folded in his lap and watched the raincalling. The children were relegated to the far side of the dance ground with people of lesser importance, and Deer Shadow was with Looks Back, conferring in whispers. Wind Caller sat wrapped in isolation, self-exiled from the Yellow Grass People by his own difference.

The children craned their necks to see past the brightness of the flames. When they were grown—which would be when Mocking Bird turned thirteen, and when the girls had their first flow of blood—they would be permitted to sit with the elders and maybe even take on some of their parents' power. But tonight they were children, held firmly in their place by the tribe. There was a sense among the Yellow Grass People that Wind Caller and Deer Shadow held too much magic between them as it was, though certainly a child did not always inherit that power. Cat Ears, the chief of the hunters, was the son of old Looks Back and had wanted to be shaman like his father. But everyone else had sense enough to know that Cat Ears was ill-tempered and prideful, and that to give him that power would be bad for the tribe.

The children of Wind Caller and Deer Shadow would not have to have their parents' power conferred upon them, and they knew it. They had it already, held it wrapped around them like a secret blanket, a shield against the cold loneliness that sometimes shrouded them when the Yellow Grass People looked oddly at them or spoke behind their hands, or when strangers at the Gathering pointed at them and whispered.

Mocking Bird was the freest of them. He could make his small flute sing to anyone, even to Follow, the coyote, who was his father's companion. But because there were others among the Yellow Grass People by now who had learned to play, there was less magic in that. It was Follows Her Father who, from the time she could walk, had padded behind Wind Caller to the maize field and sat and talked to it as if it were someone she knew.

"You have to let them have what magic they have," Deer Shadow had said, shrugging. When Others' Child had picked up a stick and drawn a puppy in the dirt because she wanted one, a small bitch from one of Follow's litters had nosed its way past the hide over the cave mouth. Deer Shadow had given Others' Child an odd look and let her keep the puppy. But Others' Child knew her mother watched her closely now to see what she would draw in the dirt.

Bitch sat with them at the rain-making, her yellow-gray nose in Others' Child's lap. Follow was lurking somewhere outside the firelight. He was old now, and he had gotten wilder as he aged, as if he were preparing to move out of this world into whatever Coyote arranged for his children after death. He stayed at Wind Caller's heels only when not too many people were around. Although his dealings with Deer Shadow had mellowed somewhat with age—she cooked him mush and stews that he could get his teeth through—and he still slept in the cave, he was leaving them; they all knew it.

Too many people had left since the dry years started. Others' Child was twelve, and she could remember when the maize grew over her father's head, the streams were full of turtles, and ducks flew overhead each spring and fall. Since the Yellow Grass People had driven the Others from the People's caves and killed many of their men, the Others hadn't troubled them, and the deer had come back to the People's hunting runs and grown fat. Others' Child and Deer Shadow's babies had grown fat with them, although Deer Shadow had had no more children. The twins had taken all the life she had to give, Looks Back had said when her only other pregnancy ended in cramps and bleeding. That, he said, was why she had been given Others' Child.

Then had come the start of the dry years. Since then Aunt Four Fingers had died, as well as Deer Shadow's father, Found Water, and one of his wives, and more of the oldest among the bands of the People.

It wasn't only the land of the Yellow Grass People that was drying up. The other bands of the tribe—the High Rock People, the Smoke People—were also growing gaunt. Even the maize didn't save them. It was withered and dry the first year and stunted the next. If the People stayed to tend it, they couldn't hunt because the game had moved; if they followed the game, the maize died for lack of water. It was a gift they would have done better not to have taken, Cat Ears had said angrily last winter after the Yellow Grass People moved up the hills to their winter caves without enough meat to see them through and eight of them died.

But Others' Child, chin on her hand, watching the rain-making, knew there was nowhere to go that the deer were plentiful. That was just Cats Ears being angry. The old chieftain, Blue Stone Man, had died in the winter, too, of the lung sickness, and the new young one, Wakes on the Mountain, was willing to listen to Cat Ears complain because Cat Ears had voted for him.

Others' Child cuddled Mocking Bird and Follows Her Father closer to her, an arm around each and Bitch between them. The rain dancers were coming, the sparks flying over their heads like red birds. Others' Child could hear the faint, thin drumming the men made with split twigs on stretched hides. The women's feet pattered on the packed earth like falling acorns. Strings of shells were sewn to their deerhide skirts, and the sound of a hard rain moved with them over the dance ground. There had been an ocean here once, Looks Back had said, and shells dug from the earth had power to bring back water.

The women danced in slanting lines like the rain walking across the purple mountains. The lines crossed and recrossed, splattering against each other, black hair flying like thunderclouds over the shell rain. It was women who could talk to the rain, sing to it with their own fertility. Deer Shadow began to dig at the earth in front of her with her drawing stick, carving droplets in it, marking out the lines of rain above the shape of Red Rock Mountain. Line on line of drops like the scars on Wind Caller's chest, like the flipping tails of fish people deep in the river.

Deer Shadow wasn't sure she could call rain. Once, when Wind Caller had first come to the Yellow Grass People, she thought she had called Coyote. She still did. But Wind Caller said he came from the south, where his people had exiled him for thinking he knew better than the chieftain-priest. A common failing of adolescent boys, he had said, amused, watching the new men strut with new spears at last year's Gathering. But the People suspected him of being at least half a god anyway. He had brought the maize, and who but a god could tame Coyote?

Deer Shadow was the woman who could make deer in the earth and call them from it. She could watch that gift flowing into Others' Child, who wasn't even born to the People. Surely that meant that the magic came from outside. Surely that meant that it would work with rain.

Behind her, Looks Back lifted his arms, burnt-dry grass tied about his wrists, showing it to Rain God in case he had been too busy with matters in the sky and hadn't seen, telling Rain God how great was their need. He wore his rain mask, which had snakes painted on it with the red dye that came from the mountains. Tied among the tufts of burnt grass were snakes' rattles that buzzed as he swayed.

Deer Shadow cut her digging stick deep into the ground, made soft with a basket of precious water from the river, carving droplets, bigger and bigger, shaping their curves like gourds, like pregnant women's bellies, like the fat husks when the maize was ripe. The women danced wraithlike to the rain drums. They were thin, their legs as fragile as the legs of deer. A faint wailing of a hungry child rose over the rain sound.

SUE HARRISON

"A remarkable storyteller...
one wants to stand up and cheer."
Detroit Free Press

"Sue Harrison outdoes Jean Auel"
Milwaukee Journal

MOTHER EARTH FATHER SKY
71592-9/$5.99 US/ $6.99 Can

In a frozen time before history, in a harsh and beautiful
land near the top of the world, womanhood comes
cruelly and suddenly to beautiful, young Chagak.

MY SISTER THE MOON
71836-7/ $5.99 US/ $7.99 Can

An abused and unwanted daughter of the First Men
tribe, young Kiin knows that her destiny is tied to the
brave sons of orphaned Chagak and her chieftan mate
Kayugh—one to whom Kiin is promised, the other for
whom she yearns.

Coming Soon

BROTHER WIND